WORMWOOD SUMMER

San Amaro Investigations Book 1

KAI BUTLER

Thank you, J.
This never would have been written without your encouragement.

CHAPTER ONE

"—YOU KNOW WHAT I MEAN?"

I glanced at the octogenarian to my right and made a slight humming sound, nodding my head. At two o'clock on a Sunday, the park was relatively quiet.

"I thought so. And they're even having their annual conference here! This week!" The woman made a *tsking* sound, surely universal, that showed her unhappiness with the situation. I echoed the sound, and her eyes slid off me, back to the ducks she was tossing bread to. Most of it was landing on the grass, but she didn't seem to notice, too wrapped up in whatever she was talking about. I'd tuned her out a while ago, content to let her continue talking and bolstering my disguise.

"Now, I'm not a bigot," she began, the words the clarion call of bigots of all stripes. "But I just think if the alchemists are so set on having a big meeting, they could go somewhere with the police force to handle the security! I heard that they're even having one of those big names come down. Oh, what's the family? The one from San Francisco."

I shrugged and raised my camera, snapping a couple of pictures.

"Did you get good ones?" she asked. "I'm sorry that the little ducklings aren't out right now."

Across the man-made pond, Dieter made another hundred dollars disappear with a handshake, replacing the bills with a small baggie full of green herbs. He looked around, his eyes catching on me and... I'd already forgotten her name. Priscilla? Portia? Phyllis? But since the San Amaro Police Department wasn't in the habit of employing retirees in matching tracksuits, he ignored us, eyes narrowing on the pair of joggers that passed behind us.

Sure, they looked more like cops, since they were running, and I looked like someone who needed a cane to get to the bathroom. After a long appraisal, he shrugged and propped himself back against the green lunch table he'd claimed for his deals. I rolled my eyes up and sighed.

"I mean, the *traffic*," Maybe Phyllis continued. "And it'll bring out all the Humans Are Humans protesters. Now *there* are some bigots."

Someone came close to Dieter, a skinny teen in a black t-shirt. It was going to be another drug deal. I'd been tailing this guy for over a week and all I'd seen was drug deals, the gym, and his pack.

Not that I didn't believe my client when she said her boyfriend was a lying, cheating scumbag. But since I'd been tailing him and seen nothing, either his girl on the side had kicked Dieter-the-Cheater to the curb or he was visiting her during the short catnaps I'd been taking every eight hours. Having watched him, it could have been either.

This was clearly a guy who could make a quickie *very* quick.

I'd taken the case a few days ago, figuring it would be easy money. Chelsea Kinney looked like a girl whose idea of a hard day would be a day when her favorite nail salon was closed for renovations. She wanted photos of her boyfriend cheating and since, according to her, he was out nearly every night, I assumed that it would be the fastest job I'd ever done. However, he'd proven me wrong, and I had hundreds of photos of drug deals and drunken revelry with his boys to prove it.

I was resigned to photographing another two men shaking hands twice as they traded money and weed, when Dieter-Dieter-Herpes-Breeder waved at the kid and headed for the sidewalk that bordered the park. Careful to stay out of his line of sight, I stood and mumbled a goodbye to Probably Phyllis. I made my way around the lake, moving a lot faster than someone with my apparent hips could move. Once I passed out of Maybe Not Phyllis's eye line, I dropped the glamour and began jogging to catch up with Dieter. My camera bag bounced on my back.

If he looked back now, Dieter would see a mid-twenties guy with tousled sandy hair and blue eyes. I tried to work out, but my job kept me from using any gym membership. Instead, I had the lean look of a scrappy stray dog.

Passing my car where I'd parked it on the street, I patted the hood fondly and slowed my pace so I was far enough behind Dieter that he wouldn't notice me. He was rushing, but he stopped to buy a bouquet from someone sitting on the sidewalk, a bucket of flowers between her knees.

Checking his hair in a storefront, he headed into one of the apartment complexes that backed the park.

Jack. Pot.

I walked into the same opening between buildings that Dieter had and pulled up short. The two stories of apartments formed a small square with a pool in the middle. Dieter went straight for the center of the square instead of one of the apartments, so I hid most of my body behind the wall.

With a slow, focusing breath, I reached into the air and waved my hand in a slow circle. It wasn't a full glamour, as that would take too much time. It was a kind of crude version of one, though. If it was a high school essay, the English teacher might tactfully call it a "rough draft." It wouldn't fool someone looking directly at me, but most people would just see the wall and their eyes would skip right over me like I wasn't there.

There was a woman sunbathing in a deck chair near the pool, and she looked about as far from my client as someone could get. She'd cut her dark black hair into chic, short spikes. Tattoos wrapped around her torso and, unlike Chelsea, she wore a literal dog tag hanging from an earring which marked her as an out-and-proud werewolf.

Chelsea, with her preppy sweater and ballet flats, looked like the soccer-mom she probably wanted to become some day. She had the air of a person that would glance askance at a werewolf with a dog tag hanging from an earring and say something that ended with "*those* people." As far as I could tell, it was an excellent cover, since she was as wolf-y as they come, and both she and Dieter were part of the South Palma pack.

Dieter's girl on the side pushed up her sunglasses and gave him a once-over, her eyes narrowed on the flowers he held. She smiled at him and waved a hand. Raising my camera, I checked settings, confident that with the glamour, they wouldn't see me.

I snapped a series of photos as Dieter unhooked the pool gate and strode in, his grin broad. He leaned down and kissed her and yes, that was the money shot because outside of some *very* niche porn, with a kiss like that, he could not claim she was his cousin or sister. It got a little heated from there, and I took enough photos to make it clear what was happening without veering into the amateur category on Pornhub.

See, I tried to be as classy as it was possible to be when I spent most of my workday photographing cheaters, going through trash, and following people. I was an *artiste* when it came to getting a photo that said, "Hey, this guy is having an affair!" without verging into prurient. I should put that on my business cards.

―――――

Parker Ferro
Private Investigator
He'll get your pictures, but not in a gross way.

———

I'd been at this long enough to know that I could probably even get some photos of them entering the same apartment. It would add that extra cherry to the evidence that Chelsea needed to prove Dieter, drug dealer, boys' boy, and cheater of the lowest class, was having an affair. She needed it to be as clear cut as it could be. See, Chelsea wasn't trying to get the apartment or the couch in the breakup. Chelsea wanted something more valuable.

Chelsea wanted custody of the SoPa pack.

When she'd explained her plan to me, I thought it was a bit extreme. I'd never heard of an alpha kicking someone out because of a breakup. But she was the pack's accountant, and Dieter was the pack's enforcer. They were both ranked high enough that they would be dealing with each other all the time.

She thought if she could show the alpha that Dieter was disloyal as a partner, the alpha might consider it to show that Dieter would be disloyal to the pack. It wasn't the worst idea I'd ever heard. I knew the SoPa alpha was touchy about stuff like that.

I had to admire Chelsea's foresight. Most women would have just thrown his stuff out on the lawn. But she'd been biding her time and playing the game. She wanted the pack and wanted Dieter left with the reputation of having been kicked *out* of his pack.

For a wolf, I imagined, that would be like getting the reputation of being kicked out of your own family. Sure, if your family was Maury-level daytime-tv crazy, everyone might shrug it off. But if your family had a reputation for being fair, playing by the rules, and being aggressively protective of its members, well, then people were going to think *you* were the one with a secret baby and the basement full of hair clippings in jars.

Someone bumped into me from behind, their bag full of liquid groceries crashing to the ground. A heavy bottle broke and soaked my jeans in dark liquor. I jerked my leg and danced away from the mess.

"Where the hell did you come from?" the guy with a liver made of steel said.

Wincing, I swore. While I'd been distracted by taking classy-as-f photos of Dieter and his non-pack-approved girlfriend, I wasn't paying as much attention to my surroundings. If I wanted to do a full invisibility spell, it would involve convincing light to bend around me, and some elements I didn't have on hand. Instead, my rough-draft version just involved convincing *people* to look around me.

Which worked great if those people didn't then walk *into* me.

"Hey," Dieter's wolf on the side said. "Who's that?"

Dieter was squinting at me, the groove between his eyebrows deepening as he glanced from my camera to my face.

"I'll tell you what he is. Dead."

I could not believe I was about to be murdered by someone who sounded like he was auditioning for *CSI: San Amaro*.

I did the only smart thing I could do: I ran. My car was on the street and he saw where I was heading and leapt to block my escape. Okay, so no car chase in my future. At least he wouldn't be able to dramatically rip me out through my windshield like he seemed to want to. I made the strategic decision to run for the park.

He paused to talk to his girlfriend, and that gave me just the head start that I needed. The park bordered the apartment complex, and some kid had clearly gotten tired of walking around the giant chain-link fence that the city had put up separating the two, because there was a gaping hole in the chain link that was perfectly child-sized.

Or, in my case, desperate-adult-sized. I squeezed down as small as I could and scrambled through, emerging in a line of trees.

As soon as my feet hit the grass, I knew I'd have a chance. Before, I'd been dealing with concrete and air, but the grass was more amenable to my needs. It's used to being crushed by people and cut by mowers. Grass is aware that its place in the universe is to be beaten down and beaten down, and when it's finally riddled with weeds, grass knows that it gets replaced with younger, prettier grass.

All that is to say grass is a salty, bitter collection of plants that made me feel like I was talking to a room full of Danny DeVitos. Will they help you? Maybe. Will they sell you out? Maybe. They'll do whatever they want and screw you for asking.

"Hey grass," I said, trying to be as light as possible. "Listen, someone's going to come through and he won't be able to see me, so he'll trample you looking for me. But, if you made it seem like I ran to the concrete, well," I shrugged. "He'll definitely get off you faster. And all I want is to make your life easy."

I could feel the curiosity and resignation. *Yeah, you got a bridge to sell me, too?* I imagined the grass saying. But, like I said, grass is irritated and constantly provoked, which leads to contrariness. So half of it said *no* and the other half said *yes*.

"Just move my scent like I went to the path," I murmured. I didn't have much time and watched with one eye as the grass shifted away from me, passing my scent blade to blade towards the walking path that circled the park.

With that taken care of, I closed my eyes and breathed in a few times before reaching out to the light and twisting it around me. It was still a rough-draft spell, but it was more like a paper that had been at least run through a spell check before being turned in.

My plan was simple. I would wait for Dieter to chase my scent to the path, where it would probably be lost with the other scents, and then sneak out the hole in the fence back to my car.

Right on cue, the fence shook as Dieter scaled it, his body a lot more massive now that I was seeing it up close. I stayed as still as I could, barely breathing. He leapt down, landing hard on the grass. I could feel the blades' explosion of annoyance and pain, like it was coming straight at me with a New York accent.

Hey, you got a problem?

Dieter's face scrunched into a frown as he scented the air, his head twisting. He slowly began to follow the scent trail that the lawn had set up. I backed my way towards the fence and it was going to be a win-win with me escaping and the werewolf chasing his own tail.

Then I heard a crunch under my foot. I'd walked too close to a maple tree and was now surrounded by a minefield of dried, crackly leaves. I could feel the amusement of the grass directly under my feet. It was ready to laugh as I got pummeled by a furious werewolf.

Dieter's head swung around and I looked for anything I could use. My eyes caught on a short hill. Squinting, I made out what looked like a dried riverbed. During the rainy season, it must be a trickle of water. Still, it gave me an idea. Now I just needed to get clear of Dieter long enough to make it work.

Shoving my camera bag to sit more comfortably across my back, I danced closer to him, keeping my body low. He was moving towards the leaf I'd crushed slowly, sweeping his eyes back and forth. When he was about to pass me, I kicked out, slamming my foot against the side of his knee as hard as I could.

He crumpled to the side with a yelp of pain and I turned and ran as fast as I could. There was a baseball game on the far side of the park, and with my head start, I probably could make it before he caught up with his injured leg. Behind me, Dieter growled. I had to make this work, because if I didn't, this was going to get very painful, very fast.

CHAPTER TWO

I CUT LEFT INTO THE WOODED CREEK BED THAT BORDERED THE park and bent to scoop up a handful of smooth, worn sand. Behind me I heard the uneven gait of a wolf with a damaged knee who was now mad enough to murder. Covering the sand with my other hand, I began to whisper.

"Hey sand," I said, panting between words. "You're so beautiful. You really do good work in this riverbed. You keep it running. You're the backbone of this whole river-thing."

The sand I was holding began to hum. It was curious, glimmering like gold in my hands. The individual grains called out for my attention.

"But, see, you used to be a rock. A long time ago. I bet if you worked hard, you could be a rock again. And then *everyone* would see how pretty you are. Because right now, you all kind of blend together. I can't even tell you apart. But, oh, man, if you were a *rock*. No one could miss that."

The sand began to twitch and hop in my hands. It was ready.

The glamour I'd cast that kept me invisible faded in fits and starts as I focused all my power on this new casting. Dieter-the-Cheater must have caught sight of me because I heard his pace quicken, and his grunts as he stumbled over the river rocks. Perfect.

With a sharp push of power, I threw the sand over my shoulder. The grains began to swirl, gathering momentum as they crashed into each other, each trying to form the biggest, prettiest rock. They pulled up more sand from the creek bed, and I heard my would be assassin, Dieter, suddenly yelp as he was pelted by sand that was flying through the air, forming pebbles, then rocks, then (if the crashes were anything to go by) slamming into each other, trying to pull the remaining sand into formation.

I glanced behind me and the rocks seemed to be attacking each other, colliding together, and there was a very pissed were-wolf caught in the middle, dodging the newly sentient rocks. There was a slight chance that I *maybe* went a little overboard. Carefully, I pulled back on the magic. Not enough to stop the spell, but definitely enough that the entire area wouldn't look like a couple of giants just had a rock fight. The stones slowed, a little more lethargic and Dieter, who was looking more wolf than man, used that as his chance to slip through.

Great. Now he was bruised, furious, and he had a case for self-defense since I threw an entire riverbed of rock at him.

"Hey, sand," I yelled. "You know who thinks that you're ugly? This guy. Hates sand. Wishes he could turn all sand into..." I had no idea what sand feared, but I took a stab in the dark. "Glass."

The rocks spun in the air, listening, and then they began throwing themselves at is-he-actually-getting-bigger?-Dieter. Smaller pebbles that I knew weren't mine got in on the action. I really had no idea that sand and rocks had such issues with being melted down and reshaped and never seeing a riverbed again— wait, no, that was actually pretty obvious.

Scrambling up the bank, I pushed through dense bushes to get to the path. I could see the field, and hear the crowd cheering. Peewee baseball, going off the numbers of parents I saw texting behind the bleachers.

I just might make it. I put on an extra burst of speed and glanced behind me to see Dieter in that awkward, half-changed state that gives most people nightmares. His legs were still human, but his torso was broader, head changing shape as his jaw actually seemed to stretch like a marshmallow that had been warmed in a campfire. He pulled up short, seeing the crowd.

Panting, I stopped near the bleachers. I felt like I was in elementary school, playing one of the infinite variations on tag. Only this one had a safe zone because no member of the SoPa pack was going to risk his good standing by attacking someone in broad daylight where there was a gaggle of baseball moms with their phones ready to film the whole thing and then complain to the police about pack wars in their parks.

Dieter shifted back, a lone, brave pebble still throwing itself at his head.

His eyes were narrowed and his eyebrows were pulled down to caveman-level. He was wondering what spell I used, maybe later he'd even ask some witch or alchemist friends, but he wouldn't find anything. The magic I use can't be found in a book. It had to be learned with experience and training only found in the Far Realm where the fae make their courts.

Chelsea did what any self-respecting paranormal would do when looking for a P.I. that could handle her werewolf boyfriend. She came to me.

My reputation in the paranormal community was a delicate balance. Witches, alchemists, and werewolves would recommend me, with a kind of *you know, he's one of us. Well, not one of* **us**, *but like 'one of us.'* Werewolves knew I wasn't a were, but they thought I was *something* not quite human. Witches assumed I was a bad alchemist and alchemists assumed I was a warlock without a coven.

I had sympathy for their uncertainty, since *I* had been uncertain for a while myself. But the truth was closer to what they thought than not. I'm not human, fae blood runs through my veins. I was trained by a witch, making me a warlock without a coven. I'm not even a little bit of an alchemist, though. The rigidity of alchemy gave me hives.

I didn't disabuse anyone about their ideas, though. Partially because who wanted to come out as fae? But also because I liked working paranormal cases. Finding the witch who cursed a client with a tail and the inability to say any word starting with *f-* and ending with *-ck* definitely beat insurance-fraud investigations.

Dieter was trying to figure out how to wring my neck without alerting all the baseball-mom witnesses. I stood up, trying to look casual and not like I'd been running for my life. The moms nearby were giving me a sort of narrow-eyed *should I call the cops* look and I pulled out my camera.

"Running late," I said. "The *San Amaro Times* sent me. Where're the kiddos?"

"For a pre-season game?" one of the moms asked, her business suit and blackberry tagging her as a lawyer.

Shrugging, I said, "Kids sell papers. Plus with everything going on, people like good-news stories."

I was vague on 'everything going on' because there's always something going on and most people will fill in the blank themselves.

Following her thumb, I headed around to the right side of the bleachers and pretended to take some photos of the kiddos. I even had a fake *San Amaro Times* press pass that I clipped to my bag. The thing about using it was that no one would ever ask why a story didn't appear in a paper. They'd be too embarrassed at how excited they'd been at the idea of being in the paper.

My eyes kept returning to where Dieter was standing, now fully human. He'd come closer. He was going to wait until I either left the game or the kids finished. Either way, he had a smirk on his face that informed me that he had nowhere to go and could wait all day. I guess drug dealers make their own hours.

The game was only in the second inning, so I had time to

figure out what my plan was. I could try to leave, but he'd probably catch me. I could try to talk the baseball dirt into making a sandstorm, but that would draw a lot more attention with all the witnesses, and the last thing I needed was Paranormal Crimes down here investigating a potential fae encounter.

One of the kiddos actually hit the ball with the satisfying sort of *thwack* that I remembered from being dragged to Dodgers games on the days when they gave out free tickets to my social worker for her caseload.

I raised my camera to catch him running to first base and instead got caught on the ball hanging in midair. In fact, everything was paused in mid-air. The parents clapping were paused, hands varying distance apart, the umpire, half bent to rest his hands on his knees was paused in a squat I wasn't sure his glutei could sustain based on how out of shape he looked.

Looking behind me, I saw Dieter frozen mid-stride. He was coming closer to me, maybe to scare me, maybe to see if he could kidnap me before anyone noticed. So, the time freeze wasn't him.

It would take an incredibly powerful coven to freeze time. Either that, or a powerful alchemist with enough time on his hands to draw layers and layers of the circles necessary to pause time. I didn't think that either would have been able to maintain the pause for... I checked my mental clock. A minute, already?

I kept scanning and then I saw him, standing halfway between the pitcher and second base, reaching up to pluck the baseball out of the air and examining it like he'd never seen one. Maybe he hadn't.

"Thistle," I said, resigned. "Of the Summer Court."

"Parker," he greeted, showing teeth that looked sharp and deadly. "Of No Court."

Thistle was narrow with a mop of cobweb-hair spiraling around his head. His face looked human until you noticed that it was as though someone squeezed his head between their hands, pushing his cheekbones back slightly, stretching his mouth too wide and leaving him with oversized bug eyes. I'd seen him look like this, uncompromisingly fae, and I'd seen him look like the most handsome man in the world, baby blue eyes and the sort of bone structure that a smart studio could build a whole superhero franchise off of. To be honest, I was not sure which was real, but I had a feeling that his fae look was his real face.

"You've been summoned by the Summer Queen," he said. That was the thing about the fae. They didn't invite. They didn't request. They definitely didn't send a text saying, 'hey. U busy?' The fae *summoned*. They *demanded*. And they definitely didn't understand that for a booty-call the correct protocol was to send an eggplant emoji at twelve a.m.

"Tell her I'm busy," I said.

He rolled his eyes to the frozen werewolf behind me. I couldn't help myself and approached him. Motionless, Dieter looked even more dangerous. He seemed like he'd gained a foot or so, and he'd somehow managed to just shift his teeth and fingers. His hands had grown claws and a light dust of fur was starting to grow on his skin. Man. This guy was going to *murder* me.

"I see," Thistle said. He raised his hand. "The Queen asked I remind you of your debt."

I spun to look at him and wished that I had Dieter's hands so that I could have ripped that smug expression off his face. He had a mild smile that gave the impression that we were playing a children's game and I'd just lost.

"The *Queen* owns my debt, Thistle. Not you. She can summon me herself if she wants," I said.

"So, should I return and tell her that you do not wish to come?" Thistle asked. He whispered a word and time shifted forward for a moment. It was like watching a film shudder to the next image. Dieter lurched forward, his frankly terrifying hands grasping for me. The noise rose as the adults applauded for a second.

Thistle spoke low, and time froze again.

What most people don't realize is that time is an entity. It's like rocks or grass. It exists. And for a strong enough fae, it would be possible to use time the same way we can use any other natural entity. Not for too long, but long enough. Time is an ocean of power. It moves forward always, but it could stop.

Only the most powerful could do that, though.

Inhaling a long breath and then exhaling all the air from my lungs, I turned back to where he was standing, looking at the child who'd turned to stare at the random man who looked like he'd just appeared in the middle of the field. I took another breath and counted to ten. My old children's therapist would be so proud of me for using a healthy coping mechanism. I put away my camera and adjusted the bag on my shoulder.

"All right," I said. "I'll hear her out."

Thistle took a long moment to smile, his teeth tinged green and sharp as knives. He reached out into the air and opened a door. Space is more flexible than time. Walking between the realms was as easy as convincing them that they were next to each other, and then just taking that step between them. You could convince space that it was closer than it thought, but you couldn't convince your stomach that the experience of jumping between realms would be pleasant.

I groaned and made a face.

With a bow, Thistle hissed, "Parker."

I forced my shoulders down, because I could look relaxed, even if everything in my body was telling me to turn around because a half-shifted werewolf was going to be safer than what was beyond the door. Ignoring the reasonable voice that was telling me to stay where I was, I walked through and found myself knee-deep in grass.

It was nighttime, the moon hanging heavy and full in the sky, like a ripe peach. I had a feeling I could pluck it from the sky and take a bite, letting moonshine drip down my arm like nectar. Shaking off the urge, I turned to see Thistle closing the door behind us, his fingers running along an invisible seam in the air, leaving a glow like sunlight behind each stroke.

The magic in the Far Realm was thicker; it seemed to seep up from the ground and into my skin. In a horror movie, this was when someone would say, "I don't like how this looks." But instead of admitting that my hair was standing up like I'd shoved a fork into a wall socket, I turned to Thistle and said, "Where is she?"

CHAPTER THREE

HE CHITTERED, THE SOUND GIVING GOOSEBUMPS TO MY goosebumps, and pointed with a long, bony finger. In the distance, lights danced, and voices rose and fell. I began wading through the grass. Thistle, the show off, glided through it smoothly, while I was wishing I had a lawnmower or a sharp machete.

Halfway to the fete, someone came up beside me.

"Parker," he breathed, his voice a brook tumbling over rocks. He looked like he was ten, an impish nose rounding out a child's face. Blue patterns had been painted on his bronze skin and he wore golden rings in his pointed ears. "Parker, you're back."

"Hey, kid," I said. "You grew up."

"Only a little bit," Larch said, wrinkling his nose. "Not as much as you. You got *old*."

"I'm not that old," I said. "You'd think I was a hundred."

"*Are* you?" he asked, dancing up on his tiptoes, and poking my nose. I paused in my slog through the grass to swat at his finger.

"Get out of here," I said. "Go bug someone else."

"*I'm* fighting a buck," he said. I watched as he leapt up, the bottoms of his bare feet brushing the top of the grass. The kid walked on top as though he was flying, and I forced my way through.

"You aren't," I said. I made a face. "Why?"

"Why do we do anything?" he asked, and his eyes flashed white, matching the heavy moon. He looked to Thistle and then lowered his voice to a whisper. "To curry favor with her."

Exhaling, I said, "Well, good luck."

"You, too," he said, and then danced across the grass back towards the lights. Everywhere his feet landed, colors exploded, a rainbow of light left in his wake. I wasn't even sure how he was doing it. What was he manipulating? The light? The air?

Shaking off the questions, I focused on my own feet, continuing to follow Thistle.

By the time I made it to the fete, my shirt was clinging to my back, and I'd been swatting away some very persistent bugs. I knew that I must have looked like a crazy person, sweating and flailing my arms. The smirk that Thistle was wearing made me think that must be the point. I jerked my chin at him where he was waiting for me at the edge of the clearing and was rewarded with a slight flinch. Then he narrowed his eyes and chittered again.

Ignoring the sound, I looked around. It was more beautiful than I remembered. Globes of light were suspended mid-air, and a thousand dancing fireflies flittered about.

The air was thick with the scent of ripe peaches and nectarines, a perfume that blanketed the gathering. They had planted long poles in the ground, and morning glory vines crawled up them and then across wires or magic to build a living canopy with glowing flowers. The tables were laden with food, an entire summer's harvest on display.

A quartet sat in a corner of the clearing played music, and there was a group of fae dancing together, a complicated pattern of switching partners and clasping hands and spinning. The music paused before the next song, and I saw her.

The fae match the beauty of their surroundings. Golden skin kissed with luminescent accents, hair in every shade of the rainbow, eyes dark and light. For all the features that mark them as different—the teeth, the uncanny movements—they are still beautiful by any standards.

No one more so than the Summer Queen. She had a narrow nose, high cheekbones, and cupid's bow lips so perfect that they would bring even the god of desire himself to his knees. Her hair glinted like the gilded page of an illuminated manuscript and had been braided around the heavy crown on her head. Shards of gemstones and gold were set together, and in the firefly-light it glinted, drawing the eye. Her neck seemed to grow longer as it bore the weight.

The Summer Queen's eyes were the color of a perfect summer's sky, pure blue, and when they cut to mine, all I could feel was fury. I shoved down the emotion, unwilling to give her any sign of what she drew out in me.

She smiled, and the expression turned every head at the fete.

"Parker of No Court," she greeted, her voice airy and filled with power. "Welcome."

"I accept your welcome," I said, pacing closer.

"You do not address me as 'Your Majesty'?" She raised one perfect eyebrow, and her smile grew broader, as though she knew how much even being here was torture.

"Should I?" I snapped. "After all, I knew you before you wore that crown."

She made a soft humming sound. "As do many who address me by my title."

I could see where this was going to go. I would continue to refuse her and she would use the debt to force me.

Showing my teeth, I said, "Your Majesty."

With a slow nod, she acknowledged the greeting.

"I thought you'd have more emissaries, given the season," I said. The fae in attendance looked to all be Summer Court, their allegiance shown by the golds and blues they wore rather than any physical difference. When appearance could be changed with a glamour, making sure that you were flying the colors was key to showing loyalty.

"The other Courts will join us tomorrow. Even the Windrose will grace us this year," she said, an amused twist on her lips. "It is not yet the solstice, Parker."

"So you have one more day until you have to worry about a knife in the back," I said. I wondered what it meant that the Windrose, the neutral arbiter of justice between the courts, was attending this year.

The curl of her lip dropped, and she narrowed her eyes. Looking to the lady-in-waiting standing beside her, she said, "How kind that Parker still worries for me."

She turned those blue eyes back to me and said, "I had thought your affection grown sour. I am glad you proved me wrong. Have faith that I will win any challenges to my throne."

I nodded and dug fingernails into my palm to stop myself from rolling my eyes. "Thistle said you wanted to see me."

"I require you to find someone," she said. She lifted her hand and projected the image of a young woman above it by magic. Her skin was a dark, sandy brown, and her dreadlocks were pulled into a heavy braid that hung over her shoulder. I felt a heaviness form in my stomach. The kid looked like exactly the sort that would entice the Summer Queen.

I was about to see a kid taken the way I was seven years ago.

"She lives in the human world," the Summer Queen said, focused on the girl. "I will have you deliver her before the summer solstice."

"I'm not bringing you your next victim," I said, shaking my head.

The Queen leaned forward, her crown reflecting the light back and forth in the gemstones until it looked like flames. Her eyes crinkled in the corners as she hissed, "Do not presume my intentions."

I opened my mouth to tell her I wouldn't do it, but a pain in my chest stopped me from speaking. My knees trembled, and I kept my feet only by tensing every muscle.

"You will find the girl and you will deliver her to me." The Queen gestured to me. Two fae, larger than the others and dressed in plain blue tunics, came up from behind me, their hands grabbing my elbows and shoulders. It only took slight pressure from them to get me to my knees.

My chest felt as though the Queen had reached in and wrapped her fist around my heart, ripping it out through my rib cage. I could feel the stutter in my heartbeat, and my breath came short.

"The debt you owe me is not as fickle as you are," the Queen said. "Yield."

I was going to die because she was going to kill me. And I'd given her the power to do so.

She had saved my life and freed me from the Far Realm with her coup against the old Queen. For that, there was an obligation.

A fae might talk the trees into bending to the ground, or a sunset into washing the sky with more colors, but the only way that a fae could cast on humans or other fae was through obligation. In fairy tales, the gifts that the fae brought were always tainted. Rumpelstiltskin wanted a child for his gift. The wicked fairy's naming gift was death for Sleeping Beauty.

The Summer Queen had gifted me my life, and until I had repaid that debt, I *owed* her. She was calling me on it, and reminding me that until we were square, she could just as easily take my life back.

I gasped out the words she wanted to hear. "I'll find her."

Immediately the pressure eased. I collapsed to my hands, panting, and hated her with every fiber of my being.

"Good," the Queen said. I saw her gesture out of the corner of my eye, and the same fae that had forced me to my knees now helped me to my feet.

I stumbled, but stayed upright when they released me. The music seemed suddenly loud, there had still been dancing while the Queen had showed me how easy I would be to murder.

"What's her name?" I asked.

"Acacia," the Queen said. She raised her chin and regarded the moon. "You have until the solstice to find her."

"A week," I said. "That's not a lot of time. If she's managing to hide from you, then I'll have to work to get her."

"I want her by the solstice." The Queen lifted an eyebrow, and she didn't even need to twist my insides to remind me again. She knew that she had me beat.

"I accept your commission," I said, the words glass in my throat. I would swallow them down and they would slice my insides to shreds.

"We thank you for your service," she said. "You're welcome to stay and enjoy the fete."

Shaking my head, I jerked my thumb in the direction of the door that Thistle had opened to bring me here. "I'll get to work on the job."

"Stay," she ordered. "We have entertainment."

At her words, the lights lowered and everyone applauded, a delicate sound that grew when Larch danced into the circle that the dancers had cleared. His feet still left rainbows in their wake. The paint on his body was glowing. He'd taken off his shirt, but left on his pants. In the darkness, the design revealed itself like a tiger's stripes.

Despite his slender pre-pubescent body, he looked like he was ready to hunt.

A scream sounded, and it was so inhuman, so confused, that it sent a shiver up my spine. The pounding of hooves grew louder,

and a buck galloped into the circle. It pulled up short, a fluorescent snake twisting in front of it.

The buck was a creature made of nightmares. It stood easily eight
feet tall. Heavy antlers that curved upwards ended in sharp points,
stained brown from blood. Its eyes glowed red, and then a second
pair blinked open on the front of its face, creating a disconcerting
image that sat wrong in my stomach. Sharp fangs were on display as it
reared, screaming again, ready to stamp the snake to death with its
heavy hooves. This was an animal that could kill someone.

In the presence of the buck, Larch looked even smaller, a child
playing with something beyond his ken.

As the buck pounded its hooves down on the snake, the
serpent disappeared, a glamour that left the animal taking a few
steps backwards. With a soft hushing noise, Larch waved his hand
and a faint green line colored the outside of the circle. Pulling out
a flute, Larch began to play, dancing around the buck.

Confused, the animal stilled, its muscles trembling. After a
moment, it swayed, its front legs bending as though it was bowing
to the Summer Queen. A round of applause went through the
crowd again, and the Queen smiled, her eyes as sharp as knives.

Larch began a complicated tune, a snake charmer in the darkness. He began casting shadows, small glamours that appeared
just long enough to send the buck panicking and leaping across
the circle. It was beautiful and horrible at the same time, like so
much of what the fae could do.

None of Larch's glamours could be considered a rough draft.
Not a single one would be broken by a drunk coming home with
more hair of the dog. Larch was doing what I could do if I took
the time to practice any of the things I'd learned at the hands of
the fae.

Finally, after the buck was panting and exhausted, boxed in by
nightmares that Larch painted in time to his music, Larch drew
out a long, high note. He was using the vibration like a blade, and

it sliced cleanly through the buck's neck. The animal collapsed forward, its heavy antlers digging into the soft soil.

It had never even come close to crossing the pale green boundary that Larch had painted.

As the lights came back up, the crowd turned to observe the Summer Queen, silent as they waited to see her verdict. As the pause turned from moments to seconds, to almost a minute, Larch's expression grew tense, his smile more teeth than joy.

The Queen nodded. "Very good, Larch. You're a credit to your teachers."

The applause was thunderous, a wave that Larch rode as the music started up again and two of the Queen's guards dragged away the cooling corpse. I watched it go and realized that grotesquely, I was like the buck. Trapped by the fae, forced to do what they wanted until I got killed for her entertainment. My only chance was to survive long enough that we were even.

When I'd paid my debt, she was going to find out it wasn't just the other courts that she needed to watch out for, because I was going to come for her.

Jerking my thumb back towards the field, I said, "I need a ride. Is Thistle taking me back, or should I call an Uber?"

From his place next to the throne, Thistle hissed, his face narrowing even more. He looked more like a snake than a man, but at a chilly glance from the Queen, he settled back down with a clenched jaw.

Stalking towards me, he stood beside me.

"Work quickly, Parker of No Court," he murmured. "Or you will find the anger of our Queen is no laughing matter."

Using two fingers, he drew a door, the invisible lines glowing like sunlight, making the fae around us wince at the sudden brightness. With a flourish, he threw open the portal and bowed me through it.

I stepped through, the target on my back more pronounced than ever. Find the girl. Easy, right? When were things ever easy?

The door closed behind me, and I was so blinded by the light that it took me a moment to realize that I wasn't back at the park. I wasn't even on the same street. Thistle had dropped me on the opposite side of San Amaro, practically on the edge of town. Hills covered in dry grass were on one side, an industrial park on the other, and overhead screamed the 101.

No bus stop and my phone was dead from the fae realm. I started walking.

CHAPTER FOUR

W<small>HEN</small> I <small>FINALLY GOT TO MY PLACE, THANKS TO THE</small> functioning bus system, my legs felt like they were about to fall off. Between the terrified sprinting that I'd done to get away from Dieter, the wading through grass, and the hike it took to find a bus stop, my poor legs had been through a more intense workout than they'd experienced in months. I was looking forward to a long shower and a dinner of whatever frozen entrée looked most calorie-filled.

Still, as soon as I got to my apartment, I could tell something was up. I lived in a squat four-floor building with the optimistic name *Las Vistas Manor.* At one point, it had been a chic yellow, but the sun had faded the paint to a dirty off-white. It was a remnant of a time when the Avenue was a happening place in San Amaro. Now the Avenue means something else entirely.

San Amaro Avenue is a street that stretches all the way across town, dividing the city in half. With the ocean on one side and the fire starter hills on the other, the city of San Amaro's borders stretch wide rather than out like Los Angeles'. The wealthy exist on the boundaries of town, with beachfront houses and hillside mansions, leaving the rest of the city divided into neighborhoods that each have their own name and flavor.

Technically, "the Avenue" could mean anywhere along San Amaro Avenue's long route, but the reality is that it meant the five blocks or so between Figueroa Street and Southwind. It was an area thick with crime, everything from vandalism to drugs. It was not my ideal office location, but it was cheap enough that most months I could afford rent.

My office-slash-apartment was on the second floor of my building, and, when I moved in, I had enough money to add a fancy sign to my door that said, "Ferro Investigations," but not enough to put that sign on anything more pricy than one of the cheaper apartments on the Avenue.

Because there were so many people coming and going, putting up wards of any sort would have been expensive and pointless. So instead, I used what I had on hand: a fine layer of dirt spread over my entryway. And that blessedly cheap substance was disturbed.

I bent down to look like I was tying my shoe. Nothing quite says, "This dude is nuts" like having a conversation with the ground, but if I crouched it maybe just looked like I was furious at my shoes and did not need the cops called. The charade probably didn't convince my neighbors, but it gave us all a good amount of plausible deniability.

"Who was it?" I muttered.

Big. Angry. Took a lot of dirt. I noted the scuff marks and had a sinking feeling that I knew who had stomped around, pounding on my door for a while before giving up.

Standing up, I rushed to put my key in the lock, but it was too late. I could hear his cheap leather shoes squeaking all the way up the hallway, even as the dirt that he'd taken with him was rejoicing at coming back to its home. Before he could touch me, I spun to face him.

"Parker Ferro!" Jeffrey Jenkins said. His voice was so loud that it echoed off the walls, rattling the other doors in the hall. He stopped a few feet away and crossed his arms. "Your rent is late."

"Jeffrey," I said. "It's only two weeks late. Give me a break. Have I ever been late before? I'll have it."

Jeffrey Jenkins was what you'd get if you gave a slug a cheap suit, a few run-down apartment buildings, and an inflated sense of self-importance. He practically left a slime trail as he rocked back on his heels. Worse, since he knew that my specialty was working with paranormals, he had it in for me. Every minor infraction was a warning letter, including things that weren't even my fault.

"No can do, Ferro," Jeffrey said. "Two weeks late is late. And in two more weeks, you're going to owe me even more rent. How're you planning on paying that if you can't pay last month's?"

He tsked and scrunched his eyebrows together, but a giant grin blossomed on his face. After a moment, he pulled his lips down into a sympathetic frown. "Sorry."

"Okay," I said, rubbing my fingers over the rough teeth of my keys. "Just give me a couple of days to wrap some stuff up and I'll have a check for you—"

His head was shaking before I'd even finished and he pulled out a thick envelope. He slapped it on my chest and I grabbed at it, my other hand forming a fist with the keys between my fingers.

"When you moved in here, you said you were quiet," he said. "You said that you ran a clean shop."

"I do, I do," I said, turning the envelope in my hand.

"But I see the kind of people you have visiting you," he said, pointing a thick finger at me. "I know your kind, Ferro."

"My *kind*," I said, arching an eyebrow. "You wanna be clear what you mean by that?"

Jeffrey bowled right through that verbal landmine with a roll of his eyes. "You work with people who should be in jail. You think I can't smell a *dog* when it drags itself through my hallway? You think I don't know you work with broom—" Realizing that his next word was going to turn his little speech into a hate crime, he put air quotes around his next words. "'Practitioners of witchcraft'?"

"None of that is illegal," I said. "I can have whatever guests I want over."

"Yeah," he said, eyes narrowed, grin sharkish. "But they aren't guests, are they? They're *clients*, which is against your lease."

"You just said you knew I was going to run my office out of my apartment!" I exploded. "You said it was fine before I even moved in!"

Jeffrey tutted, shaking his head. "You should read your contracts, Ferro. It says in real clear print that you can't run your business out of your apartment. We're not zoned for it, and I don't have the insurance to cover it."

"That's not what's written in the contract," I said, my voice low. "I read every word."

Jeffrey shrugged. "Maybe the old one got some water on it. Maybe the one I have says that you can't be running a business in my building."

My blood felt like it was on fire. There's a reason you don't renege on a deal with a fae. Contracts, agreements, word games, they all *mean* something to the fae. It's in our nature to abide by them... and to use them to trap poor suckers who think that in a deal with the fae, they'll come out on top.

"Don't pursue that," I said. "Because I know what I signed."

My voice was low and laced with the oldest magic there is. I didn't even say the words so much as they seeped out of me, deep and low, and I saw Jeffrey pause, mouth hanging open. Something in his little lizard brain must have told him that he was walking along a narrow path and another step would send him careening down into something ancient and more dangerous than he knew.

Swallowing, he shrugged his shoulders back like a bird ruffling its feathers. "That's a pay or quit notice, Ferro."

His voice squeaked on my name. He shrugged again and

seemed to get back some of his strength, his chest expanding as he got on more solid legal ground.

"Come up with the month's rent or I'm sending you your eviction notice on Friday." His lip peeled back from his upper teeth in a sneer.

"That's four days from now!" I snapped, doing the math.

"Be grateful," Jeffrey said. "I only *had* to give you *three* days."

"Oh, thanks for the extra four hours," I said, sarcasm under my tone like a razor blade. "There aren't even any banks open right now."

"That reminds me," Jeffrey said. "No checks. Money order or cash, only."

"You want a thousand five hundred in cash?" I said.

"A thousand eight hundred with interest," he corrected. "See you Friday, Parker."

One of the doors down the hallway opened, and I saw someone poke their head out. It was Malcolm, his white hair cropped short like always. As far as I knew, he'd been living in the building since back when *Las Vistas* was considered somewhere you'd *want* to live, rather than somewhere you'd ended up.

I'd been in his apartment, and I'm not sure if he used some alchemy or if it was just what a place looked like when you'd been in it for decades, but I'd swear it was bigger than the floor plans for it were. I was pretty sure it even had a whole extra bedroom that wasn't on the blueprints.

"Jeffrey Jenkins," he said. Stepping out into the hallway, he left his door open a bit. "Parker Ferro. Thought I heard shouting."

Jeffrey showed his teeth and ground out, "Just a minor disagreement over the rent, Mister Pride."

Malcolm tutted. "You know I don't like shouting."

He took unsteady steps towards us, his carved wooden cane moving along the hallway carpet with heavy thumps. In the hallway light, his skin looked only a shade lighter than the polished walnut of his cane. When he got to us, he looked up, eyes squinting.

"Almost called the police," he said.

Malcolm was the other reason that wards would have been wasted. Who needed expensive magic when they had a septuagenarian neighbor with the police on speed dial?

"No need for that," Jeffrey said. "Parker and I came to an agreement. Didn't we, Parker?"

"That I'll pay you when I can?" I said, forced cheer coming through gritted teeth.

"That you have until Friday," Jeffrey corrected. He nodded at Malcolm and stomped down the hallway.

"Let me see," Malcolm said, tugging the envelope out of my fingers. He huffed as he pulled out the papers and scanned them rapidly. I noticed that his eyes were a lot sharper when he wasn't performing for Jeffrey. "Looks like it's in order. You having trouble with your bills, son?"

I sighed down at my shoes. "Just a little cash-flow issue. Don't worry, I'll handle it."

Malcolm nodded. "He's going to serve you the eviction papers on Friday if you don't pay. But bring them to me before you do anything. He might get sloppy."

"Thanks, Malcolm," I said. He offered me back the papers and patted my shoulder, his hand weighty.

"You're a good boy, Parker. It'd be a shame if you get evicted." He shook his head. "I don't like Jeffrey much. His mother was a good landlord, but he's too greedy."

"You need help back to your apartment?" I asked, offering my elbow.

Malcolm waved me off, but I still ambled beside him as he made his way back to his apartment. With the door ajar, I got a peek inside as he stepped back in. That place was definitely larger than it should have been.

"Glad I came out when I did," he said. "You know, he pulled

the same trick on a nice girl running a bakery out of her apartment. Delivered cupcakes, I think. Always had a few extra cookies for the kids in the building. He said that her paperwork got coffee spilled on it, and when he presented her a new contract, it said she couldn't run a business out of her apartment."

He tutted again, hand tightening on his cane. "You know, I just don't like people who break contracts."

My head hurt for a minute, and I felt like I was facing something dark and massive, a storm above me. Shaking my head, the hallway spun slightly before righting itself. My blood sugar was plummeting from not having eaten since lunch.

With an unsteady step backwards, I waved my hand. "Thanks, Malcolm."

"Oh, before I forget, some cop came by your place before Jeffrey showed up this afternoon," Malcolm said.

"A cop?" I asked, frowning. My mind flipped to the only cop who might be looking for me. "What did he look like? Handsome, but with an air like he follows every regulation in the manual? The type of guy who doesn't jaywalk even when there's no one around?"

Regarding me, Malcolm said, "I'd say a little taller than you, so just over six feet. Nice suit. A fine young blood. Asked me if I needed any help getting up the stairs."

So definitely Detective Nicholas King, then.

"Did he say what he wanted?" I frowned, trying to figure out what SAPD's finest would want with me.

"No," Malcolm shook his head. "He did say he'd try again later."

"Okay. Thanks again," I said.

He watched as I made my way back to my door, shutting his only when I slotted my key into the lock. Stepping inside, I released a long sigh. Had it only been a single day?

I tossed the open envelope onto my desk, the addition threatening an avalanche of other papers. Hanging my camera bag from a coatrack near the door, I took quick steps towards the kitchen and pulled a glass out of the drying rack, filling it from the sink. I drank it down in one long swallow and then filled it again, taking a little more time with the second glass.

The rent would have to be dealt with, and it burned my blood to remember *why* I was so broke. Derek McCallum might have thought he got away, but he and I had a *contract* and he would *pay* and then pay some *more* for breaking faith. I didn't need to check my bank balance to know that after the payment I had to make to Laurel in a few days, I'd only have five hundred left.

Looking around, I was irritated all over again at the outrageous rates that Jeffrey could charge for such a crappy place. My apartment was one room, the living and dining room taking up the same rectangular space. A narrow kitchen was separated from the two by a tiled island with a sink and dishwasher in it. The bedroom was a small square with a bathroom and a closet.

I'd set up my desk in the middle of the living room and put a couple of folding chairs out for clients. That squeezed my couch and tv to the side, but the type of clients that came to me didn't mind the awkward Feng Shui.

Marco would have hated it.

I stripped off my shirt and pants, picking them off the kitchen tile and tossing them towards the bedroom as I enjoyed the chill for a moment before following my clothes into the bedroom to take a shower. Kicking the clothes towards the overflowing laundry hamper, I headed into the bathroom and turned on the shower, letting it heat before stepping in. The spray was a sharp relief and I could feel individual muscles relaxing as I soaped up.

My vision was getting spotty again, so I made the shower quick. Wrapping a towel around my waist while I was still dripping wet, I headed to the kitchen. At the freezer, I selected a tray of macaroni and cheese from the stacks of blue and orange boxes, and tossed it in the microwave. I squinted at the microwave clock, shaking my head. It was already close to nine thirty.

While the food heated, I pulled on some sweatpants and a cotton t-shirt from my high school gym class that was more comfortable than fashionable. The logo was a leaping tiger, and I made a face at how much of it had peeled off.

I'd been in high school when Marco had first taken me to his office. It was a nice storefront about as far from the Avenue as you could get. Not in one of the ritzy neighborhoods, but a nice working-class area for a nice working-class guy like Marco. It had been part of the deal when I went to live with him and Shannon. I got to do the fun P.I. stuff with Marco if I kept up with my magic lessons with Shannon.

After the last foster home where they would lock me in a closet any time my magic got out of control, it had seemed too good to be true.

The microwave beeped that my two thousand five hundred calorie dinner was done when someone knocked on the door. Three polite taps. I sighed up at the ceiling and opened the door.

CHAPTER FIVE

ON THE OTHER SIDE OF THE DOOR STOOD SOMEONE I WOULD not have pegged as the type to visit me at nearly ten o'clock at night.

Chelsea Kinney was wearing a short pea coat over a hunter-green blouse, the ensemble wrapped up with skinny jeans and high heels. Her smile had the bland banality of someone about to make a public comment in front of the city council. She clutched her oversized handbag, swinging it in front of her knees.

"Chelsea," I said, frowning. "Hey, come in."

"Thanks," she said, stepping past me. She glanced around the apartment, eyes noting the overflowing paperwork and laundry still visible in the bedroom. I moved to shut the bedroom door and gestured to one of the folding chairs in front of my desk.

The last time she'd been over, the place had been cleaner. I always attempted to make sure things looked nice when people came for a consultation. Just because I was working out of my living room, didn't mean that I couldn't have *some* pride.

"What's going on?" I said. "Did you want an update?"

Taking the offered seat, she perched on the edge, arms

wrapped around her bag. Licking her lips, she said, "I'm here to pay you."

"I still have some of your deposit left," I said, shoving the pile of paperwork to a more stable angle before flipping through, looking for my notes on the hours for her case. "I think you're good."

"No, you don't understand. I'm here to call off the hunt..." Shaking her head, she winced a smile. "I mean, you don't need to keep looking into it. It's fine."

"It's fine," I said, one of my eyebrows creeping up.

She looked around the apartment, her eyes catching on a dirty plate I'd left on the couch. The microwave beeped again to remind me about my dinner and she jumped.

"I got photos of him. There's no way he can pass it off as anything other than cheating," I said. Standing, I grabbed my bag and pulled out my camera, turning it on and looking at the viewfinder as I searched for the right pictures.

When I had them, I passed it over to her, and she released her bag to take the camera. For a few moments, she stared at it. I watched her toggle to the next picture and the one after. Her lips pinched together and then she shook her head.

"It doesn't matter. Now that he knows you were there, I can't take the pictures to the alpha," she said, handing back the camera.

I huffed a breath. Turning off the camera, I pulled out one of the two SIM cards and turned it between my fingers.

"I don't get it," I said. "You were so sure a few days ago. What changed?"

Her spine straightened, and she glared at me. "He *saw* you. He saw you and when he got home, he called a whole council meeting and made a big stink about it. Dieter thinks it was some other pack, but if he—if *they* find out it was me, it'll look like *I* betrayed the pack by letting someone into our business."

She leaned back in the chair and winced. I narrowed my eyes, scanning her. "What's wrong with your back?"

"Nothing," she blurted.

In my gut, I knew it wasn't nothing. There was no bruising visible, but she was a werewolf, she'd heal fast. Probably fast enough that she even convinced herself that it wasn't really abuse because it wasn't like he did any *permanent* damage.

I tapped the SIM card on the desk and said, "Anyone else know?"

"Know what?" she bit out.

"About your back," I said. Looking her over, my eyes caught on her out-of-season jacket. "And your arm."

Drawing herself up, she gave me the haughty look I remembered from our first meeting. The icy glance was enough to make me reconsider my first impression of her. Her bad day was a lot worse than her favorite nail place being closed.

"How much money to make you forget about this?" she asked, pulling out a checkbook.

I almost said one thousand eight hundred. But I could feel what Marco would have said to that. He would have called it blackmail. It would have *been* blackmail.

"I can forget it, free of charge," I said. I leaned forward and placed the primary SIM card on the edge of the desk. Usually, I wiped the backup SIM card after a case was done, but this time I decided I'd keep it. "In case you decide to use the pictures."

She picked it up and tucked it into her bag. For a moment, she glanced back at the dirty plate and then her eyes cut to me.

"Dieter got a whiff of your scent when he was chasing you," she said. "I don't know how you got away from him, but now that he has your scent, he's going to try to track you."

Shrugging, I said, "I can take care of myself."

"*Can* you?" she asked, looking around the apartment at my stacks of paper, the door closed to cover up piles of laundry, and the dishes left out. "Dieter's planning to kill you."

"I'm sure I'll be fine," I said, which was not really an answer, but I wasn't about to get into a fist fight with the guy. I'd lose for certain.

"He called the entire council together," she said. "He even got the alpha involved."

"Yeah?" I asked. "You're worried."

"I know *exactly* what Dieter's capable of," she spat. Her knuckles went white where she'd wrapped her hand around the strap of her bag. "Do you?"

"I mean, he's a big guy," I said. "I can imagine he'd mess me up."

"Malik agreed that you should be questioned and dealt with," Chelsea said. "That's how Dieter spun this."

"Malik is the alpha?" I asked. "No, he's second, isn't he?"

Huffing, Chelsea rolled her eyes. "How would you know what our power structure is?"

"I try to keep on top of things." I shrugged, crossing my arms over my chest. "And last I checked, Malik was second. What happened to Nate?"

"He retired." Her tone was flat.

I tried to relax my eyebrows, but I saw the problem. "Nate got killed, didn't he?"

She pursed her lips and stared at me.

"Okay, so he got killed by another pack. Recently?" I drummed my fingers on my bicep.

"In May," she said. "The cops said it wasn't suspicious. Because why would they look into the death of some pack alpha?"

I could imagine what the police would have said. Something along the lines of, "just let them work it out, they're only killing each other" and "you know how *dogs* are."

"You don't think it was another pack," I said, making it a statement.

She rubbed at her arm and winced a little. It might have healed on the surface, but the pain of whatever Dieter did when he was mad hadn't faded.

"Dieter thinks it was another pack," I said, guessing. "And you think it wasn't."

Her lip curled, and I saw some wolfishness in her display of teeth. "Why would another pack start with our alpha and then do nothing else? I even had most of the others agreeing with me."

"Until Dieter saw a photographer who was trailing him. And he spun it that I'd been photographing him doing pack activities." I leaned back and rotated my chair a bit. "So, now he has evidence that it was some other pack, trying to move in on SoPa territory."

"You said you were going to forget about it," she snapped. "Why does it matter?"

"Hey, if I'm going to be kidnapped, tortured, and murdered by someone, I want to know why." I tilted my head and smirked at her. "Call it my nosy nature."

Chelsea snorted, and I saw a hint of a smile on her face.

"And you don't think that Malik would listen to you if you tried to explain why you were having Dieter followed?" I asked. "He's a reasonable guy. More than Nate ever was."

Nate was the one who'd pulled SoPa from the lower level to one of the most powerful packs in the city. If he had them selling drugs and weaponry to do it, well, as far as he saw it, that was just the cost of doing business. Malik had been a loyal right hand as they cut a swath through their competition, but I was curious to see what kind of alpha he'd make.

Curious from a distance, mind you. I had no interest in getting personally involved in pack politics. Not that I had much choice at the moment, because it seemed like I was going to be getting a front-row seat to how the new alpha managed his territory.

She shook her head. "He's not going to have a choice."

"Because he needs to prove he's strong enough to lead the pack?" I scoffed. "Didn't he have any challengers? Didn't Dieter challenge him?"

She shook her head. "No. No challenges."

Most alphas got the title through bloodshed. It was how they proved they had the strength to lead the pack. It was rare to see someone take power through politics alone, though if anyone could, it would be Malik. He was always too smart for his own good.

"He's going to prove he's worthy by cutting off my head, isn't he?" I groaned.

"Dieter will do the actual decapitation," Chelsea said.

"Great. So much better," I said. Rubbing my eyes, I banged my head on the back of my office chair. "How likely is he to forget my scent?"

For a moment, Chelsea was quiet, and I opened my eyes to see her thoughtful. "You could try that angle."

"Saying they got the wrong guy, meaning that he lost my scent?" I said. "That'd put a black mark on his rep, right?"

"Yeah," she said, tapping one of her fingers on her bag. "It might work."

"What about taking pictures makes this a death sentence?" I groaned again and answered my own question. "Because Dieter's convinced them that I was involved in the old alpha's death. Because if I was photographing Dieter, then I was obviously going to kill him next."

I wanted to swear, but cut it off at the first sound, because Chelsea looked like a person who would get a taste-of-lemon face at foul language. "I'll stay out of his way. He can't kill what he can't find."

"I just thought you should know," she said, standing. "He seemed serious about it."

She started towards the door and stopped with her hand on the door handle. "Who was the girl?"

"Dieter's wolf on the side?" I shrugged. "No idea. I thought you might know her, since she looks like she'd be in a pack."

"We don't all know each other," she said, rolling her eyes. "And I thought the cops were bad."

"I didn't say you all know each other, but I'll be honest, you seem like a person who has a binder for each of the other packs in the area with biographical data for every member you know about."

She snorted again, but didn't correct me. After a pause, she said, "I'd be careful with the Five Dragons, then, too."

"Noooooo," I whined the word, and banged my head on the chair again. "The Five Dragons?"

"I was hoping you were going to say she was just a wolf bunny or someone hoping to join the pack," she said. "I don't know for certain."

Offering her a tight smile, I said, "Are you going to be okay?"

With her hand wrapped protectively around her left arm, she nodded. "I know how to take care of myself."

Wetting my lips, I said, "You know where I live if you ever need anything."

She jerked her chin and pulled her shoulders back, as though putting on a layer of armor. When she looked back at me, she was a senior member of the SoPa pack. There wasn't any evidence of the soccer mom her outfit painted her as.

"See you around," she said, opening the door and stalking out.

I rose to lock the door behind her and slid the chain home as I thought about the past few hours. Between the Summer Queen and losing my apartment, Dieter Rossi wasn't even at the top of my list of problems. Still, it would be bad if I got caught by the SoPas.

The microwave beeped and my stomach didn't rumble so much as turn over like a tractor engine in the dead of winter. I swore my intestines twisted in hunger. Grabbing the mac and cheese, I picked a clean fork out of the drying rack and plopped down on the couch. I watched my blank tv screen as I ate, thoughts chasing each other around my brain until I flipped on the tv, just to have the noise.

Marco never would have gotten into this mess. Or if he did, he would have been able to get out of it with some story that started with, "You know..." He'd never have owed the Summer Queen anything, and he'd never paid a bill late, though. Hell, he'd have just sat Dieter down and convinced him that cheating was wrong and he should leave Chelsea and think about his life choices.

I fell asleep like that, slumped on the couch, until I woke up to infomercials at three a.m. and dragged myself to bed.

CHAPTER SIX

I DRAGGED MYSELF OUT OF BED WHEN THE LIGHT FROM THE window was bright enough to nearly blind me, which meant that the sun had already crested the building next door, a rent-by-the-hour hotel that was half-full at any given hour of the day. Squinting at my phone, I made a face at the time.

The coffeemaker gurgled and spat out dark, caffeinated manna when I slouched into the kitchen. Coffee in one hand, dry bowl of cereal in the other, I ate at my desk as I sifted through the paperwork that had gotten backed up when I was staking out Dieter, the guy who now wanted to kill me. A few people had finally paid their bills, but when I counted up the checks it was barely one thousand, not enough to cover the money I'd need by Friday.

Still, money was money. I set them aside to cash later and jerked at someone pounding on my door. Coffee spilled over a copy of a police report on a car accident, and I mumbled, "Coming, coming," as I mopped it up with the hem of my shirt. When things were mostly dry, I walked over to the door, peeking out the peep hole to see an empty hallway. At the corner of the lens, I could see a shadow.

Normally, I would assume it was just a nervous client, maybe someone close to bolting. But given that I was a wanted man, I called out, "Who is it?"

"SAPD, Ferro, open up."

The shadow in the corner moved closer, holding up a badge and ID to the door. I blinked. I was about to be faced with a man who'd occupied more than his fair share of my thoughts recently.

Flipping the deadbolt, but leaving the chain on, I opened the door a crack and sure enough, there was Detective Nicholas King standing in my doorway. He raised an eyebrow, and I closed the door enough to slide the chain free. I pushed open the door and leaned against the jamb.

"Detective King," I greeted.

He looked like a cop from a CBS procedural. Not the veteran silver-fox head of the unit, but the young, hot new guy who shows up in episode one as the audience surrogate. One sad backstory later and he's the fan favorite and when he dies in season six rescuing a bus full of orphans, everyone points to that as the moment where the show jumped the shark.

Which was a long way of saying that he was tall and hot, with warm amber skin and hair that was buzzed regulation short. He had a build that showed careful attention to leg day and arm day. Since I'd had my coffee, I could admire that for all that he must only make a cop's salary, his suit had been tailored to fit perfectly.

"Ferro," he greeted, his lips pursed.

"Should I ask to see your warrant?" I asked. "Or is this a friendly chat?"

"This is about police business," he said. He gestured to the hallway where a couple of doors shut as he glanced around.

"Did you bring your handcuffs again? You know I like it kinky," I said. Since last time the cuffs had included a trip down to the station and being booked (although not charged) with trespassing, I actually wasn't in any hurry to repeat it.

The lines around his mouth deepened, and he shook his head, muttering about a mistake. I bit the inside of my cheek hard and then gestured like I was presenting a prize. "Come in. I don't have anything to hide from the SAPD."

He stepped in, nearly brushing me, and he had to go and *smell* good, too. Some sharp aftershave that left me with the impression of clear mountain lakes and redwoods.

The first time we'd met, I'd thought it would lead to a drink and maybe a quickie afterwards. The second time had ended up with me spending the night in lockup until Laurel came and bailed me out. Needless to say, it had spoiled my hopes for Detective King.

Surveying the apartment, he made a face similar to the one that Chelsea had, except hers was more: *This is the guy I hired?* And King's was more: *This is how you live?* His eyes caught on the same plate that had tripped Chelsea up last night, and my face heated at the reminder that I'd still forgotten to put it in the sink.

"Nice place," he said, crossing his arms and *hello biceps*. "Looks exactly how I imagined your apartment would look."

I bristled at his words and pointed to the chair.

"Take a seat," I ordered.

He drew his shoulders back and shook his head. "This isn't going to work."

Swallowing down the urge to scream, I said, "You came to *me*."

"Yeah," he said. He exhaled and pushed back his jacket to put both hands on his hips. His lips were pursed, nearly white. Finally, he huffed a sigh and sat on the chair.

At the surrender, my own irritation deflated. "Let me get you a coffee."

In the kitchen, I took out one of the good mugs and filled it with what was left in the carafe. Placing the mug in front of him, I sat down in my office chair. He examined the blue mug, the words *This Is My Happy Place* on it in cheerful teal letters.

Neither one of us spoke and when he took a sip of the coffee, he winced, but didn't say anything. I finished my own coffee and tapped my spoon on the edge of my cereal bowl.

"What're you doing here, King?"

"There's a case," he said. "I thought you might be able to tell me if it's fae."

"Why do you think it's fae?" I asked, dropping my spoon back into the bowl with a clatter.

"Because it's not alchemy or witchcraft as far as I can tell," he said. "So I need to rule out everything else."

"And I'm next on your checklist?" I asked. Of course King would have one. He was meticulous and ordered. He probably ironed his underwear every morning to make sure that there wasn't a wrinkle he didn't want to be there.

I'd blame it on the fact that he was a practicing alchemist, but most alchemists I knew were only that conscientious about their casting. Their lives were as messy as the rest of ours. Granted, most of the alchemists I knew were through my work, and most people were in one of the messier places in their lives when they contacted a P.I.

"Yes," he said, eyes narrowed. "Unless you think I should contact the *other* fae expert in San Amaro?"

I snorted at his snark and said, "Okay, point."

He wouldn't have come to me if he'd had any other choice. As far as the SAPD knew, I was the only person who'd survived a visit with the fae without ending up a vegetable or institutionalized for life. Of course, they didn't know that the reason my visit to the Far Realm hadn't ended in the San Amaro asylum was because my blood was half fae, even if my parentage was a mystery.

"What's the case?" I asked.

"A couple of werewolves have been murdered," he said. "And drained of their magic."

"What?" I leaned forward, resting my elbows on my desk. "You mean they were used in spellcraft and their magic was low."

"I mean that they didn't have a drop of magic left in their body," he said. "None."

"They're werewolves," I said. "That's impossible. Their *nature* is magical."

His lips tightened. "Yeah."

"Can I see them?" I asked. He narrowed his eyes, and I held up my hands. "I believe you, but it would be easier for me to recognize if it was a fae spell if I could see it."

"Just tell me if you've seen them use anything like that," he said.

I started to answer, but paused. "Am I consultant on this?"

"Officially?" he said. "No. You're just an expert that I'm speaking with."

"But it could be a consult I billed for, right?" I said, aware that it sounded more like a whine than anything else.

"How much?" he asked, leaning back in his chair. He crossed his legs, his ankle resting on his opposite knee. How did he always look like he was posing for a *GQ* photo shoot?

"Eighteen hundred," I said, immediately. "That'd be... thirty-two hours?"

"This is a twenty-minute conversation. How are you going to stretch it to thirty-two hours?" he said, raising an eyebrow. He'd shaved down to a heavy stubble and on me it would have looked like I couldn't afford a razor, but on him it looked like it was on purpose. Like every day, he spent twenty minutes getting the right length on his hair and beard.

"What if I followed you around?" I asked. "The SAPD has deep pockets, I could follow you around and act as a guide."

"You want to do a ride along and pretend that it's something you should bill for?" he asked, a small smile on his face. He licked a lip and tilted his head, and I had to admit that it was ridiculous. "What do you even need the money for?"

"Nothing," I said. I rubbed a hand over my face, my palm catching on my own non-designer stubble. "Never mind."

His lips twisted, and he sighed. "I can't let you bill for the hours since this isn't an official consult. But, if you found information that led to an arrest ... my bosses *are* offering a reward."

"How much?" I asked.

"Ten thousand," he said. He waited, and I tapped the spoon on the bowl again, the *clink* loud in the room. "If it leads to an arrest."

"You said this is a *werewolf* case," I said. My eyes narrowed as I thought. "Is this about Nate Charles getting killed?"

He straightened, his foot dropping off his knee. "How do you know about that?"

"I try to keep up," I said, shrugging like it wasn't a big deal.

"Do you know who killed him?" he asked.

"I heard that you think it was another pack," I said. "Why's there a reward if it was just pack politics?"

King nodded, as though acknowledging I'd scored a point. "We did, yeah, but the CGPD sent it to the Paranormal Division when they found out about the magic being drained out of the vics."

Holding up a hand, I guessed at the acronym. "Criminal Guys... Problem Department?"

King actually laughed at that, and maybe I'd guessed a little wide of the mark to see if he'd crack. "One out of four. Criminal Gang and Pack Division."

"The Gang Squad," I said. My familiarity with the police was, thankfully, tangential.

Despite my ignorance of police politics, I knew the CGPD by their street name, the one that had most wolves spitting. They said that once the Gang Squad had you in their crosshairs, you couldn't drop a gum wrapper on the sidewalk without being arrested for littering.

With a shrug, King nodded. "The Gang Squad."

"They passed something on to you?" I asked. "Doesn't it usually go the other way with them taking Paranormal cases?"

"We're getting off topic," King said, lips twisted at the mention of collar stealing. "Do you have information or not?"

"I've never seen a fae drain magic before," I said. "But I can ask around and find out for certain."

Huffing, King checked his watch. "Twenty minutes. And that's definitely not enough to earn ten thousand dollars."

"Don't count me out yet." I held up a finger. "I'm a P.I., with my own sources. Ones that don't like to talk to cops."

"Oh, yeah? You cultivate a lot of informants on the cheating husbands and child-support-evaders beat?" He looked so smug, with his lip quirked and his eyebrows relaxed.

"I do other cases," I said. "Like background checks and fraud."

"Sounds like you know a lot of people who'd be able to tell you about werewolf murders," he said.

I wanted to snark back, but the more I antagonized him, the less chance he would tell me enough about the murders that I could give him his culprit gift-wrapped. On the other hand, he was just so cocky I couldn't resist one last dig.

"Yeah, Mister Paranormal Lead Detective? Seems like none of your leads panned out either, if you're coming to me. In fact, I'd say that I have a leg up, since I haven't even started yet and your informant pool is already dried up."

Smirking at him, I raised my eyebrow, expecting him to snap back. Instead, his face flushed and he ducked his head a little, examining some papers on my desk with interest.

"That's because you're the first one I've come to," he muttered.

I was so surprised that I gaped for a minute. King? Came to *me* first?

"Tell me about the killings," I said, finally. "Maybe it'll shake something loose."

He rolled his eyes up, like he knew that I was just pumping him for information, but he started talking. "The first werewolf was found up off Calgary, in the old meat-packing plant. CGPD was tagged in because it was in Five Dragons territory, and when the SoPa alpha showed up dead in the same way, they were ready to call it retribution and were going to close the case."

His tone dripped acid, and I could tell there wasn't any love lost between him and CGPD. His mouth pursed, and I waited a few long beats. My stomach rumbled.

Digging the spoon into the bowl of cereal I took a bite. There was a huff of air and I looked up to see King staring at my bowl. "Is that *dry* Choco Wolf Crunch?"

"We can't all eat plain oatmeal every day at six a.m. after our morning workout," I accused.

"I put raisins in," King said. "At least I'm not eating raw sugar."

Taking a heaping spoonful of the dark flakes, I shoved them in my mouth and chomped, the sound like a garbage disposal full of rocks in my ears.

"That is *disgusting*," he said.

"So, CGPD was going to bury it?" I prompted. "Why'd they decide to pass it on?"

"Because the SoPas were making so much noise, the coroner had the department alchemist come in to do a scan. She was the one who discovered the magic drain, and the coroner remembered that the other wolf had been low on magic when he ran the basic bloodwork," King said.

"And two dead werewolves both without magic makes it a serial," I said.

"It makes it suspicious," King corrected. "But I won't be calling it a serial killer just yet. And *you* won't be, either."

I made a finger gun and winked in a way I was pretty sure would drive him insane. "Not a serial killer making his way through San Amaro's werewolves, got it. I'll ask around, and see if I can bring you your arrest. Have you looked into other paras?"

"What do you mean?" King asked. His gaze went slightly

distant, eyes squinted. I could see the thoughts already going behind his hazel gaze.

"I mean, wolves aren't the only ones with magic in their blood. It might be worth it to check on vampires and fae creatures," I said. "The selkies probably won't talk, but incubi? Brownies?"

King leaned back, eyes narrowed and mouth twisted. I made a show of looking at my wrist, where there wasn't any watch.

"Huh, would you look at that? Thirty minutes and counting."

Rolling his eyes, he stood. "Thanks for the tip, Ferro."

"Hey, if we're working together, you should call me Parker," I said. "And I'll call you... Nico?"

I took a guess at the nickname and watched as his mouth pulled down, a deep groove forming between his eyebrows. He practically growled, "Detective King."

"Nick?" I guessed again.

"Call me if you find out anything," he said, standing. He buttoned up his suit jacket and opened the door, sweeping out.

I grinned. Nick, for certain.

CHAPTER SEVEN

AFTER NICK LEFT, I GOT DRESSED AND FINISHED MY BOWL OF cereal. It felt a bit like spite to continue eating it dry, since I discovered that I *did* have milk that hadn't gone bad when I opened the refrigerator. While I was crunching on the last of the chocolate flakes, I ran through a list of all my informants, trying to decide who would know anything about werewolves being killed.

My phone buzzed as I mentally crossed off most of the list, and I glanced at the screen. Seeing the name displayed, I bit down extra hard on the last bit of cereal, catching a bit of my tongue and tasting blood. I swallowed down the salty mess and watched as the screen went to black, then buzzed to life again with a text.

I groaned.

As slowly as I could I washed all the dishes in the sink, even going so far as to retrieve the one abandoned on the couch. The amount of dishes created a precarious Jenga structure in the drying rack, but then I ran out of housework, and I had to read the text.

Answer your phone.

I opened the app and texted back as slow as my fingers could type:

Coming by. Now okay?

My stomach dropped as I watched the three dots showing that she was answering. After nearly a minute, she replied. *Yes. Meet me at work.*

Well. At least there would be free food.

Scanning through the closet, I chose a clean, blue button-up shirt I used for depositions, and a pair of jeans as close to slacks as I could get without looking like I was trying too hard. Out of habit, I grabbed my bag, checking that everything was there: wallet, keys, camera, extra magic supplies.

When I left, the hallway was quiet, and I paused outside Malcolm's door, but decided that I'd have to check back with him later. My car was still outside Dieter's girlfriend's apartment. If I was taking a bus, it'd add an extra half hour to my travel time, and she was already pissed at me.

Luck, or some transportation demigod, was on my side and I caught the right bus just as I was stepping up to the bus stop. The trip to the east side was uneventful, except for a couple of alchemists that started in on a witch holding a large copper cauldron. I was going to step in, but the witch glared and began muttering a spell that had both of the alchemists scratching at their arms like they'd been through a clump of poison oak.

No one else commented, and I swung down the bus steps at the next stop, landing on the sidewalk a few storefronts down from a cheery cafe with a cat shingle hanging out front.

―――――

Laurel's Cafe and Patisserie
Come in and find your next favorite dessert.

―――――

Stepping into Laurel's felt like stepping into a garden in the warmth of spring. Everything was green and calming. A few people with laptops had claimed the power outlets along the walls. There was a couple chatting near the window, and almost everyone else was reading. The dark wooden floor absorbed the sound of my footsteps as I came up to the counter.

Laurel was behind the counter, her stark black hair pulled into a bun held in place with a pen. As I approached, she pursed her blood-red lips and crossed her arms. I stopped a few feet away from the counter, watching as she looked me up and down.

"Is that Parker? Parker Ferro? He's not dead?" Laurel said.

The barista working beside her gave her a side-eye and silently grabbed a broom and moved out into the cafe.

"Laurel," I said, tucking my hands into the back pockets of my jeans and leaning back on my heels. "Place looks good. Did you repaint?"

"No," she said. "I guess it's just been that long since you were here."

One of the guys with a laptop stepped between us, dropping coins noisily into a tip jar and waving at Laurel, "See you tomorrow!"

She acknowledged him with a small smile and a wave, before returning to her assessment of me.

"I'm surprised," she said. She uncrossed her arms and moved over to the brightly lit dessert case. Without looking at me, she pulled out two fruit tarts and a pastry shell filled with some sort of creamy chocolate filling.

"Why?" I asked, following as she took the plate to one of the empty tables near the large plate-glass window.

Catching the barista's eyes, she gestured back to the counter, and the woman nodded, taking quick steps back to her post. She watched the woman and spoke without looking at me. "You usually don't come around this close to the solstice."

"Yeah," I said. "Well."

Digging in my satchel, I pulled out my wallet and removed a folded check. I pushed it over to her. For a moment, she stared at it, and then drew the check closer to her, lifting it to examine the details.

"Have you seen her?" she asked. "It's almost her birthday."

"No," I murmured. "She's not there."

"Oh, she's most definitely *there*, Parker," Laurel said. "We're both paying a lot of money for her to be there."

"You know what I mean," I said.

"She'd like to see you," Laurel said. "I know she would. Go visit her."

"Maybe," I sighed. "I'll try."

"Good," she said. She nudged the white plate towards me, the bottom scraping across the wooden table. "Eat."

I took a tart and bit into it. The berries on top were bitter and a perfect contrast to the sweet pastry cream filling. I groaned.

"This is why I don't come here," I complained. "You're going to make me fat."

Laurel snorted and smiled, the expression barely a twitch of her lips. "Liar. You don't come here because you're worried I have a case for you."

"Do you?" I said, suspiciously. Glancing down at the plate of delicious pastries, I narrowed my eyes. "Are these bribery pastries? Are you trying to get me to do more pro-bono work?"

"No, they're not *bribery*," she said. "They're a gift. From a loving sister."

"Oh, really," I said, still looking at the tart in my hand with suspicion. "What do you want, Laurel? Another one of your coven members need help finding a lost familiar?"

"I'm not allowed to worry about you? You work too much, especially this time of year. And you never visit," she said, grouchily, stealing the other tart. "And you don't have any friends."

"I have you, don't I?" I said.

"That doesn't count." She shook her head and the loud scream of the steam wand started as the barista began making a drink for a new customer.

"It does count," I said. "Because we could just pretend that we don't know each other like everyone else from the system."

"Head priestess?" someone said, approaching us from the front door.

"Kalie," Laurel said, glancing at me. "Can this wait? I'm talking to my brother."

"Sorry, of course, I just wanted to drop this off before tomorrow," she said, holding a bag aloft. I could smell sage and cinnamon. Laurel gave her a brilliant smile with all of her teeth and it was her politician's smile, the one that was for people whom she didn't want to offend.

"Thanks," Laurel took the bag and slid it under our table.

Kalie gave me a smile. Her head tilted slightly, like she was waiting. Laurel's smile became more teeth than honesty and she said, "I'll see you later, Kalie. Love and light."

"Love and light," Kalie said, turning away.

"What's up with that?" I asked, watching the redhead leave the cafe. "She's a little... enthusiastic."

"She's a little new, so she's overzealous. I think her last coven broke apart because of infighting, so she's really eager to find her place with the East Side Witches." Laurel polished off her tart and nudged the plate towards me.

"She's gunning for your job, isn't she?" I said.

"How do you do that?" she said. "You only met her for ten seconds!"

"So she *is* trying to become head priestess?" I asked. "You want me to look into her? Find out what her story is?"

"No," she said. "I'll deal with her myself. I'm a little old for my big brother to be taking care of my problems."

"Never too old for me to worry," I said, grinning when she pretended to gag at the sugary sweet sentiment.

Picking up the chocolate treat, I tried to savor it instead of devouring it instantly. With her foot, Laurel prodded the bag out from under the table and brushed her fingers through the ingredients inside. She was even younger than I was, and that made it even more incredible how much she'd made of herself.

To give her credit, she'd worked hard for all of her success. She was the head priestess of the Kitchen Witches of East San Amaro, which was a mouthful of a coven name that always got shortened to the East Side Witches if you liked them and East Side Bitches if you didn't. It was enough to give an older brother a complex, except that we weren't actually blood relatives and it was impossible not to be proud of the woman she'd grown into. She could also take me down hard if she wanted, so I liked staying on her good side.

The thing about witches is this: they are way more destructive than alchemists.

I don't mean that they're more powerful or that an alchemist couldn't pull down the house if he wanted to. But alchemists are a little like a sniper rifle. Everything has to be precisely so, the right circle, the right incantation, the precise amount of materials. When everything is *just so*, an alchemist will take the proverbial head off a guy with the precision of a marksman.

Witches are more like shotguns. They can take a handful of random stuff you find in your junk drawer and do a lot of damage. In a fight, I'm always going to put my money on the witch.

"So, Laurel," I said.

Huffing, Laurel flicked her eyes back towards me and arched both of her eyebrows. "You're using your conniving voice. What do you want?"

"How do you know I want something?" I asked. "Maybe I was just going to say that you looked nice today."

"Were you?" she asked.

"No," I said. "But it really hurts me you're so suspicious."

"What do you want, Parker?" she asked, her red lips curling into a smirk. "I don't know anything new about Derek McCallum, but I've been keeping an ear out, even though I think you should steer clear of him."

"He broke a contract," I said. "He's going to pay."

At the talk of McCallum, I felt the warmth I'd been enjoying chill. He was the reason I was in this mess now with my landlord. He was the reason that the business I'd built was in danger.

"Okay," Laurel said mildly. She tapped the table, and I refocused on her. "So if it's not him, what is it you want?"

"You heard anything about the SoPa alpha getting killed?"

Her eyes narrowed. She drummed her short fingernails on the table as she considered the question. "Why?"

"I'm curious," I said. "You know I like to keep up with the werewolf news."

"I know that you're smart, so you stay *out* of pack drama," she said. "And unlike me, you don't have to keep up with it all, so I'm curious why you're asking."

"The cops want a consult," I lied. "And they asked me about magic being drained out of wolves. I thought that you might be able to give me some background."

Laurel twisted her lips, her nails still drumming on the table. Finally, she said, "I think you should stay out of it, but from what I know, they found the alpha out of SoPa territory. SoPa doesn't think another pack killed him, but there are a lot of rumblings about retribution. I told my people to steer clear."

It wasn't any more than I knew before. I must have made a face, because her eyes narrowed again. "What's this about drained magic?"

"The cops want to know if it's fae, but it didn't sound familiar and I know I've never been able to drain magic," I said. "Can you?"

Laurel was trained as a kitchen witch, which was a little like being the MacGyver of witches. I'd seen her turn a handful of flour, a pair of scissors, and twine into a spell that took the head off a vampire. Like I said, my money is going to be on the witch who can turn an empty soda can into an IED.

As the head priestess for her coven, Laurel had unlimited access to their power. Unlike alchemists, who believed that their power came from the purity of their magic, witches pooled their magic, which gave even lesser users the ability to do massive spells. Of course, they could only do those big spells with a group of their coven members. For every witch as strong as Laurel, there were a dozen users who could barely make a pop-rock explode.

"Kind of," Laurel said. "When we shift magic to the coven, it's a drain, but that's consensual. You need the participant's permission. And we'd never take all of their magic."

"What about binding spells?" I asked.

"Maybe," she said. "But we only *temporarily* bind powerful kids, the ones who need training wheels before they can control their magic. Even then, it's not a drain so much as a... floodgate. I've never heard of it being used on an adult, and *never* on another paranormal. No." She shook her head. "Whatever this is, it's not witchcraft."

"You think it was another pack?" I asked.

Shrugging one shoulder, she said, "Malik doesn't think so. He'd know."

"Do you think an alchemist could do it?" I asked.

Just because Detective Nicholas King, upstanding, by the literal book, perfect alchemist, didn't believe that it was alchemy didn't mean that some shadier, less upstanding alchemist hadn't done it.

Laurel snapped her fingers, the sound nearly drowned out by the steam wand going again. "You need to talk to Professor Woolworth."

"Who?" I asked.

"That UCSA professor, the one that used to be in the coven when Shannon was head priestess. She'd come by, borrow Shannon's books? She tried to give you a lecture on energy circles?"

Laurel tilted her head like she was waiting for the moment I remembered the person.

I shrugged, scratching at the hair behind my ear. "No memory of her."

"Anyway, she quit when Shannon... well. She quit the East Side Witches, and I think she went into solitary practice? She's big into researching non-standard alchemy and witchcraft. Go see her." Laurel managed to make every suggestion sound like a directive. Normally, the high-handedness set me on edge, but in this case the information was good and I didn't make a fuss.

"Thanks," I said, standing. I slung my bag back over my shoulder again and smiled at her.

"Come by more often. I worry about you in the summer," she said.

"I know, I know." I waved off her concern.

"And go see Shannon," she said.

Standing, she drew me into a hug, her head hitting below my shoulder as she gripped me tightly. For a moment, I curled my arms around her before dropping them. She stepped back and shoved me, shaking her head in mock irritation.

Walking out the door, backwards, I waved at her from the sunny sidewalk, but she was already back behind the counter helping her next customer.

CHAPTER EIGHT

STANDING OUT IN THE CALIFORNIA SUNSHINE, I DUG IN MY satchel, pushing past the debris of my wallet, camera, and a collection of fast food napkins before finding a pair of cheap black sunglasses, my keys caught on one of the legs. I sighed when I put them on with one hand, my other hand weighing my keys.

I needed to go get my car.

Unless it had gotten towed, it was still outside the apartment complex, but there were a lot of ifs there. Dieter might have scented me on it—I spent enough time in it that it probably reeked of me—and that could only mean that I was walking into a trap. A group of teenage girls was heading towards me on the sidewalk and at their pronounced stink eyes, I moved out of the way, stepping onto the curb, nearly in the bike lane.

One of them had dreadlocks, and an easy smile when she turned back to her friends. I rolled my eyes upward and sighed. Acacia. The Summer Queen's new interest. Another thing I had to deal with.

Shaking my shoulders until they weren't up around my ears, I made a list.

1. *Car*
2. *Find Professor Woolworth*
3. *Get paid*
4. *Find Acacia*
5. *Keep her out of fae hands*

It would be foolish to go get my car without being sure whether Dieter knew it was mine, so I decided to go to Professor Woolworth first and then see if I could get my car later. I looked at the bus routes in my phone and saw that I could take a direct one to campus. It might take me all day, but at least I could avoid Dieter.

Twenty minutes later, when four werewolves got onto the bus, I was rethinking that decision. I wasn't sure how they'd tracked me, or if it had just been bad luck and timing, but I was pretty sure I recognized them from my week of being stuck to Dieter like a tick behind his ear. So, now it was me, four SoPa members and a bus full of civilians.

An older woman sat a row ahead of me, a crochet hook dancing in her fingers. A SoPa wolf sat in front of her, sprawling over both seats. Another took the seat behind her, leaning forward so that he was well in her space. A third boxed her in, grabbing the handrail above her seat.

The fourth slouched in the seat across from her, his cell phone in hand. They weren't looking at me, so I wondered if it was just a coincidence. Maybe I was reading too much into them taking the same bus as me. For all I knew, they were college students. Sure, college students without backpacks, books, or anything indicating that they were on their way to class, but maybe they were *bad* college students.

The woman's crochet hook slowed, and I saw her glance at the wolf penning her in, then back at the wolf behind her. I didn't need a wolf's nose to know she was afraid. She moved as though she was going to stand, and the wolf standing above her didn't move, so she shrank back, pressing herself as close to the window as possible.

The bus squealed to a stop and someone else got on. Dieter. He looked even more massive in the small aisle and he jerked his chin in the greeting common to men who think it looks cool because they watched too many gangster movies as children. The wolves around the woman echoed the movement like a synchronized boy band whose only songs were, "I Don't Deal With My Feelings Well" and "Scarface Was the Best, Right?"

Dieter stood in the aisle and all along the bus there was a slight shiver. I noticed more people beginning to get the nervous look of a rabbit who senses there's a hawk nearby, even if it can't see where. From his position in the middle of the aisle, up from me, Dieter smirked and met my eyes.

There were two options. I could ignore them and assume that their implicit threat against the woman in front of me was just a show of force. In that case, I'd ride the bus all the way to campus and get off there. They'd get off, too, and we'd have our showdown surrounded by a student body already filming it for upload to the social media site of their choice.

The other option was clearly what they wanted. I'd get off now, and they'd leave the poor woman alone. She was glancing between the three of them now, her bag clutched to her chest. Trembling, she hunched her shoulders higher.

With a look out the window, I came up with a plan. We were close to Dieter's wolf on the side. Close enough that I knew my car was around the corner. If I could draw them off the bus, but then get to my car before they caught me, I'd have a chance of getting out of this mess without fighting.

Reaching up, I tugged on the pull cord and the bus pulled up at the next stop. Without a backwards glance, I trotted down the stairs at the back of the bus and exited. Once my feet were on the ground, I sprinted for my car.

I was the rabbit at a racetrack, and the greyhounds behind me were out for blood. The park from the day before was a blur to my left as I ran for my car, grabbing my keys out of my bag.

There weren't any baseball games today, but the playground was filled with strollers and moms busy on their phones while their children reenacted *Lord of the Flies*. With the metal keys in hand, I reached out with my other hand, my satchel making the movement awkward.

Fae magic didn't mix well with witchcraft, but if I needed to, I could throw up a passable shield.

I felt movement behind me, and spun, throwing up a shield with a shouted, "*Aegis!*"

The shifted werewolf slammed into it, the impact making a crackling sound like thin ice in winter. Both his bones and the shield gave, his face distorted from a broken cheekbone and the shield displaying its cracks in bright white light.

Reinforcing the spell with a request, I thickened the surrounding air. It wasn't enough to stop something coming at full force, but it would slow any direct assaults. The air was unhappy at being forced into stillness, and I knew I could only hold it for a minute at most.

The wolf on the ground twitched, already recovering, and I rushed towards my car, unlocking it with a cheerful *beep-beep*. I yanked at the door and slid inside, locking it before the door had even finished closing. Jamming the keys into the ignition, I saw four people surrounding the car, just far enough away that I couldn't hit them with the door.

I wasn't sure why they hadn't approached me closer, and I twisted the keys, the engine choking to life. Something heavy landed on the hood of my car, denting it and cutting short the assurance that I'd get out of this alive. Dieter, a demented grin stretching his mouth to reveal teeth that looked more wolf than human, crouched on my car.

Raising his fist, he slammed it into my windshield, cracks shooting out from where he impacted the glass. I scrambled for the door handle, unlocking it and falling out onto the street as he punched again, breaking through, his grasping fingers just missing my shirt.

"Get him," he roared, and I crab walked backwards, my satchel tripping me up as I pushed myself upright and dodged around one of the wolves. I reached out with my magic, shoving as much as I could into the sidewalk. It turned to quicksand under the wolves' feet as I convinced it that staying solid wasn't in its nature. But the sidewalk was only a few inches deep, and they waded through, their strength and size playing to their advantage.

I reached the corner and made a hard right, the park within sight. There were trees at the park, and grass, and *rocks*. If I could get close enough to the baseball diamond, they would find themselves in the middle of a sandstorm.

At this point I would even take the risk of dragging a group of werewolf enforcers into the playground for the safety of a half-dozen moms with cellphones and the cops on speed dial. There was a growl from too close behind me, and I reached down with my magic, feeling for earth or... there. *Water.* A pipe burst at my request and water came straight up, slamming the wolf behind me backwards. It soaked the sidewalk, gallons of it spraying up and then turning to steam as I convinced it that our nice, balmy eighty two degree day was hot enough to boil water.

It wouldn't last, and the more water that came out, the more it resembled baby bath water, both in temperature and in pressure. I glanced back and saw that I now only had three pursuers, the other two still stuck in concrete. Of the remaining three, one had been slammed into a car by the water, and another was moaning and clutching at his scalded face. Dieter, face red and blistering, was gaining on me, though.

My hand touched the chain-link fence, about to swing myself into the gate, when he caught up, throwing his massive weight on top of me. He bore me down and I couldn't move under his mass.

Wrapping an arm around my neck, he held tight, as my vision began dotting from lack of oxygen.

No. I was not letting this steroidal excuse for a werewolf take me down. I dug my fingers into the dirt and felt for my magic.

Witches and alchemists rely on human magic, which is finite and dependent on the person. Some people have less and some have more, like Laurel. The only difference between the two is in how they practice their art.

Werewolves, vampires, and most other paranormals don't practice magic, because they *are* magic.

Fae, though, we take the magic there is in the world and twist it to our will. Sometimes that's through cajoling and convincing, through manipulation and trickery, even bargaining with the beings and magic you want to use. All that takes a mix of your own innate magic and your own charisma. I've seen fae with no innate magic, but enough charisma to seduce a whole monastery combat a fae with plenty of magic, but the charisma of a wet newspaper.

So, I drew deep and pulled at my remaining well of magic, clawing at the ground. I could feel soil caking beneath my nails. Something was under there. Some spirit resided under the dirt, under the pipes funneling electricity and water and sewage. The impression was massive, a resting giant slumbering.

What was it? The park? The spirit of the park, that used to be a vast swathe of undeveloped land? Would that be enough to save me?

My magic was low, nearly empty after the stunt with the water main, but there was enough to make a request.

I entreat you, who have seen yourself carved smaller and smaller, who are now bound by concrete and buildings, who have seen metal and plastic pipes run through you like swords.

The answer in my mind was slow and deep. I was waking something that had been asleep for years. It tasted like copper and grit in my mind.

Child of the Far Realm. Why have you interrupted my rest?

Dieter pulled my head back as he yelled at the wolves trotting up behind him. My heartbeat was loud in my ears and I couldn't hear anything else over the sound of it. I took a shallow breath when he accidentally loosened his grip.

I would entreat on your generosity. The ones here mean me harm.

Your nature entreats on my generosity. The voice was final, abrupt, unhappy.

You know my people. You know we do not reside here. But they do, and they would do me harm. Will you help me?

In exchange for what?

A favor freely given. A favor from a fair-folk must have value to you.

The noise the voice made was low and thoughtful. It felt like dragging fingers through my brain.

What is your name, child of the fair-folk?

Parker Ferro.

I heard tires, they were pulling a van up. If I didn't get away, they were going to kidnap me and my gruesome murder would be next.

That is what you call yourself. What is your name?

That's the only name I have.

I accept your terms, child of the fair-folk. You will be in my debt.

What do I call you?

The voice didn't answer, but the ground rumbled.

"An earthquake? Are you kidding?" one of the wolves said.

The shaking intensified, the ground seeming to ripple under us. It tossed me and Dieter aside, breaking his hold around my neck. I gasped, the air feeling like ice as I drew it into my burning lungs.

If the wolves noticed that it was only where we stood in the park that was shaking—that the sidewalk and street beyond were still, they clearly didn't know what it meant. Stumbling to my feet, I took two unsteady steps towards the interior of the park.

Dieter moved to follow, his gait more steady since he hadn't been recently starved of oxygen. A crack formed in the earth, a canyon in the making. Dieter stumbled into it, his leg falling hip deep.

I scraped every bit of magic I had left and fed it to the ground. The spirit consumed it, intensifying the quake. It felt as though my bones were rattling.

Two of the wolves went to help Dieter, and the two that had been stuck in concrete arrived, their jeans torn and covered with gray dust. They approached me, but I was faster, letting myself roll with the movement of the ground. If I could get farther into the park, I could hide, or let my scent fade and let the air hide me. I sprinted for the grove of trees that bordered the fence and almost made it.

The rolling of the ground faded as the spirit tired, and my magic wasn't enough to prevent it from fading.

Something tackled into my legs and something else slammed into my back, driving all the air from my lungs. Dieter was shouting, "He's got some magic going, knock him out."

The two concrete-dusted wolves pulled me up, dragging me towards the van that was idling near the entrance to the park. I kicked my feet, trying to dig my heels into the ground, but it didn't help against their physical strength. I was reminded of an old racist joke:

———

What do you call a weightlifter who goes hand to hand with a werewolf?
A chew toy.

———

Like I said, not the most politically correct joke.

Dieter held open the sliding door of the unmarked white van. He grinned at me, "Good work, pack."

Tossing me in like a sack of laundry, they didn't even bother to take away my bag. I reached in and drew out a butterfly knife that I flicked open. Before they could move, I stabbed the knife into the calf of the closest wolf, yanking it out at an angle that sliced his Achilles' tendon. He went down and screamed.

The other one turned, and I knifed in his thigh, trying to get at his groin before he got my wrist and yanked back until my hand loosened on the blade. It thudded to the floor of the van and then I had two wolves sitting on me to keep me still.

"Jesus, who is this asshole?" one of them asked Dieter.

In the distance, near the playground, I saw a couple of moms pointing at the van and I realized that they *had* called the police. It looked like a couple of uniforms had answered and they began to jog towards the van, guns out and talking into their radios.

The wolves piled in as the cops drew closer, shouting for the werewolves to freeze.

Dieter was the last one in, and he shouted, "Go!"

The van jerked into movement, sending us all sliding backwards. The wolves regained their balance, while I bounced like a pinball between them. Producing a thick coil of rope, Dieter snapped. "Just knock him out."

"Night night," one of the cement wolves said, his arm pulled back.

I felt a solid hit to the back of my skull and that was it, camera off, curtain dropped, lights out.

CHAPTER NINE

I woke up in the back of an auto shop. The place was still and quiet, even though there was some afternoon sunlight streaming in the large bay windows. A mustang was up on one of the lifts, and there was an Acura with half its engine on a large sheet next to it.

All the lights were off, and at first all I heard was my own ragged breathing. I had no idea what time it was, but the color of the light painted it late afternoon, hours after my lunchtime meetup with Laurel. My head ached, my body felt like someone had hit every muscle I had with a sledgehammer. Even my fingers hurt from where I'd dug them into the ground.

They had tied me to a chair, and I was grateful. They could have strung me up from my arms, which would have been more painful and more deadly. From having watched him, I knew that Dieter operated from a playbook entirely derived from bad nineties movies.

Wiggling my fingers, I was glad that they hadn't cut off my circulation, although pins and needles danced across my forearms where they were strapped to the arms of the chair. A car battery, logo in bright yellow, was on a cart in front of me, with jumper cables attached already.

Whether this was out of convenience or if he was trying to scare me, I couldn't tell. The message worked, though.

I swallowed, spit painful as it scraped down my dry throat. Checking my magic reserves, I found that they were still low. Whatever rest unconsciousness had provided hadn't been rejuvenating enough to replenish my supply. Plus, most metal was almost impossible to work with. It was too far from its natural state, or too often an alloy and so mixed with something else. The spirit, the essence, whatever you wanted to call it, was too diminished to be much use.

"He's awake," someone called.

"Get Dieter," a voice growled.

Two wolves stalked into view from behind me. I heard a door slam open, and I raised my eyebrows.

"Really nice place you've got here," I said. "Where is everyone? Isn't it Monday?"

"Smart mouth," one said. "Can't wait to show you what we do to smart mouths."

"Give us a set at open-mic night?" I guessed.

His eyes narrowed. I thought he might be one of the wolves that spent most of our fight being encased in concrete, but I wasn't sure. Both of them were in different clothes, and if the boiling water had hit either of them, they'd already healed.

"We'll see how fast you can run your mouth without teeth," he growled. Leaning forward, his eyes flashed a canine yellow, and I grinned at him, showing my mouthful of pearly whites.

"You know, torture isn't an effective method of information gathering," I said, my shrug awkward with the tight ropes. "In fact, they say that at a certain point the victim will just lie and tell you whatever you want to hear in order to stop you."

I heard the door slam open again and the squeak of rubber

shoes on the concrete. Dieter came into my field of vision, his face still pink where the water had hit him. It took a moment for him to talk, as he forced his mouth back into human shape.

The razor-sharp teeth disappeared, but the smirk warned me that he was ready to provide me some incentive to lie in the form of hours of agony. No matter what my mouth was saying, I didn't like my chances. Even if they were her pack, I couldn't turn Chelsea over to them. They'd rip her limb from limb for her betrayal.

"So, why don't we skip the pain part and you just tell me what you want to hear and I'll make it sound good." I wrinkled my nose as though thinking. "Or I could just start saying whatever comes into my head and we'll see if any of it is what you want to hear."

"I want to know who sent you," he said. He leaned down, and I could smell something sour and alcoholic on his breath.

"Don't know what you're talking about," I said. "I'm a photographer. All day long, all I do is street photography."

"Who. Sent. You?" he asked.

"No. One." I said.

"Try again," Dieter said. "You were photographing me doing a drop off, and someone else told you to do it."

"Is that what we're calling it now?" I asked. "I didn't know that drug deals involved flowers."

He leaned in and I saw his eye twitch. His breath was warm on my face and I squirmed back. "Now, we can do this easy or hard."

I knew the score. If I kept pressing with his affair, he was going to pass it off as a lie and I'd get the car battery to my testicles.

"I want to talk to Malik," I said.

He shoved back, making my chair screech across the concrete. "Right. How do you know about Malik?"

"I know people, and I know that if he knew you had me, he'd

like to talk to me personally." I raised an eyebrow. "Unless you want to explain to him why you won't let me talk to him."

Shaking his head, Dieter crossed his arms. He looked at one of the wolves slouching against the Acura and jerked his head towards me. The guy stood, all six feet of him, and slunk towards me. Pulling back his hand, he slammed a fist into my stomach.

I grunted. As much as every muscle hurt, I knew that he'd probably liquified some of my organs.

"Really," I said. "I'd love to talk to your alpha. Who you're supposed to listen to. Not this jackass."

I directed my words at Mister Six Foot and Dangerous, and he shook his head, slugging me across the face.

"Jupiter's balls," I muttered. I saw stars for a moment.

"Who sent you?" Dieter asked.

"No one sent me," I said.

"He's a P.I." The wolf who hadn't just punched me in the face was holding my wallet aloft, my P.I. license tucked in the front near my ID. Dieter walked over and looked through my wallet, taking out the cash and tucking it in his own pocket. He smirked when he came to a yogurt loyalty card that was only one punch away from a free one.

"You go to Yogurt Palace, don't you?" He offered it over to Six Foot Yogurt Stealer, and the wolf took the offered card and glanced at me.

"Thanks," he said, a smirk curving his lips.

"Awww, man," I whined. "Not the yogurt card. You guys suck."

Dieter grinned and began pulling other stuff out of my wallet. The receipts got examined and dropped on the ground. He put my ID aside to check my address later. I had a gift certificate to a hair place that Laurel had given me for my last birthday, which he passed to the wolf that had found my P.I. license. All my other cards got tossed on the ground.

"I thought you guys were supposed to be tough enforcers, not muggers," I complained. "This is baby crime."

Shaking his head, Dieter came close.

"Tell us about Nate," he said.

"I don't know anything about Nate," I said. "I don't mess around with wolf politics."

"Someone hired you, and I would bet it was whoever killed Nate. I bet now they're coming after the strongest living SoPa wolf." Dieter leaned back on his heels, crossing his arms. My eyes darted behind him, but the two wolves lounging against the car didn't even blink at his claim.

Oh.

Oh. Him and his four buddies had been looking for me, and were willing to intimidate random women on busses to get to me. So, either they knew about Dieter's girl on the side, or they believed him without question. Either way, it meant that he had wolves that were loyal to him and not Malik, wolves that would back him when he made his move to grab power.

What game was he playing? If he wanted to pin the murder on me, or make it seem like I knew who the killer was, then he would be the hero who caught Nate's killer. Malik would be the failure, the alpha who couldn't even avenge his predecessor.

That seemed a little deep for Dieter, though. Maybe he just was waiting until Malik established himself, so that Dieter would seem more powerful taking out Malik, an established alpha, instead of like Dieter couldn't take on Nate so he was taking on his weaker successor.

This was why I stayed out of wolf politics. It always became either too *Hamlet* with motives inside motives, or too much of a cage fight.

Apparently, I'd taken too long to answer, because Dieter jerked his chin towards my hand. "Break it."

Nosy werewolf came forward and grabbed hold of my left pinkie finger. I struggled, trying to make fists with my hands, and with a casual efficiency, he bent it backwards.

I screamed, the sound tearing itself out of my chest. Panting, I looked down and saw the finger twisted at an awkward angle. This was bad.

"Who hired you to follow me?" Dieter asked.

"No one," I said. "I was just in the area. I take pictures of people kissing in case it comes in handy for blackmail later."

"You're lying," Dieter said, his eyes flashing yellow. "I'm going to drag it out of you. You might as well tell the truth."

"I'm not, I'm not," I said. My finger throbbed in time with my heartbeat. My entire attention was on that finger.

"Who killed Nate?" Dieter asked.

"I don't know," I said. "I didn't even know he was dead before you said it."

"Break the next one," Dieter said.

I couldn't make myself watch as the wolf grabbed my ring finger and yanked it back. Normally, I'd check if it was a clean break, something that a healer could fix, but a lightning bolt of pain danced up my arm. Nothing mattered beyond that pain.

"No, no," I moaned, slumping forward.

Closing my eyes, I panted, breath shallow and barely filling my lungs.

"Let's let him sit with that," Dieter said. "Give him time to decide to tell us the truth."

"How're we going to know if it's the truth? What if he just tells us what we want to hear?" one of the wolves asked, reasonably. I guess my speech on the downsides of torture had sunk in.

"I'll know," Dieter snapped. He must have already decided what he wanted to hear, then. He'd already picked out someone that he was going to hold accountable for Nate's murder, regardless of the truth.

Footsteps crossed the garage, and when I forced my head up, I saw that only Six Foot Yogurt Stealer was still in the garage with me, leaning next to the back door. His eyes were on his phone. They'd propped the door open, and Dieter and Nosy Werewolf must have gone outside.

I felt the shallow puddle of magic in me soak into my skin, calming the chaos of pain in my body. Softening my breathing, I tried to focus, to hear anything around me I could use.

There were water pipes underneath us, but I didn't have enough magic to call on it. No plants were nearby, and the air wouldn't listen to me when I couldn't hold a breath.

Time seemed to stretch and condense because the next thing I knew my chin was resting on my chest and it was dark outside. All three wolves were back with me. Had I passed out?

Dieter kicked at my feet. I dragged up my head, the room spinning as I got oriented. Counting two henchmen and Dieter, I wondered what happened to the fourth werewolf. Was he more loyal to Malik than Dieter? Or was he just squeamish about torture?

"Who hired you?" he asked.

"No one hired me," I said. "I just take blackmail pictures."

"See, it was Gomez who hired you. I don't know why you're being so loyal to him, he isn't going to come save you," Dieter said.

"Who?" I asked, confused. I blinked, squeezing my eyes shut to get myself together. "Who the hell is Gomez?"

"Look at him," Dieter said. "I bet he's some Westside bitch. I'll bet he rolls over for all them."

Ah. Of course. Westside was a minor pack that ran alongside SoPa territory. The constant scuffles between the two had only gained momentum when Nate made it clear that he wanted Westside gone.

"What? You don't think that I'm Five Dragons?" I asked, I made my eyes focus on Dieter's face as I spoke.

His eyes narrowed, and he stepped forward to slam his fist into my stomach again. I grunted and slumped forward. Heat returned, and I recognized that it was magic, but also blood. I was bleeding internally.

"Please," I said. "Please, just let me talk to Malik."

"Malik isn't going to hear from you," Dieter said. I heard the satisfaction in his voice. "In fact, I think I'm going to take care of you right now."

"You are?" a new voice said. "Because I thought *I* was the alpha, which means that I do the thinking for you."

Both wolves with Dieter turned, their eyes wide. They were kids caught with their hands in the cookie jar, and now Daddy was home.

Malik stood inside the door, flanked by two female wolves. One had her hair pulled back in a sculpted ponytail, her clothes a pair of black cargo pants and a tight black tank top. She sneered at Dieter, showing a pair of sharp canines. The other was dressed in jeans and a loose flannel shirt, her arms crossed. Her expression was blank, but her eyes flicked to the wolves next to Dieter, then to me, then the car battery, like she was taking inventory of everything in the room.

Dieter stepped back from me and turned so he could glance at Malik over his shoulder. He glared at his alpha and made a show of slapping me lightly across the cheek.

"I don't want you to have to deal with liars and dangerous people," Dieter said. "That's what you have me for, *alpha*."

The disdain in the word made the wolf in black step forward, but Malik held up a hand. He smiled pleasantly at Dieter. "Thank you for the consideration, Dieter, but I'll make my own choices. And I'd like to hear what he has to say."

Dieter pulled his eyebrows lower, his teeth bared. Malik stood with the casual confidence of Michael Corleone.

If Michael Corleone was into snug gray undershirts and jeans with a slight sag. Malik's dreadlocks were pulled back from his face in a half ponytail that left the bottom half of them brushing his shoulders and upper back. His cheeks had a slight shadow, like he didn't shave that morning, but his air was that of complete competence.

The two wolves with Dieter went still, the rigidity of prey

when faced with a greater threat. Dieter might huff and puff and pound your house to rubble with his bare hands, but Malik was the more dangerous of the two because he had *control*.

"Get his stuff," he directed Flannel. Jerking his chin towards me, he turned to the dark office. "Get him."

CHAPTER TEN

BLACK CARGO PANTS STEPPED FORWARD AS FLANNEL BEGAN grabbing all my stuff off the ground. She tucked most of it back into my satchel and then looked at the two wolves trying to fade into the shadows. Without speaking, Flannel opened her hand and twitched her fingers. Neither wolf moved, gone still again.

Then Six Foot Yogurt Stealer dug in his pocket and pulled out the yogurt card, handing it over and glancing at Nosy Wolf, who pulled out the gift card. Examining the two, she shook her head, "Real mature, guys."

The wolves cringed, and I realized with some glee that the only wolves that Dieter could get to his side were *lame*. They still would have murdered me like it was nothing, but clearly they were not the pack's A-team.

Black Cargo Pants pulled out a knife that was black, sharp, and deadly. I was seeing a theme with her. She cut the ropes that held me to the arms of the chair, then moved on to my legs, and the ropes around my chest. Standing, she looked down at me as she re-sheathed her knife.

"Can you stand?" she asked.

I curled my arm over my stomach and felt the roar of agony return.

"Probably not," I said.

Bending, she got my free arm over her shoulders and lifted me up, keeping me steady as I managed a few steps. It wasn't as bad as I thought, and by the time I reached the office, I was mostly under my own power.

The office was decently sized, and Malik was leaning against the desk, watching as Dieter paced in front of him.

"—and you know he did it! Why else would he be sniffing around pack business? They're going to think you're too weak to take care of your own pack," Dieter snarled.

"You've made it clear what you think," Malik said, voice icy. "And now you've caught him. So you're done."

"I should stay," Dieter said.

Malik raised an eyebrow and huffed a laugh. "I'm sorry, are you suggesting that I'm not safe with Tara and Celia both here?"

"*I'm* the pack's muscle," Dieter said, pulling his eyebrows down.

Staring at him, Malik said, "Put him on the couch and get him some ice and splints."

Black Cargo Pants helped me over to the couch, lowering me carefully. She flicked her ponytail over her shoulder and looked at Dieter with narrowed eyes, before stalking out. Flannel came in and dropped my bag on the desk next to Malik. Then she leaned against the door, arms crossed. Her nose twitched, but other than that, she was still.

"You're excused, Dieter," Malik said. He tilted his head towards the door.

Huffing, Dieter slammed his open palm against the doorframe above Flannel's head as he left. She didn't even flinch, turning a raised eyebrow to Malik.

"I know," he said, sighing. "I *know*, okay? Go make sure he and his boys don't hang around."

Flannel opened her mouth, her eyes cutting to me, then back to Malik.

He shook his head. "Not you, too. I'll be fine. Parker and I go way back."

Nodding, Flannel swept out of the room with all the noise of a ghost. Malik turned to me, his gaze assessing.

"Dieter got you good, huh?" he asked. "Parker Ferro. It's been a long time."

I nodded, "When was the last time? That summer camp for foster kids when we were seventeen?"

"Sounds about right," he said. "Thanks, Tara."

Black Cargo Pants—Tara—arrived with two ice packs and some gauze.

"He'll need a doctor," she judged, efficiently wrapping my fingers with a small popsicle stick. I tried not to scream at the fresh pain, but only muffled the sound. "If we aren't going to kill him."

My eyes widened, and I made another muffled sound. Malik tilted his head, examining me.

"We're probably not killing him," Malik said. "I'm good. Close the door behind you. Go help Celia with security."

"Sure, boss," she said. The door shut behind her with a definitive *click*. I leaned back into the soft couch cushions and regretted it, as my stomach started to ache again, even with the ice pack Tara had provided.

"Parker Ferro." Malik walked around the desk to a small refrigerator tucked against the wall. He pulled out two waters and offered one over to me. I held up my injured hand, and he opened the top before handing it over.

Accepting it, I brought it to my lips and drank long swallows of cold water that felt like heaven. When the bottle was almost empty, I sighed. Already feeling better, I met Malik's eyes.

"Thanks," I said.

"What am I going to do with you, Parker?" Malik asked.

"I didn't kill Nate," I said. My words rushed on top of each other. "You have to believe me, Malik. I didn't even know he was dead until last night."

"Why were you following Dieter, then?" Malik asked.

"For a case," I hedged. An idea came to me, and I tested it out. "I can't tell you the details, but one of his clients has a hillside mom who wasn't happy that her son was getting pack drugs."

Malik uncapped the second bottle and offered it over. I finished mine and tossed it towards the trash, missing the can. With my now-free hand, I accepted the bottle.

"And?" Malik said. "Why did she want pictures of Dieter? Were you going to tip off the cops?"

"She wanted proof of what was going on so she could shove her kid into rehab. Dad didn't believe it. She wanted to have photos to give to their neighborhood security company so they could keep him out. Neither one of them wants the cops involved. You know how hillside parents are," I said, the implication sitting between us. Rich, entitled hillside parents didn't let their kids get arrested. They sent them off to rehab as many times as it took until the kid was old enough to be out from under their parents' thumbs.

"You're going to delete those pictures," Malik said. "You know I can't have anyone knowing pack business like that."

"Fine," I said. "But you should know. That wasn't why Dieter went after me. He wasn't pissed I photographed his deals."

Crossing his arms, Malik's cheek bulged as he ran his tongue across his molars. "Okay, I'll bite. What is he up to?"

"To me? It looked like an affair with someone in Five Dragons," I said. I pointed to my bag and Malik tossed it over to me. Catching it with my good hand, I cradled the bag to me and dug out my camera.

After I found the right photos, I offered over my camera. Malik stood and took it, his face inscrutable as he toggled through the photos.

"I thought you stayed out of pack business?" he said. "How'd you know she was Five Dragons?"

"Her tattoos," I guessed. It would make sense. The twisted scales tangled together were dragons. I'd taken them for an ouroboros, spanning across her rib cage and back, but as Malik squinted at the pictures, I realized that my guess was right.

He made a thoughtful humming sound and set the camera on the desk. His eyes turned back to me and they were flickering, gold and brown as something inside him shifted. My eyes went to the door, but it remained shut as his betas kept guard for him.

"What are you going to do?" I asked him.

"See, I have a problem now," Malik said. He leaned back against the desk and tapped a finger on the edge. "Maybe you didn't kill Nate, maybe you did. But Dieter is going to tell everyone in the pack he caught the killer. So I can't just let you go."

"You can't kill me," I breathed. "We go back, I was in your *pack*, Malik."

It was the truth, but our past wasn't enough to keep me safe. We met when he was fourteen and I was twelve, and back then he was just another werewolf in the foster system, unwanted because they considered him dangerous. They had kicked me to a state-run home because I'd accidentally set fire to my foster home—untrained magic and anger issues don't mix. He was there because no humans wanted werewolves, and back then the state denied all werewolf foster parents as a matter of course.

He was always one step ahead of the bigger boys, and even though he was only a kid, it was clear that some day he was going to be an alpha. Every were-creature there was willing to let him be in charge, and even some humans wanted in on his little mini-pack. *I* wanted in on his little pack.

"Key word there is *was*," Malik said. "See you left—"

"I got a foster placement," I argued. "You even said it was better for me to go—"

Raising his palm, I automatically quieted. That was how he was. A mild correction and even I felt like a puppy with his tail between his legs.

"I'm not saying it wasn't a good decision for you," he said. "But you left your pack. You put yourself first, instead of us. That's the difference between you and me. You look out for you. I look out for my pack."

"Your pack isn't going to be any safer if you kill me," I said. "Because I didn't kill Nate. And whoever did is still out there."

"Killing you would be a lot easier for me," Malik argued. "And later I could just say that you were working for someone else."

"How can I convince you not to kill me?" I asked. "How can I convince you none of this is my fault?"

Scratching between two of his dreadlocks, he said, "I'm not sure you can. I know you, after all. I know what you can do."

The problem with Malik was that he knew me before I got trained. He knew me when my magic was a vicious tool, a shiv I had sharpened on the cruelty of a system that didn't care about me at all. If I'd stayed with him, I might have ended up worse than Dieter, because where Dieter was strong and dumb, I was cunning and my magic was always going to give me the advantage of manipulation.

Silence settled between us, broken by something metal being dropped on concrete out in the garage. Malik watched me, his eyes golden and assessing. I tried not to break his gaze.

"I can help you," I said. "The cops came to me about your dead werewolves."

Standing, Malik walked around his desk and slumped into the office chair, lacing his fingers together over his stomach. He raised his eyebrows. "And what do the cops want with dead wolves? They made it clear that they thought we got what we deserved."

"Nate's case got passed over to Paranormal Crimes along with the other wolf killed in Five Dragons' territory," I said.

"Tanya," Malik said. "She was Five Dragons. Why did the Gang Squad give it up?"

"Something to do with the magical signature," I hedged. "It wasn't right. Anyway, I'm consulting on the case. I could feed you information. I bet that Five Dragons might back off if you were giving them cop intel."

Malik pursed his lips and gave a slow nod. "They've been testing the waters. They want the head of whoever killed Tanya, and they think they'll find it in our pack. I know they won't, but it's made things tense."

"So, if you let me go," I said. "I can give you any info that the cops have."

"The name," Malik said. "I want the name of whoever killed Nate."

"Pack justice?" I asked. "Him getting arrested isn't enough for you?"

Shaking his head, Malik said, "Your head for his head."

"Okay," I said. "I'll get you a name."

This was going to be a mess. I needed Nick to arrest the guy so I could pay my rent. But if I didn't give Malik someone, then I'd end up on the wrong side of a car battery again.

"Be smart about this, Parker," Malik said, like he was reading my mind. "I'm offering you a good deal. Dieter's going to make a lot of noise about me *not* killing you."

"It'd be easier to kill me and say that you'd taken care of business?" I groused.

"Yeah, it really would be simpler," Malik said. "As it is, you're handing me an enormous mess to clean up. You had to know he was going to come after you. Why the hell did you get caught?"

"I was following a lead," I muttered. I looked at my damaged hand and it was looking worse, the fingers turning a gruesome purple.

Rolling his head, Malik rubbed at his eyebrows. "You were

following a lead right through *SoPa territory*? Take a cab next time."

"Yeah, well, hindsight is 20/20," I said.

"Don't take too long with the information," Malik said. "Because I know where to find you and I know how you hide."

"Thanks," I said. His words pricked my pride. "I could hide from you."

His eyes squinted in an invisible smile, and Malik tapped his nose. "We can smell you, Parker. You don't smell human. Even if you hadn't been dumb enough to be seen on a bus in our territory, he would have sniffed you out. We sniff all you out."

"Gross," I said, but I could feel my heart pounding. Most wolves didn't have their abilities when they weren't shifted. But for wolves like Malik, talented ones, or ones who practiced a lot, they could shift piecemeal. Sniffing me out without going full canine would be easy. "What's to keep him from killing me now that you're letting me go?"

"Let me worry about cleaning my own house," Malik said. "You just get me the guy who killed Nate."

I saluted Malik with my good hand. "Yes, sir, alpha, sir."

Standing, Malik went to the door and opened it. "Celia."

The wolf wearing flannel appeared. She looked at me, then her eyes flicked back to Malik.

"Drop Parker off at home and make sure he doesn't have any unwanted visitors. He's going to find Nate's killer for us," Malik said, handing me my camera. "Apparently, he's got an in with the cops."

My eyes widened as I accepted the camera from Malik. He hadn't deleted the photos. Was he testing me? Was he trying to make sure I would delete them or was something else going on? Did he want me to keep them so he had some evidence of Dieter's dirty little secret?

This was why I hated dealing with wolf politics.

"Sure," Celia said. She bent down to offer me her shoulder, but

I waved her off and stood myself. I held my satchel awkwardly. There was no way I was going to get it back around my shoulder.

She led the way to a Jeep out in front of the shop, and I accepted her help into it. Neither one of us talked on our way to my apartment, which suited me just fine. She pulled up out front and stopped the car, but left the engine running.

"I'll do a check of the neighborhood before I leave," she said.

"Thanks?" I said, unable to help the question in it. Was it really likely that Dieter would show up here now that Malik knew about me?

"If you have any security, I'd put it in place," she said. "But Dieter's going to wait a few days before coming after you again."

Awkwardly, I opened the door with my good hand, juggling my bag as I slid out of the Jeep. I landed on the sidewalk and caught myself before falling on my ass. Celia glanced at me out of the corner of her eyes.

"Work quickly. I don't want to have to come back here," she said. She pulled out before I could close the door, the movement of the car slamming it shut.

I sighed heavily and rolled my eyes up to the sky. With the city lights, you could only see a few pinpricks of stars. The cool evening breeze made me shiver, which caused every single one of my injuries to hurt again.

Staring at the door to my apartment building, I began shuffling towards it. Behind me, I heard a car door slam and someone yelled my name. My breath caught in my throat and I spun, trying to think of any way to defend myself.

CHAPTER ELEVEN

THE MOTION MADE MY HEAD SPIN, AND I STUMBLED, CAUGHT BY the man who'd called me. Detective Nicholas King held my shoulders with both hands. His eyes were wide, and he was panting.

"What are you doing here?" I asked.

"What happened?" he asked. "Are you okay?"

"I think I should sit down," I said. I started to lower myself to the inviting pavement, but Nick held me up.

"You're going to the hospital," he said, pulling me away from my apartment.

In the middle of the street, I saw an unmarked car, driver's side door open, lights on, still running. I looked at him and frowned. "Why are you here?"

"A couple of officers saw someone getting kidnapped by werewolves." He huffed a sigh and narrowed his eyes. "I knew it had to be you."

"Because I'm so helpless?" I groused.

"Because I don't know anyone else who's dumb enough to go talk to the SoPa pack about the murder of their alpha," he said. "C'mon, hospital."

"Can't," I said. "No insurance. Just get me inside. I'll call someone for a healing spell."

Pursing his lips, he shook his head. Pointing at me, he said, "Stay. Here."

A few cars were waiting behind him and one leaned on their horn. He smiled and waved, getting back into his car and pulling into a spot along the curb. I locked my knees to keep steady when he came back.

"You know," I said. "I think I'm okay, you checked on me, I'm fine."

"You aren't going to file a police report, are you," he said, voice flat. "You're just going to let them get away with this—"

"Hey," I said. "Help me inside."

I let him wrap his arm around my shoulder and pull me close. He smelled ridiculously good, and this close, I could feel the heat from his body seep into mine. I better not be getting a fever from the beating that Dieter had given me.

"Careful," he said, guiding me through the narrow doorway. The elevator was working for once and it groaned as it took us to the right floor.

We managed a slow walk to my door, and my trembling fingers made the keys jangle against each other. Fitting the key in the lock, I opened the door and tried to step away from him, but he kept me with him, his body snug against mine as he guided me to the couch. I groaned as I lowered myself down.

I'd have to call Laurel. She was the only one strong enough to deal with the mess Dieter had made of my body. I couldn't feel the slow seep of blood into my abdomen anymore, so either my own magic had healed it or I was losing sensation.

Stepping back, Nick rested both hands on his hips for a moment. I looked up at the motion and saw a frown carved between his eyebrows, his eyes narrowed.

With a glance around the apartment, he began clearing a large space, pushing my desk back against the wall, moving my coffee table. Checking my bag to make sure I had most of my stuff back, I glanced at him.

"I get that my room wouldn't pass a fire inspection, but what are you doing?"

"If you won't go to a hospital, then I can at least make sure you don't hire some back-alley witch that will leave you high as a kite and still injured," Nick said. He surveyed the space he had made and nodded to himself.

Smoothly, he pulled off his jacket and draped it over my desk chair. He unbuttoned his sleeves and rolled them up to his elbows. When he pulled his tie loose and then off, I swallowed the saliva pooling in my mouth. My throat felt painfully dry.

Then he took a marker out from his jacket and started drawing on my floor.

"Uh, I *do* have a security deposit," I said. "But I'd prefer to get it back."

Even as I said it, I shut my eyes for a moment, a wince of anger. I *didn't* have a security deposit. All my deposit money had been spent on rent, and even if it hadn't, I knew that Jeffrey Jenkins would find a way to keep every penny.

Rolling his eyes, Nick said, "It's washable."

"Okay," I said doubtfully as he drew a large circle. The motion was fluid and practiced. He drew an outer circle a few inches away to limit the spell and then drew four circles between the two larger ones, at the four points of the compass to anchor the spell-work. Inside them, he wrote distinct alchemy symbols.

Shannon, the witch who'd trained me and Laurel, had only taught me witchcraft, and in craftwork there were plenty of different ways to design spells. Written circles were just one of them.

Alchemy was different. It was precise and relied on its own language of spellwork, a mix of medieval symbols and Latin that most alchemists memorized before they even used their magic to light a candle. I'd heard of alchemists that could do spells without writing anything, but it was higher-level stuff because they had to keep the language and symbols clear in their minds, as though they'd *written* them down.

Nick's writing was clear and meticulous, even on my laminate flooring. I watched with curiosity as he filled in the gaps between the two smaller circles with even more writing. Not even a single line was out of place.

"You're pretty good at this," I noted. "You've been practicing long?"

He glanced up at me, squinting, as though trying to read me. "Are you serious?"

I shrugged. "I've seen a few alchemists practice, and they weren't this precise."

He turned back to his writing and I could see half a smile on his lips. "Yeah, I've been practicing a while."

Bending closer, I tried to read some of it, but my Latin was limited to the basics taught in a few foster-kid after-school programs where alchemist studios would volunteer to get the good PR. *I go to school* kind of stuff. Whatever he was writing was a lot higher level than *eo ad scholam*.

He began writing a third circle outside of the larger one, and I hadn't seen that before. Then a fourth, and finally he bounded it with a last circle. By the time he finished, I was pretty sure that even if it was washable, I'd just be leaving a giant alchemy mess when I got evicted.

"Come over here," he said. His voice seemed lower, somehow more resonant.

"You should get undressed," he said. "You can leave your underpants on unless they did some damage there."

I looked down and sighed. Awkwardly, I tried to pull my t-shirt over my head one-handed, and startled when his hand covered mine.

"I'll help," he said.

I was aware of how close he was. We were almost the same

height, but he had a few pounds of muscle on me. He gripped the bottom of the shirt, and we got it off without too much extra pain.

He hissed when he saw my chest, and it looked bad. Purple stained my rib cage and abdomen, yellow and brown lining the outline of fists and feet. It was a stark reminder that I hadn't been supposed to survive the night.

Nick's plush lips opened and I could see him start to make another argument for the hospital, but I spoke before he could. "I don't have an extra twenty thousand dollars for a hospital visit without insurance."

The floor creaked as he shifted his weight and unbuttoned my jeans. Over the course of our rocky relationship, I had to admit that I'd thought about him unbuttoning my pants before. Of course, in all of those imaginings, it had been more hurried, and we'd both been thinking about a more pleasurable end to the evening.

Still, I felt myself getting goosebumps as he pulled my pants down, his fingers brushing my thighs as he crouched to help me out of them. I rested my hands on his shoulders. The sight of his head at my groin was exactly as exciting as I thought it would be. Luckily, the residual pain and exhaustion was enough to quash any physical arousal.

It was *not* the time to be perving on the hot, uptight cop, I reminded myself. I wasn't even sure why I trusted him to heal me, except that he was confident that he could do it and I knew that he was too by-the-book to offer if he wasn't sure that he'd be more help than harm. It'd go against the Boy Scout code or something if he didn't leave me better off than he'd found me.

He stood, and we were inches away from each other. My body heated at my near-nakedness while he was still fully dressed.

"Can you step over the circles?" he asked, eyeing my feet and the expanse of writing. It was about a foot and a half put together.

"I'm not *that* injured," I lied. Still, I was careful not to touch the black lines as I entered the circle.

"Lie down," he directed. "Head north, feet south, hands angled."

I took a guess at north and settled down, my arms angled away from my body. He walked around me, then crouched and touched my left hand, adjusting it so it was brushing the inner circle near the western anchor of the spellwork. His hand was hot against my injured fingers, and he gently undid the wrapping around my palm. Tossing the bandage and popsicle stick aside, he held up my hand for a moment, and sucked in air through his teeth.

"I'm going to position them so they're easier to heal," he said.

"You do you," I said, bracing for the pain.

Quickly, he moved them so that the broken bones were better aligned with the knuckles and I cried out, panting as he finished.

"This shouldn't take too long," he reassured me. He closed his eyes and when he opened them, they glowed a soft green as his magic flowed through him.

My eyes widened a bit as I examined his changed appearance. I'd never seen an alchemist with that much power in person. The most I'd seen was an alchemy instructor at a studio who had faint lime green lines around his irises when he started using his power.

Nick's eyes lost their hazel coloring and flashed hunter green. I could practically see the magic flowing through him as he reached down and pressed his hands on the outer circle. The black lines lit up the same green as his gaze and I saw the color spill through the words and circles getting closer and closer to me until they reached the anchor points and then his magic hit me like a wave.

I'd never felt anything like it before. When I practiced spellcraft with Laurel and Shannon, magic flowed between us. Because some of the magic had started in me, it always felt like my own, just flavored with Laurel or Shannon's signature.

This was entirely different. Nick's magic overwhelmed me. It flowed into me, filling every part of myself with him. I noticed him in a way that felt more intimate and close. This wasn't just a flavor of him, like the scent of familiar cologne in an empty room. This was all of him, every feeling he had, every aspect of his personality.

"Whoa," I breathed. I closed my eyes and let myself taste the magic in me.

I could tell how much pressure he put on himself, how much work it took every day to live up to his own expectations. Underneath, I could tell that he had a moral compass that would definitely give me headaches, as my own was more flexible.

"They did some internal damage," he said, his voice going straight into my mind. "Don't move."

His magic traced through my veins and organs with the same speed that it had made its way through his circles. I could feel the spellwork fixing as it streamed into me, a warm river of healing. It reached the bruises on my chest and the agony dissolved, the skin fading back to a more normal appearance.

My fingers took longer. It felt like my hand was submerged in a warm bath, and even as I heard crackling and noises that made me want to clench my teeth, none of the pain reached me. Curious, I tried to reach out to him with my magic, but it bounced back. Even though he was working *in* me, he'd drawn a tight boundary around my magic, keeping it separate from his own.

"You alchemists really *don't* like mixing magic," I noted. I tried to look at him without moving, but his head ducked as he focused on a part of the circle, murmuring in Latin.

When he looked up, I saw a sheen of sweat on his forehead, and the hunter green in his eyes was flickering with hazel, creating the impression of a muddy olive green. With a huff, he clenched his eyes closed, opening them with a flash of pure green.

"Almost done," he said.

Slowly, his magic receded like the tide revealing a naked beach.

As he pulled back, I could feel him being careful, untangling the spell when it stuck to different parts of my body, the ribs that had been apparently cracked by one of the hits or kicks, the skin tender from being healed. It would have been easier to just pull it all out, and leave behind some minimal damage, but he was leaving *no* damage behind, which took a tremendous amount of care.

"Done," he said, leaning back on his heels. He stayed crouched next to the circle, panting from the exertion. His ragged breath slowed through effort.

"Wow," I said, sitting up. I stretched my neck. I hadn't even noticed the knots and tension that had been residing in my shoulders until they were gone. "That was intense."

"What did you expect?" he asked, raising an eyebrow. "Me to just slap a magical bandage on you and call it a day? It'd be too much paperwork if you died on your couch and they found out I'd just left you there."

Laughing, I said, "I bet you love paperwork. I bet you take your paperwork to bed with you and look forward to all-day seminars on new forms the department makes you fill out."

He shook his head. "You need help getting up?"

The circles he'd drawn had shriveled up, and when I brushed at the edge of one with my thumb, it smeared like soot. He leaned back and sat cross-legged next to me, his eyes tracing over my body, as though looking for any imperfection he'd left behind. I reached out and covered his hand with mine.

"Thanks," I said. "I could have handled it, but this was a lot better. Maybe I should call the cops more often."

He didn't say anything, and he hadn't moved his hand. In fact, when I focused, I saw that he trembled a bit, his muscles spasming under his tight shirt.

"Are you okay?" I asked, wrapping my hand around his still one and turning it over.

I could see faint dark marks on his fingertips, as though he'd

"It's still drinkable," I muttered, crossing my arms.

He shook his head, but I caught a slight twist to his mouth before he forced it down.

"Now that you're not dying, you're going to tell me what happened and how badly you screwed up my case," he said.

CHAPTER TWELVE

"HEY, I DID *NOT* SCREW UP YOUR CASE," I SAID.

He pursed his lips and raised an eyebrow, waiting.

Throwing up my hands, I said, "Why do you think I screwed up your case?"

"I came to you, let you *in*, and the next thing I know you're being kidnapped by the SoPa pack," he said, ticking off the events on his fingers.

"I never said they were SoPa," I said, narrowing my eyes.

"You think I can't recognize a description of Dieter Rossi, SoPa enforcer?" He exhaled a long breath through his nose. "What did you tell them?"

"I didn't tell them anything!" I snapped, crossing my arms over my chest.

"Really," he said. "Because let me tell you what it looks like happened. You asked the wrong people about my werewolves because you wanted the ten thousand dollars. Dieter got wind of it and he kidnapped you and you got away because you told them everything I'd informed you about."

It was a little too close to the truth, and I felt my stomach tighten because of the agreement I'd made with Malik. Fae nature is finicky with promises. I'd tried to word our arrangement carefully, so that I didn't actually have to betray Nick, but I could feel my own magic tugging at me.

"Well, just so we're being honest," I said. "He wanted me dead for other reasons."

"Sure. And what were those reasons?" Nick asked.

"I have some photos of him cheating on his girlfriend," I said.

"You're *blackmailing* Dieter Rossi?" Nick said. He rolled his eyes up to the ceiling. "Are you kidding me?"

"I wasn't blackmailing him!" I said. "The photos were for a case."

"What case?" Nick asked, his mouth a flat line.

"I can't tell you," I muttered. "Client confidentiality."

"Of course," he said. "Client confidentiality."

I poked him in the chest and said, "Hey—"

A sharp knock interrupted us and we both turned towards the door. Nick's hand drifted towards where he usually wore his gun, and then his eyes snapped to the chair where he'd put his jacket and holster. Holding a finger up, he crossed the room to the chair and pulled his gun.

He nodded at me and I went to the door, saying, "Who is it?"

"Pizza," the voice on the other side called out. "A large pepperoni?"

My shoulders relaxed, and I opened the door, signing the receipt as the guy slid the pizza out of the insulated bag. He handed it to Nick and accepted the clipboard back from me.

"Have a good one," he said, heading down the hallway.

After I closed the door, we stared at each other for a bit, the smell of fresh pizza wafting between us. My stomach growled loudly, and I said, "You should eat. You used up all the healthy calories from your salad at lunch healing me."

"I didn't have a salad," he said, heading to the kitchen to put the pizza on top of the stove.

"Let me guess, a whole grains bowl? A veggie wrap?" I said,

opening the cabinet and handing him a plate. They had a delicate blue pattern around the edge, and they'd been Shannon and Marco's before we moved her into the care facility.

He shrugged, and admitted, "A hummus plate."

Laughing, I flipped open the lid, and we each took two slices. I scarfed my first one down right at the stove, reloading before I'd finished chewing the crust. Nick leaned back against the counter, but made quick work of his own slices.

At the second plate, we made our way to the couch, Nick grabbing his soda while I filled a glass of water from the tap. I was surprised he didn't snark at the meal choice, but we'd both used up too much magic to eat anything other than a high-calorie dinner.

With a stomach full of greasy pizza, Nick looked a little more relaxed. He must have been starving. He wasn't joking about healing being precision work. The wrong spell could do more damage than help. You could end up with an extra set of kidneys or blood clean of any white blood cells.

"How did you get away?" Nick asked.

"I know Malik Bell," I admitted. "From when we were kids."

"Same neighborhood?" Nick guessed. He licked some grease off of his thumb and I watched his pink tongue slide across the pad of his finger.

"No," I said. "We were at a boys' home together for a year or so when I was between foster families."

"And he was ok with you taking photos of his second?" Nick asked.

"You're behind on the news," I said. "I don't think Malik trusts Dieter any more than you do."

Nick's brow furrowed. "That's going to be bad news for South Palmas."

At first I thought he was talking about the pack, which would have been pretty progressive for someone whose job was to break up dangerous packs. Then, I remembered who I was talking to.

He was talking about the actual neighborhood. The territory that SoPa controlled. Of course, he was the kind of guy who worried about the people he'd pledged to serve and protect.

As I was ruminating on what terrible luck I had that I was so into a guy who was so straight-laced, so genuinely *good*, I saw his chin dip and spring back up. His eyes drifted closed again and then snapped open. I took his plate from slack fingers.

"I'll be right back," I said.

Standing, I padded to the kitchen and put our plates in the sink as quietly as I could. I murmured to the air, using the barest hint of magic to convince it that it was warmer than the thermostat suggested. The apartment warmed. Not hot, just enough that the next time Nick's eyes shut, they stayed closed.

Air was mostly a party trick because it never lasted long without genuine effort. Still, when I walked back to the couch, Nick had slumped over, his chin on his chest. I nudged him into a more comfortable position, laying sideways on the couch. Grabbing the throw blanket that Laurel had given me for Christmas a few years ago, I draped it over him.

His features relaxed in sleep, and he looked younger. Without the tension from the pressure he put on himself, he was even more attractive. Shaking my head at myself, I sat down beside him and closed my own eyes.

———

I woke up to sunlight blinding me. Squinting, I listened for the soft noises of someone in my apartment. The apartment was empty, Nick's jacket and gun gone. Disappointment raced through me before I realized how ridiculous that was. He had his own life, a job to get back to. I should just be grateful that he'd healed me instead of dropping me at the hospital despite my protests and leaving me with a twenty thousand dollar medical bill.

Keys scraped against the lock of my front door and I sprung up. It couldn't be Jeffrey Jenkins. I still had three days to come up with the money.

The bag from the bakery around the corner came through first and then two styrofoam coffee cups, the white lids on tight. Nick bumped the door shut with his hip and smiled when he saw me awake. I mirrored his expression and felt my cheeks heat.

"Borrowed your keys," he said, offering over my key ring.

I accepted them back, and he walked to the kitchen, setting down the coffees and the bag. Trailing behind him, I could feel my eyebrows going up, even as something warm settled in my stomach.

"I got a call this morning from the ME," he said. "Your tip was good."

"What tip?" I said, watching as he tore the bag open to reveal four donuts and a couple of croissants. With a loud grumble, my stomach let me know that it was still hungry after all the magic I'd used the day before. I snagged a croissant and tore into it.

"About werewolves not being the only ones made of magic," Nick said. "I sent some unis to Sintown to check for bodies. They found an incubus stashed behind a dumpster. Who knows how long he'd been there, since the garbage guys never reported a body."

Sintown was a few square blocks on the west side of San Amaro. Even if they'd seen the dead body, the garbage collectors might not want to report it since then they'd be on record and no one wanted to be on the wrong side of the pimps and madams who ran Sintown.

"And?" I asked. "Was he drained of magic?"

Nick nodded and, to my surprise, grabbed one of the chocolate covered donuts. I ate the last of my croissant, licking the flakey crumbs off of my fingers.

"I figured you were a bran muffin kind of guy," I said.

"Usually," he said. "But these looked like something you'd like."

I squinted at him, and a faint flush colored his warm brown skin. He avoided my eyes, grabbing a coffee. Pointing at his clothes, I said, "That's a different suit."

"Of course," he said. "I keep a change in my car."

His tone was amused, like it was a thing to have a second expensive suit in the car just in case you spent the night on some P.I.'s couch.

"The job *can* get dirty. Don't you have spare clothes in your car?" he asked.

The last I'd seen of my car, it had a giant hole in the windshield and was in Five Dragons territory. If I was lucky, I still *had* a car. More than likely, I now had a parking space where I used to have a car.

"Jeans and a t-shirt," I said. "Not an Armani suit!"

"Tom Ford," he corrected, the flush darkening his skin again.

"I'm going to change," I said, stuffing a donut in my mouth. "Into normal-people clothes. Since I don't have a five thousand dollar suit in my car."

"Find something decent," he said. "I thought you could come with me to the morgue."

"What?" I said, the donut muffling the word. I swallowed and spoke around the food, ignoring his wrinkled nose of disgust.

"You've been helpful," he said. "Given how you're living, you must need the money for something. I thought, maybe you might want a... leg up."

Squinting, I said, "You're just afraid if you let me go on my own, I'll get kidnapped again."

"That healing did take a lot out of me," he said. "I can't do another. So, I figured I'd keep you close. Plus, if you see the body, maybe you can tell us if we can discount fae magic completely."

Suspiciously, I said, "I'll go find something decent."

"Anything other than your usual hobo-chic will do," he said.

Just to spite him, I chose my best jeans and a t-shirt for a local grunge band. I found one of my only suit jackets to throw on top of it, so he couldn't say I didn't try. When I came out, his eyes traced down from my tousled blonde hair to my bare feet.

His tongue darted out, but then his lips tightened. He huffed a sigh. "Fine."

"Not good enough?" I asked, grinning cheekily at him. I turned in a circle with my arms out like I was modeling. "You don't think it's classy enough to look at dead bodies?"

He shook his head. "Put on some shoes, Parker. Let's go."

I grabbed my boots and a pair of socks and laced them up as he finished his portion of the donuts. I grabbed the last donut and my coffee, before realizing that I'd need supplies if I was going out in the world.

Even though I'd survived, my run in with Dieter had thrown me a bit. I wasn't as good at working with metal as I was with nature, and I didn't want to be helpless again. Plus, no matter what Malik's people thought, Dieter still wanted me dead sooner rather than later.

Opening one of the kitchen cabinets, I rifled through my supplies. I began grabbing things, balancing the coffee, donut, and some sticks, a rock, and a bottle of my favorite dirt.

"Here," Nick said, coming up beside me. He held out my satchel, and I shoved all the supplies into it. "Do I want to know what that's for?"

"Security," I said. "I *can* take care of myself."

"Obviously," he said. "I mean, people who can take care of themselves often get kidnapped by dangerous werewolf packs, beaten to an inch of their lives, and let go because they happen to know the pack alpha."

"Key word there is 'let go,' and an inch from death is still not dead," I said. Swinging the bag over my shoulder, I grabbed my keys and took the coffee back from Nick.

"So, I should have let you just bleed internally because an inch from dead wasn't actually dead?" Nick said. He held open the door for me and I walked through, locking it behind us.

"Sure," I said. "I could have handled it."

In the hallway, I got a better look at Nick and muffled a groan. Even though he'd spent the night on the couch like me, he didn't look like he had a crick in his neck or a day-old stubble. Instead, his close cropped hair and light beard made it look like he was showing off that he hadn't slept at home.

He rolled his eyes up and muttered something about black-market witches and back-room alchemists. We headed down to the street and I tilted my head to examine his Mustang, the black paint shiny and clean in the morning light.

"Whose car is this?" I asked. "Do you have a cooler older brother that you borrowed it from?"

"Well, my boring sedan was in the shop," he said. "This was all they had for a loaner."

His deadpan humor startled a bark of laughter out of me and I climbed in the passenger side, arranging my bag on my lap and shoving the whole donut into my mouth before I could get any crumbs on his detailed seats. Despite his joke, it was obviously his car, from the public radio that came on as soon as he started the engine to the light and siren that he had stowed in the back seat. His suit from the day before was hung neatly in the back.

"You know," I said. "They have therapy for people like you."

"Fully functional adults?" he said. He pulled a pair of sunglasses out of the car's sunglasses holder and slid the aviators on. "Yeah. That's how we get to be fully functional. I'm pretty sure they have tv shows for people like you."

"Cribs? My Glamorous Life?" I said.

"Hoarders. Queer Eye," he said, buckling his belt. He pointedly waited for me to snap mine on before heading out.

As we passed through San Amaro, I tore open the coffee lid, taking a sip of the bitter blend. It was a perfect antidote to the slight haze of exhaustion I was still feeling.

"Why are you inviting me?" I asked. "You could have just left me a note."

After a long beat, he glanced at me, his eyes a quick flash of hazel visible in the gap between his sunglasses and his cheekbone before staring back at the road.

"I know you can be helpful," he said. "And you clearly need the reward money for something. Call it a favor."

Already I was shaking my head, the weight of the favor bearing down on me. "No, I don't like owing favors."

"I meant for me," he said. "After all, if you help me get a quick arrest, I'll look good with the captain."

"Fine," I said. "I can help with that. But only because you said that I can be helpful. Gosh, what a sweetheart saying such nice things about me. You *liiiike* me."

"Forget it," he said. I caught the flash of hazel again as his eyes looked towards me, while his head stayed firmly facing the road.

CHAPTER THIRTEEN

THE CITY MORGUE WAS A GRAY CUBE WITH A PARKING LOT THAT Nick had to swipe his ID for us to get into. The chainlink gate buzzed loudly and squealed as it trundled open. He found us a spot near the entrance and I took one last swallow of my coffee before leaving the empty cup in the cupholder.

When I glanced over, he was straightening his jacket on his shoulders, his expression blank and *that* was the Detective Nicholas King that I knew, not the one who rolled up his shirt sleeves and healed me, when normally he could barely stand to be around me. He jerked his head towards the building and I trailed behind him into the clean white entrance hall.

The receptionist made us both sign in, taking down my driver's license number on the sign-in sheet. She gestured to the waiting-room chairs, but I saw Nick stay standing, sliding off his sunglasses and tucking them into his jacket pocket. I wandered over to the art on the walls that clearly hadn't been updated since the eighties. Tangerine-colored flowers and a teal background was not modern art.

After a few minutes, an assistant came by to collect us, leading us to a large, concrete room with drawers for dead bodies covering one wall, and a few tables for autopsies. An office was tucked to the side, and I watched a bald, portly man finish a mug of coffee at his desk before grabbing a clipboard and coming closer to greet us. He pushed a set of narrow rectangular glasses up his nose with the knuckle of his forefinger, like he was used to adjusting them when his hands were covered in bodily fluids.

Before Nick could say anything, the man pointed at me, "Who's this, Detective King?"

"Parker Ferro. He's a consultant on fae matters," Nick said.

"Doctor Rictor," the ME introduced himself. He didn't offer to shake my hand, and given what he touched daily, I was grateful. I raised my hand in a small wave.

"Is this fae-related?" Rictor asked. "I didn't get any F.E. paperwork."

"There isn't any," Nick said. "We're trying to figure out if it *is* fae-related."

Shaking his head, the ME said, "Well, it's *something*-related. I've never seen magic readings like this, and I've been here for years. I even had the department witch come in to verify my findings."

"What did you find?" Nick said.

"Here, I'll show you," Rictor pulled back the sheet and revealed a slender, gorgeous man. If he didn't have a Y incision marking his chest, I wouldn't have known he was dead.

Succubae and incubi are creatures from the Far Realm. They share an unnatural beauty with my kind, although they aren't able to practice any of the complicated magic that fae can. Instead, their magic comes from carnal pleasures. They draw power from sex and sexual desire, and while fae are limited in how they can use magic on humans and other living creatures, succubae and incubi can use their magic to do a number of spells.

Most of them are sex and pleasure-related, which makes them excellent prostitutes.

"Okay, we're looking at a who-knows-what aged incubus. I

asked around and the closest I can guess is seventy years old." Rictor looked down at his notes.

"We don't get a lot of fae-creatures in here. Most of the time, they get left in the hills to get picked up by the fae if they die and I don't know what the fae do with them in the Far Realm," Rictor said. "But, anatomy-wise they're similar to us. There's some strangulation marks, but I don't think that was what killed him."

"No?" Nick asked, frowning down at the body.

"In fact, I couldn't tell you the cause of death. Unlike the werewolves, where you could see physical injuries, this guy seemed to just... stop," Rictor said. He pulled out a rectangular device that looked like a Geiger counter and offered it over to Nick. "This is what we use to test for residual magic so we can find out if someone's death was due to a spell. I've never used it to look for a lack of magic before. But, when I ran it over the werewolves, they should have pinged at a four out of five. Basic, baseline magic for wolves. They were at a zero."

Nick waved the device over the incubus and the arrow stayed stubbornly at zero. "What's normal for an incubus?"

Rictor shrugged. "Not a lot of studies on it. But definitely not zero."

"Anything else suspicious?" Nick asked.

"We have some markings here, on his chest," Rictor said. "It's faint, but you can make it out. Looks like an alchemist's circle, but I've never seen one like this. You?"

Nick squinted at the lines. They formed a broken circle, and where anchor points should be, there were instead open V shapes. Unlike all alchemy spells, there wasn't any closing circle enveloping and limiting the spell. Instead, it was just a circle of words.

"Is it Latin?" I asked Nick.

He shook his head. "No. Not Greek, either. And the witch didn't recognize it?"

"Nope, she thought it might be older alchemy." Rictor held

out his clipboard and Nick took it and skimmed the witch's report.

Passing back the clipboard, Nick turned to me. "So? Fae magic?"

"No," I shook my head. "The fae don't need written spells to cast."

"So we still don't know anything other than that it's not just affecting werewolves." Nick raised his eyebrows, looking between me and Rictor.

I stepped close and took a better look at the spell. It wasn't like anything I'd seen before, but when I got close enough, I could almost smell the glamour on him. I grabbed a pair of gloves from the head of the examination table and slid them on before leaning close again and touching the edge of the spell.

"What's this written with?" I asked.

"Honestly? If I didn't see it in front of me, I would tell you that there wasn't anything written there," Rictor said. "It's not ink, it's not even alchemy paint."

That must have been what Nick used in his spell last night.

"I think the spell is missing pieces," I said. "The writing part isn't fae, but I think it was written *with* fae magic. Look, it's a glamour."

I brought my hand over the incubus's chest and using a minor glamour connected the broken lines so that the inner circle was whole. The spell flashed, and I saw the lines move.

The spell slithered across the incubus's body, like a snake that had been warming itself in the sun. It raced towards me, arcing the distance between my finger and his skin even as Rictor pulled us apart. I felt a drain immediately on my power. The spell was a leech that had attached itself to my magic, sucking it so quickly that I had no protection against it.

The spell grew fat with the influx of magic. It swelled and consumed more and more. I screamed, feeling the magic twist itself around my neck, cutting off my voice.

Picturing the sticks I'd put in my bag, I reached into my satchel and blindly grabbed for them. My desperate fingers wrapped around them, and I croaked out, "Help me, old one."

Here's the thing about trees. I don't want to cast any aspersions on Shel Silverstein, who I'm sure was a nice guy, but most trees won't voluntarily give you everything down to their trunks. But—and here's where I admit that I don't know any other books with a tree main character, so I'm going to turn to movies—if you look in the right place and ask around, you can find a tree like that talking one in *Pocahontas*.

A wise old crone of a tree, who'll give you cryptic advice. A tree that could also save your life if you need it.

The branches in my hand exploded into growth. The ends grew down through the concrete, shattering it under my feet, searching for a connection to the earth. The body of sticks twisted together, thickening into a trunk and then rising into a canopy of leaves. I pumped all the magic I could into the wood, even as the spell hunted across my torso, searching for the bubble of power I was using.

Nick was yelling something, his gun out, but he was keeping the barrel down, clearly unsure where to aim it. When he caught my eyes, he holstered it and pulled out a small silver blade and a white handkerchief. The blade was carved with miniature alchemy circles and two lit up as he began chanting. He bent, grabbing his pen from inside his jacket and started drawing quick circles around me, trying to contain or end the spell.

I didn't have the voice to explain that I could feel the end of the spell, and it was when it had drained me dry and left me a magicless husk like the incubus on the table. I coughed instead and saw Rictor pulling out an honest-to-god wand and starting his own counter spell. A closet warlock hiding in the morgue. What a headache for the department.

The tree roots finally reached the earth and found the deep pool of magic that exists there. It's not one that I could access on my own, but the tree could drink it like literal water. When the tree hooked in to the good stuff, it spoke.

"Parker Ferro," it said. "This spell you are toying with is dangerous. What's your plan here? Let it kill you? After I've invested so much time in making sure you don't grow up to be one of those who would cut my kin down?"

Rictor stopped chanting, his mouth hanging open as he stared at the massive tree dripping sarcasm like sap in the middle of his morgue. Nick had wrapped up the alchemist's circle on the floor and grabbed my arm where one of the spell's lines wiggled across my forearm. With a quick slash, the silver blade made a shallow cut across my skin and the line died off. But it was only partial, plucking off one leg of a spider, leaving the bulk of it limping and hungry, crawling over my chest.

"Not mine." My voice was a hoarse croak. Nick cut across my neck, barely a paper cut deep, but it worked and left my voice free. I gasped and began coaxing the tree. "It'll kill me before I can plant more of your seeds."

The tree *hrumphed*, and her voice was the brush of leaves on a windy day. "And how many have you yet planted? And how many of those survive?"

Still, she grew branches to cradle me close, enveloping me in an embrace, winding me into her trunk until we were one and the spell calmed for a moment, feeding on the deep, pure magic of the earth. The tree wound her own magic into the spell, and then, like a root cracking the pavement, she ripped the spell apart. I felt it shatter and used what was left of my own magic to stomp out the wriggling remains—smothering them like the sparks that jump off a campfire.

"In exchange, you will plant more of me," she intoned, and released me, dropping five small seed pods into my hands before stilling. "I see a new debt on your soul. You should be careful who you pledge your favors to, young one."

Her trunk opened, the light a brilliant white after the safe darkness. Two hands reached in and pulled apart the gap, forcing it wider. The tree sighed, opening farther, even as her being seemed to shrink until I couldn't hear her anymore.

Nick grabbed me as soon as I was free and pulled up the hem on my shirt, his knife ready to slice at any bit of spell that remained. I held up my hands and said, "Whoa, whoa. We're good. The spell is gone."

"Shirt off," Nick commanded. "I need to check."

I shrugged off my jacket and pulled my shirt over my head. His fingers stroked firmly down my neck to my hip. He spun me and checked my back with equal thoroughness. He even parted my hair to check if the spell was hiding there.

"What was that?" he snapped.

At the same time, Rictor said, "This is a sentient tree."

His glasses askew, he carefully brushed a finger over a leaf nearby. The leaf fell. The tree itself shrank, cracking like old paint. Like a prop built for some children's play, the whole thing caved in. After a few moments, the only thing left was the sticks I started with and a giant hole in the ground.

I scooped up the sticks and stowed them back in my bag with the new seeds.

"That tree talked," Rictor said. "What—Why—How?"

"The universe is vast, warlock," I asked. "And my comprehension is incomplete."

It snapped him out of it. Some covens rely on accepting the mystery of the universe, their tenets claiming that for every piece of knowledge there are additional questions and pursuing them rather than accepting truth is the way to madness. He shook his head like he was clearing a fog, and then he looked between me and the incubus on the table. The incubus looked the same. Only the spell was missing.

"The universe is vast," he said. "My comprehension is incomplete, but ever expanding. I seek knowledge over answers."

"What happened?" Nicholas interrupted. He pointed at me.

"What was that spell and what was that magic? I've never felt anything like it. Was that witchcraft?"

That sort of question has dogged most of my childhood. Half the foster homes that kicked me out were because of what I could do with my magic. The other half were just a "bad fit" or "no longer willing to be foster parents." Which I translated pretty clearly as not liking me.

"I have no idea what the spell was. I'm pretty sure that the spell must have broken apart when the incubus died. Maybe even before whoever cast it got what he wanted, because I could still feel some of the incubus's magic sliding around in there," I said. The incubus's magic felt odd with mine, oil and water, taking up space together, but I doubted I'd be able to use it. I'd have to drain it out somehow.

"Okay, well," Nick shook his head. "Crap."

"*Crap*?" I snorted. "I almost got killed and the best you can manage is 'crap'?"

"Hey, according to you, *almost* doesn't even count!" he said.

"Well, it counts now!" I said. "You were slicing and dicing me!"

"To save you from a spell that had killed an incubus!"

"Stop!" Rictor said, holding up his hand. "The paperwork on this is going to be a nightmare. In the meantime."

He walked back to his office and returned with two clipboards with a thick stack of blank paper on each. "Start on your statements."

CHAPTER FOURTEEN

WE ENDED UP AT THE MORGUE FOR ANOTHER TWO HOURS, lunch delivered by a frightened medical examiner's assistant. Crime Scene techs had to show up again, although Rictor said that was mostly formality. After a brief discussion, none of our stories included a talking tree, as that would get Rictor and Nick put on administrative leave while the department checked them for narcotics and then made them get cleared by a psychologist.

"Is there an answer?" Rictor asked when he walked me and Nick out to Nick's Mustang.

"The tree?" I shrugged. "More things in this world have spirits than most humans believe."

"Does that mean that *all* trees are sentient?" he asked. "Or all plants? Or—"

"I don't know," I said. "Think of it as part of the great mystery."

He pushed his glasses up with his knuckle and closed his eyes, "The great mystery contains us all."

When we were in the car, safely buckled in, Nick said, "I wonder if he's registered."

"Rictor?" I asked. "What, are you going to tell on him?"

"He should be registered," Nick said.

"Yeah, because that's gone great in the past. I thought that with all the anti-discrimination lawsuits, witches and alchemists didn't have to anymore."

"Law enforcement is an exception since it could affect their ability to perform their job," he said, eyes straight ahead. Glancing at the dashboard, I smirked. We were going exactly the speed limit.

When we pulled up in front of my apartment, he parallel-parked with the expertise of a valet. I got out and leaned down in the open door to say my goodbyes, only to see him unbuckling his seatbelt. He closed his door and locked the car. Silently, he trailed me to my apartment, a couple of steps behind me.

The thin carpet muted our footfalls, yet I was hyper-aware of him, I heard every step he took. My key missed the lock twice before I managed to get it in. With the door open, I turned. He was close, so close that I could feel his touch like an echo on my skin.

"Seeing me to my door, you gentleman?" I asked, smirking.

"I'd like to kiss you," he said. His tongue traced across his plush bottom lip and I had had *fantasies* about that lip.

"You don't even *like* me," I said. "I'm the annoying guy who breaks into your crime scenes."

"It wasn't a crime scene," he said, stepping closer.

"I still ended up in cuffs, didn't I?" I asked. I reached out, but stopped before I touched his chest.

"We shouldn't," he said, taking another small step forward until my hand made contact and I could feel his pec through his white dress shirt. It tightened and, yeah, I could get used to touching that.

"Why?" I asked.

"I'm pretty sure it's just adrenaline from your almost dying," he said. "And you're consulting on the case, so it'd be a conflict of interest."

Shaking my head, I said, "You're not paying me. So, as far as I can see, I was just a guy you interviewed who didn't know anything."

The flat look he gave me made it obvious that the excuse was thin. Still, he took another step towards me, backing me into the apartment. His foot kicked the door shut.

I took two steps still facing him, fisting my hand in what was a very expensive shirt. Pulling him with me, I walked backwards into my bedroom, glad that I'd done laundry this week so the sheets smelled clean, even if I'd left them rumpled on my unmade bed.

"You should kiss me," I said.

"I can kiss you," he said.

He leaned in and pressed his lips against mine. The sensation sent sparks of pleasure across my skin and I wanted more. With both hands, I grabbed his ridiculously expensive jacket and pulled his body snug against mine. The muscled planes fit in a way that sent a jolt of pleasure up my spine.

He slid his palm under my t-shirt and up my back. The sensation of his warm, smooth skin on my skin made me shudder. I pushed closer to him and the kiss turned heated as I licked open his lips and slid my tongue inside.

We swayed there for a few minutes. Each time one of us would press forward, the other would answer and it was an erotic dance that made me want more sensation. I pushed back and enjoyed the sight of him leaning forward, unwilling to let me go. His mouth was slightly open, and he blinked a few times, coming back to himself.

I yanked off the satchel still crossed over my chest and then pulled out of my jacket and shirt. When I refocused on him, I saw he was neatly laying his jacket on the bed, unbuttoning his shirt. Squashing the desire to rip open his shirt and send all the buttons flying, I toed out of my shoes and shimmied out of my pants.

He stilled, his eyes scraping over my body. I raised an eyebrow and threw myself back on the bed, lounging with one hand behind my head and the other massaging my dick through my underwear. His swallow was audible in the quiet.

"You going to join me?" I asked. "Or are you just going to stand there?"

"Yes," he said, stuttering. "Yeah, let me just."

One of his expensive buttons hit the wall with a soft click as he hastened out of his shirt, pulling the undershirt off with a hand at the neck of the white t-shirt. He unbuckled his belt, and his pants slid down his legs like water. He had to bend to untie his shoes, and I grinned.

For all that he was competent and great at his job, he was so awkward here that I felt affection for him leaking out of me. The moment I'd met him, I'd known he was my type, even when he wouldn't admit the house we were in was haunted. When we'd met up later, I couldn't help but think that he was handsome, but way too arrogant to demean himself with me.

Maybe he was still that, but he laughed with me when he finally got the shoes undone, and then he was all grace and power when he slid over me on the bed. His muscled arms framed my head as he hovered over my mouth.

"Hey," he said, a grin wrecking the coolness of the line. "Can I kiss you?"

"Took you long enough," I said, lifting my head to kiss his lips. "Thought I'd die over here."

He leaned down and his body was heavy on mine in all the right ways. His kisses moved from my lips down to my neck, making me shudder. The feeling sent blood straight to my dick, and I groaned.

As he rubbed his body against mine, I felt something stir inside me. The latent incubus magic, unable to mix with my own, was sparking between Nick and me. I felt it heightening each sensation, making everything feel just slightly *more*.

"What is that?" Nick asked, pulling back. His eyes were cloudy, flaring green and then clearing.

"I absorbed some of the incubus's magic when the spell shattered," I said. "I think we're both in for a ride. You okay with that?"

He frowned a moment, clearly trying to decide.

"Is the magic the reason that we're doing this?" He drew back, frowning.

I shook my head. "No. It's just heightening everything. I mean, you wanted me *before* this, right?"

"Yes," he nodded. "I really did. Did you want me?"

Licking my lips, I realized he was going to make me say it. The pause stretched, and he started to back away from me. I grabbed his arm and held him close. "Since I saw you in that bulky, yellow rain jacket. Since then."

"That was the first time we met," he said, a warm flush spreading across his face and down his chest.

"You're telling me," I said. "You still in?"

After a bit, he shrugged. "I've never had sex with an incubus before. You'll have to give me pointers."

"Hey! I am an incubus virgin here, too, pervert!" I said, pointing at him. He licked the tip of my finger and then sucked it down, teeth scraping against the pad of my finger.

Oh. *Oh.* This was why people went to Sintown, then. Everything in my hand felt like it was directly connected to my dick. I moaned in pleasure.

Pushing up my hips, I ground our dicks together through the underwear. The friction was amazing, and I did it again, enjoying it when Nick bit down too hard in his pleasure.

"Want to fuck me?" I asked. My mind was shooting fireworks and all I could think about was how much more pleasurable it would be when he was inside me.

"Yes," he said. "Yeah, I want that."

I rolled out from under him and slammed open my bedside

table, grabbing lube and a condom. He was on his back, lifting his hips to slide off his blue boxer briefs, and I enjoyed the sight for a moment, condom pinched in my fingers and lube rolling on the bed between us.

"How do you want me?" he asked. His hand gripped his hard cock and pumped once. I watched it grow longer and thick at my gaze.

"Let's start like that," I said. I pushed down on his shoulder and he lay back, his hands framing my hips as I swung a leg over him. "Here."

The lube was in a slim gray bottle and he popped it open and coated his fingers in the viscous liquid. It had been a while since I'd gotten laid, and that was usually just in a car outside a club or a quickie from someone off Grindr. I couldn't remember the last time I'd had sex with someone I wanted to see after we both got off.

"Hey," he said. "You okay?"

"Yeah," I said. My hips jerked forward as he rubbed a knuckle into my perineum, and I groaned when he increased the pressure. It made my cock jump, nearly touching my stomach.

He slid a finger inside and it felt perfect as he pumped it in and out, adding more lube before sliding a second finger in. I closed my eyes and ground down, enjoying the stretch.

"More," I said. He obliged, adding a third finger and more lube. For a while, he just rocked his fingers in and out, and I enjoyed the pressure against my prostate.

Languidly, I opened my eyes and saw that he was biting his lip, his eyes fixed on my face. When our gazes met, his grin turned wicked, and he curled his fingers, rubbing small circles against my prostate. I shuddered, pulling up. His fingers followed, and I said, "Condom. Now."

Ripping open the condom with his teeth, he slid it on and then coated it with more lube. Watching him, I realized that whatever magic the incubus had left in me had burnt out. This pleasure was all him.

I reached down and helped position his cock at my entrance. Holding it steady, I slid down. The head of his dick felt so much larger than his fingers, and it took a moment to slide in.

Pausing above him, I let myself enjoy the sensation of just the tip of his dick inside. When I looked down, he was panting, hands fisting on the sheets. I gave in, bearing down until he was fully seated inside.

We both moaned, and he brought one hand up to grasp my forearm where I was braced above his head. His hand tightened, and he licked his lips again. Unable to resist, I leaned down and kissed him.

The kiss was clean and sweet, and I rocked, getting momentum going. Pushing back up, I let myself ride him, enjoying the pressure and stretch, the feeling of foreignness inside of me.

Eventually, I reached down and began pumping myself, a spark of pleasure exploding when he dug his short nails into my hip. I wanted more.

"I want you to fuck me," I said, opening my eyes to see his hazel eyes wide.

He nodded. "Yes, yes."

He flipped us, rolling on top of me and slinging my legs over his shoulders before slamming his hips home.

"Is this okay?" he asked.

I gasped. "Yeah. Yes. More like that."

He moved again, and I enjoyed the impact of our bodies meeting. He reached down and tugged on my dick, some remaining lube lessening the friction. I came, suddenly, unexpectedly, and felt my whole body tighten around his dick.

He shuddered, going stiff as he trembled above me. I felt him try to shift off and reached up with both arms to pull him down on top of me.

We breathed together for a few minutes, his breath hot on my neck. Finally, he pulled out, careful with the condom. Rolling over, he relaxed next to me, his hand finding mine in the tangled sheets.

"I should take care of this," he said.

I looked over to find him on his side, face half hidden in my pillow, his visible eye watching me. Using our intertwined fingers, I tugged him closer, and he came easily, nestling his face into the curve of my neck.

———

We must have drifted off, because the next thing I knew, my shower was on and I was alone in bed. I savored the soreness in my ass and the faint bruising I could feel where his hands had been just a shade too tight against me.

The water shut off, and he came to the doorway, my towel wrapped around his waist, a few stray droplets sliding down his chest. He smirked at me.

"Your shower is disgusting."

"Are you offering to clean it for me?" I asked. "Is this a full-service hook-up?"

"I'm saying next time clean the shower before I come over," he said. "And maybe I'll be in the mood for another round instead of wondering if that level of mildew is safe to be around."

"I'll have you know that my mildew is perfectly safe to be around. It's decorative," I said.

"It's disgusting." He sidled towards the bed, leaning down like he was going to kiss me and then pulling up and grabbing his phone out of his pants pocket. "I was going to order dinner. You have a preference?"

"Is it dinner time?" I asked, squinting at the window where the orange light showed it to be evening. "I don't know. Anything, really. Pizza?"

He gave me a flat look and then patted his stomach. "Two days of pizza means four days at the gym."

"Oh, eww," I said. "No. You just burned a thousand calories healing me yesterday, and we had to have burned another thousand right now. I can't believe you're thinking about the gym."

Sitting up, I pointed at him. "You're one of those guys who gets up at five a.m. to go workout, aren't you! And then you eat your bran muffin! You tried to trick me into believing you were a donut guy."

I shook my head and *tsked*. He laughed.

"How about some Chinese food?"

"Like that is healthier!" I huffed and slid off the bed. Getting close enough to kiss him, I grinned and then grabbed my towel off his hips.

His breath hitched and his eyes locked onto my lips. I could see his dick jump a little in interest. With a wink, I breezed past him into the bathroom.

"Just get me whatever!" I called, turning on the water.

He swore slightly under his breath and I cackled as I stepped under the hot spray.

CHAPTER FIFTEEN

WHEN I GOT OUT OF THE SHOWER, NICK WAS ACCEPTING A couple of bags that smelled delicious and handing over ten dollars in tip. He'd pulled on his pants and undershirt and even though both were perfectly neat, it was like seeing a whole different person than the suave Detective King that I was used to.

In the kitchen, he pulled out boxes of Chinese food, dividing up fried rice and veggie dishes.

"No Kung Pao?" I whined.

He shook his head and hid a small grin before opening the remaining three boxes. Delicious, heavy scents filled the kitchen, and he spooned some Kung Pao chicken onto my plate, and then some orange chicken. He added some seafood dish to his own and then split a box of spring rolls, two for me, two for him.

We settled on the couch, arguing over whether he should have sprung to have beer delivered, too. I watched him as he ate and blushed hot when he caught me staring.

"I thought you didn't like me," I said. "You said you didn't!"

"I never said that," he said. "I think I said you were a pain."

"That means you don't like me." I narrowed my eyes and

pointed my fork at him. "That's what it always means when someone says that!"

"Well, I do." He crunched on one of the spring rolls, neatly wiping away crumbs with a napkin. "I like you."

Shaking my head, I said, "So what is this? A hook-up?"

He poked at some squid with his fork and didn't look up at me. "Is that what you want?"

With a rising suspicion, I tested a theory. "Was the morgue visit a *date*? Was that your idea of romance? Were you trying to seduce me with *dead bodies*?"

"No!" He laughed. "But it worked, didn't it?"

"I almost died! You almost killed the guy you like!" I bit into a spicy pepper and had to take a long drink of water.

"It wasn't a date, but you seemed to need the money," he said. "And I felt bad that I couldn't pay you your fee for consulting."

"So you admit I'm consulting," I said. But the mention of money had brought me down. I still only had three days before I needed cash.

It also reminded me that I had another case hanging over my head, too. The Summer Queen wouldn't take it well if she found out I was prioritizing another case over hers. In fact, it would get me a painful reminder of what happened when I resisted her directions.

"What was that, back at the morgue?" Nick asked.

I wet my lips, ready with a lie.

"I know that wasn't witchcraft," he said, forestalling me. He squinted at me. "What you use, it's fae magic, isn't it?"

"What're you talking about?" I asked. My mouth was dry, and I felt my heart beating twice as fast as it should.

No one should know I was fae. Only two people did, and one was bound to secrecy, and the other was a vegetable. Malik suspected, maybe. But he couldn't be sure, and that was enough to make it doubtful that he'd talk to anyone about it.

"I know the reason you're an expert in the fae is because they took you. You were eighteen, I saw your file," Nick said. His eyes were piercing me, searching for truth. He must be a defense attorney's nightmare during an interrogation.

"Yeah, they took me," I said. "But you can see I'm human."

"I'm not accusing you of anything." Holding up his hand, Nick said, "They taught you their magic, didn't they?"

I exhaled. So Nick didn't know. My stomach felt tight, the Chinese food sitting sour and heavy.

If I lied about that, Nick would get suspicious. I'd banked on him not knowing enough about witchcraft to suspect anything. In fact, in the past, I'd even made sure not to do anything a witch couldn't do around him. That had all been thrown out the window when the spell latched on to me.

"Yeah," I said. I was reminded of Malik and how he'd said that he could sniff me out. He made it sound like I wasn't alone, but as far as I knew, I was the only one living here in San Amaro.

If I hewed close to the truth, maybe Nick would buy it. Maybe he wouldn't ask too many questions and then I could get away with continuing my life as it was. Because if he knew that I was fae, even part fae, not only would he not want to date me, he'd want to lock me up and throw away the key.

"I was in foster care from when I was little. They found me in front of a fire station when I was three, and I could just never find the right home. Not until I was fifteen. I got taken in by this amazing couple who ran a group home. Shannon was a head priestess, and she taught me how to use my magic. If I did all my work with her, Marco would let me help out on cases."

Getting taken in by them had been the best thing that ever happened to me. Marco was an old hand with foster kids, and the way that he made even *me* feel bad about some of the stunts I tried to pull had been nothing short of a miracle. Shannon had been more nurturing, but that was only until I started lessons. She required perfection in magic, because anything less could be dangerous.

"When I turned eighteen, I went out partying with some friends and we ended up out in the hills. It was around the summer solstice, so we knew the fae might be there. We were a little drunk and... I don't know what we were thinking. They all made it back, but I didn't. The fae took an interest in me."

Which was to say, I woke up in a room made of silver tree branches and drank water out of a golden goblet, and by the time a servant showed me to the Summer Queen I thought that staying there might be a little fun. A few nights couldn't hurt. And Shannon had recognized my magic for what it was: fae. In my mind, I would learn about my people and then go back to Marco and Shannon and my life in San Amaro.

"It didn't feel like long, a few months, maybe. But what no one tells you is that time in the Far Realm passes differently. It kind of matches up with our seasons, but it also doesn't? It's hard to explain. I knew the summer solstice had passed and then the winter solstice, but it seemed like one long afternoon. Everything was so beautiful, all the time. There was always something fun to do, some game to play."

When we weren't engaging in revelry, I could learn magic with the most experienced of fae. I started with the children, the crèche, but after only a few weeks, I was already doing higher level stuff. All the groundwork that Shannon had laid out for me worked just as well with the fae as it did with witchcraft.

I knew that I was an oddity. The Summer Queen—the *old* Summer Queen—used to enjoy having me attend at her side. I was her most favored entertainment. My surprise and joy at all the Far Realm had to offer delighted her. It took me years to realize that her amusement acted like manacles around my wrists. I would never be free until she grew tired of me.

And once I began to bore her, my life would be very short afterwards.

"Yeah, I learned magic from them. I could pick it up and I think they thought it was amusing to see me try." I avoided details. Nick was leaning forward, his eyes on mine, a frown between his dark eyebrows. He smiled when I paused and then reached out, covering my hands with his.

I had been clenching my fists so tightly that when I opened them, there were crescents from my fingernails carved into my palms. Gently, Nick pulled my hand to his lap, lacing our fingers together.

He was buying this. It made me ill. Leaving out my fae nature made the story different—a human trying to survive in the Far Realm, outnumbered, out of his depth. Because I was a fae, the real story was of going home, learning about my kind, learning to be as manipulative and conniving as the rest of them were.

"Like I said, time *felt* different there and one day, one of the Summer Queen's court came to me and told me that even though it had only seemed like a few weeks, I'd actually been there for years. Two years. Which meant that I'd just abandoned Shannon and Marco and the other kids that lived with us. I'd just left. They probably thought I'd run away."

Swallowing, I felt the same fury rise up in my throat. The terror at realizing that as much liberty as the Summer Queen gave me, I was trapped.

"Lilacina—that was her name—she told me that she'd set me free, but only as a favor. I would owe her my life."

I let that sit between us. My debt was something that weighed on my soul, a tie that bound me to Lilacina until I had paid it off. There was no way out; even my own death wouldn't free me from that obligation.

"In FET," Nick said, "I mean, Fae Encounter Training, they tell us to never accept any gift from the fae. And to never make promises."

"Yeah," I said, my grin unhappy. "That would have been smarter. But I had to get free and she could open a door I couldn't. So, I took her up on her offer. I came home, and I found out that while I was away, Shannon and Marco had been in a car crash. He'd been killed, and Shannon was in a coma. Or, I don't know, something. She can open her eyes and they say that she can hear you, but I don't think there's anything there."

I used my free hand to rub at my eyes, a scratchy hot feeling under my lids. When I'd gotten back, I'd been so angry and bitter that I hadn't even mourned them. Even now, I wanted to shove the emotion down into a box and forget it existed. Swallowing, I continued.

"So Laurel—she was one of the other foster kids that Shannon and Marco had taken in—she and I pool our money every month and pay for Shannon to be in a nice facility. Because Shannon was good to us. She shouldn't be stuck in some state facility where they only check on her once a day.

"What I didn't know was that Lilacina wasn't helping me out of the goodness of her heart. When I left, the Summer Queen went a little nuts. Every guard, every servant was sent to search for me. She was convinced that one of the other courts had taken me. The Summer Queen almost went to war with the Autumn Court over it."

I pulled my hand back from Nick and he let it go. Pressing my hands together, I trapped them between my knees.

"With her weakened, with her guards out of court, Lilacina made her move. She killed the old Summer Queen and ascended the throne. I was just a distraction. She probably would have let me go even if I hadn't promised her anything."

Bitterness dripped from my words, acid in my mouth. I reached out and grabbed my glass, drinking deep. Nick rubbed my back.

"So you owe the Summer Queen your life. Do you think she's going to collect?" Nick asked.

Of course he was going to be practical about it. I'd just told him I'd been an idiot and willingly accepted a deal with one of the most powerful fae, and he'd probably ask to see the contract next. He'd want to talk it over with a lawyer.

"She already has," I said. "A few minor jobs over the years. She called me before you did. Wants me to find a girl. So now I need to figure out how to find her and fulfill my obligation to the Summer Queen without actually *giving* her the girl."

"Did you find the girl the Queen wants?" Nick asked.

I shook my head. "I haven't had time, in between being kidnapped by Dieter and almost getting sucked dry by that spell."

"Give me the details," Nick said. "I can help you track her down."

Frowning, I glanced at him, trying to read him through his open expression.

"Hey." He put a hand on my knee. "It'll be okay. I can help."

It would be nice to have one less thing to worry about. Slowly, I nodded. "Okay. Yeah."

"But, maybe in the morning." He moved closer, and his body heat was like a banked fire. My bitterness faded, and the terror I'd felt when I thought he might expose me melted as he pressed his mouth to mine.

"You don't have to do this alone," he said, lips brushing mine as he spoke.

My heart hurt. I wanted to believe him, but I knew that when every word out of my mouth was a lie, all I would be doing was taking advantage. I was the worst sort of fae. The kind who could take the truth and twist it and mold it until up was down and left was right. He should apply every warning about the fae to me, and Nick didn't even know it.

Pulling back, I said, "You should be careful with me. Fae magic is dangerous."

He huffed a breath and leaned back, a smirk pulling at his cheeks.

"I don't know if you know this, Parker, but I'm a pretty powerful alchemist. I think I'll be okay." His eyes flashed green as though emphasizing his point.

Closing my eyes, I tried to convince myself that I should just let him think that. There was no reason to show him otherwise. Guilt forced me to speak.

"Okay, fine," I said. I picked up his empty can of soda and headed to the kitchen. Opening the refrigerator. "Can I gift you another one?"

He didn't even blink at the phrasing. "Yeah, thanks."

I pulled it out of the fridge, and if he remembered that we had drunk the last two cans, he must have just thought I had a secret stash somewhere. Walking over, I handed him the soda, standing over him as he accepted it.

The obligation settled over him like a rope binding him to me. He didn't realize it, but now he owed me. And I was going to collect.

Using my magic, the obligation glowing between us, I said, "Hit yourself in the face."

CHAPTER SIXTEEN

Nick raised his hand and slapped himself across the face.

His eyes were wide and his mouth opened in a choked off protest. I stood, fists clenched at my sides, feeling like I was a million miles away from him.

"What was that?" he asked, pulling his hand back and staring at it. Opening and shutting his fingers, he made a fist.

He turned back to me, eyes narrowed. "What did you do?"

"That was fae magic. The talking tree is just part of it. The real stuff is what they can do with obligation. I gifted you something." I gestured to the soda in his hand. "You owed me."

He dropped the soda, the can rolling back and forth on the laminate floor. Squinting at me, he said, "Explain."

"You're the one with Fae Encounter Training," I said. My face felt hot. I knew that I *had* to show him, but that didn't mean that I had to do it like this.

Nick was getting too close. He wanted to *help*, and he didn't want anything in return. When he heard my story about how I got in deep with the fae, he didn't think I was an idiot and deserved what I got. I could tell by his expression that he felt *sorry* for me.

With an eyebrow raised, he waited, and I thought again that he must be the best interrogator the department had.

"Fae magic doesn't work on people. Not like it does on things. It can convince water to boil, but with people you need more than charisma and power. You need an in. You need an obligation."

"Why does a sense of obligation make a difference?" he asked.

"No, not a *sense* of obligation. If a fae gives you a gift—something you want, something you've given permission for them to give you—then you owe them. You have to give them something equivalent when they ask for it," I said.

"Have to how?" he asked. "Could you have made me do something worse than hit myself?"

"Not for just a soda," I said. "The bigger the gift, the bigger the obligation."

"So, your obligation to the Summer Queen is your life. That's major. How will you know when you've paid it off?"

His eyes narrowed, and he frowned slightly. I hadn't scared him, he wasn't thinking over every one of our interactions to figure out if he owed me more than a coke. He was *thinking*, trying to work out the limits and boundaries of a fresh problem.

"You're not understanding," I said. "I'm dangerous to be around. My magic is dangerous."

"So is carrying a gun," Nick said. "How about you let me worry about my danger tolerance, okay?"

Shaking my head, I threw myself on the couch next to him. I covered my face with my hands and huffed out a sigh.

"You should run," I said, voice muffled by my palms.

"Because you picked up some mean party tricks with the fae?" he asked. "I should run because you don't keep any food in your house and I'm going to starve. And if your bathroom is any sign of how often you clean, then we're going to have issues."

"I'm trouble," I said. "Why are you still here?"

For a long beat, Nick was silent. Finally, I lowered my hands and saw that he was looking at me, a small smile on his face.

"I told you. I like you," he said.

"That simple?" I asked. I wanted it to be. Deep in my bones, I wanted it to be that easy for us to just fit together like two puzzle pieces.

"Does it have to be complicated right now?" he asked.

"My life is always complicated," I said.

Nick leaned over and pinned me against the couch, his hands pressing my shoulders back into the cushion. "Let's make it easy. I want to stay the night. Maybe have sex again. Do you want that?"

I should say no. Everything in me said that I should send him on his way, back to his square little life where he cleaned his bathroom regularly and had more than ketchup in his fridge. Unfortunately, I liked him as much as he claimed to like me.

Somehow I'd have to figure out how to protect him from the chaos I seemed to attract. The fae, the SoPa pack, my landlord, and whoever else wanted a piece of me this week would all have to get in line because I had someone I wanted to keep safe.

"Yes," I said, finally. I stretched up, and he leaned down and our mouths fit together.

———

Parker Ferro, you live.

I woke up, my heart racing. The voice in my head was familiar. Deep and cold, like water underground. My heart pounded in my ears.

Who are you?

You know who I am. I am the one who you now owe. I see I am not alone.

Something tugged on the web of debts and promises I owed or was owed. I shuddered. Next to me in bed, Nick snuffled and nestled closer to me. His muscular arm wrapped around my chest and pulled me close.

Carefully, I pulled loose, sitting up on the edge of the bed. My hands tightened on the bedsheet. Breathing deeply, I tried to gain control again.

What do you want?

Survive this trial ahead and I will call in your debt. I have doubts that you can fulfill my requirements if you cannot live through what comes.

The voice faded as swiftly as it had appeared. My arms trembled where I'd propped myself on the edge of the bed. Standing, I padded out to the kitchen to get a glass of water.

Thistle sat at my desk, his face narrow, eyes squinted as he read over a sheath of papers. It was the envelope with the eviction paperwork. Silently, I drew the bedroom door closed, holding my finger up in warning when he looked at me with a malicious grin.

"What are you doing here?" I asked, my voice quiet.

"These are poorly phrased," Thistle said. "If you took this to Court, they would tear through it with a few choice words."

He wasn't talking about San Amaro's court. I headed to the kitchen and grabbed a glass out of the cabinet. The tap water was icy when I drank it down, and I refilled my glass as Thistle stared at me.

"Why are you here?" I asked.

"The Queen requires an update," he said, placing the paperwork down. In the moonlight coming in through the windows, he looked nearly pearl, his hair made of spun silver.

"It's only been a couple of days," I said. "And, believe it or not, it's hard to find someone based on a basic description and no photo. What does she even do? What's her full name? Where does she live?"

Thistle chittered, his teeth growing long. He stood and pulled out a small rectangle from his jacket pocket. Sweeping across the room with a liquid grace, he stopped in front of me where I was leaning against the counter.

He held out a picture pinched between his forefinger and

middle finger. Raising an eyebrow, I took it from him. When I flipped it over, it was the same girl that the Summer Queen had shown me, this time her hair braided and pulled back into a rough ponytail.

She was grinning at the camera, her smile open and wide. It was taken close up; she must have known whoever was photographing her. On the back, someone had scrawled an address.

"That is where she lives," Thistle said as I took it in.

When I looked up, he was staring at the picture, not at me, his expression gone blank. I looked between him and the girl. Then, casually, I tossed the picture onto the countertop.

"Thanks, I'll get to it before the solstice," I said.

His eyes caught mine, and everything about his face sharpened like a knife. I watched him turn feral as he snapped, "You will get to it *now*."

"Why do you care?" I asked. "She's just some human the Queen wants, isn't she?"

Thistle's hands twitched, and he brought them up to grip my cheeks. His nails had gone long and sharp, although he kept his claws from cutting my face. He brought his face close to mine.

"Acacia is not just *some girl*," he hissed. After a long beat, he released me, my jaw aching from where he'd held my face tight. "She is the one the Summer Queen wants. That should be enough for you to hasten to find her."

Rubbing at my cheeks, I picked up the picture again and said, "Does the Summer Queen know that you have a crush on her newest toy?"

Instantly, Thistle had snatched the picture from me. "How *dare* you?"

"Oh." I grinned. "More than a crush. You love her. That's dangerous, isn't it? A fae loving a human?"

"She's no more human than you," Thistle snapped, the picture cradled in his hands.

My stomach dropped and the glass of water trembled in my fingers. I had to gasp a breath of air before I could speak. "What?"

I was the only one. That was something I'd known my entire life. I was a changeling, a fae left behind in the human world, who had never been brought back home. After so long in the human realm, I didn't even resemble a fae to the rest of my kind. That was why I'd remained unclaimed by any family when I went to the Far Realm.

I was the *only* fae living in the human realm.

"You thought yourself unique?" Thistle hissed. "You are not unique, merely unwanted. Abandoned. Cast out by your parents. Unlike Acacia. *She* is precious."

"Are there others?" I asked. "Others like me?"

"Not like you," Thistle said. "The others of our kind who reside here have lived in both realms."

"What do you mean?" I set the glass of water on the counter with a heavy thunk. "Explain."

"You forget yourself," Thistle said. "I answer to her majesty, not you."

Narrowing my eyes, I watched as his sharp teeth grew long and then he pulled back, placing the picture tenderly on the counter. Thistle had been one of the old Summer Queen's most loyal courtiers. At one time, I'd thought he was a friend, as he was the one who taught me enough to move onto higher level magic.

The next time I saw him after I returned to the human realm, he was firmly in the new Queen's good graces. Just as obsequious, just as loyal to his new mistress. His hatred of me was the only change.

"Because if you fall out of grace, she might not let you court her daughter," I said. "Acacia."

Thistle hissed, his claws grabbing me around the throat and lifting until my toes dragged on the floor. I grinned, even as my breath became labored. Wrapping my hand around Thistle's wrist, I choked out, "Let me down."

He dropped me and I landed heavily on the floor, my bare feet unsteady until I gripped the countertop tight. I smirked.

"That's why you betrayed the old Queen. Lilacina has you over a barrel," I said. "You love her daughter and now she's the only one who can give you permission to... what? Marry her? Court her?"

The glare he threw me would have made anyone else in San Amaro cower. It was the sort of look that started a good number of fairy tales. A kind of, *I'm going to mess you up* look.

"The Queen isn't here," I said. "Tell it to me straight and maybe I'll work on getting Acacia back before the solstice."

"I owe you *nothing*," he hissed.

Raising an eyebrow, I waited, confident that he'd give in. I finally had something he wanted, or at least I would as soon as I found Acacia.

"Acacia is the Queen's daughter by a human. A half-blood. She grew up in the human realm, but trained with her mother. When she was merely a member of the court, Lilacina sent her here to live and to act as her mother's agent. After you betrayed the previous Queen, I was sent to help Acacia adapt to her new position. A Queen requires more from her people than a courtier." Thistle's words were a hiss in the darkness, his gaze fixed on mine. "She is better than you in every way. More capable, more intelligent, more loyal. Her grasp on our magic is not your rudimentary wielding."

"Great, so she's practically perfect in every way," I said. "Get to the important part."

"Acacia has regular meetings with the Queen, and missed the last two," Thistle said. "The Queen sent me to find her."

"And?" I asked.

"Nothing. No sign of her," Thistle said. He twisted my shirt in his hand, threatening to lift me again. "Do not fail me as you failed the late Queen Aster."

"I didn't *fail* her. I was offered an out. I didn't know that Lilacina was going to use that as an opportunity to commit regicide," I said. But in my stomach, the words felt like glass, slicing at all my newly healed organs. Because it wouldn't have mattered if I had known. Malik was right. I only looked out for myself.

Thistle huffed a harsh laugh that twisted his lips. "You lived with us for years and you claim ignorance of even the most basic of fae politics. I hope you are more effective as a hound sniffing Acacia's trail than you are as a fae."

"Hey," I said, wrapping my hand around his wrist. "I have to find her. Lilacina made sure of that. I'll take care of it."

I wanted to promise him that Acacia was fine, that she was just blowing off steam or running away from her regicidal mother, but that would have been a lie. Fae were the most frightening thing in San Amaro, but there were plenty of other things that could get you killed.

"Why didn't the Summer Queen just tell me it was her daughter?" I asked. "I thought she was planning to kidnap some poor kid."

"The court knows Acacia is a fae agent in the human world, but her origin is unknown. The Queen has let the assumption that she is the bastard of some other court flourish." Thistle released me, but continued to stand too close for comfort. The rage seeped out of his pores.

"Does she love you?" I asked.

"It's irrelevant," Thistle snapped. "My feelings are my own until her mother consents."

Shaking my head, I said, "You know she won't, Thistle. She's got a hook in you and she's going to keep you on the line until you don't have anything more to give her."

"What would you know of it?" Thistle asked. "You have so

little loyalty that you betrayed the Queen who gave you everything."

Bile ate at the back of my throat and I clenched my teeth. He was *not* going to make me feel guilty for leaving, even if it had resulted in the Queen's death. Sure, she'd given me a lot of nice things, magical curios that most alchemists and witches would sell their firstborn for, but all that was at the cost of my freedom.

I held up my hand, and said, "Let's focus on what we have in common, okay? You want Acacia, I have to find her. Do you have any other ideas where she might be?"

"No." Thistle's teeth chattered, the sound like two forks scraping together.

"I'll let you know as soon as I find anything," I said. "Try not to break into my apartment again. I have a doorbell."

Hissing, Thistle disappeared, his body snapping out of existence in a moment. I blinked. That was new magic. I'd never seen a fae do that before.

After I found Acacia, I'd have to ask him about it, and hope that he was in a good enough mood to be honest with me. Putting my glass into the sink, I picked up the photo and examined it again.

She was pretty and had an openness you didn't see on fae that often. I wondered how much of her loyalty to her mother was earned and how much was manipulation on the Summer Queen's part. Walking to my desk, I put the picture in the center and then headed back to bed.

CHAPTER SEVENTEEN

I woke up wrapped in the hottest blanket. Nick's breath on my neck tickled and when I swatted at him, he roused with a sound that was something between a growl and a moan. I didn't want to make fun, but couldn't help trembling while trying to contain my laughter.

"I'm up," he said, eyes closed, mouth still on my neck. His dick was stiff against my hip.

"Yeah, you are," I said.

He chuffed a laugh and rolled onto his back, releasing me. How did I know that he was a cuddler? He seemed like the type that would complain about not sleeping well if his partner wasn't in bed with him. Mushy stuff that I'd always relegated to the list of things that other people got, but I couldn't have.

"Last night was fun," he said. He propped himself up on his elbow and gave me a soft look that I didn't deserve.

"We should do it again," I agreed. "You want to take a shower?"

He shook his head, and I noticed that after two days without a razor, his look was getting shaggy. Running my finger along his beard, I enjoyed the rough feeling on my skin. He nipped at my fingertip when it crossed close to his lips.

"How about breakfast?" he asked.

I was going to suggest breakfast in bed, but his phone buzzed on the nightstand. Immediately, he reached for it and flicked his thumb across the screen.

"Detective King," he answered. On the other end, I could hear someone speaking rapidly, their voice deep. "Text me the address, I'll be there in thirty."

He slid to the edge of the bed, and I got a glorious view of his ass when he stood: round and toned and perfect. With his boxer briefs on, the temptation was immediate to pull him back to bed and strip them off.

"Sorry," he said after he hung up. "Looks like we found another victim."

Frowning, I said, "Who?"

"What," he corrected. "A vampire, and they don't decomp like the rest of us, so the ME wants to call in an expert to see how long it's been dead. Maybe he'll give the department a discount and tell us about the incubus, too."

He rubbed a hand over his head, but the smile was awkward.

"Sorry," he said. "I have to go."

Swatting at his thigh, I said, "Get out of here, go see your dead vampire. Ugh. Vampires. Sociopathic talking rats."

"I'll call you later," he said, pulling on his clothes.

"Now, I have to know, do you have a *third* suit in your car?" I teased.

"No, but I don't think anyone saw me yesterday," he said. "So, I'm good."

I walked him out, locking the door behind him. Crossing to the kitchen, Acacia's picture caught my eye again, and I walked over to my computer, opening up a small scanner I had tucked next to the monitor. I ran the photo through and uploaded it to the cloud so that I'd always have a copy. Then I put it in my satchel, just in case I needed it.

After changing and choking down some dry cereal for breakfast, I ordered an Uber. If I couldn't go with Nick to the crime scene, at least I could make progress on the only lead I had. The guy who showed up had Lyft and Uber stickers on his front window and rolled down his window. "Parker?"

With a nod, I opened the car door and slid into the back seat. The driver called back, "You have a music preference?"

"Whatever," I said, and he turned up the jazz station that he was listening to.

"You a college student?" he asked.

"No," I said, staring down at my phone.

He seemed to get the message, and the rest of the trip to the university was silent.

The University of California, San Amaro was set towards the edge of town, and had spread across the flat plain between a highway and the hills. The campus consisted of the original buildings, all boring gray blocks that had been built for functionality in the forties. As the campus grew, buildings were added and the architecture on these varied widely depending on the decade, purpose, and financial backing.

Over the years, the city had crept up around it, student housing first and then laundromats, cheap food, and bookstores. It still was its own enclave, colloquially known as the College Quarter.

On most major holidays, the Quarter turned into one large street party. Drinking, revelry, and some incredibly illegal things happened, which had led to more than one showdown between college kids and SAPD cops. Every city council meeting before Saint Patrick's day, Cinco de Mayo, July 4th, Halloween, even Memorial Day for some reason, had citizens lining up to worry about the crime increase if a party happened.

Between bouts of bacchanalia, the area was quiet. College kids going about their business for the most part.

The car pulled up inside the campus, in front of a confusing building. I wasn't familiar enough with architecture to try to label the style. It was tall, tan, and had windows inset from the exterior, with each window framed with alternating white and grey rectangles. Tall beams sprung from the top like ribs that were caged in by more of the rectangular pieces. To be frank, it was the sort of place that gave me a headache just looking at.

After thanking the driver and hopping out, I adjusted my satchel and stared up at the building. It was shaped like a giant C, two short legs backed by the longer central building. I headed into the entrance, large double doors under a sign reading "Sallow Hall."

Inside, I searched the directory with the accompanying map. I'd checked out the department website in the car and it looked out of date compared to the rest of the university's pages, but it listed Professor Woolworth's office on the fourth floor of the building.

After getting lost twice, due to the fact that apparently both wings of the building had different entrances than the main structure, I finally found the right floor. The walls were decorated with artistic photos of different witchcraft and alchemy ceremonies. I was pretty sure I was in the right place.

The office was on the eastern facing side of the hall, and shades pulled halfway down blocked the morning sun. The view from the fourth floor was expansive: the rest of the campus spread out, ocean in the distance, cars zipping along the highway nearby.

I was a little confused not to see the elderly woman I'd been expecting. A man sat at the desk that took up most of the office. His chin-length sandy brown hair fell in his face as he read through some notes. He looked slightly pink, as though he'd just come off a treadmill, although his breathing was steady.

"Professor Woolworth?" I asked.

His head snapped up, and he squinted at me in the doorway. After a moment, he said, "Office hours are by appointment."

"I'm not a student," I corrected. Stepping inside, I offered over my hand. "Parker Ferro, I'm working with the police."

"Mark Woolworth." His hand came up, and he squeezed mine. "How can I help you?"

Settling into one of the chairs across from his desk, I said, "I was actually hoping to talk to the, uh, *other* Professor Woolworth."

The smile dropped off his face. "I'm sorry, my mother passed away in February."

"Sorry for your loss," I said automatically. "I hadn't heard."

His lips pinched. "Thanks."

For a moment, we sat in silence, and then I said, "My questions are more general magical-studies questions, maybe you could help me out?"

"Always happy to help the SAPD," he said. "What's this about?"

"Just a quick question about the provenance of a spell," I said. I pulled out a notepad from my bag and sketched out the spell that had been on the incubus. I left the broken bits intact.

Passing it over, I watched as he examined it, rotating the notepad as he read. A frown pushed his eyebrows together. "You know, my mother would have been the better person to ask. She made her career studying the roots of alchemy and witchcraft."

"Yeah?" I asked.

He nodded, reaching behind him and pulling down four books. He passed one over to me and I saw the name *Dr. Adelaide Woolworth* emblazoned on the cover. The title was an obscure reference to the first spell most witches and warlocks learned.

"*We Are One?*" I asked.

"Yeah," Woolworth said. "She thought that witchcraft and

alchemy used to be the same practice, taught to us by the fae. Over time, the two split into distinct practices."

"You don't agree?" I asked, flipping through the book.

"I think my mother saw a shared past as something that might unify us now, when I find the reality is that one allowed magic use to become complex and deeper while the other stayed superficial and kept to those naturalistic roots." He shrugged. "I think it's far more interesting to study what's currently happening in magic than to focus on the past."

His tone made it clear which practice he preferred, and I glanced at him out of the corner of my eye. There was a certain tone of voice you could use that would say, "hey, I'm one of you" even if your words weren't saying that.

"Alchemy," I said, pushing a confidence into the words. "Right?"

He snorted and cocked his head. "Yeah, I dabble. To help me with my research."

If it was just about his research, I'd eat the thick book I was holding. He was one of those alchemists that couched their preference for the practice in pseudo-intellectualism. *Oh, of course both practices are valid, but, you know, only one allows you to practice complex, higher level spells. But they're both valid! Just one is better than the other.*

"I thought your mother was a witch?" I said. "Wasn't she part of the East Side Witches coven?"

"She was. When they lost their head priestess a few years ago, she went into solo practice," he said. "She always thought there was a lot more to be learned in actual practice than in research alone."

"So, the symbol?" I said.

"Actually, it resembles something in one of our textbooks for this semester. I'm teaching Comparative Magical Practice and Cross-Cultural Roots of Power. I took it over when my mother passed," he said. He pulled out another one of the books, a textbook that his mother had co-authored, and passed it over. "Check out chapter ten."

I flipped through and found the right chapter. Skimming the text, I found a few diagrams that closely resembled the one I'd drawn. In fact, with a few different symbols, it was identical. The caption listed it as a spell found etched in an ancient Roman waterway.

"That does look similar," I said. "Is there anyone else other than your mother who could tell me anything about this specific spell?"

"Unfortunately, my mother was one of the top experts on this. There's a few other professors who study some of it. Mostly at Harvard and in Europe. I can give you their contact information, if you want," he said.

"Thanks," I said. He turned to a new page in the notepad and began writing some names. I paged through and found more symbols that could have been pieced together to make the one that had attacked me.

"Must be hard to be teaching your mother's class," I said.

"Well, she did literally write the book on it," he said, frowning as he added another name. "And the only reason it's being offered at all right now is that it was a two-semester class. Fortunately, it's just a seminar, and the college is considering not even offering it next year."

"So this isn't exactly common knowledge?" I asked.

"No, no," he said. "Even when my mother was teaching it, it was a niche study. I mean, this time there's only," he paused to count a list of students in a nearby grade book, "twelve taking it."

"Is that the list of students? Could I get a copy of that?" I asked. He snapped the book closed.

The murders had started after a semester of this class, in San Amaro, where one of the few experts in the field lived. There was a pretty good chance that one of the students knew something, maybe the dead professor had mentioned something. It would wrap things up neatly if it was one of them, but that might be hoping for too much.

"I'm sorry, do you have a warrant?" he asked, looking up from the notepad. "Don't you need a warrant for that information?"

"I'll get one," I said, accepting back the notepad. Skimming the list, I saw a couple of professors at Harvard and Georgetown, three at Oxford, and one at the Sorbonne.

"Can I keep this?" I asked, holding up the textbook.

"Of course," he said, collecting the other books.

Standing, he began putting them back on the shelf and knocked over a picture. It rotated as it fell, turning face down and landing on the corner of his desk, glass shattering with a crunch. Mark spun, gasping. He reached for the picture, but I'd already picked it up.

I frowned at what I was seeing. It was a teenage Mark Woolworth in a practice uniform, in what looked like an alchemy studio. He was standing between two serious looking men, both tall and wearing dark uniforms, showing them to be higher level alchemists.

To one side stood a much younger Nick. He was staring into the camera without a smile, matching the men's expressions. Looking between them, I could see some familial resemblance.

The broken glass featured a circle of some sort etched in. I had no idea what it powered, but it looked more commemorative than functional. The frame was obviously as valuable as the photo to Woolworth.

"Hey," I said. "No worries, I know a little bit of spellcraft. Do you want me to fix it?"

The offer was like a siren song. All fae offers were. There was a reason that the children followed the pied piper. Sure, he offered them treasures beyond their imaginings, but also something in the offering was tempting in a way that made most people lose just enough reason to consider accepting.

It was how people found themselves obligated to fae. Not that

I would ever pull on someone's strings like that. With my own obligation riding me, I didn't want to put anyone else in that position. The idea made my skin crawl.

"Yes," Woolworth said. "Fix it."

Saying a quick chant of mending as a cover for the fae magic I was using, I talked the glass into melding back together. When I finished, there wasn't any damage at all. The circle was unbroken.

It was like I couldn't help myself. Something in my nature maybe was just as terrible as the rest of them were, because even though I didn't want to, I still let that obligation stretch between us. He *owed* me. The only thing I had was a promise to myself that I *wasn't* like them, so I *wouldn't* call in the obligation. I had to be better than that.

Ignoring his suspicious squint, I handed over the picture to Woolworth. "Was that your old studio?"

He tugged the picture out of my hand. "I trained at one of the other King studios, the one that used to be here in town before they closed it. This was at a special weekend class I was able to take with the actual King family."

I made a soft humming noise to keep him talking, and he tapped the older man in the photo. "This is Robert King. He's the greatest alchemist of his generation. Probably even the greatest alchemist from the past hundred years."

"That must be his son?" I asked.

"Yes! Both of them, actually," he said. "Andrew King and Nicholas King. It was amazing to be able to learn from the greats."

Reverently, he placed the photo back on the shelf.

"I'd love to have met them," I said. "Sounds like it was a once in a lifetime experience."

"Usually, he works with presidents, CEOs, but he was very generous with his time," Woolworth said. "And Andrew took over as head of the organization this year, so there's little chance of learning from Robert again. Although I've heard he still takes a few select students every year."

"You think he might take you as a student?" I asked.

Woolworth's face fell, his lips twisting like he'd tasted something sour. "No, no. I don't have nearly enough magic to make me interesting."

Amount of power was everything to an alchemist. Unlike witches who could consensually share power, and thus use their coven's collected magic to power larger spells, alchemists were strict about keeping themselves pure. The only magic they had access to was what they produced themselves.

An alchemist with a small amount of magic would be limited for their entire lives. They might be able to do more complicated spells, but it would take years of powering each element. There were more than enough men who spent more time arguing alchemy nuance on the internet than they actually spent using their insignificant power to do any spells.

It was a timely reminder, though. The amount of power needed to perform the spell that killed the incubus would be beyond a lot of alchemists, and most witches would need permission from their coven to access that amount of magic.

"Thanks," I said, standing. I saluted Mark with the notebook and walked out the door.

I needed the names of the students from his seminar. It was too convenient that the murders began now, when a new crop of students had just learned about similar spells.

CHAPTER EIGHTEEN

WALKING OUT OF THE BUILDING, I SQUINTED UP AT THE CLOCK tower visible throughout the campus. It was eleven a.m. If I was going to break into Woolworth's office, I'd need to wait until everyone had gone home for the day.

I might as well get some work done on the other case that had fallen into my lap. Plus, getting into Acacia's apartment would let me brush up on my breaking and entering before I had to do it later tonight.

Pulling out the photo, I searched for her address and found it on the border between the Quarter and San Amaro. I started to call another car, but decided to grab food first. Using magic always made me hungry, and I'd be using a lot today.

While I was eating two slices of pizza from one of the off-campus pizza parlors, I thought back to the picture of Nick. The men in the picture had been severe. For that matter, Nick had looked so serious in the picture that he didn't resemble the warm, snarky guy I'd slept with last night. Still, it was unmistakably him.

I'd always taken him to be some do-gooder from a nice middle-class family: mother a teacher, father middle management. He'd always given me the impression that he'd become a cop because he had one of those moral compasses that didn't break, no matter how much money you threw at it or how much terrible stuff he saw.

I'd never asked. I'd just assumed. More fool me, I thought.

What I couldn't get over was that I'd seen him, an alchemist with the last name King, and just never connected the dots. Because the Kings... well, they were a family that even *I* had heard about. They had the money and connections that came from generations of being in politics, business, and anywhere else power flowed.

While I couldn't name any of them on sight, maybe I hadn't wanted to ask why a San Amaro cop could afford expensive suits and cars. I finished off the crust of my pizza and sighed. I felt vaguely betrayed; the one decent thing in my life had just been snatched away from me.

The fact that Nick was alchemy royalty was another reason I should keep him at arm's length. What would he say if he ever found out I wasn't as human as I looked?

I couldn't help but want to hear his explanation, though. Why hadn't he ever said anything?

Tossing the greasy paper plate into the trash, I looked at Acacia's address on my phone again and judged it to be reasonable walking distance. The exercise would do me good, I decided. Even if it was hot enough to cook an egg on the sidewalk.

Halfway to Acacia's apartment, I regretted my decision. By the time I arrived, I was a sopping mess, sweat dripping from every part of my body. Blotting at my face with my shirt, I saw that her building had a phone plate and, unlike every other apartment building in the Quarter, no one had left the door propped open with a brick.

Squinting at the round silver buttons, I began at the top, pressing every single one. In a college town, someone had probably ordered food and didn't care about safety enough to bother to check who was ringing the intercom. My assumption was rewarded with a reverberating buzz as someone let me in. Apartment 3B should take building security more seriously.

I took out my keys as I walked, hoping that I had one that would fit into the lock. If not, things were more complicated. At Acacia's door, I glanced around, but no one was in the hallway, so I began going through all the keys on my ring, starting with some that I kept just for this purpose. The lock looked like a deadbolt, one of those built in with the handle, a long rectangle of metal connecting the two, so that if you turned the handle from inside, it would unlock the door.

One of the keys slid home, the right brand, even though the teeth were all wrong. This was where it got tricky.

Metal is nearly impossible to talk to, because most metal is an alloy of several elements. Brass, steel, trying to talk to a hunk of them is impossible. There are a few exceptions, though.

If the metal has enough of a purpose and it's been used regularly or intensely, it might start to have an essence not as its elements, but as its product. For example, a fork that someone uses every day begins to think of itself as a fork first, steel second. Every day, someone touches it and that person thinks "fork" and their belief becomes the fork's belief. After enough time, the fork thinks, "Oh, yeah, I *am* a fork."

It doesn't work with everything, but things that people use often enough—doors, flatware, clocks—start to have that essence. The problem is that they're hard to wake, you have to pump a lot of magic in to make them notice you, and also they get really stubborn.

Sure, you could talk to a spoon and try to convince it to bend, but the spoon would just get confused. *Bend? But my purpose is to hold things, and I can't do that if I'm bent.*

All that was to say, a lock's job is to open and shut. It's keeping things safe. That's the energy people put into locks. That feeling of terror when you turn your key and realize that you forgot to lock your door? Locks remember that. They know what their job is.

With the keys hanging in the door, I pulled out my phone and propped it on my shoulder, so it looked like I was talking.

"Hey lock," I said. "You're super good at your job, aren't you? I mean, I bet a lot of people have tried to pick you, but you're just so strong."

I felt the lock wake. It was older, like the rest of the building. I wasn't sure how long since they'd installed the lock, but it had been long enough that there was a purr of energy when I pushed magic into it.

"I know so many other locks that you can pick with a credit card. But you, you're great. And I bet you and the handle both are in sync. I mean, if I just *turn* the handle, you unlock." With confidence, I reached for the handle and tried it.

The lock hesitated. It really wanted to show me how in sync it was. It wanted to show me what a great lock it was.

"Wow, I mean, you're even trying to keep me out!" I praised. "And you *know* I'm supposed to be inside! I mean, that's awesome! You should be proud of yourself."

The lock settled, smug leaking through. I twisted the keys and pretended to be surprised. "Oh, man, lock! I think there's a mistake! These keys work, but you're not turning."

I frowned and hummed as though confused. "Maybe I should bring some oil for you? I mean, that would get sticky and drippy inside of you. Man, it's too bad that you're stuck on these keys."

Gently, I twisted again and the lock slowly, slowly clicked open. Pulling out the keys and twisting the handle to open the door, I let the magic fade from our connection while still praising.

"My mistake! You're such a good lock. I don't think I've met a better one!" I felt the smugness return even as the lock faded back into neutrality as I cut off the magic and let my phone drop back into my hand.

"Hey!" someone said behind me, brightly.

Turning, I saw a short girl with a pixie haircut on the staircase between floors. The building was narrow: only three apartments on each floor, a winding staircase took up the area where an apartment might have gone across from Acacia's door. I smiled, friendly.

"Hey," I said. The trick to being where you're not supposed to be is not acting like you're doing anything wrong.

"Are you Acacia's friend?" the girl asked. She'd streaked her hair with rainbow hues that shimmered when she cocked her head.

"Yeah," I said. I held up my keyring. "She said I could stop by to pick up some stuff."

No one ever asks to see the right key, even if they are pretty sure that that's not the keyring they remember their friend having. She squinted at me, and then looked to the keyring, her face relaxing.

"So you've seen her," she said, shoulders falling.

Wetting my lips, I smiled. "No, actually. I talked to her by text and she dropped off the keys in my mail slot. Why?"

Over the years, I've discovered that the last thing you want a witness to remember is that you claimed to see a missing person. If they turn up dead, then you're the last person to have seen them alive, or, more commonly, the suspect the cops want to pin the whole case on. If the missing person doesn't turn up dead, then their friend asks them about the weirdo that *said* he saw them.

Marco always said that you want to be as honest as possible when working the job, but he was also better at it than I was. Granted, he never had to deal with missing bastard fae princesses.

"So you haven't seen her either?" the girl asked, arms crossing.

"No." I shook my head. "What's up? Is something going on?"

I frowned, like I was very concerned. This girl had to know something. Anyone who talked to Acacia enough to be worried about her, had some insight into her disappearance, even if they didn't know it.

"She hasn't been home in two weeks," the girl said. "I'm getting kind of worried. Sorry. I'm Skylar."

Extending my hand, I shook hers and said, "Parker."

Glancing at the open door, I said, "That's so weird. Yeah. I just talked to her via text. She borrowed some books of mine and I need them back for class. I figured she'd just bring them, but she said I could get them myself. I was going to just leave the key in her mailbox, but maybe I should keep it?"

Skylar bit her lip and looked past me into the apartment. "Maybe if you see anything suspicious, you should call the police."

"You could call the cops," I said, holding up my hands like I didn't want to. "If you're so worried."

Huffing, Skylar said, "I tried. They said I need to stop calling them so often and that she was probably just staying at her boyfriend's for a few nights. But I've met her boyfriend. She said he doesn't live in town. He always comes to stay with her."

"Really?" I said. "Who's her boyfriend again?"

"Tall guy? Looks like an actor," she rolled her eyes to me as though that was of some significance. "I think she said his name was Thomas?"

Thistle. Had to be. The guy couldn't just pick a normal glamour. He had to choose one that left people thinking he was famous.

"He come over a lot?" I asked.

"Usually on weekends," she said. "He might live in L.A.?"

With a nod, I said, "I might have met him. I don't talk to her a lot this semester, I'm so busy with classes."

"Could you ask her to call me?" she said. "I'm getting some... terrible... energy. I'm just worried about her."

Around her, the air seemed to waver a bit, like it did in the heat. The magic was leaking out of her, and my eyes widened.

There were few humans whose magic didn't pool in them, waiting for use.

"You're an oracle?" I asked.

"How'd you know?" she groaned. The magic in the air seemed to absorb back into her, and the short hair of her bangs stood up like she'd touched a Van de Graaff generator. Sharply, she shook her head, and it settled back down.

The hair color, which I'd taken for a very unicorn-punk expression of style, was some of her excessive magic escaping the only way it could.

"I can just tell," I said. Leaning against the door, I eyed her up and down. "What terrible thing do you see with Acacia?"

Biting her lip, she sighed. "Before she left, I felt this kind of dark energy around her, like a wolf hunting its prey. I tried to warn her, but she didn't listen."

"A literal wolf?" I asked.

Immediately, she shook her head. "No, it just felt *like* a wolf. And then she didn't come home, and I tried everything. I tried reading the cards, I tried tea leaves. All I get is big flashing danger signs, but no specifics."

I pondered the problem. It definitely meant that she hadn't just run away from her responsibilities with the Summer Queen. But 'danger' wasn't a big clue to go on. There was another option, but I was even more hesitant about it.

"Hey, let me grab my stuff from Acacia and then maybe you can read my cards? I'll look for her, so maybe that will give us a clue?" I asked.

"You'll look for her?" she said, relief loosening the tightness around her eyes. "Awesome. Thank you. I'm up one floor: 3A."

"Sure," I said. I walked into Acacia's apartment. "I'll be right there."

She waved at me, grinning, and hopped up the stairs.

I shut the door and looked around. It was pretty typical for a college student's apartment. Furniture that looked more cheap than sturdy, enough snack food to fill a convenience store. There wasn't anything that screamed where she'd gone.

Experience made me quick to thumb through the paperwork on her desk, but there wasn't anything other than bills and college papers there. I picked up a gas bill and squinted at the name.

"Hello, Acacia Clarke," I said. "Where are you hiding?"

On her desk there was a rectangle free of clutter with a power cord trailing off her desk, but the laptop that should have gone there was missing. Her trash was rank after two weeks and, when I poked through it, was mostly food waste.

I grabbed a photo album off a shelf, and a couple of books that looked like journals. Other than that, her place was free of clues. She didn't even have any wards or dirt like mine to guard her space.

Closing my satchel, I locked the door and headed upstairs to Skylar's apartment. It was exactly the sort of space I expected. Scarves hung from everything, covering the windows so that light filtered in in colored shadows. Fairy lights trailed across the ceiling, tangling in each other as they came to the ground at plugs.

She was sitting on a meditation cushion in front of her coffee table and gestured for me to sit across from her. I sank to the ground and watched her deal out the cards.

When she flipped them over, they weren't cards that I knew. She hummed as she looked at the spread, tracing her fingers between the cards like she was spinning a web.

"You'll find her," she said, sighing in relief. Then she paused, frowning. "But, I'm not sure how or when. Or..."

Uncertainty gripped my stomach. This had been a bad plan. Skylar dealt another card, and then a final one. "...or if she's alive. You've got a great weight coming to you."

"Like a trial?" I asked, thinking of the voice in the dark.

She hummed. "Like a new responsibility. Something life altering. You'll have to decide if you want to take it and be free or live as you are: chained."

"Any more specifics?" I asked.

She shook her head, biting her lips hard. "No. If I get specific, she might be dead. And, if I say she's dead, then she's *dead.* Maybe —maybe if I just don't read it, then she could still be alive?"

A fat teardrop landed on a card showing a Pan dancing in the field. She shoved her hand up her face, wiping away snot and tears.

"Okay," I said, quickly. "Skylar. I'll look for her and I'll find her alive."

I couldn't make a promise because I was fae, and a promise *meant* something if you're fae. Instead, I just tried to make her believe it. If she believed it, I could believe it.

A sense of dread settled over me. I had to find Acacia alive. If I found her alive, the Summer Queen wouldn't rip my heart out through my throat.

CHAPTER NINETEEN

AFTER CALMING SKYLAR DOWN, WE EXCHANGED PHONE numbers, and I told her I'd have Acacia call her as soon as I found her. She walked me out, humming under her breath.

"Give me something," she said. "A tithe."

"Uh," I thought of my slim wallet. All the cash I had had been stolen by Dieter, and everything in my bank account was earmarked for Shannon's care facility.

"Anything," she said.

I dug through my satchel and pulled out a bird's feather. It helped me make my magic look like witchcraft if I carried around some of the accouterments.

She ran her thumb along the blade of the feather, ruffling it. Nodding, she grabbed my hand swiftly: a snake striking. With my palm pressed between hers, the feather sandwiched between our skin, she closed her eyes and whispered.

Magic rolled off her in waves, breaking against me. I was careful to keep it out; I had no desire for a repeat of my experience with the incubus's magic. If I acquired a bit of oracle magic, I imagined all the havoc it would cause in my life.

"Be kind to your boyfriend," she said, finally, the words resonant, like a dozen voices were speaking through her. "Pictures are perfect, people are not."

She released my hand, keeping the feather tight between her fingers. Blinking, her eyes refocused on mine, rainbow hues dancing in her irises. Cautiously, she smiled.

"Did that make sense to you?" she asked.

"Yeah." I nodded. "Yeah, what—?"

"I thought maybe if you gave me a tithe, it might tell me more about Acacia. Sometimes payment helps, you know? But," she shrugged, "I mean, I guess good luck with your boyfriend?"

"He's not—Thanks," I said, avoiding unloading my complicated relationship with Detective Nicholas King, of *those* Kings, on a stranger.

She waved at me and shut the building door behind me. I checked my phone and found that I still had hours to kill before I could break into Woolworth's office. Where could I go in the middle of the afternoon on a Wednesday?

The answer came to me immediately, and I groaned. The facility wasn't more than five miles away, but I had no interest in walking in the scorching sun anymore, especially now that I was weighted down by the books I'd stolen from Acacia's place and borrowed from Woolworth. Pulling out my phone, I ordered an Uber.

This driver didn't want any conversation, which worked for me. I watched the buildings around us shift from the Quarter to the more staid-looking buildings on the outskirts of San Amaro. When he pulled up in front of a wide, two-story building painted a soft sandy beige accented with teal, I grunted a thank you and slid out of the car.

Meadowhaven was the best that we could afford, and it looked like what we paid for: a neat, well-run care facility. I tugged on my t-shirt, and dusted off my jeans, walking around the stone fountain and towards the automatic double doors.

My phone rang, and I glanced at the screen, raising my eyebrow when I saw who the caller was.

"Couldn't keep away from me, huh?" I asked.

"Just wanted to see if you were free for dinner," Nick said. "Thought I might take you out on an actual date, not just one that almost gets you killed."

"I don't know, I kind of liked our date to the morgue," I said. "You know, bright lights, dead bodies, unrecognizable spells. It had all the ambiance a guy could ask for."

Nick laughed. I wanted to ask him about his family, but given that I wasn't being truthful about my own, I thought I should tread lightly.

"Are you done already?" I asked.

"I'm headed back to the station," he said. Over the line, I heard a car door slam and then the audio was different as he switched to the car system. "The expert should be at the morgue later today and my captain will be there."

"So you won't be able to sneak in your consultant," I surmised.

"Yeah," he said. "But maybe we could grab dinner after? I could give you the summary?"

Sighing, I said, "I actually have my own lead. I need to follow up on it tonight."

"Parker," he said, voice serious. "Don't mess around with the packs. I know you think you're immortal, but the SoPa will kill you."

"Yes, dad," I said. "I hear you. Not the packs. It's something else. If it's worthwhile, maybe we can have breakfast and talk about it."

"Or a late night dinner?" Nick suggested. I could hear the whoosh of traffic in the background.

"You just want to make sure that I'm not dead, don't you?" I asked.

"Someone has to," he said. "Forgive me for wanting to make

sure you get back to your place alive. Oh, wait, shoot. We can't do dinner, I'm meeting my uncle downtown."

"Your uncle, huh?" I said. I decided to test the waters, see if he was hiding who he was or if I was just the guy who didn't know who he was sleeping with. "One of those *real* Kings? What's he doing in San Amaro? I figured our little town wouldn't be interesting to someone of his stature."

On the other end, Nick snorted. "It's the Alchemist's Society. Their annual meeting. All the major studios send representatives. It's a lot of powerful people in one room. I could stop by afterwards?"

So, maybe he wasn't hiding. Maybe he was just coasting on what I didn't know for as long as possible. Well, at least we'd have one thing in common.

"Okay, fine. I'll text you when I get home. But you better bring some dessert," I said. "And if you're asleep, then no eggplant emoji for you."

He laughed, agreeing to the deal. Hanging up, I grinned down at the phone, aware that the smile melted away when I looked back at Meadowhaven.

Classical music played, and a pleasant woman smiled at me from behind the reception desk as I entered. I approached, already pulling out my license.

"I'm here to see Shannon Ortega," I said, passing over the ID.

"Oh! She doesn't get very many visitors," the receptionist said brightly. "I'm sure she'll be happy for the company."

She wrote down my name and license number in the log book, noting the time, and then held out the pen for me to sign. When I finished, she passed over a visitor's badge and reminded me I'd have to return it when I left. I shook my head when she asked if I needed directions.

Heading to the elevators, I pressed the button to the second floor and saw someone come out of the small manager's office and check the log book, her eyes seeking me out as the elevator doors slid shut. I sighed heavily, leaning back against the mirror lining the elevator. Great. Something else to deal with.

Shannon's room was in the middle of a long corridor. The entire floor was populated by people like Shannon, who needed round-the-clock care, and those who needed less care, so were only at the facility temporarily. While some doors were decorated with photos or memorabilia, humanizing the occupants, her door only had a white nameplate reading S. Ortega.

I knocked once and then walked in. Shannon lay in her bed, eyes open. She was in a fresh dress, and the tv was on, although they hadn't propped her up to see it. It sounded like background noise, a late-afternoon talk show that was probably driving her crazy. When I lived with her, tv was a treat she doled out when someone had been particularly good.

Her hair was pulled off of her face in a braid, the color gone a mousy brown, rather than the brilliant chestnut I remembered. She breathed in and out, blinked.

"Hey, Shannon," I said.

By the time I'd gotten home, the worst had been over. Marco was dead, Shannon still in the hospital. Laurel had medical power of attorney and had been arguing long and hard with the doctors about taking Shannon off life support. No brain functions, no responses, and she wasn't even breathing on her own.

I'd gone to see her once at the hospital, hooked up to a dozen tubes and wires. With all that beeping and screaming, I wasn't sure how she'd been able to look so peaceful. Eventually, the doctors wore Laurel down and she agreed to let them pull the plug.

We'd both been there: me, a guilt-ridden mess, and Laurel, exhausted to the point of incoherence. The doctors had told us they would be just outside when we were ready. They turned everything off and... well, Shannon kept on breathing.

A few hours later, the doctors were scratching their heads and Laurel and I were trying to figure out where to go from there.

Shannon's insurance had covered the hospital, but long-term care was in our court. They'd provide a couple hundred dollars a month, but the rest was up to us.

Personally, I thought it was her magic that kept her alive. She was a powerful witch, head priestess of her coven, and there had to be some reason that she was still ticking even though every medical professional that looked at her thought she should be dead.

"You look good," I said. "I mean, all things considered. Sorry it's been so long since my last visit. Laurel got on my case. Her bakery is going really well. I don't know if she'd brag to you about it. You know how she is. Perfect is never good enough with her. Anyway, she got a write-up in the *San Amaro Breeze*, you know that weekly? You used to complain about the horoscopes?"

I watched her chest rise and fall. She blinked. Shifting in my chair, I gripped the strap of my bag, my fingers going numb.

"There's a guy who asked me out," I said. "He's a cop. We've run into each other before, on the job. He's nice. I think you'd like him. Or at least you wouldn't hate him. He's very by-the-book. Although I think he's bending the rules a bit for me. He let me go to an autopsy with him, to help me help him solve a case."

Sighing, I considered my next words.

"I don't know what to do about him. I can't tell him about me, and you always said that truth was important in a relationship. I mean, I know you were talking about you and me, but I always kind of thought you meant in general, like, for romantic relationships, too.

"And I can't stop thinking about you and Marco, too. You two were like so good together. I mean, I saw enough couples that weren't. And you guys were just... great."

Biting my tongue, I felt a spark of pain.

"But the real reason is this. He has a dangerous job, I have a dangerous job. What if I lose him like I lost you? What if we start something and he gets killed? I mean... I don't know. I don't know that I could do that.

"I think sometimes that if you'd survived. I mean, you *did* survive, but if you were aware of everything, you'd just be crying all the time. I remember how you and Marco were. If I feel this bad losing you two, how would you feel about losing him?"

For a moment, I just breathed, realizing that the air felt heavier. I swallowed.

"And he hasn't been honest with me. I know I haven't been honest with him, but he's from the King family. An alchemist. But, can you imagine if he found out about me? Even you were freaked out. I know you tried not to be, but you *were*."

Groaning, I rubbed a hand over my face. I dragged it up through my hair, aware that I'd just made it stand on end like some punk rockstar.

"I wish I could ask you what to do. There's other stuff going on, too. It's all just a mess. And there's no one I can go to for advice."

Weirdly, my mind flashed to Malcolm, and his offer to look at the eviction documents. But that was ridiculous. As far as I could tell, he was as human as they come. There was no way I could dump any of this on him. Even the relationship stuff would blow his mind, if he was as old as he looked.

"I'll figure it out. Anyway. You look good."

I reached out and patted her hand, her skin tacky and cool. She didn't move, not that I expected her to. Standing, I leaned over and straightened some hair that had gotten loose from her braid.

"See you later. I'll try to visit more often," I said.

Maybe if I got evicted, I could set up shop in her closet. We were already paying for her room and it wasn't like she'd mind.

The bland classical music was still playing when I got back in the elevator and rode it down. In the lobby, the receptionist grabbed the phone, and I took long strides towards the door. I was only a foot away from the threshold when someone called for me.

"Mister Ferro!"

Wincing, I turned, smiling my most client-friendly grin.

"Yes?"

"Victoria Hawkins, director here at Meadowhaven," she said, extending her hand. I shook it and wondered what could be so wrong that the director wanted to talk to me.

"What can I help you with?" I asked.

"I wanted to let you know that there have been a few incidents recently with Ms. Ortega and we aren't sure how you and your sister want us to handle it," she said.

Frowning, I crossed my arms. "What incidents?"

"I hope you know that we wouldn't come to you if it wasn't something... well. Her tv changes channels," she said.

"What?" I asked.

"We set it on PBS, because we find that that's the least disruptive for our residents, but we've come in several times now and found that it's on different channels," she said.

"That sounds like you have a staff member who's watching tv when they're supposed to be taking care of Shannon," I said.

"Yes, normally, I'd agree with you," she said. "But there's also the dreams."

"What dreams?" I asked.

"We've had to be... thoughtful about who we place in the rooms adjoining Ms. Ortega's. We've had a couple of residents who complained about the same dreams when they were in rooms next to hers," she said.

"What do you mean?" I asked.

"They keep having dreams of a car crash," she said. "And also about a family. *Your* family."

I blinked, goosebumps rising on my arms. "What do you want me to do about it?"

"We're concerned about the long-term viability of having a

resident like her here," she said, giving me a bland, comforting smile. "If we keep her, we would need some extra funds in order to compensate staff and residents for the disruption in their lives."

"Staff?" I asked.

"Sometimes the staff who work with her also experience... well. I won't go into the details, but it's been hard to find a staff member willing to care for her long term."

I dragged a hand through my hair. Okay. *Okay.*

"I'll talk to my sister," I said. "We'll try to figure something out."

"Good," she said, perfunctorily. "I'm glad we had this chat."

Nodding, I muttered a goodbye and walked outside, the air cooling as the sun set. What would it mean if Shannon was actually in there? How would she be faring after so long locked up in her own body?

I cursed and checked the time. I still had a couple of hours to kill, but if I grabbed dinner, that would make it eight. Good time for a college break-in.

CHAPTER TWENTY

At eight o'clock, the campus wasn't empty. There were some late classes, a few clubs meeting. Lights lit up the gym next to the stadium like a disco ball, the mirrors inside reflecting light and movement out as I walked past. The libraries were also open, and I held the textbook I borrowed from Woolworth earlier to my chest, so I looked like a student.

Break-ins were best when there was some cover. You didn't want to be the person who everyone remembers. I tried to pick a time when there were still students on campus, but all the professors would have gone home to their Masterpiece Theatre and salads for dinner.

Someone sneezed nearby me, and I spun. A kid with striking green hair wearing a dog tag from his ear had his elbow up near his nose. I squinted, trying to see if he was wearing any colors or tattoos that would mark him as a specific pack. The last thing I needed was another one of Dieter's allies or a Five Dragons member to get their hands on me.

Malik had said I'd be safe, but that didn't mean that I wasn't suspicious of anyone so openly wolf. The kid frowned at me, his nose twitching, and I remembered Malik's warning about sniffing my kind out. Turning away, I strode towards Sallow Hall.

My shoulders hunched when someone called, "Hey! You looking for the meeting?"

I turned and frowned at a blond kid, hair cropped short. With oversized biceps and a tight green shirt, he looked like he spent a lot of time at the disco-gym.

"Sorry, you got the wrong guy," I said.

"Hey, no. You don't have to be scared, man!" he said. "Humans Are Human is meeting over in the Qin building, room two oh five."

My eyebrows crept up. "Humans Are Human?"

"A group of honest Americans who don't like how werewolves and other nons are trampling all over our country," he said. "I saw how you looked at that werewolf, I know you agree."

Holding up my hand to stop him, I said, "I know Humans Are Human. I'm just surprised that they let the club meet on campus."

Especially since its premise was that people like werewolves and witches weren't human and so didn't deserve civil rights.

"Yeah!" he said. "I mean, of course we can't call the club that, but the Human Debate Society is meeting in two oh five."

His exaggerated wink made me huff a breath that he took for a laugh and he looked proud of the joke. The last of the orange sunset faded from the sky, and the HAH member looked larger in the shadows. He grinned at me.

"Listen, maybe you haven't thought of yourself as one of us before, but it's really natural to realize once you're away from home that just because a parrot can talk, doesn't make it a person. They can train a chimp to fly a space shuttle, but it isn't any more of a human than a werewolf who wears a suit." He slapped my shoulder. "You get it, man."

"I have a meeting with a professor," I said, my rage boiling my stomach. I knew that I couldn't make a scene. I definitely couldn't talk the ground into literally swallowing this trash whole without ruining my inconspicuous burglary.

"Maybe after," he said. He pulled out a blue leaflet with the meeting times and rooms. On the back were ten photos of older men and women, their faces surrounded by gun crosshairs. It listed them as the members of the Alchemists' Society. "We're protesting the Alchemist Society meeting tomorrow, you should join us!"

Walking away, I raised a hand to wave instead of smashing him across the mouth like I wanted to.

HAH was just a more public expression of a tension that had been roiling the country since the courts granted werewolves rights almost eighty years ago. The sentiment was why it took until a few years ago for California to allow werewolves to be foster parents and why so many kids in care were werewolves. And California had some of the most liberal laws on the books.

My fist ached as I imagined the muscle-bound HAHer facing anything half as frightening as I knew Malik had dealt with when he was in the system. Shifting my shoulders, I got my head back in the game. HAH was everywhere. It wasn't any of my business if UCSA was turning a blind eye to a group of them meeting on campus.

Sallow Hall was more dramatic at night. The arching pillars on the roof seemed to reach down, and with most of the office lights out, it looked like something was about to happen.

I headed in, taking the stairs instead of the elevator. My footsteps were squeaky on the treads and I checked the hallway before opening the door. Empty. The office doors were all closed, and I walked down the hall, checking for cameras, but there was nothing.

Likely, the university was more concerned about someone hacking their system than someone breaking into a professor's office. In fact, I'd guess they only had a few security people, relying on alarms and witnesses to stop most crime. Still, I kept my pace quick and when I got to the office, I dragged a breath through my teeth. I had a problem.

The door had a keypad lock. There wasn't even a keyhole for emergencies, which meant there was some master code that overrode professors' personal ones. Closing my eyes, I tried reaching out with magic to see if I could make the lock work for me, but I got back a resounding silence. The electronics were too complicated and the individual parts didn't make up a larger whole the way they did with an analog lock.

I glanced around the hallway, but there was little to help me. The ceiling might be a good entry point with its removable squares, but I had no way to get up to it. I could wait until the cleaning crew came by and try to sneak in with one of them, but that would mean a lot of waiting and the hope that they cleaned daily.

In quick succession, I ruled out climbing in through a window (I'm fae, not Spiderman), stealing keys (who from?), and trying to convince the hinges that they should open for me (they would bend the wrong way). My options were getting more limited, and every minute I wasted on this was one less minute I'd be spending tracking down the students in the seminar.

Exhaling, I thought about how Thistle zipped in and out of the world, to the fae realm and back, into my apartment and out. He had more experience than I did, sure, but we were on equal footing when it came to actual, raw power. Time had replenished my magic. I had more than enough to try something stupid.

Turning the problem over in my mind, I realized that it must be like a game that the fae crèche played during school. I'd been too old and too weird, by their standards, to participate, but between lessons I'd watched them. They weren't trying to get between realms or even between two rooms. Their goal was to cross a small pond on rocks set too far apart to walk on.

They would dance to the first one and then take a step, convincing the space between the two rocks that it was only a stride away instead of farther. To the naked eye, it looked like their bodies disappeared and reappeared in the same position, as though they were walking in an old movie with missing frames. If they failed, they only got dunked in water. If I failed, I'd end up sliced in half.

Facing the door, I narrowed my eyes. The problem didn't have to be unlocking the door. Instead, I could try convincing two spaces that they were closer than they actually were. I'd been inside the office. All I needed to do was arrange it so that the inside of the office was closer to the hallway.

Closing my eyes, I thought of Woolworth's office, how it had felt, all the spirits that lived in it. The older books had more energy than the younger, mass-produced ones. The desk was over twenty years old and had seen many a junior professor sit behind it. It was solid, grounded. The chairs were relaxed. Few people sat in them these days, but they knew their purpose.

Weaving a web of the energy, I wiped away the door, erasing it from my mind, pulling myself closer and closer to the energies inside the office. I could feel reality bending a bit. *Yes, the office is much closer to me than you think. In fact, if I take a step, I'll be inside.*

I took a long step, my eyes still closed. Forcing a breath into my lungs, I opened my eyes. I was inside. My knees gave out, but I locked them, grabbing hold of a chair to keep myself upright.

There had to be an easier way of doing that, one that left me less convinced I was going to end up embedded in a door. The energy of the office was still flowing, and I pulled back my magic, drawing it back in. Such a big spell had taken something out of me, but less than I expected.

"Okay. Let's find the class list," I said.

Woolworth's desk was an organized mess. That is to say, I'm sure he knew where most papers were, but with the stacks everywhere and the file folders only labeled half the time, it wasn't likely that he'd notice if something was out of place as long as it was mostly where he remembered it.

Starting on one side of the desk, I rifled through piles of paperwork, finding stacks of college essays, department bulletins, even some personal mail mixed in. His electric bill last month had been outrageous.

A red folder stuck out where he'd placed it on top of his keyboard. I opened it and raised my eyebrows. Bingo. Taking my phone out, I snapped a quick picture of the class list, the flash making me glance at the door. I hadn't heard anyone coming up, but that didn't mean that some mouse-footed janitor wouldn't notice the light under the door.

Under the class list was a half-completed worksheet, and my eyebrows went up when I saw what it was. Someone had filed a civil-rights complaint against a student in Woolworth's class. He'd been writing his own statement about the event, but had only managed a few paragraphs before leaving off.

The person filing the complaint was one Acacia Clarke. At the sight of her name, my eyebrows rose. I knew she was a college student; Skylar's comments and her apartment in the Quarter were enough to tell me that. What was the likelihood that she was in Woolworth's class? Did she have something to do with what happened to the werewolves? I wasn't sure I liked the implications.

She'd filed a complaint against one of the other students in the course. Apparently, he was a member of Humans Are Human, who referred to werewolves, succubi, and all magic users as "monsters" and "wastes of space."

Woolworth's own statement was interesting reading.

Several times, when Mr. Powell referred to alchemists as "non-humans," I corrected him that the term was alchemists and that biologically, they were the same as humans. This resulted in several classes lost to arguments between Mr. Powell and Miss Clarke. While I strive to keep my classes balanced in terms of viewpoints

He'd stopped writing, but even I could see that he'd just given up and let the bigot control the conversation rather than argue for the humanity of werewolves or anyone else who wasn't like him. I snapped a picture of the complaint and the form letter from the civil rights office underneath.

It looked like they were taking it seriously, and I couldn't help but wonder if that was because of the severity or their concern that the last thing they needed was a social-media reckoning. A university as old as this one probably had a few speciesist skeletons in its closet.

Powell turned out to be Timothy Powell, according to the roster. Woolworth had circled his name and Acacia's. It wasn't a lot to go on, but it was a start. Maybe the Humans Are Human supporter decided that those he didn't think were people didn't deserve to live. The way that the movement was going, it wasn't the first time that one of them had been radicalized to do more than make angry posts on Reddit.

Just to be thorough, I combed through the rest of the desk, but none of the other paperwork jumped out at me, and when I unlocked the drawers, it was mostly office supplies and some computer wires that he must use during lectures. I glanced at the bookshelf to see if anything else looked interesting.

The photo of Nick and his family was back in its place of pride. In the darkness I squinted, trying to understand Nick's expression. Skylar's words were fresh in my mind and I knew that I didn't have the whole story. All three of them, Nick, his brother, and their father looked serious, but was that unhappiness I saw in his eyes?

Woolworth had positioned a few other photos of himself in a practice uniform across the bookshelves. No personal photos, though. None of him with anyone who looked like his mother. I moved closer and squinted at one of Woolworth as a young man, standing next to an older man, his arms crossed, a groove carved between his eyebrows.

He was a familiar guy, and I tried to figure out where I knew him from before realizing it was the flier that the HAH member had just handed me. Looked like it wasn't just the King family that Woolworth practiced with. It was too bad his magic wasn't as strong as his ambition.

Putting everything back in its place, I started towards the door, freezing when I heard the harsh beep of someone entering a number on the keypad. Glancing around, there was nowhere to run. The window didn't open enough to escape out of, and I still didn't know how to climb down a building without falling to my painful death. There wasn't any bathroom to escape into.

My heart pounded, and adrenaline made everything narrow. My mind flashed with options that were each more fantastical than the last. No, I needed to keep this simple.

Raising my hand, I began weaving an invisibility spell. In the dark, it should be easier, since I could just add to the shadows, rather than trying to match the brightness of the sun. Whoever was on the other side paused entering their code.

"What are you doing here?" I heard Woolworth ask.

"What?" someone growled, and I was *intimately* familiar with that fuzzy ball of rage. What the hell was Dieter Rossi doing here?

"My office, what are you doing at my office?" Woolworth said.

"This is your office?" Dieter asked.

"It has my *name* on the door, you idiot. What did you think it was?" Woolworth said.

"I just—" Dieter started.

"You know what? I don't want to know. Do you have any for me?" Woolworth snapped.

"Not right now," Dieter said. "I might soon."

"Then what are you doing here? God, you're an idiot, you could get me fired being here." I blinked. I'd never have pegged Woolworth as a guy who would stand up to a homicidal six-foot werewolf with the strength to tear his head off.

In fact, I could feel Dieter's growl through the floor, a rumble so low that it felt like the beginnings of an earthquake. Then it stopped.

"That's what I thought," Woolworth said. "Don't contact me unless you have something for me, and even then, *never* come to my office."

"Fine," Dieter said.

I wondered what their deal was and then rolled my eyes up. What else would they have to talk about? Drugs.

Woolworth was someone who could purchase a lot of product and then sell it to his students. Magical Studies, with its reputation for studying the arcane, would be a perfect front for someone who wanted to move another sort of product. Still, he must buy a lot if Dieter was letting a professor talk to him like that.

"I'll walk you out," Woolworth said. "Wouldn't want you to get lost on the way."

Dieter muttered something, and I heard him stomp off. I listened against the door, but I didn't hear Woolworth. Taking a deep breath, I inched open the door and peeked out. No one was in the hallway.

Before they could get back, I bolted, ordering a ride as I took the stairs two at a time. When I got to the street where my Lyft was waiting for me, I didn't see either werewolf or professor.

CHAPTER TWENTY-ONE

AT MY APARTMENT, I PAUSED IN FRONT OF MALCOLM'S DOOR, then knocked twice. It was late, but he was always up. Sometimes he'd catch me when I came home from late-night stakeouts and we'd have a beer or a whiskey together.

No one answered. Frowning, I knocked again, but the door remained still. He must finally be catching up on his sleep, I decided, heading to my own apartment.

In the shower, I stared into space while I tried to make sense of the day. There was a lot going on and trying to tease apart all the different threads was impossible. I thought about Shannon, the possibility that she was still in there, haunting the other residents, and then the likelihood that Acacia just happened to be in Woolworth's class. Did something in the history of magic make her realize something about her own powers?

I had to make time to at least skim the book that Woolworth had given me, but I wasn't sure how because I also had to track down the rest of the twelve students in the seminar.

Groaning, I buried my head in my hands and squeezed my eyes shut, water pounding down on my head. When it cooled, I turned it off, and wrapped my towel around my waist as I went searching for food in the kitchen. I'd just opened a jar of pickles when there was a firm knock at the door.

After peeking through the peephole, I opened the door, raising my eyebrow at the bags of food that Nick was carrying.

"Are we expecting more people?" I joked.

His eyes strayed to my stomach and then lower, where the towel wrapped around my hips. Swallowing, he dragged his eyes up to mine and I couldn't help the wicked grin on my face.

Cocking my hip as I leaned on the door, I said, "Are you planning on coming in?"

He moved forward, crowding me back and pressed his lips to mine, a hungry want sparking between us. I released the door and grabbed his face between my hands. The noise in my head quieted, and I focused on the sensation of his lips pressed to mine, his tongue tracing the seam of my lips.

"Is this okay? Do you want to keep going?" he asked, his lips barely moving, the words a whisper against my skin.

"Yes," I said. If he wanted to ask for consent until we were both blue in the face, at least it would be a pleasurable asphyxia. I let the towel drop.

The bags he was carrying slipped to the floor, and I kicked the door shut before jumping up, wrapping my legs around his waist and, *god,* it was so sexy to feel his suit pants and belt against my naked skin. It made me feel wanton.

He grabbed my legs, his hands finding my ass, and he squeezed, his muscles supporting me. I could get behind that kind of strength.

"Bedroom," I moaned, tugging at his head with my hands.

"Yeah," he agreed.

———

After an enjoyable hour, when cuddling had overtaken passion, my stomach rumbled, waking both of us from our easy post-coital doze.

"I hope that food was sturdy," I said.

He grinned and stood, naked. "Come and find out."

Amused, I grabbed a pair of sweat pants and followed him into the living room where he was digging through a duffel bag. He pulled out his own pair of lounge pants, and I huffed a laugh when I saw an Adidas logo. If the man owned a pair of white tube socks, they were probably name brand, too.

As I watched, he picked up the two large paper bags and put them on my kitchen counter, grabbing plates out of the cabinet. A large, colorful salad came out first and I groaned.

"Is this about my refrigerator?" I asked.

"I'm just saying, you're about to die of scurvy. A few more vegetables might prevent you from losing your teeth," he said, portioning it out between the plates. He took out some tacos I was excited about until I sniffed and didn't smell that telltale rich scent of cooked meat. They must be filled with some vegetarian non-meat. I squinted suspiciously when he portioned out beans and rice, but they looked normal.

"What's in the other bag?" I asked.

"Be a good boy and you'll find out," he said. And *hello*, that *voice*. If I wasn't starving, I would have dragged him back to the bedroom.

I took my plate and fork back to the couch and poked at the salad. He sat down next to me and watched me make faces at the salad for a minute before sighing.

"Are you going to try it?" he asked. "Because I can promise it won't taste any different if you stab it into wilting."

"Fine," I muttered. "But you'd better tell me about the autopsy."

Watching me take a bite, he said, "It went about the same as the incubus. We found a trace of the spell under UV light, but it looked like whatever went wrong with the incubus's spell had been worked out by the time he got to the vampire. The expert is staying an extra day to examine both bodies and write up her report, but she said that the incubus was probably killed about three months ago, and the vampire two."

"Who was patrolling the area? Or do most cops think vampires spend all their time face down, not breathing?" I asked, frowning. With a courage I wasn't sure I had, I stuffed a bite of the salad into my mouth and chewed.

"We rarely patrol *looking* for vamps," Nick said. "But it revealed that some patrol logs had been altered to make it look like the officers did their rounds."

"What about the incubus? I mean, the garbage company couldn't have been ignoring that dumpster for three months, even in Sintown." My words came out around another mouthful of salad. I wasn't going to tell him, but the salad tasted amazing. Whatever the dressing was, it made beets and Swiss chard taste not only edible, but like something that I'd want to eat a lot of.

I finished it off and grabbed a taco, polishing it off in three bites.

"That one, I don't know. I *suspect* that his pimp was hiding the body or maybe using it... post mortem." Nick's expression went dark, but I was so hungry that even his implication that someone used the dead incubus to fulfill the city's necrophilia needs couldn't turn my stomach. "When he found out we were looking for a body, he dumped it so we wouldn't start searching the actual brothels."

Not that they were legally called brothels. No, they were all apartment buildings and gentlemen's clubs. So what if the apartments had men and women who didn't live there coming and going at all hours?

"Huh," I said, chewing on the taco. It, too, was delicious. At Nick's look, I made a face. "Okay, fine, this is fantastic."

His wide open grin was enough to take the sting off of my

capitulation. I ate the beans and rice while he tucked into his own meal, covering his mouth to ask, "And your lead?"

"I talked to a source," I said, not sure if I even wanted to tell him about Laurel. "And she said that there was a professor at the college who'd know about the kind of magic we were looking for. So I went, but the professor died earlier this spring. I talked to her son, Mark Woolworth, he's teaching her course. A course that involves a lot of reading and research about symbols that look like what we saw on the incubus."

Nick nodded as he ate and glanced up when I paused. He didn't look like he recognized Woolworth's name, but the photo of them together had been taken years ago. Now, how to explain to my by-the-book maybe boyfriend that I'd broken into Woolworth's office?

"I had to wait until tonight to get a class list because he didn't want to give it to me in front of anyone who might see," I said. He didn't want to give it to me at all, but all I was doing was *implying* that Woolworth had given me the list, not outright saying it.

"And?" Nick said.

"I got the names," I said. "And one of them jumped out at me. You know that girl that the Summer Queen wants me to find?"

Nick nodded and raised his eyebrows. "She's in the class?"

"Yep," I said. "So, maybe it's related or maybe not. But she's missing, too."

Twisting his lips, Nick made a soft, thoughtful sound. "You know, I asked about her today."

"How'd you know who to ask about?" I said, sharply.

"There was a picture on your desk," he said. "I told you I would. I didn't want to let you down. What's the point of having a cop boyfriend if you can't use him for info?"

My brain went blank for a minute, a deer with a wolf in its sight. "Boyfriend?"

"I mean, if you want," he said. "I didn't want to—I mean, *I* want, but you're really independent so I wasn't sure—"

"It's fine," I said, interrupting. "Boyfriend is fine."

"Anyway," he said, and I recognized the slight glow as a blush. He stirred his rice into his beans and took a bite. "I asked around and her job submitted a missing persons report today. The sergeant who took the report said that one of the managers sounded like he had a crush on her. He had *way* too much information about her. Like, he knew what her hair smelled like and exactly what she was wearing the last time he saw her."

"Where did she work?" I asked.

"A hotel on the waterfront," Nick said. "I can get the exact name if it's important."

I shrugged, unsure what would be important at this point. Nick stood, taking both of our empty plates back to the kitchen and opening the second bag. Even if it was more of the veggie-heavy food from the first bag, I'd happily eat it.

"So, we have a missing hotel clerk," I said. "And a class list of suspects. Oh! And Acacia was filing a civil rights complaint against some Humans Are Human member in her class."

Nick huffed. "Humans Are Human. Could they have chosen a dumber name? It's like saying Air Is Air. I feel dumber just hearing it."

He handed me the plate, which now had a large slice of cake and a melted puddle of what used to be ice cream next to it. I grinned, dragging a forkful of the cake through the cream.

"Hey, you might know the professor," I said, my heart beating fast. The wolf was watching the deer again, and I wasn't sure who was faster. "Woolworth. He had a picture of you and him with your dad and brother at some alchemy special session."

"Ah," Nick said, looking down at his own plate. He frowned. "The name doesn't ring a bell, but I can look at a picture. We met a lot of people through sessions. Most of them weren't that... exclusive."

"I didn't know that your family was *those* Kings," I said, aware that I sounded like an idiot.

"Yeah," Nick said. He bit his lip. "I didn't lie about it."

"No. You just didn't offer it up." I was aware that I was toeing a line. Even though I was pushing him for honesty here, I knew that I was the one with the bigger lie in my story. My lie could hurt him, where it looked like his just hurt himself.

"My captain knows, but I'm pretty sure that no one else does, otherwise they'd treat me like I got this job just because of my family," his lips pursed. "Which I didn't."

His eyes cut to me, narrow and suspicious. I held up both hands. "Hey, I never said you did."

"Yeah, well." He shrugged. "You wouldn't be the first who thought that."

"Okay, look, I don't know you that well," I said. "And you don't know me, either, except what I look like in cuffs. But I want to know you."

Slowly, Nick nodded. "I'd like that, too."

"Good. Now eat some of your melted ice cream. My rich boyfriend doesn't know that it belongs in the freezer and not on the ground. I guess he's always had servants who take care of that for him."

Shaking his head, Nick bumped my shoulder with his. He was smiling, but I could sense wariness when he looked at me. "What are you going to do with the class list?"

He was navigating us back to safer territory. The case was something neutral, and I wondered how hot-button his family was to him that he couldn't even have one conversation about them without freezing me out.

"Well, we know when the werewolves were killed, right? We have those exact dates. They didn't sit around for months. I'll call the students and find out who has alibis so we can clear them." I took another bite of cake, and enjoyed Nick's look of discomfort when I spoke, mouth still full. "Hey, it's even something I can do from home, no chance of a werewolf kidnapping."

"Good," he said. "Since so far you're oh for one with Dieter Rossi."

"I'll have you know," I said. "I'm one for two, okay? I got him pretty good before he got me and almost killed me."

Nick grinned and shoved a forkful of cake in my mouth. "Shhhhh. Tell yourself that."

————

The next morning, he pulled another suit out of a garment bag I hadn't even noticed him bring in. I watched him dress and groaned into my pillow.

"I can't believe I didn't realize how rich you were before now," I said. "You have eight hundred designer suits and they're all tailored."

"Well, you aren't that good of a detective, then," Nick said, tightening his tie.

"You want breakfast?" I asked.

He looked at me in the mirror on the closet door. "What do you have for breakfast, Parker?"

I bristled at the dry tone and muttered, "Dry cereal."

"Because your milk is expired?" he asked.

"Go on," I said. "Get out of here. Your invitation is revoked."

He laughed, and turned to pin me to the bed, hands on either side of my head. With a fervent kiss, he drew a groan from me. Then he stood and crossed his arms.

"Get groceries. I'll see you tonight," he said, gathering his things into his duffel bag.

"Will you get takeout again?" I begged.

"Fine," he grinned. "You should still get groceries."

I waved him off and locked the door behind him. After a quick shower, I opened my fridge, only to remember that he was right and soda or beer wasn't something I could add to the dry cereal.

Closing the fridge door, I screamed when I saw Shannon standing in my kitchen.

"Holy Hera, Parker, this is *not* how an adult lives," she said.

CHAPTER TWENTY-TWO

"SHANNON?" I SAID, FROZEN IN PLACE. SHE WAS THERE, BUT IT was like seeing an illusion. I could see almost through her, my mind trying to tell me that no, she wasn't there, even when my eyes were saying the opposite.

"Hey, kiddo," she said, lips twisting up. It was the same calm expression I remembered. It was the smile that broke me. I'd been in so many places by the time that I met her and Marco, but she could get through every one of my defenses just by being more patient with me than anyone had ever been.

I showed up late to school even though she'd dropped me in front? She'd smile and ask me what happened, not saying anything else until I confessed about the kid in first period who would kick my chair the whole class. If I swore at the table? She'd smile at me and remind me that there were kids younger than me at dinner and just because someone exposed me to language like that too young, I didn't have to be the same way.

Even when I tried using my magic on the other foster kids in the house, she didn't get *mad*, she just waited until we were alone and told me that just because people more powerful than me had hurt me, it didn't mean I had to become one. *I* didn't have to hurt people weaker than me, just because I could.

If I hadn't met her, I wasn't sure who I would be. Someone meaner, for certain. Someone who didn't care about the people he hurt or the things he broke as long as it got him what he wanted. Swallowing, I closed my eyes, half expecting her to disappear when I opened them.

She was frowning at me, her hip leaning against the sink when I opened my eyes. "Parker, do you even *do* dishes? Some of these have mold in them! Don't tell me you think that nice detective is going to stick around if you have a sink full of dirty dishes. He doesn't seem like the type who goes for slobs."

"Shannon, what are you *doing* here?" I asked. "*How* are you here? You're in a coma."

"You know I'm not," she said. "And I'm here because you asked for help."

Waving my hands in front of me like I was warding off a hive full of bees, I said, "No, no. I did *not* ask for help. I definitely didn't ask you to show up at my place! You should be in your body! If you can be here, you can wake yourself up."

She pulled her lips to the side, grimacing. "I've tried, Parker. I've tried a lot. There's only so much time I can spend listening to goddess-blessed PBS before I go insane. I mean, I think at this point I've seen the entire *Hercule Poirot* series! And all of *Inspector Morse*. Even the one with the new kid."

"So you're watching daytime tv?" I accused. "You always said that rotted brains! And you can't haunt people's dreams! That's mean!"

Huffing, she said, "That's mostly an accident. I don't know how to control that."

"Maybe by *not haunting people*." My stomach growled, and I pulled down a bowl and filled it with Choco Wolf Crunch. "I'm going to call Laurel and see if she can figure out how to get you back to yourself."

"I've tried visiting her," Shannon said. "She doesn't even see me. Tell me I raised you better than that."

I glanced down at the cereal and picked a spoon out of the drawer. "It's just when I don't have anything else to eat."

"Really," she said, her lips pursed. "And when *do* you have things to eat? Because it looks to me like you haven't done any grocery shopping in a few weeks. And is that milk even safe to have in the fridge?"

"Will people lay off my milk?" I groused. Pulling out my phone, I pressed the button for Laurel. It rang once before she picked up.

"Parker, why did Shannon's care facility call and say that you agreed to pay more for her care?" she asked before I could say anything. "We can't afford that."

"The director thinks that she's haunting people," I said. "And I never agreed to pay, I said we could work something out—"

"Great," she muttered. "I have to call them back and deal with this nonsense. Haunting. People are so narrow-minded about witchcraft these days."

"That's what I need to talk to you about," I said. "I think we might have an issue—"

"Oh, wait," she said. "That's them on the line. I'll call you back after I've dealt with this. I might even have the coven lawyer in on this call. *Haunting.* Artemis's blessed, I'm ready to see some heads roll."

She hung up before I could explain that there was a good reason people thought Shannon haunted them, and it was because she *was.*

"I'm so proud of her," Shannon said, fondly. I yelped at her proximity. She'd come closer when I was on the phone, ear tilted to listen in. "She's such a good head priestess. I'll bet *she* goes grocery shopping every week."

"I remember you being nicer," I said, glaring at her.

"You were fifteen, Parker, I had to be nice to you. You were a really messed-up kid, who'd been in situations that most grown adults couldn't handle. Even though you had an amazing amount of power, you had no training." She tilted her head, eyes crinkling in the corners in a smile. Raising her hand, she stroked it down my cheek, and I got goosebumps, even though there was no sensation. "But now you're an adult and you need a reality check."

Taking a spoonful of my cereal, I narrowed my eyes. With a swallow, I said, "Reality check?"

"You're about to lose your apartment," she said.

"No," I said, huffing. "I have until tomorrow to get the money and if I can solve the case, then I'll have more than enough money."

Wrinkling her nose, she sighed. "So, say you solve the case today. Do you think the police are just going to cut you a check on the same day? Even if they do, will it clear your bank account so you can give your landlord cash?"

"How do you know all this?" I asked. I'd talked about a lot of my worries with her, but this was more detail than she should know.

Glancing up at the ceiling, she said, "So, I might have been visiting a little before now."

"You've been *spying* on me?" I accused.

"Well, it's not like you noticed! And I do it with all you kiddos," she said. "I worry. Can't a mom worry?"

"So why can I just see you now?" I asked.

"I don't know," she shrugged. "Maybe you want to? Maybe you finally believe that you can?"

I sighed and rubbed a hand over my head. "I know I'm going to lose the apartment. But, I don't know what else to do. I have to follow this now, anyway. Acacia's involved and that means I'm bound to it."

"Who's Acacia?" Shannon asked, frowning.

"I thought you were the one who knew all my secrets," I said.

"I'm not always here," she said. "Sometimes I disappear. It's hard for me to stay in one place for long."

"She's the Summer Queen's daughter," I said. "I have to track her down."

"And she's involved in this police case?" Shannon asked. "How?"

"I don't know yet," I said. Stirring my dry cereal, I watched as the flakes spun around.

"What're you going to do, kiddo?" Shannon asked. "If you get kicked out?"

"I'll probably have to get a new place," I said, glancing around. It would be a pain to move everything, but it would be possible.

"Do something for me?" she asked.

Surprised, I looked back at her. "Sure. Anything."

"Do that pile of laundry in your closet before your nice cop boyfriend sees it. It smells like donkey balls. If he sees it, he's definitely going to leave you." She made a face that looked like she'd eaten a lemon.

Groaning, I said, "Fine! I will do laundry and grocery shop."

"You'll figure this out, kiddo," she said. "Now, don't you have leads to track down?"

"You said it was pointless, since I won't get the money before tomorrow," I said.

"You still have to make that Summer Queen rhymes-with-witch happy, and maybe you'll get the money in time to make a down payment on a new place," she said. "If you do all your work, then I'll listen to you whine about lying to your boyfriend."

"It's not whining," I said. "I'm in moral crisis here!"

"Okay," she said, raising an eyebrow. "I'll listen to your moral crisis, then."

"You used to be *so nice*," I said.

She crossed her arms and waited and how did that still work when I wasn't fifteen anymore and she was mostly dead? With a huff, I stalked to my desk, taking out my phone and sending the picture of the class list to the printer. When it came sliding out, I took out a yellow notepad and a pen and woke my computer.

Thanks to social media, it was ridiculously easy to find phone numbers for most of the people in the seminar. I started with the first name.

Using an app, I disguised my number as one of UCSA's offices.

"Hi, Isaiah, this is Zachary Byrd," I said. "I'm calling from UCSA's Office of Student Conduct. We're investigating a complaint about a student in your course."

On the other end of the line, I could hear the hesitation. "Was it Tim? God, that guy is an asshole. Is he complaining his rights were violated?"

"How about you tell it to me from your perspective," I said.

Shannon smiled from where she sat in the guest chair across from my desk. "You're doing great, kiddo!"

Rolling my eyes, I listened as Isaiah described pretty similar behavior to what Woolworth had written in his statement. Even though it was a course on magical studies, anytime someone mentioned alchemists or witches, Tim would go off on a rant about Humans Are Human.

"Professor Woolworth—um, the dead one—she was really good about handling him. This new professor doesn't really seem to care?" Isaiah said.

"Hmmm," I said. "Could you tell me more about the course? I want to make sure I understand."

Isaiah was more than happy to. He was a magical-studies major and talked at great length about everything the course covered. It sounded like a course that most kids went to college to take. A passionate professor teaching in-depth about a subject that she'd done most of the research for.

"Just to clarify," I said, glancing at my notes from Nick's case to see when Nate, the SoPa alpha, had been killed. "You were meeting May fifteenth?"

"No," Isaiah said. "I was out of town, in L.A. Was there a

special session? Why didn't anyone tell me? I'll have to contact Professor Woolworth to see—"

"Oh, no," I said. "My mistake! Anyway, thanks for your time!"

I hung up and took another bite of my cereal. I cleared Isaiah for the murders, and I had a few pages of notes on the course itself. Other than Tim, Isaiah hadn't been able to single anyone else out who'd been acting weird. Certainly no one who'd had too many questions about the details of spells from the book.

"You did great!" Shannon said, her head close to mine where she'd been listening to the call. "I don't know about the lying, but I'm very impressed. Marco would have been, too."

I raised my eyebrows and sighed. "Should I just turn on the speaker? This is kind of creeping me out."

"Only if you want," Shannon said, raising her hands. "You're the P.I., here."

The next few phone calls were much the same. My image of the class became clearer. It was just esoteric enough that only magical-studies majors and minors wanted to take it. Dr. Adelaide Woolworth, recently deceased, was a passionate, dedicated educator who wanted her students to be as invested in her subject as she was. She brought actual artifacts to class, including ones that bore symbols similar to the one drawn on the incubus.

Her son, Dr. Mark Woolworth, was not as invested in the course or his students. He read lectures directly from Power-Points and spent most of the time focusing on the ascendency of alchemy, his focus of study. Under him, Tim's aggressive HAH tirades had gotten more frequent and less coded.

Acacia had been the student most likely to stand up to him. Everyone seemed to suspect that she was the one who'd filed the complaint.

Unlike Isaiah, most students could name a couple of others who were *very* interested in studying the original spells that Dr. Adelaide had brought into class. Unfortunately for me, none of them overlapped in their suspicions. Still, after talking to nine of the students, I could clear all of them.

That left only three that I couldn't get a hold of: Acacia, Tim, and Charlotte Evans.

"I liked him," Shannon said, after I hung up on the last student. "Seems like a nice boy. He should go into research."

I rolled my eyes up and shook my head. Shannon had labeled almost *all* the students "a nice kid." The exceptions were a student who swore while on the phone with us and another one who made it clear that she agreed with Tim's HAH views, even though she was too polite to say it outright.

While thinking of my next steps, I entered a grocery order in on my phone, adding some vegetables at Shannon's pointed, "A lot of carbs on your list, aren't there?" Just after I pressed confirm, my phone rang, and I saw it was Charlotte Evans, my missing student.

"Zachary Byrd," I said. "Office of Student Conduct."

"Mister Byrd? This is Charlotte Evans," she said. "I got your voicemail."

"Miss Evans!" I said. "I just had a few questions about a course you're currently taking, Comparative Magical Practice and Cross-Cultural Roots of Power?"

"Is this about Acacia's complaint?" Charlotte asked. "I'm pre-law and I helped her draft it."

"Yes," I said. "We're just hoping to get information from multiple sources."

"I'm not sure that my statement will be any different from the complaint," she said. "I had the same experience that she did. Although I thought she should include Professor Woolworth in it, too."

"Adelaide Woolworth?" I clarified.

"Mark Woolworth," she said. "My family is mostly witches and warlocks, and he's said enough derogatory things about witchcraft that I thought... That is, I think he's discriminating based on magical practice, which is illegal."

"Did he do anything specific?" I asked. "Give you a worse grade?"

"No, it was just... when we were discussing witchcraft during the Roman Empire, he kept repeating that if the Romans had practiced alchemy, a lot of the underlying problems wouldn't have occurred. He didn't outright say that witches were weak, but he said that the coven power structure allowed for corruption and was equivalent to building a house on sand."

"Huh," I said, frowning. "No one else mentioned that."

"They probably didn't notice. It's the sort of thing that sticks with me, I guess because I thought the microaggressions would end at college." She paused. "I mean, it wasn't just the Roman Empire stuff. It was any time he had a chance to, he was talking about the failings in witchcraft."

I paused, but she didn't give any more examples. "Did *you* want to file a report against him?"

She huffed and said nothing. After another long pause, I said, "Listen, how about I give you my fax number and if you want, you can send me anything else you think I should see."

"A fax?" she asked, clearly puzzled.

I'd chosen a fax because I didn't have time to create a fake UCSA email, but I had a quick answer for her, anyway. "Faxes are confidential. No chance of someone hacking it."

"Fine," she sighed. "I'll *fax* you."

"Thanks," I said, listening for her to hang up.

When I put down the phone, I looked around, expecting to see Shannon cooing about what a fine young witch Charlotte was. But the apartment was empty.

"Shannon?" I called.

Someone pounded on the door. Jumping up, I checked the peephole and rolled my eyes. At least now I'd have groceries, I groused, opening the door for the delivery guy.

CHAPTER TWENTY-THREE

MIDAFTERNOON, AFTER I'D EATEN A SANDWICH THAT I MADE with actual food that I had in my fridge, I was reading through my notes about Tim. He was the sort of guy who'd cheer about a dead werewolf online, but was he the sort to use unknown magic to kill one?

In fact, despite all the students being magical-studies majors, only about half volunteered the information that they were practitioners. Of those, the only one I was suspicious of was Acacia. If she had even a portion of her mother's magic, then she was more powerful than most users.

Unlike me, she'd been trained in fae magic since she was a child which meant the glamours involved in the spellwork would be simple for her. But what would she gain from killing the SoPa alpha? The magic would sit just as uncomfortably in her as the incubus' had in me.

My phone pinged, and I grinned when I saw who it was. So, Mister Hotshot Detective wasn't playing hard to get. He didn't seem like a guy who'd follow the three-day rule or any of that nonsense, but it surprised me that he'd made time to text me when I knew he was busy with two dead bodies.

How's your day going?

I pondered how to respond.

Ruled out most of the seminar students.

Most?

There's one who I haven't been able to get a hold of, and he's my best suspect right now.

Name?

Timothy Powell.

I'll pick you up in twenty.

Raising my eyebrows, I wondered if I should call him on how high-handed he was being, but the same frisson of attraction made me quell the urge. I was so used to taking care of myself that having him take charge was exciting. On the other hand, I knew that he'd just ask for consent as soon as he got here, so it felt... safe.

Safe was not a feeling I was used to.

I gathered my things, including my camera, and was waiting in front of my apartment when he pulled up. The car rumbled, a sleek cat, and I couldn't help but make a face when I got in.

"So, the car..." I said.

"I just like it, okay?" he said, smirking. "When I was growing up, we weren't allowed to drive, there were always bodyguards and employees around. Once I was on my own, I wanted something fun to drive."

"If you say so. I was just going to say that from personal experience, you don't have *anything* to compensate for in that department," I teased. "I'd rate the entire package very satisfactory."

"You're terrible," he huffed, his face gone rosy as he pulled the car back into traffic.

There was an address already plugged into the navigation and it put us squarely in the Quarter. It reminded me about something that had been nagging me since last night, and I pulled out my camera, toggling through all the photos of Dieter I had.

Nick's glances were heavy on me, but he kept his focus on the road until I found the photos I was looking for. At the time, it had been just another drug deal from Dieter, but now that I knew who I was looking for, I could tell that it was Woolworth that Dieter was talking to. With jerky movements, Dieter had looked over his shoulder, then at everyone in the park, before handing something to Woolworth.

Having heard their conversation the night before, I wondered if Woolworth was as assertive with Dieter when he wasn't worried the pack werewolf would endanger his job. Maybe he had Dieter wrapped around his finger because he made him a lot of money?

"Something interesting?" Nick asked.

"Dieter Rossi knows Woolworth," I said. "I heard them together last night."

"Huh," Nick said. "I could tip off a detective in Vice, if you want?"

He sounded unsure what the issue was, and I couldn't blame him since *I* wasn't sure what the issue was.

"Don't worry about it," I said. "We headed to Tim's house?"

"Timothy Powell," Nick confirmed. "No priors, no contacts with police. In fact, the only thing we know about him is his driver's license number and his address."

"Isn't that most people?" I said. "Most people don't make it a habit to get arrested."

"I still like to know more before going in," Nick said.

"Well, what I know is that our baby Humans Are Human member made everyone in the seminar uncomfortable," I said. "He didn't tell anyone if he was a magical practitioner, but most people thought he wasn't, because of his views. So I'm not sure why he chose to use the spells as his murder weapon."

"It wouldn't be the first time someone used a tool they weren't familiar with to kill people," Nick said. "Still, it's a leap to go from espousing HAH views to killing people."

Shrugging, I said, "I know, but unless you're turning up leads, this is the best I've got."

Nick shook his head. "No. We're trying to track down which pimp the incubus worked for, but we don't even know his name. The cops that walk Sintown aren't any help, either."

I made a questioning sound and Nick sighed. "'It's how they are.' 'It's what they get.' That sort of thing."

"Helpful," I said, irritated. "So glad we pay you boys in blue the big bucks."

"Hey, there are some good men on the force," Nick said sharply.

"Sure, *you*." I rolled my eyes to his face. "I haven't met any others."

Shaking his head, Nick repeated, "There are good men on the force."

I crossed my arms, letting him have the last word. Unsurprisingly, my acquiescence seemed to bother him more than if I'd kept arguing. He opened his mouth to argue some more, but hushed when he saw my smirk.

We parked in front of the building, Nick using a placard that listed his car as a police vehicle in order to use the red fire zone. As we got out, I looked up. It was a four-story building, larger than Acacia's.

"Tell me there's an elevator," I said. "I'm walked out."

"Maybe we should add more cardio to your days," Nick said, voice dripping with the implication of what kind of cardio he was interested in.

My head whipped around to see if he was being as suggestive as he sounded. His face was neutral, and he arched an eyebrow at my open mouth. Pointing at him, I shook my finger.

"You, Mister Only Good Cop, are *nasty*."

With a snort, he led us into the building, using a master key to unlock the lobby. The elevator was working and Nick looked at the stairs pointedly before following me into the elevator car. He pressed the button for the third floor and we rode up in companionable silence.

At the door, Nick knocked and said, "Timothy Powell? SAPD, please open up."

"Please?" I said, raising an eyebrow. "Where are we? Tea with the Queen?"

"It doesn't hurt to be polite," Nick said. "Pounding on doors is for tv. Most people respond to a knock faster than a threat."

I opened my mouth to poke fun, when the door across the hall opened.

"Oh, good," an elderly woman said. "You're here. I called about Timothy days ago."

"Ma'am?" Nick asked.

"Timothy! I know something happened to him. He always does my grocery shopping when he does his on Sundays, but this past Sunday he didn't come over." She squinted at Nick. "You're here to do a wellness check, aren't you? To make sure he's alright?"

"We're here on another matter," Nick said. "Do you know where Timothy might have gone?"

"No," the woman said. She closed her door halfway and emerged with a set of keys, her arthritic fingers finding a brass-colored key. "Since you're here, you can check on him. This is his key. I didn't feel right going in without permission. But you're the police. You can go in, can't you?"

"Thanks, ma'am," Nick said. He took the keys and unlocked Tim's door, nudging it open with his boot. I could see his hand inching towards his gun, and I leaned over.

"You might want to wait for an actual threat, detective. Right now all we know is that he missed his grocery date, and that he's an ass," I said, sliding my eyes back towards the neighbor who was standing in her doorway, hands clutching at her floral housecoat.

Nick's lips tightened, but he led the way inside, saying, "Timothy Powell? We're here to check on you. Please let us know if you're inside."

Someone sat on the couch, head tilted back, throat exposed.

"Tim?" Nick said. "I'm going to need to see your hands."

His hand rested on his gun, ready to draw it. We circled around the couch and I swore, loudly, colorfully, using some words that I was glad Shannon wasn't around to hear.

"Is everything all right?" the neighbor called, peeking in the front door.

"Ma'am, you need to return to your apartment. I'll be there in a moment to talk to you," Nick said.

Timothy Powell's dead body stared at the ceiling, lips gone blue. He didn't smell at all, which might have meant recently dead, or, if my suspicions were right, something more nefarious.

Nick pulled out his cellphone calling in the body, and I grabbed a pen out of my bag and nudged his t-shirt down at the collar. Black circles, uncontained swirled. The spell was still active.

"Nick," I hissed. "Nick. This is a trap."

"What?" Nick asked, turning. I gestured to the spell with my free hand.

"That looks different," I said. "It looks like something that's summoning something."

Glancing around the room, Nick said, "I don't see anything. Maybe it's not functioning."

"I think we set it off by coming inside," I said. "I don't know what it's summoning, though."

Nick came closer and pulled Tim's shirt down with his hand, fully exposing his chest.

"Jupiter's puckered anus," Nick swore. Despite our situation, I felt my eyebrows shoot up. I hadn't been sure that he even knew words like that. Grabbing his alchemy pen out of his jacket, he started drawing a large circle on the floor, so quickly that he stumbled, righting himself before the line did more than waver.

"Get him inside," he snapped. "And I hope you have some defensive magic in that bag of yours."

I hefted Tim, awkwardly dropping him in the middle of the circle as he began to glow red.

"Get out!" Nick snapped. I hopped over his lines and dug through my bag, finding a handful of rocks that I sent spinning above my hand.

As Nick finished his circles, I coaxed the rocks into a new purpose. They took to it eagerly. It was one reason I'd kept them around. Rocks were usually staid in their purpose, but these ones, made of volcanic rock, were eager to explode.

As Nick began filling in the anchor points, his pen dragging across the carpet in messy lines, I saw Tim's t-shirt move. With horror, I saw a claw rip through the cotton, an arm following and then a shoulder. The head that came through was a thing of nightmares, as though a bat and a lizard had combined into a chimera.

"I'm going to need more rocks," I muttered. The creature, using its bat-like wings to climb out, finished escaping through Tim's chest, red organs and blood dripping down its scaled green skin.

It opened its mouth and shrieked. The windows rattled. I jumped, the rocks in my hand spinning faster and faster as I pumped more magic into them.

"Keep it in the circle until I'm done," Nick ordered. He didn't look up at the thing, and whether that was out of necessity or because he had faith in me, it left a lot of pressure on my shoulders.

The creature lunged for the boundary and I sent two rocks spinning towards it, the explosions knocking it back. It screamed, batting at its eyes with its claws. It had four legs like a lizard and a tail that I kept an eye on.

The long appendage swept out, crossing the circle, and I jumped over it, reaching into my bag and pulling out a handful of dried leaves. As I poured magic into them, they turned green, vines linking them, until I had an undulating palm of twisting plants.

Tossing them down on the tail, I watched as they took hold, roots digging deep through the floor, searching for somewhere to find water. Luckily before they dug all the way to the person who lived under Tim, they found a pipe and began drinking, growing thick and heavy.

With its tail pinned, the creature lunged at me again, and I shoved more magic into the rocks in my hand, splitting them into smaller pebbles. I shot a few at the creature's face, peppering it with smaller explosions as Nick began a second circle. With this one, he frowned as he wrote, pausing every few seconds.

"Seriously?" I called out. "You aren't done?"

He started to answer, but the creature turned to him, long claws reaching and grabbing his arm. Throwing himself back, he got away, but I could see blood staining his stupid expensive suit. My stomach plummeted, and I shouted to get the creature's attention.

"Hey, ugly!"

It turned to me, spit dripping down from where it gnashed its teeth. It lunged at me and I sent one of the rocks straight into its eyes, exploding like fireworks in its face.

The rocks in my hand were getting smaller as I split them again. As small as they were, all I was doing was irritating the creature rather than doing any actual damage. When we finished, I'd be able to call the rocks back together from the exploded pieces, but right now it would cost me too much energy and time.

The demon yanked at its tail, ripping up part of the floor before the vines tightened down again. It swiped at me, the long wing giving it an extended reach, and its claw caught my cheek. I felt hot blood dribble down my chin.

Time for a new strategy. If the vines had found water, I could, too.

Calling the water from the sinks, it wound towards us like a river, coming faster and faster as the water from the bathroom joined in. It swirled around the creature, staying inside the circle that Nick was finishing.

Freeze, I commanded it. The temperature plummeted, and the demon slowed as its blood cooled. The ice leapt up its legs, water following, building manacles of ice that trapped the creature's legs to the carpet.

"A little help would be nice!" I yelled, my attention on the creature as it twisted, shattering the ice. I pumped magic back into it and the ice froze up again, but the damage was done. The ice was weaker where the cracks were and it was only a matter of time before the demon was free.

"Get clear!" Nick yelled.

I drew back, and the circle lit up in Nick's familiar green magic, racing towards the anchor points. When the circle fully illuminated, the area burst into flame. The demon screamed, and it looked as though it was melting.

Wincing back, I shielded my eyes. After a couple of minutes, the flames faded. The carcass of the demon sprawled out, half bone, half burned scales in the messy circle that Nick had drawn.

Curious, I glanced at the ceiling and didn't see any black soot or char. Nick's circles had contained the whole fiery mess.

The apartment door burst open, cops flooding in. "SAPD, get down on the ground!"

CHAPTER TWENTY-FOUR

I DROPPED TO MY KNEES, FINGERS LACED BEHIND MY HEAD. Nick copied me, but slower, and he was repeating, "SAPD, I'm SAPD, stand down!"

The trigger-happy cops didn't seem to care that they were about to shoot a superior officer, and we both ended up in handcuffs.

"Are you okay?" I asked Nick, the handcuffs tight on my wrists. I leaned over, trying to see his arm. "How bad is it?"

"I'm fine," Nick snapped, his eyes narrowed on one of the cops who was radioing the situation in.

Shaking his head, Nick turned to me, his eyes catching on my cheek where the demon had nicked me. "Parker. You're hurt."

"Hey, it's barely a paper cut," I said. "You definitely got it worse than me. What was that?"

Clearly unwilling to let my injury go, Nick called out, "Hey, he needs medical attention."

One of the cops approached and examined me. He waved over another cop, and they tried to figure out if we needed an ambulance when someone spoke from the door.

"King, what the hell are you doing?"

Nick relaxed, his shoulders falling as he said, "Captain."

"Jesus Christ," the man said, a toothpick clenched between his molars. "Get him out of these cuffs."

"Sir?" The officer holding Nick's badge rushed to grab his keys, the metal jangling together as he scrambled at the lock. "So sorry, sir."

"Uncuff him," Nick said, gesturing to me. He crouched down next to me as they took off the handcuffs, and he reached into his jacket, pulling out a handkerchief, using it to wipe at my face. "Thanks for keeping me safe."

I shivered as he blotted at my skin, and almost reached out to cup his hand, but stopped myself. Nodding, Nick reached down and took my hand, pressing it over the handkerchief so I was staunching the bleeding.

Then he stood, and I saw Senior Detective Nicholas King again, for the first time since we'd started this whole adventure. His captain was a portly man, his toothpick swaying up and down as he spoke.

"Give me a report, King. What the hell happened here? You said it was a dead body. *This* is not a dead body." He plucked the toothpick out and gestured to the demon corpse before tucking it into his pocket and pulling a fresh one out of his shirt pocket.

"We discovered the body of Timothy Powell, someone I was looking into regarding the magic murders. He'd been killed, but when we entered the apartment, we must have set off the spell," Nick said. An EMT showed up, gear in hand. He looked around and zeroed in on Nick.

With quick motions, Nick rolled up his sleeve, holding out his arm for a bandage as he continued speaking with his captain. Once I saw the shallow scratches, I felt like I could breathe again. The jacket and shirt must have taken some of the attack, because those claws could have sliced down to the bone.

"What spell?" the captain asked, eyeing the alchemy circles

that Nick had drawn. "This looks like a containment and disposal spell."

"That was me," Nick said. "I realized what it was when I saw the dead body."

"Care to share with the class?" I muttered. "Enough with the suspense. What was that thing?"

"Alchemists have long believed that there are more realms than the Far Realm," Nick said. The medic finished up, and he gestured towards me. "In the Victorian era, a lot of powerful alchemists spent their entire lives searching for access to these other realms."

I waved off the medic, and Nick sent me a narrow look. Huffing a sigh, I pulled off the handkerchief, getting a good look at it. It was *monogrammed*. Nick was ridiculous, I thought fondly. Of course his hankie was monogrammed.

The medic cleaned the wound and pressed a bandage on.

"Stay here, you need to take him to the hospital," Nick said.

"You'll *both* be going to the hospital," the captain corrected.

"Captain—" Nick started.

"The demon?" I interrupted.

"What most people don't know, is that alchemists accessed some of the other realms. They're numbered, by the level of difficulty involved in opening a gateway. I saw that they'd summoned a creature from the fifth realm." He frowned. "This is high level magic, higher than almost anyone could carry out. It would require a storehouse of magic."

"Could you do it?" the captain asked.

"With time," Nick said. "Maybe. It would be much easier with multiple practitioners."

"So, you think it's related to the magic killings?" the captain asked.

"I think that if he's draining magic, he must be using it for something," I said. "The spell in the morgue sucked all the magic out of me, but it was going somewhere."

"Who the hell is this?" the captain asked.

"Sorry," Nick said. "Captain Tate, this is Parker Ferro, the source I've been consulting with."

"Ferro," Tate mused. "You took over Ortega's old P.I. business, right?"

Nodding, I said, "Yeah. I changed the name, though."

"Okay, so our mystery killer drains this kid—what was he, another werewolf?" Tate asked.

"I'm not sure," Nick said. "We'll have to look more into his life in order to tell."

"Drains him and then uses the magic he took to summon a demon. Why?" Tate said.

"He knew someone was going to come after him, maybe?" Nick suggested.

I was examining the couch where the killer left Tim. It looked staged. If he'd been killed there, he'd gone easily, which didn't seem like Tim's MO.

"Maybe it was a trial run," I said. "To see if he could."

Shaking his head, Tate said, "If he was just testing his abilities, I don't like what that means."

Nodding, Nick began going over the complicated technical aspects of the spell. As he spoke, I drifted away, examining the rest of Tim's apartment.

The living room was sparse: a few posters on the wall from big-budget action movies, a bookshelf crammed with textbooks. I looked at the titles and saw a range of subjects from math to psychology to magical studies. It also meant he had enough money that he didn't worry about selling the textbooks back every semester.

A few houseplants were sunning themselves under the window. They looked well cared for, but I wasn't an expert on ferns. Still, I could feel the happiness radiating from them, echoing in my magic like the bubbles in a brook.

Nick glanced at me and I waved him off. He narrowed his

eyes, clearly saying that he didn't want me touching anything, and I held up both hands. *Fine, fine, no touching.*

A crime-scene tech circled around me, marking on the floor where there was some blood spatter from the demon. I nudged open the bedroom with my foot and squinted in the darkness.

Using my elbow, I flicked on the lights and took in the room. Plants lined the bedroom window, flowering lilies of some sort. A sun lamp was off to the side, tucked in the corner of the room.

The bed was unmade, sheets crumpled and a pair of pajama bottoms tossed on top. I walked over to the night stand, seeing a phone charger and a couple of thrillers stacked on the wooden table. A gold chain hung out of the book on top.

Glancing back to the living room, I saw no one was looking at me, so I picked up the book, opening it to the chain. The necklace slithered out, and I caught it in my hand before it fell to the floor. My heart jumped. I could feel it slamming in my chest like I'd run a marathon.

The pendant was a series of interlocking leaves, maple, oak, poplar. It was made of gold and copper and brass with gems set into the points of the leaves. The metal felt warm in my palm.

With another glance back, I pocketed the pendant, making sure that none of the long gold chain was showing. Carefully, I put the book back as I'd found it. I examined the rest of the room and found a stash of HAH gear in the back of the closet.

When I walked back into the living room, Nick was watching the techs work with his arms crossed. He smiled when he saw me.

"Anything interesting?" he asked.

The necklace sat heavy in my pocket, a lie that I couldn't tell without my house of cards falling apart. I shook my head.

"Do you need my statement?" I asked.

"Not right now," Nick said. "You can come by tomorrow. You should go to the hospital."

One of the techs began photographing the counterspell he'd used against the demon, catching Nick's attention.

"I'll see you later?" I said, backing towards the door.

"I'll be by tonight," he confirmed. "Go to the doctor, Parker."

I grunted, neither agreeing nor disagreeing, and Nick stepped over to see what a tech was talking about, something about a secondary spell in the floor.

Outside, police cars and flashing lights lined the street. A couple of more techs rushed passed me, and the cop that had cuffed us had been assigned to guard the perimeter. He shot me a nasty look as I passed, but I ignored him.

There was a park nearby, and I wandered towards it, going against the flow of traffic heading towards the building to see what all the noise was about. As soon as my feet touched the grass, a cool relief seeped into my muscles. I found a shady picnic table and sat, shifting to pull out the necklace.

The chain pooled in my hand, and I held the pendant up. The precious metals and stones glittered in the light. It was fae, and I could even tell which fae court it came from.

The Autumn King was fond of giving pendants like this to his favored courtiers. To wear it would have been a sign of respect, of trust, as much as fae royalty trust anyone. I'd seen only a handful during my years in the fae realm.

Yet Tim had one. I shouldn't have been surprised. If the Summer Queen had her own operatives in the human realm, it made sense that the other courts would, too.

What didn't fit was Tim's interest in HAH. If he was half-blood like Acacia, or a changeling like me, then he should have felt as annoyed by the messaging as we did. After all, HAH was against us, too.

And did Acacia know who she was dealing with? Was it all part of some joint venture? Maybe if Tim got kicked out for espousing HAH views, then he'd look more appealing to more dangerous HAH sects?

Still, none of it fit, and now I'd never be able to ask him about it.

Did whoever killed him know that he was fae? They'd have to. One taste of his magic, and it'd be obvious. So, was the demon trap for the fae or the cops or both?

It brought too many questions to mind. I rubbed my finger against an emerald set into a maple leaf on the pendant and took a breath that filled my lungs. What was I supposed to do here? One fae was dead, another was missing, and a murderer was at the heart of it.

There was only one solution, one person who could help me detangle what was going on. The Windrose. The balance between the courts, who was rumored to know every trick the fae monarchs tried before they even thought it themselves.

The Windrose would have some way to get in contact with him in the human realm. In fact, I was pretty sure I knew what that way was.

Standing, I looked towards the hills, shading my eyes. There, in the distance, was a solitary oak tree. It was massive, its long arms dipping close to the ground, even as its canopy had to be seventy feet above the ground.

Looked like I was going hiking.

———

Stopping at my place, I picked up water, some snacks, and a better backpack for hiking. It shouldn't take more than an hour of walking, but I wasn't looking forward to it.

A bus dropped me close to the trailhead, and I wasn't wrong about how unpleasant it was to walk the dry hills in the baking sun. By the time I reached the oak, I'd emptied every drop of water from my bottle and eaten an entire box of granola bars.

At the tree, I paused, leaning against one of the branches. I sighed, long and low, as I looked up at the massive tree. There was some debris from other hikers. A couple of old beer cans, a few plastic wrappers that had gotten caught in the spiked leaves.

"Okay," I said. "How do you work?"

The tree was the first thing I'd noticed when I returned from the Far Realm, because it *felt* like the Far Realm. Its branches pulsed with the power and energy that moved through every living thing in the Far Realm, the sort of power a fae might take to replenish their own.

If the Windrose was here, and I knew from court gossip that he lived exclusively in the human realm, the tree would be where he was. I circled the tree, but there weren't any obvious doorways or a burrow that led to him. Even higher up, I didn't see anything that looked like an entrance.

Closing my eyes, I reached out with my magic to look for anything hidden and felt only a faint, faint line of connection. It was gossamer thin, connecting the tree to something in the distance. When I tugged on it, I felt a shift in the world.

Snapping my eyes open, I realized that I'd made a mistake. The thread acted like a doorway, and I'd accidentally stepped inside. Wherever I was, it looked like a house.

Everything was dark, polished woods. There was a small round hole in the center of the room, but other than that, the room was bare. Stained glass windows climbed up massive walls, giving the impression of a church. They featured fae, and when I turned in a circle, each window mapped to the four different courts.

Winter, first, with their pale whites and purples, the world around them covered in snow. Spring, with greens and pinks, flowers covering the green land around them. Summer, blue and yellow a harvest cornucopia surrounding them. Finally, Autumn with its reds and browns, the world falling asleep as they walked through it.

When I approached one of the regular windows set between the mass of color, all I could see outside was a garden.

"Hello?" I called out.

The fae I was expecting didn't arrive. I pursed my lips and began looking. When I exited the room, it was set apart from the rest of the house. I passed a modern kitchen with all the cleanest appliances. Then, a door leading into a library, but there was no one sleeping in the chairs. Finally, I reached a living room, with couches and a tv, the windows showing a view of an empty street.

"Huh," I said. I saw four front doors, spaced evenly across a long wall, and then I saw the dead body.

CHAPTER TWENTY-FIVE

IT WAS THE SECOND I'D SEEN IN ONE DAY AND NUMBNESS rolled up my legs, settling under my breastbone, when I looked at it. I took long strides to the entryway, knowing it was too late for me to do anything.

Malcolm lay spread out on the carpet, his cane tossed beside him, as though someone had tried to get it out of the way. I knelt, my knees landing heavily on the floor, and put my fingers at his throat. No pulse. With my magic, I reached out and tried to sense for him, but all I felt was a deep, empty nothingness.

Someone had drained him of magic and left there on the carpet like trash. Anger smashed into my chest, and I hissed out a long breath. He didn't need to die.

I settled back on my heels and looked around. Now that I knew what I was looking at, the entryway looked familiar. How had he kept his nature hidden from me? For that matter, how had he hidden the rest of this house from me?

In retrospect, I recognized the couch and the tv. But he must have been incredibly powerful if he could throw a glamour that would confuse even me. Why had he been interested in me? Was it to keep an eye on the Summer Queen?

No, Malcolm had never even once asked me about her. In fact, he'd been nothing but kind to me since we met. I felt my anxiety deflate as the grief rose up again. I didn't have many friends, and I thought he'd been one.

"What am I supposed to do now, Windrose?" I asked his corpse.

He would have had some way of summoning the courts, but I had no idea what it was. I pushed a knuckle hard into my eyeball, seeing sparks and flashes. When I opened my eyes, I saw the cane.

Squinting, I noticed some details that hadn't been clear before. Symbols for each court were carved across the top where his palm would rest. I remembered the hole in the floor in the large stained glass room.

Testing a theory, I picked up the cane, unsurprised at the weight now that I knew who'd been using it. I walked back to the seasons room and placed the cane into the hole. It fit, standing upright when I stepped back.

Nothing happened.

Narrowing my eyes, I tried calling out, "Summer Queen, I summon thee."

The room was thick with heavy potential, like rain about to fall, but nothing happened. I went to the large stained glass windows, but there were no buttons or leavers. There wasn't even a residue of magic I could examine.

Brushing my fingers against the head of the cane, I pushed magic into it. I kept the amount low, and felt a vibration come back to me, like touching a guitar string that's been plucked. Hesitantly, I increased the amount of magic and the cane sprouted roots. They plunged into the ground, but unlike my own friendly tree, no damage was done to the wooden floor. It was all an illusion or—no, that wasn't right. The tree *was* growing, but it was growing into the Far Realm.

It looked almost like a glamour, but I'd imagine that it was solid if I touched it, roots growing blue and yellow, purple and white, orange and brown, pink and green. The colored roots raced towards the stained glass, lighting them up. Doorways opened in front of the windows and I caught images of the Far Realm, the different courts glancing into the doorways.

Soon, fae came through. I expected an entourage when the Windrose summoned the courts. To my surprise, it was just one fae from each realm.

The Winter King entered first, then the Spring Queen, Autumn King, and Summer Queen. I recognized them from my time at court and felt goosebumps rise at how much power was in the room with me.

"What is the meaning of this?" the Winter King asked, his gruff voice chilling the surrounding air.

"Where is the Windrose?" the Spring Queen asked. "You. You were the Summer Queen's favored childling. What are you doing here?"

At that statement, the Autumn King stepped forward, examining me. "*You* summoned us? Explain yourself."

"Yes, Parker Ferro," the Summer Queen purred. "Explain yourself."

She didn't need to tug at the obligation between us to make herself clear. The room crackled with the power the four of them held. I raised an eyebrow, waiting to see if she'd push the issue.

She smirked at me, and waved a hand, a throne appearing behind her for her to sit in. The rest of the royals did the same, their expressions ranging from curious to dark.

"The Windrose is dead," I said. "So is Timothy Powell."

Pulling the pendant out of my pocket, I approached the Autumn King, offering it over. He examined it, turning it over in his hands, a frown etched between his brows.

"The Windrose is dead?" the Spring Queen asked, her light voice musical. "How? Who killed him? You aren't claiming to have done it, are you?"

She smiled as she spoke the last, her laughter echoed by the Winter King. The Summer Queen was scrutinizing me, her eyes narrowed, and she asked, "Did you kill him, Parker?"

"No," I said quickly. "No. It wasn't me. There's a serial killer here in San Amaro who's draining paranormals of their magic. I'm pretty sure he got to Malcolm, too."

"On what evidence?" the Winter King boomed. "No human could have killed him, he has power beyond their ken."

"Come see for yourself," I snapped. Stalking out of the room, I walked back to Malcolm's body. It was unchanged, and I stood to the side as the Kings and Queens examined it.

The Spring Queen bent over him, her hands hovering above his chest. She frowned.

"The child speaks true, the Windrose has no more magic in him." She glanced to the Winter King, and I noted the silent exchange between them.

In the previous Summer Queen's reign, the Spring and Summer courts had been allies, but with her death, it looked like that had shifted. The Autumn King examined the pendant in his hand and said, "Timothy was killed in the same manner?"

"Yeah. And someone used his body to summon a demon from one of the other realms." I leaned back against the wall, crossing my arms.

The Autumn King frowned and looked to the Summer Queen. "I had no idea that humans were so advanced in their magic that they could summon a demon. Perhaps it is a rogue fae?"

"You think between the four courts, none of us know of a rogue fae draining human magic?" the Winter King spat. "No. It is either one of our agents or it is, as the child says, a human."

For a moment, there was a tension that seemed to crackle between the royals. I looked between them as they eyed each other. The only two who seemed to trust each other were the Winter King and the Spring Queen, and even she was eyeing him with a slight curiosity.

I could see her wondering if he was so dismissive because it was one of his court, perhaps acting in some attempt to steal power from him. After a long pause, the Autumn King said, "I have seen enough."

He stalked back to the room they'd entered, and the rest followed, with me bringing up the rear. I stopped short when I entered, as the thrones had rearranged themselves, now in a semi-circle ringing the tree.

The tree itself had finished growing, an oak similar to the one I'd used to find the Windrose's house. But instead of a rough, crooked trunk, a throne had grown out of it. The seat sat empty.

I shifted on my feet, crossing my arms, as the monarchs took their thrones.

The Winter King, his throne made of ice that seemed lit from within by shifting lights, stroked his auburn beard and looked around the assembly. The Spring Queen, her throne made of vining roses, turned to him, and murmured, "The seat needs to be filled."

"I agree," the Winter King said. "It has never before sat empty."

"Balsam, we have time yet, don't you think?" the Autumn King asked, his throne of branches cracking as he moved, faded leaves shivering as he shifted in his seat.

The Winter King's eyes flicked to the Autumn King, and his lip hitched in a sneer. "Do we? Who was this Timothy Powell who carried your insignia? Perhaps he was a pawn who had outlived his usefulness and would create a suitable cover for a monarch who would tip the scales between courts."

"I agree," the Summer Queen said, her throne made of prisms that sparkled, reflecting light like a lake on a summer day. "Why does the Autumn Court want no one who might sit in judgement? Your season approaches, perhaps a war comes with the cooling weather?"

"Absurd," the Autumn King spat. "We all know which of us

here are *dogs of war*. It was not me who won my throne with regicide, Lilacina."

"Oh, no, much better to manipulate an infirm King into handing over his crown," the Summer Queen said, sugar dripping from her words. "Such a pity that his majesty passed so soon after you ascended to his throne."

"Perhaps we should refocus on the issue at hand," the Spring Queen said. "Who knows of a fae that could take the Windrose's place? Someone who has no loyalty to one court above the other."

"I know of none," the Winter King rumbled. "This is why it's always been that the falling Windrose trained his replacement. The only fae who are not aligned with a court are exiles, and I have no urge to call them back so they might sit in judgment of us."

The Summer Queen smiled, and I felt a chill trace up my spine. She motioned to me, a ballerina's graceful gesture drawing attention to where I slouched next to the Windrose's throne.

"I know of at least one who would fit those requirements," she said. "Parker of no court."

"This child?" the Winter King said. "Surely you jest. Where are you from, boy?"

"San Amaro," I said. "And I'm not your boy."

"A changeling?" the Winter King asked. "What court do you align with?"

"None," I said.

Tilting her head, the Spring Queen said, "But I saw you in the Summer Court when Aster was queen."

I noticed the Summer Queen's lips tighten at the mention of her predecessor, and I wondered how deeply I could dig the knife in before she tried to bring me to heel.

"Queen Aster was generous with me," I said. "She was a great ruler, much loved by her people."

The Summer Queen was glaring at me, but didn't yank on the reins she held, so I continued.

"I appreciated her generosity with me, but I owed neither her nor her court loyalty," I said. "I never pledged fidelity to her."

She'd only asked once. Maybe if I'd stayed longer, the pressure might have increased, but even at the time I felt like it was only a passing fancy on her part. It had seemed like a joke, and she'd never brought it up again.

"No court?" the Spring Queen asked. She squinted at me and I felt a breeze brush my cheek. "He tells the truth."

She lilted slightly on the word, and I wondered if she could see the obligation that stretched between the Summer Queen and me.

"I cannot trust someone who served, even informally, in another court," the Winter King said. "He will not have my vote."

"You, yourself, said that there is no one else. He is an outsider, an unclaimed changeling," the Spring Queen said. "Have faith, Balsam. If he is unworthy, it will become clear soon enough."

The King looked at her with narrowed eyes, and then nodded, a piece of a glacier crashing into the ocean. "Let him hang himself on the rope we provide."

"Are you comfortable with him, given that he so clearly prefers Queen Aster to you?" the Autumn King asked the Summer Queen.

She smiled, all teeth, and said, "I am. Who better to sit in fair judgement than one whose affection is to a dead woman, rather than one of us living?"

"Isn't anyone going to ask what I want?" I snapped. I had no desire to be Lilacina's puppet Windrose, finding in her favor over and over again, giving her the advantage among the courts. The Autumn King wasn't wrong that of the four of them, she was the one who could raise an army to go to war.

"What do you want, Parker of No Court?" the Winter King asked.

His eyes were blue, but unlike my own, his faded to pale

white. His auburn hair was thick and his skin flawless. Glinting scales ran across his cheeks.

"I don't want to be Windrose," I said. "I want no part in court politics. I've seen enough carnage in my life."

The Summer Queen laughed, her voice high. When she looked at me, it was a hawk looking down at a mouse in the field. Would the mouse be faster, or would it end in bloodshed?

"He speaks as the Windrose already! Was it not the Windrose who castigated us for the violence in our politics?" she asked. Reluctantly, the other monarchs nodded their assent. "He grew up away from our courts and our politics, so he will view any questions without bias."

"I am reluctant to agree with the Summer Queen, but she has a point. I'm not sure that we could find anyone else who could take the position," the Autumn King said. "Should we call a vote?"

The Winter King snorted. "Let us call a vote, then. Who votes in favor of naming this child, who understands little of the Far Realm, to the most powerful position in the land?"

I opened my mouth to protest, to say that I refused, that I understood it was an honor, but I wanted no part in it. The Summer Queen twisted the obligation between us, her face never wavering. I choked back a cry of pain. It was clear what she required of me. No matter my feelings on the issue, I would become the next Windrose or die fighting it.

"I vote in favor of him," the Spring Queen said, her eyes on mine. They were a warm pink, the first blush of color on a cherry tree. Her smile was reassuring. "I think he will do well."

Oddly, the words gave me hope, and I couldn't figure out why.

"I vote in favor of him," the Autumn King said. He looked at the Summer Queen and nodded his head, gesturing with his fingers. "I am curious how one who so clearly despises the Queen will be fair to her court."

"I vote for him," the Summer Queen said. "I thank you for your concern."

"I am outnumbered, it seems," the Winter King growled. He glared at his ally, but the Spring Queen merely smiled at him, the expression drawing a frown to his brow.

"Are you ready, Parker?" the Summer Queen asked. She tilted her head, a warning, and I nodded, my teeth clenched so tightly I was sure that they were going to crack.

"Assume your throne," the Winter King said.

CHAPTER TWENTY-SIX

I GLANCED AT IT. GROWN INTO THE TREE, IT SEEMED LIKE A living thing. The branches wove together to provide a backrest. Leaves rustled as I approached, but when I reached out, no voice from the tree answered me. If it had a spirit, it was deeply buried.

Taking a seat on the throne, I leaned back. Nothing happened.

"Parker of No Court," the Winter King said, his voice dropping the surrounding temperature. "Do you pledge neutrality in all issues in which we ask you for judgment?"

If I pledged neutrality, it bound me to that promise. The Summer Queen could twist all she wanted and she couldn't break this promise I made. I would at least be free that much.

"Yes," I said. "I pledge to be neutral in my judgments."

The room seemed to shake, a layer of ice shooting out from the Winter King's throne. It hit the tree, and the tree absorbed it. The King was binding himself to *my* judgments.

"Parker of No Court," the Spring Queen said, her smile blossoming into a grin. "Do you agree that with this rank, all ties and obligations will be severed and no new ones shall bind you? You will enter your potion as Windrose free of all debts to fae or humans?"

I thought of all the promises I'd made. I owed so many people. The Summer Queen had an obligation, Malik had a promise, Nick was just someone I wanted to help. I even owed Jeffrey rent. Did that count? Or the retribution that I owed Derek McCallum?

There was no way I could make her that promise.

Then my brain caught up with her words. She wasn't asking for a pledge, she was asking for *permission*. I looked at her face, the spark in her eye just as bright as what blazed in the Summer Queen's gaze. I'd taken her for the simpler of the monarchs, but she was trying to wrest control of me out of the Summer Queen's hands.

I nodded.

"I agree that with my assumption of the role of Windrose, all ties and obligations will be severed. And no fae or human can bind me as long as I keep my position." I watched as the ice receded and flower petals fell from the air, blanketing the dark wooden floor. Her magic was a warm bath that enveloped the tree and me in it.

It brushed against me, a warm tide washing away footsteps in the sand, taking with it all the debts I carried. I no longer owed the Summer Queen my life. My promise to Malik was no longer a tug on my heart. I was free.

Still, I could feel a few left. What I owed the tree, what I owed whatever ancient spirit lived in San Amaro's ground, those were still there. Then again, they weren't human or fae. I looked at the Spring Queen who sat, a smug smile on her lips as she turned to the Summer Queen.

Lilacina sat utterly still on her throne, lips pursed and eyes narrowed at me. If she was breathing, her chest barely rose and fell. She must have felt it when the Spring Queen wiped away the obligation binding us together. Her hands tightened to fists on the armrests of her throne.

"Do you pledge to fulfill this role until you are dead, until your spirit is released from your body, until you no longer draw breath?" She hissed the words, as though she was enjoying imagining my corpse.

The idea brought me up short. *Did* I want to promise to keep this role until I died? Malcolm had been old, although with the glamor he wore, it would be impossible to tell *how* old.

Was I comfortable being neutral for that long? Being unable to stab the Summer Queen through the heart the way I wanted to?

"I pledge to fulfill this role until another, one who is more capable, will accept the mantle," I said. "I pledge that I will not shirk my duties and will fulfill them with my whole heart until that time."

Snorting, she gestured a hand, and a warm summer breeze blew away the colored petals, leaving a dry heat in its wake.

"Parker of No Court," the Autumn King said. "Do you vow to protect fae life, regardless of what court or circumstance they come from? Do you promise that under your watch, fae will be safe no matter where they roam?"

Frowning, I tried to see the thorns in his pretty speech. His hand clenched tight around Tim's pendant, the chain dragging over his knuckles.

"I vow that I will fight for all fae, regardless of their circumstance. Under my watch, I will do my all to keep them safe no matter where they roam." Clauses inside clauses, just enough to give me wiggle room. No one could promise them safety, but the role of Windrose was more than judge and I would have to fulfill it.

That I was free from the Summer Queen was enough to make me willing to pledge that and more.

The Autumn King's magic was a crackle of dried leaves,

billowing up with a gust of wind. As they flew past me, I felt his magic tie me to my promise.

The four monarchs had bound themselves to me. They would accept my judgement and my words would be law. But it wasn't a one-way promise. If I broke faith with them, it would shatter the ties that kept my judgments followed and me safe.

I was free from the Summer Queen, but I'd just exchanged one prison for another. My chest felt tight, iron bands binding me to this new role.

"So it is agreed," the Winter King said. "We welcome the new Windrose. Stay true, for the consequences for all are dire if you do not."

A rush of unfamiliar magic hit me. It felt old, older than any of the monarchs' magic. It tasted like aged liquor and burned as it raced down my spine. I'd never felt anything like it, even when I was practicing witchcraft with Shannon and Laurel.

The room hummed with magic, and then it discharged, a clap of thunder so loud that it shook the tree.

"As your first task, you will find the one who murdered your predecessor," the Winter King said. "Do not call us until you do."

He swept out, his fur-lined cloak spinning as he returned to his realm. The Summer Queen stood, stalking through her own doorway, without a backward glance towards me.

I smirked. Oh, how losing me must burn her. They had given the pawn a position equal to hers, and now not only would she have to obey my rulings, she'd have to see my face and know that it was her fault she'd lost the upper hand.

"Let me know when you have found the one who murdered my... Timothy," the Autumn King said. "I would have his killer's judgment found in front of me."

The King peered at the Spring Queen, who remained in her throne. Her fingers were steepled in front of her mouth and she nodded at him as he departed.

I waited, but she was silent, assessing me. Finally, I asked, "Your Majesty? Was there something you wanted?"

"I am glad to hear that you still hold some fondness for the late Summer Queen. Her passing greatly unbalanced the Far Realm for some time, and it was only through the steady hand of the Windrose that it did not end in all-out war." She raised an eyebrow. "I am glad you were willing to be freed of your obligations. There are some who are more attached to their chains than to freedom."

Uncertainly, I nodded. I wasn't sure how to tell her that my "fondness" for Queen Aster was a show to bother Lilacina. She didn't seem to need to be told.

"As you are now at your own liberty," she said, "I suggest you limit who else you make promises to. The other monarchs are not as sensitive as I am, and may have missed an obligation entirely, but they will be watching you with avid attention, now. Your judgments should be above reproach."

Her gossamer gown moved like flowing water as she stood and turned. "Congratulations on your freedom, Parker Ferro."

After she left, the portals vanished, and the thrones faded. I stood and watched the tree disappear until all that was left was the walking cane. Picking it up, I hefted the thing. It was still heavy.

I walked back to where Malcolm's body was, but there was nothing there. It was as though he'd never existed. The unfamiliar magic I'd felt during the ceremony must have been him. When I'd inherited his job and his magic, it had left nothing behind.

Shaking my head, I brushed my palm across the smooth wooden floor. I made a fist and thumped the floor twice, hissing out a frustrated breath. For a moment, I rested there on the floor.

I ground my hand into the floor and pushed myself up. Being free of the Summer Queen had been my goal for three years. Now, the reality of it came at a greater cost. The role of Windrose was a trap and though I'd left room to free myself, until I found someone else to take the position, it was my weight to carry.

Looking around, I could tell that the house was larger than I'd first assumed. A set of stairs showed a second story, and there appeared to be a deck outside the kitchen. Then there were the strange doors leading out of the entryway.

Curious, I opened the first, seeing the street I'd seen from the windows. It was empty, and the porch overlooked the spread of San Amaro, the ocean in the distance. I was in the Hills, where all the rich people lived to keep themselves away from us peasants down below.

Closing the door, I opened the second and blinked when I saw my hallway. My apartment door was only a few feet away, the flickering of a fluorescent light making it feel like home.

The third door opened at the oceanfront. It looked like it was one of the abandoned fisheries that were being torn down and turned into expensive apartments. No one walked by, and I closed the door.

Approaching the last door, I felt a sense of dread. When my hand closed on the door handle, I saw that what I'd taken for a doorknob lock was actually a small round dial. It didn't have numbers, rather there were inscrutable symbols around it.

I left it in its position and turned the doorknob. It opened into the Far Realm, I knew that immediately. The magic was soothing after the day I had, and I wanted to step through and enjoy it, but I didn't dare in case I couldn't get back.

Closing the door, I studied the other symbols, but didn't turn the dial. I'd have to do more research to find out what all of it meant. The sun had set in the windows, and I checked a clock on the wall, unsurprised to see it was nine o'clock.

My stomach rumbled and while the kitchen here looked good, I hesitated before stealing a dead man's food. The fastest way to get home would be through Malcolm's door back into *Las Vistas*, but then getting back would be the issue. Making another trek up to the oak tree was possible, even if the idea made me exhausted just thinking about it.

A heavy metal *thunk* sounded behind me. Turning, I saw a set of keys, four of them. My backpack, which I'd accidentally left at the oak tree, was there, too.

"A *sentient* house?" I said. "No. No! Nothing this complicated with this many pieces could have a spirit."

I felt the irritation but didn't hear a voice. The floor swallowed my stuff. Holding out my hands, I said, "Okay. A sentient house. Do you have a name?"

It came to me instantly. "Silverwood," I said. "Okay, Silverwood. I can use the keys to get back in?"

After a long beat, the keys and my backpack reappeared, the floor smoothing out. I reached out with my magic, but couldn't get any voice, just a presence. It felt like being next to a whale at an aquarium, something massive and silent that could swallow you whole. The feeling was the sort that made small animals stand very still, so they wouldn't be noticed.

Silverwood had noticed me, though. It knew who I was and the position I had inherited. Whatever its feelings on Malcolm's death were, it wasn't going to lock me out.

Scooping up the keys and my backpack, I tossed them in the air. "I'll be back, okay?"

I exited into *Las Vistas* and walked down the hall to my door. Compared to Silverwood, my own apartment felt barren. If Malcolm had lived in his house for long enough, then he could have imbued it with a spirit. Maybe all of the Windroses had lived in the house, maybe it went back aeons. If it was that old, though, it should be speaking to me.

Shaking my head, I dug my keys out of my backpack and unlocked my door.

"Parker," someone said behind me.

Turning my head, I saw Nick and smiled. The expression was automatic. He was one of the few people who cared about my well-being right now for wholly unselfish reasons. He looked ragged, and he didn't have a bag.

"What happened?" I asked. "Come in."

We trooped inside and I dropped my backpack under the desk. He closed the door behind us and stood nearby, arms at his side. His gun was still in his holster, and he was watching me with a frown.

"Are you okay?" I asked. "You look terrible. Do you need water or something? I actually have juice, if you want it."

"Parker, I need you not to lie to me," he said.

My eyebrows went up, and I asked, "What are you talking about, Nick?"

There were so many lies right now. I couldn't tell him about my new role without revealing that I was fae. I couldn't tell him about how I'd gotten away from the SoPa pack without revealing that I'd promised to betray him. I couldn't even tell him how I'd gotten the list of students in Woolworth's class without revealing that I'd broken into his office.

"I need you to tell me what you took from the crime scene. And then we need to go down to the station," he said.

CHAPTER TWENTY-SEVEN

"WHAT?" I SAID. "I DIDN'T TAKE ANYTHING FROM THE CRIME scene."

"A tech saw you, Parker. He told me because he thought you and I were friends, and he didn't want to get you in trouble. If he'd told the captain, you'd already be arrested. Don't *lie* to me, okay?"

Nick rubbed a hand over his head, and looked at me again, his eyes sharp and narrow. Gesturing to the couch, I said, "Let's sit down."

Stalking over, Nick sat, his eyes following me until I took a seat on the other side. I rested my forearms on my knees and said, "I don't know what they saw, but I didn't do anything."

Nick snapped, "You're lying. Try again."

"Hey, I'm *not*," I said. "Why are you so convinced?"

"Because I knew, Parker." He shook his head, covering his face with his hands. He had a fresh bandage on his arm; clearly he'd been to the hospital while we were apart. "I knew you had to have found something, why else would you leave so fast? I just thought you'd follow the lead and then rope me in, but I've been calling you for hours, and you're avoiding me. What did you find?"

His tone was cracked, the words made of broken glass. Nick, the guy who was the only cop I knew who was honest and true, had been willing to let me get away with stealing from a crime scene. I'd taken someone who actually had ethics and, in three days, I'd turned him into someone who would give them up for me.

"Are you involved in this? Was that whole show at the morgue just to throw me off, make you less of a suspect?" Nick asked, pulling his hands from his face. He looked at me, his expression raw and hurt. What he wanted was reassurance, but the questioning irked me.

"I'm a suspect now? Because some tech thinks he saw me take something from the scene?" Crossing my arms, I rolled my eyes. "Give me a break."

"Just tell me what's going on," Nick begged. "Tell me what you took and we can make it right."

"Yeah, because the police are going to look really fondly on me," I said. "If *you* think I'm a suspect, they're going to take you off the case. And the next guy is going to want to pin it on someone. Might as well be me."

Nick was silent, and I laughed. "Oh, that's great. You already told them, didn't you? You're already off the case?"

Shaking his head, Nick said, "I wanted to give you a chance to explain first. Just... talk to me, Parker."

Lacing my fingers, I clenched my hands together until my knuckles went white. My chest ached. Nick was the only decent guy that I'd ever dated, and we were so new. He was upstanding and honest, and all I was going to do was drag him down with me into the muck.

But he was the one asking. And no matter what our differences, I *liked* him.

"Timothy was fae," I said, the words heavy. It felt like adding to my burden, more stones on my shoulders. "I found a pendant that belonged to the Autumn King, and I knew I had to tell the fae as soon as possible."

"Who's the Autumn King?" Nick asked. "Is he the Summer Queen's husband?"

I shook my head. "No. There are four monarchs in the Far Realm. They each have their kingdoms, but their individual power waxes and wanes with the seasons."

After a beat, Nick nodded. "Why did you have to tell them before telling me?"

"If the Autumn King came looking for Timothy, he'd tear the city apart looking for his killer. I thought if I went to the... if I went to them, I could keep them in check long enough for us to find the killer," I said. "That's why you couldn't reach me."

"You were in the Far Realm?" Nick asked.

"Kind of," I said. "I left my cellphone behind. I didn't know you were worried. I'm sorry."

The words were out before I thought them through, but I meant them. I was sorry. Maybe it was just sorry that Nick was so invested in me when I had to struggle to tell him even a hint of the truth.

"Where's the pendant?" Nick asked.

"I gave it back to the King," I said.

"Fleet-footed Hermes," Nick swore, and I felt both my eyebrows go up. I wanted to make a joke at how vanilla it was compared to the more colorful language he'd used earlier, but at his dark look, I pinched my lips together.

"We still have to go in, you need to make a statement," Nick said.

"Fine," I said.

The silence stretched between us, crackling with all the things unsaid. Staring at his hands, Nick said, "Okay, so you saw a pendant at the scene and gave it to a fae. What did he say? Are the fae coming to San Amaro?"

When the Franciscan monks traveling California reached San

Amaro, they named it that because, like the saint of the same name, they thought they had sight of paradise. There was a reason that, unlike everywhere else in California where they forcibly converted and enslaved Native Americans, there were no villages or tribes living near San Amaro.

What the monks had actually seen was the Far Realm, and a couple of them were foolish enough to enter it. Their companions never heard from them again. The monks, unwilling to recognize that this meant they shouldn't mess with the fae, built a Mission here. And despite the fact that the fae razed it to the ground, built another one, this one fully stocked with Spanish soldiers.

The history from there is a mess of violence and fae trickery, with humans at the losing end of most of it. Sometime towards the beginning of the nineteenth century, no one quite knows why, the fae backed off. They were still around. The fae still liked to snatch particularly pretty or talented kids with some regularity. Changelings like me are still a regular occurrence. But, overall, nineteen out of twenty San Amaro natives have never had an interaction with an actual fae.

So, the threat of the fae coming back loomed large for residents of the city.

"No," I answered. "I made a deal with them."

"What did you do?" Nick asked.

"I promised them that I'd find whoever was killing the fae here," I said. "And that I'd bring him to justice."

Nick's eyes narrowed. "Fae, plural. Who else got killed?"

I winced. That slip of the tongue was going to cost me.

"I don't know, maybe they count the incubus, too. They're from the Far Realm," I lied. He'd know it was a lie, and he'd leave. Maybe send someone to arrest me.

With a heavy sigh, Nick said, "I don't know why you keep trying to convince me that you're a bad person. I've been inside you, I know you're not."

"What?" I said. "Hey, just because we had sex—"

"When I healed you," Nick said. "We were inside each other, and I know that you sensed me. I could sense you, too."

"Whoa," I said, pointing at him. "You were inside my *head?*"

"No," Nick said. "You know. You felt it."

"That's not okay, you didn't tell me—"

"Would you have rather I let you *die*—"

For a moment we were talking over each other and then Nick said, "*Enough.* No, I didn't read your mind. You know how it was, though. I could sense *you.* And I know you're a good person."

"You don't know anything about me," I spat. "I've been lying to you since the moment we met. I'm not *good.*"

"Right, the first moment we met. You think I didn't know that you weren't a tourist? Or, when you broke into Derek McCallum's house. You think I believed that you were just looking to rent the place? That your realtor gave you a key, and you decided the best time to look around was at nine o'clock at night?" Snorting, Nick said, "I know you were lying about that. But just because you were looking into McCallum for a case doesn't mean that you're a bad person."

I shook my head. "Oh, it wasn't for a case. I wasn't looking into him for a case. I was working for him."

Nick pulled back like I'd hit him. "No. McCallum isn't the kind of person you work for. I've looked into you."

"Well, I was," I said.

"Then why were you breaking into his house?" Nick said. "He forget to pay his bill?"

"Maybe," I said. "Maybe he stiffed me and I was there to get what was mine. See? Not a good guy."

"Was it illegal? What he hired you to do?" Nick asked, eyes on mine.

"No," I admitted. "It wasn't. But that doesn't mean that I didn't know better taking a job from him."

And oh, how that decision had cost me.

"So you got screwed by McCallum," Nick said. "Are you afraid that if you let me get close, I'll screw you, too?"

The words hit me because I knew how true they were. When Jeffrey Jenkins showed up with papers evicting me from my apartment, I already had a bag packed in the back of the closet with everything I needed to survive. I could leave everything else here and walk away, because that's what they had forced me to do my whole life.

McCallum was going to pay not because I needed the money he stole back, or because I wasn't used to getting screwed, but because he'd broken a contract, and now that I understood my fae heritage better, I understood why it rankled. Why everything in my blood screamed that he had to pay for such a violation.

"You want to know the truth?" I said, looking at him through narrowed eyes. My lips twisted into a smirk. "I can prove you will screw me."

Settling forward, Nick watched my face. I could tell he was on his guard just in the way his shoulders were tight. "I'm not going to hurt you, Parker."

"I'm fae," I said, dropping the words like high tech precision bombs.

Nick went still, and I watched the realization hit, his eyes widening, his hand grabbing for his alchemy pen. It was automatic, and I shook my head *tsking* at him. He looked down at his hand like he was just seeing it and put the pen back into his pocket. His warm brown skin had gone gray.

"See?" I said. "You can't trust me."

"I healed you. There wasn't anything that wasn't human," he said.

"Changeling," I said. "You could send me to Rictor, and when he cut me open, I'd be one hundred percent human."

"But I've seen your file," Nick said. "The fae took you. Someone filed a missing persons report on you!"

"My foster parents," I said. "Probably the only ones who missed me."

"So, you're fae." The words seemed to drag themselves out of his mouth. He licked his lower lip, a tic that I'dseen before, but this time only increased my stress rather than my arousal. For the first time in our relationship, he was nervous. I'd gotten him on his back foot and it was rotten fruit in my stomach.

"Am I still a good person?" I said, the words laced with every venomous thing I'd heard about fae my entire life. Can't trust a fae, they're snakes. Don't let them look at you or they'll steal your soul. Be careful or the fae will take your children like the Pied Piper.

"I don't know," Nick said, his voice quiet. "Are you? You tell me. You're so intent on proving that I don't know you, that you aren't good... I came here because I knew you wouldn't just steal from my crime scene when you knew it could hurt me."

I watched as he swallowed.

"But you did. I want to be mad and think it was wrong, but department regulations would have us lock up that amulet. If the Autumn King or whoever came looking for it, he'd assume it was our fault that Timothy was dead." Rubbing a hand over his head, the short hair making a soft rasping sound against his palm, he squeezed his eyes closed. "You're fae, and that means if I were on the job, I'd have to report you..."

"What do you mean, if you were on the job?" I said when he trailed off.

"It's almost ten o'clock at night, Parker," Nick said. "I got off work hours ago."

"What about me having to come down to the station and all that?" I said. I watched as he looked down. "Was that just to scare me?"

"No," Nick said. "You do need to go in. Just not right now. I can't believe you're fae. You don't act like it."

Both my eyebrows shot up, and I snapped, "Oh, really? You've met a lot of us, have you?"

Nick laughed, which felt so weird that I joined in. It was like gas being let out of a balloon, and we both began gasping for air. He shook his head and his laughter faded out.

After a beat of silence, he said, "Thanks for telling me. I should go. This is a lot to process. Come to the station tomorrow and make a statement."

"What about the amulet?" I asked.

"She just said that she *thought* she saw you take something, that you were acting suspicious," Nick said. "It's not enough that she'd take it to anyone higher up."

"Are you going to tell anyone?" I asked.

"That I've been sleeping with a fae?" Nick said. "No. It's off the clock, you aren't doing anything wrong."

"You don't know—"

"Stop," Nick said, firmly. "Living your life isn't a crime. You aren't a bad person and I don't know how to convince you of that."

Rolling his shoulders, he said, "I'll talk to you tomorrow. I just need to figure out what this means to me."

I watched as he stood and glanced back at me. His lips tightened into an expression halfway between a grimace and a smile.

"Oh," he said. "Acacia's work called. The manager found a video that he wanted us to see. I figured you might go check it out before the officer on the case takes it."

"You're breaking all sorts of rules for me," I said.

"*Look*," Nick said, giving me a steady look. "If the tape is missing, then I *will* arrest you, Parker."

"There's the Nicholas King I know," I said.

"I'll check in with you tomorrow," he said, opening the door. He pulled it shut behind him and I pushed myself to my feet to lock it.

"That could have gone worse," Shannon said. She was standing in the doorway to the bedroom and she was wearing a different outfit. I'd barely noticed the first time, but she'd been in the same dress she wore at her facility.

Now, she was wearing jeans and a white tank top, an oversized flannel shirt completing the outfit. Her sleeves were rolled up, and I half expected her to have her spell book handy because it was the same outfit she used to use when training me and Laurel. She gave me a sympathetic look.

"How do you feel?" she asked.

I waved off the question. "Were you here for the whole thing?"

"Some," she said. "I heard you tell him the truth. I've never heard you tell anyone that you're fae before."

Letting that observation slide, I headed to my restocked fridge, staring at the vegetables and wholesome ingredients I'd bought hoping Nick would make me something with them. Shutting the fridge, I opened the freezer and pulled out a TV dinner. As it spun in the microwave, Shannon moved towards the kitchen.

"I need you to call Laurel," she said. "I think the facility is trying to kill me."

CHAPTER TWENTY-EIGHT

"WHAT?" I SAID.

"I'm sorry that telling your cop didn't turn out like you wanted," she said. "Normally, I'd suggest ice cream."

"I'm not five, Shannon. He didn't push me off the swing at the playground," I said. "I'll be fine."

"No, you were honest with him and he ran away. After telling you he didn't think you were evil. So, kind of a mixed bag, I guess," she said. "At least he's not going to tell the cops about you."

"Yeah," I agreed. I couldn't help but wonder why. Fae in San Amaro was exactly the information that any good cop would want to make sure someone knew about, and Nick's Paranormal Crimes Captain was the perfect higher up to foist the information (and responsibility) on.

After having spent a few days together and a few memorable nights, I couldn't imagine that he'd changed who he was in his core. When we'd first met, I'd gotten the impression that he wanted to be a captain someday, and chief of police after that. He had that sort of upright energy.

Leaving my place, though, it was clear that he had no intention of telling his superiors about me. In fact, he'd been trying to reassure *me* I was a good person. It was one thing to think that the mantras of Humans Are Human were nonsense, but pretending the fae aren't dangerous was downright suicidal.

I couldn't parse out why I wasn't grabbing my go bag and getting on the next bus for L.A.

"It looks like you're doing a lot of great reflection," Shannon said. "And maybe realizing you aren't unlovable and not everyone is going to reject you and all that other stuff that Marco and I tried to teach you. And I hate to break that up, but, I really am afraid for my life."

"Tell me who's trying to kill you," I said, shaking my head.

"They hired a new night nurse," Shannon said. "She's a little religious."

The microwave beeped, and I grabbed a fork from the drawer before pulling out the TV dinner and stirring it all together. Rubbery vegetable pasta mix. Yum.

"At first I thought that they'd changed my medication, because I'd be somewhere, and then I'd just kind of disappear," Shannon said. "But one time I was in the room and I saw her inject me with something. Something that isn't on my chart."

"What does it have to do with her religion? She might just be an Angel of Death or something," I said, talking around the salty mass of food in my mouth. Despite how unappealing it was, I was starving and had already finished half the meal.

"I think she's in one of those HAH cults," Shannon said. "Her entire family does nightly prayers about preserving the purity of Earth for humans and her pastor does some frightening end-of-the-world sermons."

"You followed her home?" I asked.

"She's injecting me with something suspicious! What would you have done?" Shannon asked.

"Okay, so she's a nut," I said. "Are you sure it wasn't just a medication change?"

"Parker." Shannon's voice was quiet. I looked up from the tray, trying to decide if I was so hungry that another two-thousand-calorie plate of food would be worth it. "I'm scared. I don't know what happens if I die, if she kills me. What if this is it?"

"Okay," I said. "I'll have Laurel look into it. Why don't you want me to deal with it?"

"You've got enough on your plate, honey," she said. "And tomorrow you need to start figuring out where you're going to live."

My stomach tightened, and I dropped the empty TV dinner tray into the sink, the fork bouncing out with a metallic ring. Digging through my backpack, I was relieved to see that my cellphone had survived the day's events.

There were ten missed calls from Nick and five voicemails, I deleted all of them without listening and dialed up Laurel. She answered, her voice sleepy.

"What's wrong?" she asked.

"I have something to tell you," I said.

On the other end of the phone, she shifted and clicked something on. "Tell me."

"I've seen Shannon," I said.

"Yeah, I know," she snapped. "I asked, and this was the first time you've shown up in months."

"No," I said, cutting her off before she could reprimand me more. "I mean that I've been *seeing* her. Her spirit, her ghost, whatever. She's here, right now, in my kitchen."

Silence echoed back on the other end of the phone.

"Whatever this is, Parker," Laurel said, evenly. "It's not funny. I already took our lawyer to Meadowhaven, and he says we have a good case for discrimination. Shannon's not haunting you. She's not dead."

"I'm not joking," I said. For the second time that night, I was afraid someone I cared about would reject me after I told them the truth. "It started after I visited her at Meadowhaven. She followed me home, I guess. Either I'm going crazy or she's here. Ask something that I wouldn't know."

Laurel sighed and inhaled a long breath. "What happened when I turned eighteen?"

Glancing over to Shannon, she had her eyes narrowed and tapped her finger on her chin. Laurel would have turned eighteen while I was with the fae, and we hadn't talked much about what happened while I was gone. It was too fresh, too hard for both of us.

"We went out to the islands, just the three of us. Marco insisted that we go kayaking, but we didn't know Laurel couldn't swim. We capsized, and she panicked," Shannon said. She frowned down at her hands. There was more to the story, but, with all my secrets, if neither one of them wanted to tell me, I had no right to push.

"Shannon said you went out to the islands and Marco took you guys kayaking. You didn't know how to swim and so when you capsized, you panicked," I repeated.

With a gasp, Laurel said, "How did you know that?"

"I told you, Shannon is here," I said. "She has something she needs you to do. I can't do it, because I've got a lot going on right now, but I think it has to happen soon."

"What?" Laurel said.

"Her night nurse. She says the woman is injecting her with something dangerous, it's going to kill her," I said. "She followed the woman home and the woman's part of some Christian doomsday cult."

"We have to get her out of there," Laurel said.

"Yeah, I agree," I said. "But where can we put her? Mead-owhaven is going to warn anywhere else about her haunting everyone."

Laurel groaned. "I was *so rude* to that woman. I called her a bigot. And Shannon actually was haunting everyone."

"Well," I said. "You didn't know."

"*You* did," Laurel said. "You would have let me walk around showing my ass—"

"Hey, she was bigoted," I said. "It could have been anyone else, but she thought it was Shannon. Anyway, where can we move her?"

"I'll have to think about it," Laurel said. "Can she stay with you?"

"Uh," I said. I wouldn't even have a place for me to live soon, much less my ghostly foster mother. "I don't have any room. You've been to my place."

"Yeah," Laurel said. "Okay. Is the nurse on shift tonight?"

I glanced at Shannon and she shook her head. "No."

"So it's something we can deal with tomorrow," Laurel said. "I'm going to be up all night thinking about this."

"It won't help your reputation at the facility if you show up looking insane," I informed her. "Try to get some rest."

"Thanks," Laurel said. There was a beat, like she was trying to find a way to politely ask why me, why the prodigal son rather than the dutiful daughter. "Love you."

"Love you, too, sis," I said, and waited to hear the empty line when she ended the call. Looking at Shannon, I spun my phone between my thumb and forefinger. "You sticking around?"

"I'm going to go check on Laurel," she said. With a wave, she faded out, leaving me alone again.

Sighing, I headed for the bedroom, kicking off my shoes along the way. I collapsed face first onto the bed. Unlike Laurel, who I knew would stay up all night baking, worrying, or both at the same time, I fell asleep and didn't dream of anything.

———

I woke up to someone pounding on my door. Groaning into my pillow, I checked my phone for the time, but it had died in the middle of the night, so I plugged it in. The knocking was joined by yelling.

"Ferro, I know you're in there! Come out!"

Through the peephole, I saw my landlord and let out a sigh. Pushing back my shoulders, I opened the door.

"Jeffrey Jenkins," I said. "What can I do for you?"

"You Parker Ferro?" a short man standing next to Jeffrey asked.

"In the flesh," I confirmed. He handed me an envelope, marking down some notes on a clipboard. "You've been served."

"What is this, Jeffrey?" I asked.

"You're going to get kicked out," Jeffrey said, his mouth stretching into a joyous grin. "I'm not going to have to deal with you, or your dogs, or whatever other inhuman *things* you're doing business with anymore."

"Could you sign here?" the process server asked.

Taking his pen, I signed my name with a flourish.

"You have dogs?" the process server asked. "This building allows pets?"

He looked around and nodded his head like he'd have to consider it. Why anyone would take a look at *Las Vistas* and think, "Hey, I could live here" is beyond me. Desperation drove me, and cheap rent is all the neighbors mention when I asked.

"He means werewolves," I said, jerking my thumb at the positively ecstatic Jeffrey.

"Oh, man," the process server said. "No. That's not cool. Werewolves aren't dogs. That's derogatory and a myth. Werewolves are just as human as you and me."

"I didn't say they weren't human," Jeffrey said. "But I don't like crime around my buildings, and the type of people you work with aren't on the legal side of the law." His lip twisted up, and he said, "It's for the safety of my tenants."

"Sure," I said. "How about that black mold in the stairwell?

That going to get fixed soon, then? For the 'safety of your tenants'?"

"No one's reported any mold to me," Jeffrey said. He narrowed his eyes. "You going to try to fight this with made-up accusations?"

I held up my hands and said, "What, you want me to bring video evidence of the living conditions here to the judge?"

"Yeah? And I'll drag in all the CCTV of every one of your 'guests'—"

"Anyway," the process server said. "Sorry about your eviction, man. Good luck."

He headed down the hallway and I waved at him. Showing my teeth to Jeffrey, I said, "Nice guy. You should use him again. Maybe he can be a witness to the death traps you're running when everyone gets together and sues."

"Where are you even going to go?" Jeffrey asked. "No one's going to hire a P.I. with no office."

Ignoring him, I looked at the information on the documents that the process server had given me. "When did you even get these? Doesn't the court only open at seven-thirty?"

"First one in line," Jeffrey said, jerking his thumb towards himself. "I wanted to make sure you got them as soon as possible."

"I could have your money for you," I said.

"Do you?" Jeffrey asked, both eyebrows going up.

"No," I said. "But I might have gotten the money."

"Sure, and monkeys might fly."

"I'm not going to miss seeing you around," I said. "I always need to wash after we chat."

Showily, I wiped my free hand on my jeans. He laughed, a quick grunt that made him sound more like a pig than a person. Raising his eyebrows, he pointed at the paperwork.

"Ten days to respond, Parker," he said. "Tick-tock."

With the stack of paper, I saluted him and watched as he moved towards the elevator. I was reminded again of a slug.

Heading inside, I skimmed through the paperwork. Remembering how he'd tampered with the lease, I double-checked, but everything looked in order, which left me stuck. I had the two weeks to get in my rebuttal and then we had a court date. After that, things moved quickly.

At most, I'd get a month or two of respite. As long as he didn't try something like turning off my water or electricity, I could live here until then. Still, it wasn't a long-term solution.

I'd have to actually move somewhere else.

I checked my phone and decided that there wasn't any time like the present to go look at the video at the hotel. Nick had mentioned that it was one of the ritzy places on the oceanfront, and I was pretty sure I'd seen a paystub from The Ala Mar hotel when I was searching Acacia's place.

"Might as well look the part," I said to no one.

When I left, I was wearing a suit jacket over a button-up shirt and nice slacks. It wouldn't get me into any of the fancy country clubs in Montecito, but I'd pass for someone who should be allowed to see the video they were holding.

I sprung for another rideshare because the hotel was far enough away that I didn't want to walk, and I wasn't sure when the cops would come to take the video into evidence. The blue sedan deposited me in front of a hotel that cost more per night than any place I'd ever stayed. Wondering what the daughter of the Summer Queen could find working here, I wandered inside.

Looking around, I realized exactly what she'd found. People who thought that money was no object wandered through the lobby, dogs or expensive handbags under their arms. I saw someone I recognized from the HAH flyer as a member of the Alchemists' Society on the phone, his voice carrying to where I stood near the door.

"Don't come here, I'll come to you," he said. "You know why. No. Fine, I'll see you there."

If there was one place information and secrets would flow, it'd be an expensive hotel in a vacation community. If she befriended some working girls that were there often, she'd have enough blackmail to take down a lot of people.

Now the question was, what did the Summer Queen want with human politics?

"Can I help you?"

CHAPTER TWENTY-NINE

A BEEFY SECURITY GUARD WAS GLARING ME DOWN.

"I'm here about Acacia Clarke? There was some video you wanted us to see?"

The security guard crossed his arms and said, "Do you have any ID?"

Before I could tap dance my way through his doubts, an older man pushed past him. He'd cropped his graying hair short, and he had muddy brown eyes that widened when he saw me.

"Do you have any news about Acacia?" he asked.

"We're following a few leads," I said. "Are you her manager?"

"Bret Numburg," he said. "She's worked for us for a couple of years now."

"What sort of work did she do?" I asked.

"Hospitality," he said. "We have a lot of guests who are very particular about their stays, and she was excellent at making accommodations and making all our guests feel valued."

His enthusiasm made his speech almost impossible to understand, but I realized he was saying she was one of the fixers that expensive hotels had for guests with more money than sense. Need tickets to a sold-out show? Call her. Need a car to get home from a party? Call her. Need hookers or booze or some other illicit things? Acacia could get them all for you.

"You said there was video?"

The man nodded, his head bouncing like a bobble-head doll. "Yes. This way."

He led me into a back room, the security guard trailing us like a storm cloud. In the security office, he pulled up a video and gestured for me to take his seat. Settling in, I said, "What am I seeing?"

"A few weeks ago, Acacia said she was worried someone was following her." The man wrung his hands together. "It's happened before, but not with her. Sometimes guests get interested in staff."

"Was it a guest this time?" I asked.

"No," he said. "Here, you'll see."

I watched Acacia come in through the front doors, looking professional in her hotel-issued suit. She checked her oversized bag, but from the camera's angle, you could see she was actually looking out at the street she just came in from. After a moment, she continued on past where the camera saw her.

We watched for a few seconds and then a very familiar figure came in, sunglasses doing little to hide who he was. Dieter. I shifted in my seat, leaning forward.

"Xavier, here, caught him and threw him out. We almost called the police because he stayed across the street watching the entrance. I drove Acacia home because I didn't want her having to wait for a bus," Numburg said.

"Did he come back after that?" I asked.

"No," Xavier responded.

I leaned back in my chair, eyeing him.

"Do you think you'd be able to get me Acacia's work schedule?" I asked Numburg. "For the last few months?"

"Her work schedule? Of course. Do you think it will help?" He was already half out the door. "I'll just be a minute."

After he left, I spun the chair to face Xavier. "Numburg likes Acacia?"

Xavier said nothing, his face twitching slightly. I nodded. "He like a lot of the girls, or just this one?"

Squinting at me, Xavier said, "No one's ever complained."

"Acacia didn't complain?" I asked.

Xavier shook his head, a mountain moving. "No."

"Maybe her work schedule was the best one out of all the concierge staff?" I asked.

His linebacker shoulders lifted and dropped. "She could take care of herself."

"But you still had to throw out her stalker?" I said. "She tell you what it was about?"

"She didn't have to," he said, eyes squinting at me. "My job is to keep her safe."

Rocking the chair back and forth, I watched him and tried to figure out what he was seeing in the hotel. "Maybe you fell down on the job. She's gone, after all. And she wasn't the sort to disappear, was she? On time, every shift. Attentive with guests. Nice to other employees. I'll bet that Numburg wasn't the only one who liked her special."

Xavier shrugged again.

"What was different about the wolf? Usually you let her fight her own battles," I said.

"He was big. And he was trying to get her alone," Xavier said. "He didn't take any hints."

"Unlike the hotel guests," I said. "Who take her brush-offs without any problems."

"Yeah," Xavier agreed.

Because she could use fae magic to muddy the situation with guests. Distract them, give them gifts, until they were under an obligation to her. They'd do what she wanted and not even know why.

What I couldn't figure out was what Dieter wanted with her.

They had nothing in common, as far as I could tell. Their only link was Woolworth. Was Woolworth worried that the student who'd gone and tattled about the HAH'er in his class was going to tell on him about his drug dealing?

"She ever talk to you about school?" I asked.

"No," Xavier said. "She'd meet with some classmates here, sometimes, though."

"Blonde guy?" I guessed. "Tim?"

"Yeah, him," Xavier said. "On her lunch break."

"Numburg didn't mind?" I asked. Maybe the overly helpful manager did have a reason to kidnap her.

"Nah," Xavier said. "He's married."

Snorting, I said, "Of course he is. You know anything else?"

Xavier appeared to be weighing my words. "I expected the werewolf to come back. He was heavy when I threw him out."

"And persistent," I said. "But he didn't show up?"

"Just the one day. After I tossed him out, nothing." I weighed his words. It wasn't like Dieter, who'd stalked me through the city, tortured me, and lied about me to his pack, to give up after one setback.

The door rattled as it opened, Numburg returning with a handful of papers. "This is her schedule for the last year. You think it had something to do with the guy following her?"

"We're following up on leads," I said. "Someone will be by later to take the video back to the station."

The look Xavier gave me made it clear he didn't buy that I was a cop for a second, but at least he seemed to believe that I was trying to find her. And I certainly had more motivation than the cops did, since I'd made a binding promise to the four courts to protect their people.

Plus, I was pretty sure that Thistle would skin me alive if I tried to shirk my duties.

Walking me out, Numburg couldn't stop talking about what a valuable employee she was, and I hoped his wife knew how much he valued his much younger female employees. Not my business, though, and I shook his hand as I left.

On the street, I slid on sunglasses and considered my options. In order to talk to Dieter, I'd have to go through Malik. Malik was going to want an update on the case, and I didn't want to risk my relationship with Nick by letting anything slip. Plus, it was just bad business.

My stomach rumbled, and I thought about stopping for a snack before deciding what to do next. No good decisions came on an empty stomach. At least that's what the five-year-old in me said. Plus, after the week I was having, I deserved some empty calories.

The temptation was there to call Nick and see if he'd be willing to go out right now. Maybe have the long-promised date that wasn't at a morgue. He'd asked for space, though, and I wouldn't intrude when it was so clear that my presence was unwanted. In fact, he hadn't contacted me at all yet. That had to be his way of saying that he could deal with a P.I. who had a fridge like a graveyard, but he couldn't deal with a fae changeling who lied to him all the time.

I decided to kill two birds with one stone by having Malik take me out to an early lunch. My phone was dialing him when a familiar white van pulled up in front of me. I looked around, catching sight of two men standing at the corner, suspiciously still as they stared at me.

Clutching my phone, I turned and sprinted down the street. As I got to the corner, my hand rummaging through my bag for anything I could use, another car came barreling through the intersection, heading straight for me. There was just enough time to throw up my hands and thicken the air around me before it slammed into me.

The impact threw me back, the air acting like a pillow that took the brunt of the crash. Unfortunately, I got hit hard enough that I hit the building behind me. The blow knocked my breath

out and I couldn't get any air back into my lungs. My vision
grayed at the corners, and I struggled up to my hands and knees.

To my left, I saw Xavier running towards me from the hotel
lobby, a gun drawn. No, I realized. A taser. That would be about
as useful as a Nerf gun against a werewolf.

I pushed up, crawling away from the car, even as I heard a
door open.

"Get him," a woman's voice said from the driver's seat.

One-handed, I blocked a boot that was aiming for my head,
and reached with all my magic to sink their SUV into concrete.
For a moment, the ground wavered, but then I felt fifty thousand
volts of electricity enter my body. Xavier had fired his taser from
a good fifteen feet away, somehow missed the wolves standing
over me, and hit me instead.

Laughing, the one closest leapt, lifting him up by his throat
and throwing him ten feet. The poor guy went down hard. On the
sidewalk, I twitched, drool coming out of my mouth. I probably
could have shaken off the taser, but coming so close after being
hit by a car, my body was still in shock.

With a groan, I pushed myself up to my hands again, and the
woman in the driver's seat said, "Jesus, get him *down*."

A boot came straight for my face and that was the last I
remembered.

———

I woke up in a frighteningly similar situation to a couple of days
prior, when the only thing that had saved me from death by werewolf was that at one point, Malik and I had been friends. By the
tattoos that these guys were sporting, I wouldn't have as easy a
time in this round of Parker-the-torture-victim.

A pit formed in my stomach, acid roiling. I wouldn't have a
hot cop to heal me afterwards, either. I'd end up in a hospital in
even more debt and wasn't that just my luck. I'd survived one

werewolf encounter this week; I refused to let a second one kill me. There had to be a way out of the situation.

"He's awake," someone said.

Swinging my head up, I assessed my situation. I was tied to a chair, my bag on the ground a few dozen feet away. We weren't in a body shop, which meant that this whole encounter wasn't because Malik was tired of waiting. In fact, based on the lighting and the meat hooks that swung from the ceiling, we were in cold storage.

Two werewolves were playing cards on a table across from me and a third was standing at the door. He'd been the one who spoke and was listening to whoever was on the other end of the white earbud in his ear.

"She's coming down," he said to the two werewolves playing poker.

They dropped the cards, scrambling to put them into their box, and then lifted the table and brought it closer to me. One pulled out two cases, spreading a series of tools out on the table. Medical scissors, a bone saw, a meat cleaver, a few screwdrivers and pliers, some others that looked like sex toys I didn't want to play with. It was not shaping up to be my afternoon.

The door to the cold room opened and the three wolves straightened, doing the wolf dance of submission without fur. It was a weird contortion of the neck, as though they wanted to bow, but knew that wasn't right either.

The woman that entered was shorter than all three of them. She had warm bronze skin like Laurel, but that was where the similarities ended. Her hair was a curled brown tangle down her back and her eyes were dark brown, almost blending into her pupils. Turning, she murmured to the man with the earpiece. Without wolf hearing, I couldn't make anything out.

She had a loose tank top on, and I could see a tattoo similar to the one that Dieter's girlfriend had. Only hers was larger, taking over her whole back with the shape of it. The tattoo itself seemed to move, and I wasn't sure if it was the head injury or her abilities, but it looked like it was about to leap off her and bite me. When she turned to look at me, her mouth was sharp with carnivorous teeth.

I blinked, and they were normal human teeth, but now I couldn't pretend I hadn't seen the predator lurking under her skin.

"Who was your next target?" she asked.

Shaking my head, I said, "Who are you?"

Her lips went flat. "I'm asking the questions."

For a second her nostrils flared and then she spat on the floor. The two wolves without the earpiece flinched back. She stalked towards me, leaning in close and dragging her nose up my cheek.

I could smell brimstone on her breath. My stomach dropped. I wasn't talking to some high ranked member of Five Dragons. I was talking to *the* highest member. One of the dragons that the pack was named after. My heartrate must have skyrocketed because she smirked at me.

"Your kind hasn't wanted war with mine for some time," she said. "What court would send you to incite it?"

By the glance that the other wolves shared, she usually didn't talk like a fae. Her words, though, were court language, which made me wonder how old she *was*. The fae had been hands-off the human world for over two hundred years. Had she known them back when they made war with San Amaro?

"I don't know what you're talking about," I said. "I know Dieter convinced you I'm killing werewolves in San Amaro, but I'm not."

At a wave of her hand, one of the wolves went scurrying for a chair almost identical to mine. He brought it for her and she sat, leaning forward and grabbing my chin.

Her eyes shifted gold, the pupil a narrow yellow slit as she examined me. "You won't fool me."

"I'm not trying to fool you," I said. "I'm trying to convince you not to kill me because I didn't kill any wolves."

"Fae, you can't lie to a dragon," she said. "I smell your fear."

Behind her, the wolves stiffened. I knew better than most that most people were so afraid of the fae they believed even the most ridiculous of rumors. Fae could send you into an endless slumber, fae could trick your heart into stopping.

Maybe some of it was true, but I knew *I* couldn't do any of it.

"No lies," I said. "What do you think I did?"

"You killed the wolves to start a war between the packs so you could make us slaves in the old ways," she said. "But we've freed ourselves, we're not going be the fae's pets."

"Well, good," I said. "Because as far as I know, no one in the Far Realm wants to deal with the whole slavery thing."

The dragon laughed, a trail of smoke curling from between her lips. "And what would you know? You're a pawn that some monarch is using. None of your kind has even shown up to save you."

"Why would they?" I said. "They don't know I'm here."

"You admit to acting alone," she crowed. "I will enjoy your death."

"I said they don't know I'm here, not that I killed the werewolves," I said.

"And why would I trust you?" she said.

"Because if you kill me," I said, "there *will* be war. And all you'll have left of your pack is corpses."

CHAPTER THIRTY

"A WAR OVER A PAWN?" THE DRAGON CROONED. "I DON'T THINK so. I think your masters will say they did not know what you were doing and wash their hands of you."

Digging deep, I found that well of magic, the one I'd used when Jeffrey threatened to break the contract. It flowed through me and my words dripped with the power of whatever made up fae magic. Promises, contracts, charisma, whatever it was, rolled through my voice as I spoke.

"I am the Windrose," I said. "There are no masters I cleave to. And as the balance between the four courts, I promise you that if I die, the war that will roil this world will take everything you hold dear, Jimena Torres, dragon of old."

She shot up, the predator in her recognizing an equal power. The three wolves moved towards us, but she held up a hand, and they stilled.

"How do you know my name?" she asked, hands curled into claws, red scales growing up her forearms.

The truth was, I had no idea how I knew her name. But I didn't want to reveal that whatever had come with the promotion to Windrose was new to me, too. So I did what I did best. I lied.

"I'm the Windrose," I said. "My powers are more than some fae courtier's."

Her eyes narrowed, the dark slit of her iris going paper thin. "A new Windrose? Since when?"

"Since the same person who killed your wolves killed him," I said. "We're allies in this."

Someone thumped against the door and Dieter pushed his way through. He snarled, "What's going on? He should be dead. Torres said she'd kill him."

With the beefy werewolves in the way, Torres was short enough that he hadn't seen her. At Dieter's aggression, her entire body gave a reptilian shiver, and she gestured for her pack to make room. They practically flung themselves out of the way.

"You'd tell me what to do?" she spat at Dieter, her tongue flicking out and back. "With my own pack?"

Dieter took a half step back, his hands going up. "No, no. It's just that Malik had him delivered to you, so I wanted to make sure that you weren't having any problems. Ferro's tricky, he can convince anyone of anything. He's fae."

He said the last like a trump card and I frowned. Dieter shouldn't know that. Malik didn't even know that, and he had a much better reason to suspect me than Dieter.

"Malik can wait," Torres said. She pointed at him, the curled finger of her claws making the gesture into a threat of disembowelment.

"He's not speaking for Malik," I said. "Whatever else he told you, you have to know that's a lie."

"You shut your lying mouth or I'll rip out your tongue," Dieter said, his chest going wide as he took a step towards me.

Torres's hand slammed into his chest, her claws drawing blood as she shoved him backward. He hit the wall, his head snapping back, and then he surged forward, a growl contorting his face.

"You're in my territory," she said. "Behave or I'll show you what I do to werewolves who piss me off."

She spun back to me. "Explain. Quickly."

As Dieter grumbled, held back by two of the werewolves in the room, my mind raced. Dieter shouldn't know I was a fae. If he did, then was he tracking Acacia for the same reason? Because she was fae?

"Malik doesn't trust him," I said. "He's trying to prove Malik isn't worthy and take his spot as alpha, but he's not strong enough to do it in combat."

"I've met Malik," Torres agreed. "He'd be good in a fight."

"So, I'll bet you talked to Malik when the whole wolf killing went down," I said. "And he said he was looking into it. He'd find the killer."

Torres's eyes flickered between human and reptile, and she crossed her arms. I noticed her hands had shifted back to human, and I had to assume that was good for me. If she wasn't turning into a dragon right this second, then at least I had a chance of convincing her that I was telling the truth.

"And then a few days, maybe a week or two later, Dieter shows up and says he's come from Malik and that he's there to help, and you think he's an idiot," I said. "But you don't want to offend Malik, because good neighbors are hard to find for packs in the same city, so you let him stay."

Torres said, "Close. He came a few days ago."

I grinned. "Because that's when Dieter couldn't convince Malik to off me. So he thought, 'hey, you know who's violent and will kill whoever I point her at? One of the five dragons.'"

"He's lying," Dieter said. "Malik said that this guy was the killer. He used his fae magic to kill the other wolves without leaving a mark."

"Who're you going to believe?" I asked. "The Windrose, or some *beta* who's trying to steal the job from his alpha?"

"You don't have any proof that you're the Windrose. He *is* in Malik's pack," she said. With a glance at her pack mates, her chair was righted, and she took a seat in it, appearing like one of the fae monarchs I'd just met with.

"True," I said. "That's true. And maybe I know your name because I was stalking you, ready to kill you next. But I think I've finally figured out why Dieter is so eager to have me killed."

I smirked at him. "See, I thought it was all about the fact that it'd be hard to keep your position once it came to light that you were cheating on your SoPa girlfriend with a Five Dragons member. But that wasn't it at all, was it? You just figured if I had photos of you and your girl-on-the-side, maybe I had pictures of you with someone else."

Dieter's eyes narrowed and his chest bulged as he gnashed his teeth together. "I don't know why you're letting him lie to you."

"Quiet," Torres ordered.

"You figured I had a picture of you with the killer. Now, maybe I didn't know anything, or maybe I did. Maybe, depending on how long I'd been tracking you, I saw you give him Acacia Clarke. Maybe even Tim Powell. Because it was them or you, wasn't it?" I said. The pieces fit.

Dieter, who bristled at Malik's control, would never accept some human giving him orders unless there was a very good reason. But Mark Woolworth, alchemist professor of Magical Studies, had discovered old spellwork and used it to suck the magic from incubi, werewolves, and whoever else he wanted to. He'd probably had Dieter's head on the chopping block until Dieter convinced him he could find Woolworth a sweeter prey.

That prey being the fae living in San Amaro. It wouldn't be hard to imagine that Dieter hadn't even known we were fae, just that we *smelled* different. Woolworth, clearly the smarter of the two, had been the one to figure out why. The pieces clicked together like a jigsaw puzzle.

Dieter wasn't following Acacia because Woolworth wanted to keep her quiet. He was following her so he could feed Woolworth his next meal. The only part that didn't make sense was why he hadn't tried to send Woolworth after me.

"What I don't get is why you didn't give me to the killer," I said. "I mean, that would have solved the problem for you, wouldn't it?"

Torres's eyes crinkled in the corner, like she was smirking. "Not the problem of his leadership. If he delivered you, the pack would be his. Even if he delivered you to *us*, he might gain Five Dragons' support for his coup."

Nodding, I said, "Or, maybe he even has you kill me and then comes back a few days later and reveals that it was Malik behind it all along."

"Not the brightest of plans," Torres said. "But about what I'd expect from a SoPa member."

Dieter's eyes were wide, and he was looking between us. "Why are you *believing him*? He's *lying*."

At the curl of her finger, the werewolves brought Dieter closer to Torres. She jerked her chin, and they kicked out his knees so he collapsed down hard on the concrete floor. He snarled, but between the two of them, they kept him subdued.

"There's a simple way to tell," she said. "I propose a contract, Windrose."

My suspicions grew, my stomach knotting even as the magic in my blood stirred. Contracts were where the fae *lived*.

"What contract?"

"You agree to deliver the killer to us, in exchange for your life" she said to me before addressing Dieter. "If he can't agree to it, then maybe he's lying. Maybe you're right and this insignificant pawn brought down a member of my pack and your alpha."

Dieter was beginning to smirk. I puzzled through why. Malik must have made it common knowledge what I'd promised *him*. It was impossible to deliver the killer to two people. Bowing out of the contract would give Torres a reason to kill me.

"Or you could just call Malik," I suggested. "And ask him if Dieter is here as his representative, or if he's here because he's a lying snake."

Torres flicked out her reptilian tongue again and said, "Snakes are no more prone to lying than fae, fool."

Still, she pulled out her cell phone and dialed. The phone rang once, and I heard a tinny voice on the other end.

"Alpha, is Dieter here as your representative?" Torres said without any introduction.

A massive explosion that took out the refrigerator wall closest to me cut off whatever Malik said. The concrete the fridge was built into seemed to crumble into its elements, and the rebar *melted*. And it was all in a perfect circle.

Nick.

Nick stepped through, gun in his hand, badge swinging from a chain around his neck. "SAPD. Get down!"

Torres, who'd flinched back from the initial noise and light, was already half shifted and she gestured with her other hand for her pack to attack Nick. He threw down a fine white powder and it formed a perfect circle around me. He was in his suit pants and a black t-shirt, and he'd covered every inch of his skin in alchemy circles.

"Can you get out?" he asked.

The attacking wolves slammed into the barrier created by the powder, but as more of them poured into the room, summoned by the guy with the earbud, I saw cracks form. Torres was stalking behind them. Her eyes narrowed as she barked orders I couldn't hear. The barrier seemed to muffle sound, and it gave loud electrical snaps whenever a wolf hit it.

"No," I said. "What are you doing here?"

"Talk later," Nick said, muttering a spell under his breath. He slapped his hand to the rope on my wrists and it slithered apart, a neat cut slicing the knot open. He did the same with my other wrist and ankles. By the time he got to the rope binding my chest, I could see the circle he'd drawn on his palm was cracked and fading, the magic he'd poured into it breaking apart the spell.

"I got it," I said, scrabbling with the knot. After a moment, I gave up and debated slamming the chair back to break it, but Nick handed me a long knife he'd pulled out of what seemed to be thin air. It slid through the ropes like butter just in time for me to meet the first wave of wolves who crashed through Nick's barrier.

They went for Nick first, which made sense because he was the one with all the impressive firepower, but he held them off, slapping at a spell on his bicep that exploded out, shoving them back until they crashed outside the circle again. He firmed up the circle with a second toss of powder.

Narrowing my eyes, I said, "Are all these *non-lethal?*"

I tried to be quiet, but Nick rolled his eyes and said, "I'm not cleared to even *be here*, Parker. I'm not going to lose my badge for killing civilians when there are other options."

"Okay," I said. "Glad that we're going to have to get out of here without killing everyone. What's your plan?"

"I figured once you were free you could do that thing, the slap-yourself thing, and we could walk out of here," he said. "Or like a pied-piper thing. Whatever works."

"Are you *kidding me?*" I said. "You thought that I'd use some fae magic that I don't even have to get us out of here? I am planning all future rescues, Nicholas King."

"You can't do the hit-yourself thing?" Nick said.

"What *gift* have I given these wolves, other than a new window into their torture chamber?" I said, gesturing to the hole in the wall behind me.

Nick swore and brought his gun up again. "What're we going to do?"

The concrete was malleable, but I wasn't sure I could do a big enough area to get all of them, and it was only eight inches deep or so. But I could feel something else. The water, I realized.

When Nick took out the wall, he'd broken a few pipes, and they were spraying water all over the sidewalk. It took only a little energy to convince them to spray into the fridge. I examined Nick's arms.

"Is any of that electricity?" I asked.

"Why?" he asked, eyes narrowed.

"It'll be non-lethal," I promised. And it probably would, too. Wolves heal quickly.

"Yes, I have electricity," he said. He slapped a hand on his shoulder and I saw one of his circles power up.

"Give me a second," I said.

"Not too long," he warned. "Or *I'm* going to get electrocuted. Good luck getting out of here if you have to drag me."

"Don't worry," I said. "I'll leave you behind. Every man for himself."

Nick cracked a smile. "Next time, I'll bring the handcuffs. Can't leave me behind if we're cuffed together."

Kneeling low, I closed my eyes and began singing to the water. You can talk to it, sure, but water is, by nature, social. It puddles, it looks for itself. And, for some reason, when it gets together, it sings. Do not ask me why.

I crooned to it, and convinced it that it should avoid me and Nick, and all it needed was enough to lap around the ankles of the surrounding wolves. Just enough to soak their socks, their shoes, anything that it could get into. I hummed about how it would get electricity if it did it well enough.

The water answered. I saw the wolves shifting and swearing as the water continued pouring in, and they sloshed through it, their mouths moving even though I couldn't hear them because of the barrier.

"Now," I said. "There."

Nick was sweating, his forehead a shining as he spoke his spell, extending his arm to where I'd pointed.

"Is this going to work?" he asked between words.

"Probably," I said.

Sighing, he said a word that caused his entire body to twitch and a lightning bolt slithered down his arm almost too fast to see, landing in the middle of the assembled wolves.

CHAPTER THIRTY-ONE

THE CRACK OF THE LIGHTNING BOLT MADE THE WOLVES JUMP
back, but it was too late. The water had done its job and most of
the wolves were twitching from electrocution, falling into the
water, which only increased their exposure to the voltage. Nick
sent another two bolts into the water before the spell faded, the
ink peeling off his skin.

"Any more?" I asked.

He shook his head, and I hummed to the water, singing of its
sister, ice. Amiably enough, the water hardened into ice, leaving
most of the wolves trying to break themselves out of the frigid
prison. We were in a refrigerator, and the insulation helped keep
the water ice for longer.

A few wolves had already recovered from the electrocution
and were pounding against the barrier. I even saw that the water
had washed away a bit of it and the barrier was weaker there. My
glance gave it away, and the wolves pounded against the weaker
part until it gave in.

Then it was a free-for-all. I used the knife that Nick had given
me to slice at the wolves, going for their weak spots. Eyes, the
groin, anywhere that they weren't sure would grow back.

Nick became a whirlwind of movement, powering up and tossing spells without hesitation. He had to know where each spell was and exactly what it did without looking. I would have admired how capable he was, but a wolf that had been in the room with me when I woke lunged for me.

He was tall and thinner than I'd thought. His frame was perfect for attacking, because he could dart in and get out without having the weight of larger muscles. As he crouched lower and sprang forward, I spun along his arm, getting in as close to his core as I could and stabbing into his stomach.

With a surge of power, I heated the blade, and he screamed in agony. A stabbing he could have shaken off. A hot shard of metal in his abdomen was a threat on his life.

As long as I didn't make too much of a mess, he'd heal from it. So, I pulled the knife out cleanly and danced back, using his swaying frame as a shield between me and the wolves behind him. Someone caught him and tugged him out of the barrier.

My next attacker was smart, working in coordination with another wolf, their glances speaking as they tried to circle me. They'd made the mistake of dripping water all over the concrete and, with a thought, I froze it. Their shoes slipped at the sudden change in friction and it only took a sweep of my leg to have them on their backs, trying to get back on their feet.

They crab walked backwards, and I took the time to get closer to Nick.

"Plan?" I yelled.

"My car is outside," he said, tossing a spell that seemed to shift the whole room forward an inch, jostling wolves so that they fell together. The shift in the crowd let me see what was behind them and our need to get out of the room, safely or not, was suddenly more important than anything else.

Behind the wolves, there was a dragon. Torres had shifted, growing taller than a Clydesdale. She looked halfway between a nasty garden lizard and a bird. Feathers framed her face like a mane, and sharp teeth snapped at the air. In clear irritation, she swished a tail that ended in bright white feathers.

She roared, the sound so loud in the enclosed space that even the wolves winced away from it. It was clear what her message was. *Get out of my way.*

The pack scrambled away, dragging their wounded behind them. I looked at Nick, who was wilting. Half the spells I saw had faded or peeled off. At my glance, he firmed his shoulders back.

"You good?" I asked.

His lips went white as he pressed them together, but he nodded quickly.

"All right," I said. I saw my bag, kicked to the side of the room and knew that if I got it, we might have a chance.

Nick followed my glance and nodded. He sent out a series of spells that hit Torres in her face, explosions that had about as much impact as sparklers. Still, it gave me an opening, and I sprinted through the shreds of the barrier for my bag. A couple of wolves tried to grab me, but I sliced at their knees and they danced back. One handed, I grabbed my bag and pulled it over my head, securing it across my body before sliding on the slick ice back towards Nick.

Torres flicked her tail, and it slammed into me, sending me to my hands and knees. She raised her tail, and I used all my magic to yank some water up, so that her tail came down on shards of ice. A couple pierced her skin, and it gave me the time to scramble over to Nick.

He was panting, sweat darkening his shirt. I didn't ask if he was ok; it was clear he wasn't. Coaxing the ice back into water, I reached into my bag and pulled out a handful of leaves. I tossed them on the ground and began pouring my magic into them.

They grew. I'd found them growing green and verdant at the edge of an abandoned property, no water, barely any nutrients in the soil. Here, with enough water and concrete they could sink their roots into, they grew fast and thick. I didn't even know the name of the plant, and they were too starved to do more than take and take.

Still, within a few moments, we had a waist-high hedge of thorny, thick brush. Enraged, Torres lunged at us, the low ceiling preventing her from opening her wings. Nick sent a spell that flew like a frisbee, rolling along her side and leaving a shallow cut in her scales.

The brush began growing up the legs of the assembled were-wolves and, in their panic, they shifted into their wolf forms. Their desperation must have had some effect on Torres because she whipped her head back and forth, growling. Then, like a lion protecting her pride, she broke through the thick brush, the stubborn wood of the branches and trunks tearing her scaled skin as she ran towards us.

At the last moment, Nick pressed his hands into the ground and the shield solidified just in time to take her charge. She crashed into the barrier, making it halfway through. I yanked out a box of salt from my bag and threw it up in the air, sending it unerringly for her open wounds.

Roaring in pain, she withdrew, lashing her tail as the salt dug deeper. I tossed another handful into the air and it found every open cut: the one along her side Nick had made, the ones in her feet that the brush had torn open, even the nicks that my ice shield had made earlier. As effective as it was, I still felt guilty that I was literally pouring salt into her wounds.

"We should go!" I shouted, dragging Nick up and towards the door he'd created in the wall.

He scrambled to his feet, and we stumbled towards the wall, almost getting out when a stream of new wolves came through, half-shifted and ready for trouble. For a moment, I thought the Five Dragons reinforcements would be the last thing we saw. Then, inexplicably, the Five Dragons attacked them.

"What—" Nick said.

"Don't care. Move," I said, shoving him forward. We managed another two steps before a couple of the new wolves attacked us.

Nick was tapped out. He pressed a hand to one of the spells remaining on his forearm and it gave a half light before fading. As he raised his gun, I saw the resignation in his eyes.

I slapped my hand on the spell he'd been trying to activate and pumped my own power into it. Rather than Nick's pure green, it lit a brilliant yellow and his eyes caught mine. Alchemists don't share power. The most they'd do was cast separate spells towards the same goal. I hoped he'd take my magic in that spirit rather than an assault on his way of practicing.

He began the incantation, sending the spell spiraling towards the wolves. For a moment, it spun around them, and then they swayed, their eyes spinning dizzily.

"Is this an inebriation spell?" I huffed.

He didn't have time to answer before another pair of wolves charged us, and then it was a desperate scrabble to survive. After a while, I couldn't tell who we were fighting anymore. The new wolves? The Five Dragons? It all blurred together as I activated spell after spell for Nick.

We got more fluid as we gained practice. I thought it would feel weird powering up an alchemist's circle. But for all that the spellwork was unfamiliar, it felt exactly like Nick: precise, controlled, and something I wanted to sink into.

I activated a spell and watched him spin what looked like webbing around three wolves. Reaching deep, I grew brush around them, until a hedge encased them. Nick slammed the butt of his gun into the temple of a wolf coming up behind us, and I swept his legs out from under him.

"How're you doing?" Nick said.

"Good," I admitted. I knew I should have been drained a few times over, but I somehow still had some magic left.

It had to be a side effect of becoming Windrose. My well of power had expanded, or changed. Whereas before I was powerful,

I now felt even more so. Like I'd had blinders on, and when they'd been taken off, I could see the universe.

"Here," Nick said, tapping his chest.

Slapping my hand to his shirt, I couldn't see the spell, but I could feel it. It was larger than the rest.

"What is this?" I asked.

"We need to get out of here," he said, eyes darting around.

I powered it up, and felt it sapping almost everything I had left. As it took my magic, I was a little relieved to know that there was a boundary, that being Windrose hadn't changed me to the point of being unrecognizable.

Nick began chanting, and I felt the spell pull more from me, dragging out every last dreg of my magic. Around us, the brush shriveled and died off as I couldn't give it any more magic. With the area clearing around us, I finally got a good view of the melee.

A sleek wolf darted around the room, his teeth tearing as he bounded from fight to fight. He leapt and used his weight to bear down an opponent, and I recognized that move.

"Stop," I said, gesturing to Nick. I dug deep and found the voice that I'd decided to call my Windrose voice. "*Stop.*"

It echoed in the room, booming with power and resonance. A few of the wolves winced back, yelping. Torres tossed aside a half-shifted wolf she'd been holding in her claws and hissed at me.

"I think there's been a mistake," I said. My voice was back to normal, but some echo of the power must have remained because no one went back to fighting. "Malik, why are you here?"

His shift was so fluid that you could blink and miss it. He squinted at me, "Parker. What the hell is going on?"

"You're here to help your allies, the Five Dragons, right?" I asked. "You were on the phone with one of their alphas and you heard her get attacked."

He'd been bounding around Torres too fast for it to be obvious that he'd been trying to protect her. And with all the chaos of two packs attacking each other, all anyone could tell was that they were being attacked and needed to have their own claws out or they'd be eviscerated.

Malik looked around the room and hissed. He jerked his head and his pack mates pulled into a tight formation behind him. A few injured were leaning on their fellow wolves.

Torres shifted slower than Malik, but she was more massive and watching the enormous dragon become a petite woman again left me with an odd sense that the world wasn't right. She was naked and didn't seem to care.

Placing her hands on her hips, she whistled and the Five Dragons moved towards her side of the room.

"So, a misunderstanding?" she asked.

"We thought since our alliance was so new, we'd offer our help promptly," Malik said.

"Well good job almost killing your allies," she snorted. Snapping her fingers, a female werewolf appeared with a robe she draped over the alpha. "Tell him about Dieter."

She directed the last at me.

"Dieter is working for the killer," I said.

"What?" Malik said, and Nick turned to me, his eyes wide and lips pressed tight together.

"He showed up here and tried to get the Five Dragons to kill me, but I think his long-term plan was to get them to kill *you*, Malik." I glanced at Nick and shook my head slightly. He narrowed his eyes, but said nothing.

"Where is he?" Malik said. "We have to question him."

Torres turned to look at the two wolves that had been holding him down. They were both injured and whined in submission at her dark gaze.

"He, uh, well, when the wall went down, we, uh," one of them stuttered.

"He escaped," Torres said. "You *let* him escape."

They whimpered.

"Who's the killer?" Malik asked.

"I need to go through my photos," I hedged. "It'll take some time."

"Why was he helping the killer?" Malik said. "It doesn't make sense."

Shrugging, I said, "If the killer threatened to take his life? If the only way out Dieter saw was by handing over other magical creatures?"

Torres was watching me with narrowed eyes and she smirked. "So you lie even to your allies?"

"What's he lying about?" Malik asked.

"Ask him what magical creatures he's concerned about," Torres advised. "And ask him why."

Malik glanced at me, his eyebrow raised. I sighed.

"I'm fae. The killer found the old Windrose and killed him and they gave me the position," I said.

"The what?" Malik said. Around him, the wolves shifted at the mention of my nature. I hoped that their fear would last long enough for Nick and me to escape without any more bloodshed.

"He's the arbiter of justice in the fae world," Torres said. She shook her head. "Even if he knows the killer, he will only bring him to *fae* justice. Not pack justice."

"Not if we find the killer first," Malik said, glaring at me. He pointed at the two women that I'd met the night Dieter had tortured me. "Go find Dieter and find out who he's working for."

"With them," Torres said, pointing to two of her own people.

The small posse left, and I raised an eyebrow. "Good hunting."

"Leave, Windrose, before we decide to keep you here and wring the truth out of you," Torres said, smoke rising from her lips again.

Nick was pulling my arm, and I didn't wait to be told twice. We ran.

CHAPTER THIRTY-TWO

WHEN NICK SAID HIS CAR WAS OUTSIDE, HE MEANT *RIGHT* outside. He'd driven half up onto the sidewalk, and I recognized the area of town we were in as an industrial park halfway between a shopping mall and a freeway overpass. I snorted to see the building labeled as a butcher's. There were assorted other cars parked in the street, clearly SoPa members who'd rushed in to help the Five Dragons, only to end up making the mess worse.

Nick paused next to the driver's door, panting a bit as he dug in his pocket for his keys. His badge swung from his neck, flashing silver in the sunlight.

"You want me to drive?" I asked.

He shook his head. "I got it."

"Okay," I said, sliding into the passenger seat when he unlocked the car. "If you pass out and crash, I'm going to give this whole rescue thing a one-star rating."

"What's the rating right now?" Nick asked, cracking a smile as he slammed the car into reverse, just barely missing a sedan that had pulled in behind him.

He sped off, only slowing when we passed a cop car going in the opposite direction. The car didn't have any lights or sirens going, and I wondered if that was because no one had called the cops on the fight we'd just had, or because the police knew the area was Five Dragons territory and just didn't want to bother with pack violence.

"I was going to give you five out of five, since there was a pretty good chance I was going to get killed by an actual dragon, but you didn't exactly stick the dismount, did you?" I said.

"Everyone's a critic," Nick complained.

"When my life is on the line?" I said. "Yeah, I have some *notes*."

"What's the Windrose?" Nick asked. "She said it like it meant something. Who is he? Why does Jimena Torres think you're him?"

Staring out at San Amaro, I said, "We have to talk about this?"

"Since you're going around telling everyone you're whatever it is, yes," Nick said. "What happened between yesterday and today?"

I winced, and he clearly caught me because he said, "You were *already*—No. Explain."

"The four courts are always fighting over power. And way back before, it was even worse. The sort of wars that destroy kingdoms and leave nothing left behind." I picked at my cuticle, staring down at my fingers to avoid looking up at Nick. "So, they decided to have a mediator, a judge, someone who makes decisions that they all have to abide by. It's important that the judge doesn't come from any one court."

"And you grew up here, so that would make you a good candidate," Nick said.

"Yeah," I said. "I went to visit the Windrose because I had to tell him about Tim, remember? But when I got there, he was dead. The fae kings and queens wanted to fill the position before one of them used it as a chance for a power grab, so..."

"They grabbed the nearest, non-affiliated fae?" Nick said.

"Exactly." I glanced at him, expecting to see anger or irritation, but instead his eyes were half-lidded and he looked like he was about to pass out on the steering wheel. "Hera's daughters, you okay? You sure you don't want me to drive?"

"We're almost there," he said. We were a block away from my apartment, but I kept my eyes on him the whole time, sure we were about to crash and kill ourselves violently.

When he pulled into an empty parking spot against the curb, he sighed, leaning his head forward so that his forehead touched the wheel. I could see his breath coming in short pants. His pallor was almost gray.

"What's going on?" I asked. "This isn't normal exhaustion."

"Magic depletion," Nick said. "I'll be okay after some food."

"Let's get some," I said. "I have a fridge full of it. Between you and Shannon, I was getting a complex about my lack of real food."

Together, we stumbled into the building and then into the elevator. Jeffrey wasn't around. The last thing I needed was him gloating right now. Propping Nick against the elevator wall, I pressed three and the creaking elevator rose. The groaning of the machinery distracted us from conversation.

At my floor, we got out and headed down the hall. I saw Laurel before Nick did and waved at her with the hand I wasn't using to stabilize Nick. She'd been pacing in front of my door, gnawing on her thumbnail. Frowning at us, she took quick steps to get on his other side.

"What happened? Are you okay?" she asked.

"Yeah, we're fine," I said. "What are you doing here? Why didn't you use your key?"

"I wanted to talk to you before you went inside," she said.

I stopped in front of my door, keys held in my fingers. "Laurel?"

"So, we had to get her out of Meadowhaven since the director didn't take my allegations too seriously," Laurel said.

"*Laurel*," I repeated. "What's inside my apartment?"

"I'd take her with me, but I don't have an elevator," she said.

Opening the door, two things struck me. The first was that I no longer had a living room. I had a couch, a desk that Laurel had shoved into the corner, and *Shannon* in a *hospital bed*. She took up most of the room, and at least what little space there was left wasn't taken up by monitors or anything else that beeped or wheezed.

The second thing was the disconcerting image of Shannon, the ghost, standing next to her body, squinting at it, her nose wrinkled. She looked like she wanted to say something, but the whole situation was so far from okay, that I shook my head. With a shrug, she raised both hands and mimed zipping her lips.

When we were teenagers and being annoying, she would actually reach over and pretend to zip our lips shut. It had been horrifying as a sixteen-year-old to have your foster mom do something so juvenile, so at least for me, it had worked.

"I brought food!" Laurel said. She helped me get Nick inside and we squeezed past the bed to let him collapse on the couch. "He doesn't look good, Parker. Is he a cop?"

She was eyeing the badge with a frown. I nodded, "Nicholas King, Laurel Perez, my sister. Laurel, this is Nick. My, uh—" I wanted to say boyfriend, but were we still together? "The guy who rescued me from the Five Dragons."

"The *Five Dragons?*" Laurel hissed. "Athena's *tit*, Parker. You said you were staying out of wolf politics."

"Look, can we do this after he gets fed? He said something about magic depletion," I said. "Where's the food?"

"Kitchen," she said. "Magic depletion? You're going to need more than a sandwich."

Pulling out her cellphone, she texted someone and then leaned over to grab Nick's wrist, taking his pulse while staring at the clock app on her phone. "Let me guess, alchemist?"

"Nicholas *King*," I called from the kitchen.

"Nicholas King," she said, smiling. "Hi, I'm Laurel Perez, the head priestess of the Kitchen Witches of East San Amaro."

"Hi," Nick said, his face waxy, a slight sheen of sweat on his forehead. "Nice to meet you."

"You can't do anything by halves, can you, Parker?" she muttered, grabbing the plate of food I'd prepared. She must have felt really guilty about saddling me with Shannon because she'd brought every type of pastry her shop offered and half the sandwiches on the menu.

Giving the plate to Nick, she hovered her hands over his head, then his chest and traced down his legs. Sucking in a breath through her teeth, she muttered, "You used every single drop. I thought they taught you Kings better than that."

"It was kind of an emergency," Nick said. Some color was coming back into his face and he didn't look quite so gray anymore. His eyes cut to me. "Someone reported a cop was kidnapped. It took a little untangling to realize that it was only a P.I. pretending to be a cop."

"How'd you find me, anyway?" I asked, eating one of Laurel's croissant sandwiches. I was pretty sure she made it with actual manna, but she said it was just homemade aioli.

"Uh, a tracing spell," Nick said. He flushed, his warm brown skin going slightly pink. He looked up at the ceiling, avoiding my eyes.

"Wait, a tracing spell?" I said, eyes narrowed. "What did you have of mine? Did you take my underwear or something pervy?"

"You were in my car," Nick huffed. "I found a few strands of your hair."

Shaking my head, I said, "Pervert. I bet you stole my toothbrush or something."

"You *use* your toothbrush?" Laurel said, doubtfully.

I glanced at her and rolled my eyes. "I *am* an adult, Laurel."

"Sure," she said, eyes on her phone. She texted rapidly, and I glanced back at Nick, nearly dropping my sandwich.

"Jesus Christ," I swore.

Laurel and Nick both frowned at me, the tension in the room

skyrocketing as they looked for whatever danger had set me off. I waved a hand, and they relaxed.

"Mom, you can't do that," I said.

Shannon had stuck her head into Nick's chest, and when I spoke, she yanked herself out and looked at me in surprise. "You called me Mom."

"A slip of the tongue," I said. "Get out of his chest."

"Tell Laurel to make sure she doesn't forget the spices if she's doing a magic smoothie," Shannon said, stepping back from Nick.

Nick's eyebrows were up in confusion and Laurel had that picked-last-for-kickball look that meant she was trying to make the best of a bad situation. "Shannon's here?"

I pointed to the middle of the living room where Shannon had retreated to stand next to her body. Laurel squinted, like she was trying to see, but eventually her shoulders slumped.

"Shannon, your foster mom?" Nick asked. "Oh, yeah, what's up with the body in your living room?"

With his color returning, he was back to being a cop who was actually good at his job. His eyes ran over the whole setup, and he tilted his head, the inevitable question of if she was supposed to *be* here arising. He glanced at me, a frown wrinkling his brow.

"I don't know, ask Laurel. This morning, Shannon was at her very expensive facility and not messing with my Feng Shui." I gestured with my sandwich, a few greens falling out of the croissant before I protectively brought it close again.

"Well, Parker told me that Shannon's night nurse was trying to kill her," Laurel said to Nick. She pointed at the plate in his hands. "Keep eating. So I went to her facility to check, but they don't take the word of incorporeal spirits, so my only option was to take her home with me."

"How did you even get her out of there?" I asked.

"It wasn't a big deal," Laurel said. "I wanted to take her to my apartment, but you can see that would be hard since I don't have an elevator."

"She rented a U-Haul," Shannon said. "Strapped me into it like I was a refrigerator."

"A U-Haul?" I said to Laurel. "And you're always complaining that I'm the irresponsible one. Why'd they even let you take her like that?"

"She's *literally haunting* them, Parker. They'd have helped me put her into a wheelbarrow if it got her off the property." Laurel went into the kitchen and grabbed a bag of artisanal potato chips.

"Wait, how did you know her night nurse was trying to kill her?" Nick said. "Why didn't you report it to the police?"

"So, a few days ago, I began seeing Shannon's spirit. Ghost?" I said, looking to Shannon, who shrugged. "Anyway, she told me."

"No," Nick said. "I'm done. You're telling me that you're seeing your foster mom's ghost." He looked at the body and amended, "Spirit. Who told you that her night nurse is trying to kill her. Why?"

"Some sort of cult," I said. "I'll be honest, with everything else going on, I figured I'd get to the cult thing when Shannon wasn't in danger anymore."

"If she's killing residents, then the police should investigate," Nick said stubbornly.

"Can we have a time out?" I said. "Laurel, Shannon can't stay here. I'm getting evicted."

"No!" Laurel pointed at me. "*You* have a time out. You're getting evicted? Explain! And since when do you have a hot alchemist just chilling on your couch? And what's this nonsense about the Five Dragons? I mean, SoPa is one thing, but I don't even like *driving* through Five Dragons' territory. Do I need to be setting up wards? I should call the coven."

When she paused for breath, I waited to see if she had any more hysteria to get out. She shook her head, lips tight.

"Okay," I said. "So, this is Nicholas King. He's almost dead on my couch because a few days ago, he asked me to look into a serial killer draining paranormals of their magic. I went sniffing around and it turns out that Dieter, the SoPa I was looking into for work, was feeding the serial killer fae. Then he tried to get the Five Dragons to kill me before I could expose him to Malik. And you probably don't need wards because one of the Five Dragons alphas let us go, so I think we're good."

"So, Mister Hot Cop decided to rescue you out of the goodness of his heart?" Laurel said, raising an eyebrow. "Really?"

She squinted at Nick and crossed her arms.

"I don't know, we *were* dating for a while," I admitted.

"Can we talk about that later?" Nick asked. He looked better, but still a little like a half-drowned kitten. "Maybe with less family in the living room?"

"I mean, it's up to you if you want a kitchen witch thinking you did me wrong," I said. "I don't even like for her to think I was the one who left the toilet seat up."

Someone knocked on the door and Laurel shuffled around Shannon's bed, opening the door before I could warn her to check who it was first. On the other side was a petite redhead who I immediately recognized as the witch gunning for Laurel's job.

She grinned at Laurel and the expression was a far cry from the Machiavellian menace that I'd seen at the coffee shop. It was, instead, a little girl looking into a toy store. Hopeful and yearning all at once. *Oh.*

"Thanks, Kalie," Laurel said. She reached out and clasped Kalie's hand, causing the other woman to blush hot. Glancing down at their entwined fingers, she tightened her grip and bit her lip.

"Do you need help?" Kalie asked.

"No, no," Laurel said. "My brother can handle this."

"You're sure?" Kalie said.

"Yeah, I'll call you later," Laurel said. She held the door open and watched Kalie walk down the hall.

I exchanged a look with Nick. He seemed mostly confused,

but when I wiggled by eyebrows, he shrugged. The man, for all his good qualities, didn't know Laurel like I did, though.

She closed the door and slid the chain back on. Her smile was one of those sappy sweet expressions that deserved a lot of ribbing, so I obliged.

"Just to be clear, you're giving me crap about my love life, and you *slept* with your arch-nemesis?" I said.

"You," Laurel said, eyes narrowing, "are the *worst*."

CHAPTER THIRTY-THREE

LAUREL STALKED OFF TO THE KITCHEN TO MAKE HER MAGIC smoothie, taking the reminder of herbs with an eye roll. "I'm not a *novice*, Shannon," she muttered.

Nick was slowing down his eating, his eyes sharp and alert, even if he still didn't look like he could lift much more than his head. I settled next to him, my own sandwich platter balanced on my stomach. For a while, we ate in silence, interrupted only by the click of my stove being turned on and Laurel's mutterings about the state of my herb collection.

"You wanted to talk about what happened yesterday?" I asked.

Nick nodded. "I thought about what you said. And I realized that if you're going to keep trying to push me away, then I have to assume you don't want to be with me. But if you're just doing it because you're scared that I'm going to leave you? I'm not."

Swallowing the suddenly dry sandwich, I asked, "What does that mean?"

"You're fae. You're the Windrose, whatever that means. You're a foster kid, and I bet you don't think that you can be in a relationship because you think that everyone who you meet is going to leave you." He spoke with the confidence of someone used to being right about this sort of thing. He was a cop, and it looked like his ability to read situations was as good as mine.

I stuffed the rest of the sandwich in my mouth to avoid answering him.

"I like you," he said. "I want to make this work. But, like I said, if what you really want to tell me is that you *don't* like me, then I hope we can still work together because clearly someone needs to keep an eye on you before all the other packs in San Amaro kidnap you just to see what the big deal is."

The sandwich was flavorless, and I chewed and swallowed, the feeling of food scraping down my dry throat. My mind was racing. What *did* I want?

The answer was painfully clear: Nick. But I wanted him so badly that the idea of him leaving me, the idea of opening myself up when it wasn't to win an argument, left me feeling like I'd taken a knife to my own gut.

"Okay," I said.

"I don't know what that means," Nick confessed, his brows tight. "Does that mean you just want to be co-workers?"

"I'd like to try a relationship," I said. "Try the boyfriend thing now that you know everything."

"Do I know everything?" Nick asked. He gave me a searching look, and I nodded. "Alright. Yeah. Let's try it, then."

He leaned over, our sandwich plates clinking together, and pressed his lips against mine. They were dry, like he was dehydrated, but he smiled into the kiss and I wanted more.

In the kitchen, Laurel turned on the blender. I pulled away from Nick and glared at her, ignoring her sugary sweet smile. "Get it," she mouthed, the sound impossible to hear over the roar of the machine.

"So, who's the serial killer?" Nick asked.

I thought about obfuscating, doing the tap dance I was used to to keep everyone at arm's length and me with all the information. Instead, I said, "Mark Woolworth."

"The professor?" Nick said. "How do you know?"

"I heard him ordering around Dieter, and also Dieter was tracking Acacia. I thought it was just because Woolworth was worried she'd file a complaint about him, but Dieter knew I was a fae," I said. It seemed tenuous, but I saw the pieces clicking for Nick, too. "And *no one* knows I'm a fae. I think Woolworth must have given him something that smelled like fae, which is how he was tracking us."

"We could find out if there's any evidence he was tracking Tim, too," Nick agreed. He accepted a glass of smoothie from Laurel with a nod. "Why now, though? Why start killing like this now?"

For a while, we mulled over it, and then I stood, picking up the textbook off my desk. I paged through until I found the photo showing the ancient spell. Moving back to the couch, I handed it over to Nick.

"Look familiar?" I said.

"This is really close to the one we found on the incubus," he said. He thumbed through the rest of the book, stopping when he got to the author's picture on the final pages. "Woolworth. Related to our serial killer?"

"His mother," I said. "He took over her class when she died a few months ago. Maybe he didn't know about the spell until now?"

"So," Nick rolled his eyes up to the ceiling, thoughtfully. Laurel cleared her throat, and he took another sip of the smoothie. "Mom dies, and he's distraught. Maybe he goes through her research and discovers the actual spell used? And, what? Tries it?"

Picking up another sandwich half, I took a large bite and thought about it for a minute. "He tries it on what, though? It's a huge leap to go from academic study of magic to murder."

"There must be something we're missing," Nick said.

"I didn't know Professor Woolworth even had a son," Laurel

said. She'd collected the leftover smoothie in a second glass and pried the remaining sandwiches out of my hands, replacing it with the drink. Standing over me, she watched until I took an unhappy sip.

Of course it was delicious, Laurel had made it. Still, I preferred the sandwiches over the slightly grainy texture of the drink. "Do I want to know what's in this?"

"Something that's good for you," she said. "Don't think I can't see that your magic is dangerously low, too."

"You didn't even check me," I said. She gave me a flat look and sitting on her hospital bed, next to her body, Shannon was giving me the exact same one. "I'm feeling very attacked here."

"We should check his house," Nick said. "Maybe we can even catch him there."

"He knows we're after him. Dieter would have run to him," I said. "Where else is he going to go? The SoPa and the Five Dragons want his head."

"We can still check it out," Nick said, giving me an arch look. "I'll call my captain to get an address."

He tried to stand up and Laurel shook her head, shoving him back down with one hand. "You're going to rest. Maybe even take a nap. You're lucky you didn't go into shock."

"Are you sure that you're his sister?" Nick said. "I don't think I've ever heard Parker sound that responsible."

"Foster sister," I said.

Nick settled back and finished his smoothie, handing over the empty glass when Laurel gestured and accepting his sandwiches in return. "Tell me exactly what you heard. I want to try to get a warrant."

I rolled my eyes. "Can't we call it a wellness check? Maybe see if we don't hear some screams when we get there? I can throw my voice really well."

Granted, it took a bit of magic and convincing the air that the vibrations had come from the other side of the door, which wasn't a big deal.

"No," Nick said, his lips pulled down slightly in the corner. "We have to do this by the book. This guy is a serial killer. If he gets off because we didn't do things right, then that's more dead people on our hands."

"God, the book, the book. I think you love the book more than me," I complained, hiding my smile in my glass. I'd met a lot of cops in my time in the system, and it was rare to find an honest one who actually cared about the people he was supposed to be protecting and serving. Most just wanted things to be easy, even if that meant that they weren't following the rules they enforced.

Laurel looked between us, a smirk on her face. She raised an eyebrow, and I shrugged. Okay, so maybe I liked him a lot. Hex me.

"I was... uh..." The conversation I'd heard had been from when I was breaking the laws that Nick held so dear. Pulling back my shoulders, I tried again. "I was on UCSA's campus when I saw Woolworth. Dieter came by and Woolworth got really pissed. He didn't want them seen together and told Dieter that he shouldn't come back unless he had 'something' for him. I thought he meant drugs, but now I'm thinking he meant another fae."

Nick nodded, writing on a notepad.

"Seems suspicious," he agreed. "Not enough to get a warrant."

"You're just going to let him go?" I said, narrowing my eyes.

"No," Nick said. "Of course not. I trust your judgment. If you think he's the guy, then we put on the pressure. But we just can't search his place unless he lets us in."

"What's the likelihood that a guy who's killed five people is going to just let us in?" I said. "This is a fishing trip. He's going to attack us."

"If he attacks us, then we definitely have a reason to detain him and search his place," Nick said.

I grinned. "Okay. I see what you're thinking."

"I'm not thinking anything," Nick said, frowning. "I'm telling you how the law works."

"Sure," I said, tapping my nose. It seemed to make him even more irritated, and he began listing all the different legal ways that you could search someone, and explaining them to me. It was kind of adorable.

"I'll leave you guys to it," Laurel said. "If I think of anything else, I'll text you."

"Thanks, sis," I said.

"Parker Ferro," she said. "Dropping all the family titles today."

Sliding her bag onto her shoulder, she leaned over and kissed my cheek. "Be careful. Call me if you need backup. And both of you keep eating. I'm going to send over another bag of food. Eat all of it."

"Yes, ma'am," I said. "We won't even leave a single crumb."

After she shut the door, I looked over at Shannon and sighed. "What are we going to do about you?"

"It's not ideal," Nick agreed. "But you can keep her here until the end of the case at least."

"Yeah," I said. "Well, about that. I really am getting evicted."

"What?" Nick said, sitting up. He frowned down at me. "Why?"

"That's not important," I said. I didn't want to get into the mess that was the job I'd done for Derek McCallum and how it had left me broke, angry, and ready for revenge. "I'm just not sure how long she can stay here."

"You'll figure it out, kiddo," Shannon said. "I believe in you."

Nick was frowning. "I thought we said no secrets. You *just* told me I knew everything."

Groaning, I dragged a hand through my hair. "Fine. Okay. No secrets. The job I did for McCallum ended badly. You knew that. I lost everything in my savings and then some. What I had left, I had to use to pay for Shannon's facility. So, no rent, no apartment."

At the mention of McCallum's name, Nick's nostrils flared.

"See?" I said. "This is why I didn't want to bring it up and ruin a perfectly good evening."

"The perfectly good evening where I'm recovering from magic depletion and you're looking half dead?" Nick said.

"Okay, well, I resent that," I said. "I am a paragon of beauty."

Some of my magic was returning, and I put up a glamour, the sort that fae were known for. I couldn't hold it long, but when Nick looked over at me, he looked struck. Shocked.

I'd turned my skin from California-tanned into a golden lustre that made it look like I'd bathed in body glitter. My lips glistened like I was wearing shiny lip gloss. The ears were easy because everyone thinks that fae have pointed ears straight out of Lord of the Rings, so I'd done those, with several silver rings lining the cartilage. My eyes were the crowning glory, though.

They'd always been blue, a washed-out sky blue that one of my lovers told me made him think of long summer days. But with the glamour I deepened the color, pushing the blue as far as it could go until they were the color of a sapphire ring. Then I told the color to shift so that the blue was never quite the same each time you looked into my gaze. It was the aurora borealis of eyes.

Nick reached out and brushed a thumb across my cheekbone, his mouth hanging open slightly.

"What is this?" he asked.

"A glamour," I said. It was a familiar look, one that I'd worn nearly my entire time in the Far Realm.

"I like how you were," he said. "I like how you look on your own better."

I felt the words in my chest. Dropping the glamour, I watched Nick's expression go from patient to affectionate as he leaned close and pressed a kiss to my cheek. His lips were warm. When he spoke, his breath tickled my skin.

"Much better."

"You don't like the full get up?" I asked. "Most people are attracted."

"I like the look of you right now," he said. "If you want to play dress up, I can get into it, but the whole look isn't what I got into this for."

"What'd you come for?" I asked.

"Obviously the guy who likes handcuffs and can't keep anything in his refrigerator."

Shoving him, I laughed. Someone knocked at the door and when I checked the peephole, it was a guy wearing one of Laurel's Cafe shirts. He handed over two enormous paper bags of food and then offered over a cooler filled with the expensive pressed juices that Laurel sold.

When I got back from putting everything in the kitchen, Nick was on the phone with his captain, telling him our theory about Woolworth.

"Yeah, I understand," Nick said. "I agree. But we need an address for that." He listened for a moment and nodded, "Yes, that's a good idea. Tomorrow morning." After a beat, he said, "Okay, thanks, Captain." Hanging up, he grimaced at me. "The captain doesn't think that it'll be enough for a warrant, either."

I swore. "So, our plan is just to hope that he lets us into his house?"

"We'll go over tomorrow. The captain is going to have some people on standby, but we can't depend on them because they'll be a few minutes away. He's sending over Woolworth's address now," Nick said. "He thinks Woolworth wouldn't kill us because so far he's only been killing paranormals."

"Of which, I am one," I pointed out. "And if Woolworth was powerful enough to take down the Windrose, I'm not really eager to face him on my own. Can't backup wait around the corner or something?"

"The captain wants us to treat it like we don't know he's the killer," Nick said.

"And a raid team of cops would give it away." I looked up to the ceiling. "Okay, I mean, it feels like a bad plan."

"Hey, you think we can't handle him? We just fought off two of San Amaro's top wolf packs," Nick said. "We know who he is, we know what he's capable of. We've got this."

I shook my head, "And here I thought *you* were the responsible one."

CHAPTER THIRTY-FOUR

THE NEXT DAY, AFTER A BREAKFAST THAT APPEARED VIA another employee of Laurel's, we got in Nick's car and headed to Woolworth's address. Nick had drawn an alchemist circle on both of our chests and powered them both up with his returning magic. When asked what the circles did, he said they were lower profile than a bulletproof vest.

Nick was putting on his holster and gun when his cell phone rang. After checking the number, he rolled his eyes and shook his head. Still, he answered it.

"What is it, Sam?" Whoever was on the other end spoke rapidly, and I took my time packing my bag, trying to eavesdrop out of habit.

Nick sighed. "He's probably just out. You know how he is. If you're that worried, call 911. I'm in the middle of a case, but I'll call you this afternoon if he hasn't shown up."

He hung up and slid the phone back into his pocket.

"Everything okay?" I asked.

"Yeah, that was my dad's secretary. He came to town with my uncle for the conference. Apparently, my uncle went out this morning and hasn't come back yet, and Sam's worried he won't make his presentation this afternoon." Nick checked his gun and then clipped it into his holster.

"You aren't worried?" I asked.

"My uncle can handle himself and Sam worries too much," he said. "I'm actually surprised my dad sent him to the conference. It's not really his thing. Even when I was little, he'd disappear for years and then he'd show back up. He wasn't interested in the family legacy until I was in junior high."

"If you're sure," I said.

"Yeah," he said. "Let's go find a murderer."

Woolworth's neighborhood was in one of the older areas of San Amaro. The houses were all Spanish style, with white walls and red ceramic roofs. Large, heavy trees lined the streets, giving the impression that we were in a whole different century. Most of the houses were set back from the street, so when we parked, we had to walk up a couple flights of stairs to get from the sidewalk to the front door.

There was magic on the way up the steps. I could feel myself brushing against it like stepping through a cobweb. It didn't feel anything like the hungry, sharp magic that I'd activated in the morgue. If I had to put it into words, it reminded me of Shannon's magic. Warm, friendly, familiar.

"Ready?" Nick said.

I nodded. He brought up his hand and pounded heavily on the door.

For a moment, there was silence, the dark wooden door standing still. Then it opened a crack and an older man poked his head out. His eyes were sleepy, and there was a crust of salt on his cheeks and beard. By the stiff quality of his graying hair, I pegged him as a surfer.

"Can I help you?" the man asked.

Nick glanced at me, but I shook my head. Whoever this was, he wasn't our professor. Maybe Woolworth had a partner?

"SAPD. We're here looking for Mark Woolworth," Nick said.

He pulled out his badge and flashed it. The man held out his hand and Nick passed over the badge for examination.

Looking at the guy, he fit into the counter culture role, up to and including questioning all authority. Returning Nick's badge, the guy sighed and ran a hand through his hair.

"Mark isn't here right now," he said. "Is everything okay?"

"Yes," Nick said immediately. "We're here because one of his seminar students was killed, and we were hoping to ask him a few questions."

"Come on in," the guy waved.

We stepped in as he walked through the house, passing an open sitting room and heading into a remodeled kitchen. He leaned against the granite countertop and served himself some coffee. "You want any?"

Nick shook his head. I was curious why we were getting the royal treatment from someone who was clearly suspicious of police out of habit.

"You think he had something to do with the death?" the man asked.

"Why do you ask?" Nick said.

Sighing, the man scrubbed his hand through his hair and examined his cup of coffee. "He's an odd kid. When he moved back, Adelaide thought maybe he was trying to mend fences."

"You were Adelaide's boyfriend?" I asked.

"Partner," he said. "For almost ten years now. Mallory Silva."

I leaned against the counter across from him. "You don't think he came home to make peace."

Nick stood back and I could feel him scanning the room, looking for any clue that would give us a legitimate reason to conduct a search.

"I think he came back because the job was here," Mallory said. "There's not many places hiring magical studies professors these days, and Mark got a junior position on staff."

"So he and Adelaide didn't get along?" I asked.

Mallory shook his head. "No. They had a falling out before I met her and barely talked."

"What was the fight about?" I asked.

Mallory sighed. "Magic. He blamed her for being such a weak alchemist. I don't know why he thought it was her fault."

"What happened after he moved back?" I asked.

"It was tense for a while," Mallory said. "Especially when he'd pick at her for doing witchcraft. She was between covens, and so she'd do solo practice out in the backyard."

He jerked his thumb towards a giant bay window that over-looked a garden. It was overgrown, full of herbs and bushes that would make any kitchen witch happy. You could probably do almost anything with what was back there.

"He's still living here?" Nick clarified.

"Yeah," Mallory said. "He hasn't said anything, but he inher-ited her half of the house. I offered to buy him out, but he's been... odd since she died."

"What do you mean?" I asked. I let myself slip just a little bit. Part of obligation magic is that you have to know what people want, what their deepest desires are. I knew that this guy's deepest desire was to have someone listen to him. It took just a brush of my magic and he was pouring out the entire story.

"Adelaide had been sick for a while—cancer, the big C, you know," he said. "But she was on the mend. She'd just finished another round of chemo and was home on bed rest. I was here most of the time—I sold my company and retired a few years ago —but I had to go out to get this bone broth that she'd fallen in love with."

I waited, the listening ear that he craved. No judgment for how much he disliked his stepson, no commentary, just a vast cavern of listening. Behind me, I could feel Nick's confusion. He wanted to ask questions, but the web of listening I was casting only let him hear.

"Mark was home, and I asked him to look in on her and make

sure she didn't need anything. He said he would and when I got back... well, he said he went in to check on her, and she'd passed away. He even called 911, but because Adelaide had a DNR, they said to just call the mortuary." Mallory sighed and rubbed at his face. "It's not that I don't believe him. The doctor warned us she was going to be weak and there could be complications. But... he had black marks on his fingers like he'd been using an alchemist's marker. I didn't see any circles, so it might have just been for work, for one of the classes he was teaching. Still... I can't stop thinking about it. And then, he started keeping his room locked. He bought a new lock and didn't give me the key. I'm worried about him. I think maybe he saw something when Adelaide died, and it changed him."

He stopped and for a moment, the kitchen hummed with the silence. I broke it. This poor schmuck didn't even know that he owed me now. I could feel the thin ribbon of obligation tying us together. There was another one, too, faint enough that I almost missed it.

Woolworth. He owed me. Not a lot, barely even a favor, but enough. What had I done that was a gift for him?

"Do you mind if we take a look in his room?" Nick asked. If we got the homeowner's permission, we were golden. We were *legal.*

For a moment, Mallory was silent. He was going to say no. He might not like Mark, might even think that he had something to do with Adelaide's death, but he didn't want to think of himself as a guy who would give up his stepson.

In my head, I swore. We were about to lose him. Angrily, I pressed my knuckles into the countertop and without looking at either Mallory or Nick, I said, "You should let us see his room. It would help."

With the words, I pulled on the obligation and felt it unravel under the pressure of the request. Slowly, Mallory nodded. "Yeah. If it would help you."

His confusion was apparent in the frown on his face, and he said, "This way. I want to help you."

He said the latter to himself, as he led us up a staircase and down a long hall. Nick came up beside me, his eyes narrowed. "What did you do?"

"He thinks Mark did something," I murmured. "All I did was nudge him."

"Like you nudged me to hit myself?"

"Maybe," I said.

"That's illegal," Nick said. "That's not consent, Parker."

I ignored him, my back stiff. I knew. I knew it wasn't right, but it was in my nature. I was just as bad as the rest of the fae, and now I had proof. When it came down to it, I'd do what it took to win.

At the door to a bedroom, Mallory stood back, his mouth tight. He pointed at the deadbolt above the handle.

"See?" he said.

Nodding, Nick pursed his lips. He tried the knob, and it easily turned. My stomach tightened. Glancing at me, Nick's brows were drawn together and I could read the uncertainty in his gaze. It was too easy.

Still, he nudged the door open, careful not to step inside. There weren't any obvious alchemy circles on the floor, which was bare wood like the rest of the house. The room itself was chaos.

Books were stacked everywhere, and what had once been a pleasant blue wall, perfect for a guest bedroom, was covered with papers. Woolworth had hung a whiteboard on the wall next to the bed, and there were drafts of circles on it, the same symbols repeating in different patterns. I glanced at Nick, but his eyes were darting all over the room, looking for any danger.

We were both on edge, it seemed, after the attack at Tim's place. Mallory pushed past us, and Nick grabbed at his arm a second too late. He stepped into the room, his eyes wide. He spun in a slow circle and said, "It wasn't like this a few weeks ago. Before he put the lock on it. It wasn't like this at all. This is—"

He shook his head and pushed his toes into a stack of papers. "I don't even know what this is."

"Sir," Nick said, his commanding voice on. "I'm going to need you to step out of the room."

"Oh," Mallory looked around again and shuffled out, his socks silent on the wood. "Of course."

He covered his mouth with his hand and leaned against the hallway wall.

Nick glanced at me, and I shrugged. There hadn't been any obvious magic when Mallory entered the room. Maybe Woolworth had just left the house too quickly to set up a booby trap.

"When was the last time Mark was here?" I asked. "Exactly?"

"He left last night," Mallory said. "He was here at dinner time, I think."

Deliberately, I took a step into the room, but nothing happened. Pulling out my phone, I started snapping pictures of everything. The whiteboard, papers, the stack of books, all of it recorded on my phone in case we needed it later. Nick followed behind me, pulling a pair of blue gloves out of his jacket pocket.

He snapped them on and then handed me another pair. Juggling my phone, I slid my hand into them and continued recording the room. Most of it looked like variations on what was in the textbook, but some of the books looked old. I picked one up and thumbed through it.

"That's one of Adelaide's research texts," Mallory called out. "She had it here on loan, but I know I returned it to the university after she passed. They were supposed to return it to the private collection it had come from."

Woolworth had scribbled notes on the pages. Whatever book Mallory had returned to the collection, Woolworth had either outright stolen it or replaced it with a copy. It looked like the book was written in Latin, and I didn't read it nearly well enough to make out what it said, but the diagrams told a pretty good story. Several circles that were similar to the one we knew were diagrammed on the pages.

The difference seemed to be that unlike modern alchemy circles, these were broken, missing the clean lines that would keep spells contained and magic conserved. Instead, they were messy, half witchcraft, with an uneven split of the words of power across the diagram. I put the book down and picked up another. This one was in English, although it looked over a century old. The typeface made me squint, but I got the gist that it was an apocryphal alchemy text which posited that anchor points could be used to do more than maintain a spell's integrity and limit its scope.

Nick was methodically going through the papers on the wall, the grooves on his forehead deepening into a frown that made my stomach clench.

"What?" I asked, low.

"He was experimenting," Nick said. "The incubus was the second, and Woolworth drained him on purpose. But, the spell still wasn't right, so he did a different iteration on the vampire. I think it wasn't until he got to the Five Dragons werewolf that he perfected it."

"Who was his first?" I asked, thickening the air so that the sound wouldn't carry to Mallory.

Glancing at the doorway, Nick raised an eyebrow. I shook my head. He shouldn't be able to hear us and with our backs to him, he couldn't read our lips.

Looking at me, his eyebrows up, Nick said, "Adelaide. Although the way he writes about it, it might have been an accident."

"No," I said, using my phone to scratch at my hairline. "No, how do you *accidentally* drain your mother of magic?"

"Practicing one of these ancient spells, bringing it in to the in-house expert," Nick suggested. "It seemed like initially he was just trying to upstage her."

I began snapping pictures of the notes that Nick was referencing, wanting to get as much on camera as possible. A notification popped up on my screen. Skylar was calling.

I swiped it away, only to have a text pop up when the call disappeared.

YOU ARE IN DANGER. CARDS SAY BAD. GET OUT.

A moment later, she texted again.

Are you already dead?

"Uh," I said. "We need to go, Nick."

"What?" He was holding his phone to his ear, I assume calling his captain.

Pushing him in front of me, gathering Mallory along the way, I said, "Move. Now."

The explosion happened as soon as we left the room. Our backs were to it, so neither of us got any protective spell up. We knew exactly who the killer was, and he wanted us to die with that knowledge.

CHAPTER THIRTY-FIVE

Nick's bulletproof-vest spell shielded me some from the initial blast, but it threw me forward into him, the explosion leaving both of us scrambling for more protection. The shrapnel of wood and drywall from the walls, and some extra metal that Woolworth had clearly fashioned into an IED, ate away at the protective circle Nick had drawn on my chest, and I felt the heat of the flames at my back.

When I looked over, Nick's mouth was moving, but all I could hear was ringing in my ears. He rolled over and checked on Mallory. I struggled to my feet, pulling the air in tight around me, weaving as much protection as I could from it. Then I started trying to contain the fire that had resulted from the blast. I stepped in close and pulled all the air out of the room.

Fire needs air. Drop a lid on an oil fire in a pan and suddenly you just have a charred dinner and a screaming fire alarm. But air is hard to control. I could pull it away from the flames for maybe a couple of seconds. I had to hope that was enough.

Digging deep, I wondered how much magic I had left. Laurel's smoothie and the endless supply of her delicious sandwiches had helped refill some of my magic, but I didn't have the reserves I was used to.

A whirlwind began surrounding me, pulling all the air from the bedroom. The flames flickered and then subsided. Out. I sighed in relief.

Releasing the air, I took a step closer to the bedroom, wanting to make sure. Nick grabbed me and pulled me behind him, dropping what looked like a quarter on the ground. A shield shimmered into existence, Nick feeding it with his green magic, gasping for breath and going to one knee at the drain.

Another explosion rocked the house, and this time I got a front-row seat to what we'd survived. It looked like the entire floor was blowing up, the wood splintering, and now I could see what Woolworth had done. He'd made his circle out of metal and somehow placed it underneath the wood. The spell was literally tearing itself apart, exploding as sloppy spellwork released the magic it contained.

My expertise was in fae magic and witchcraft, not alchemy spellwork, but I could tell that it was going to keep exploding until the entire circle destroyed itself and demolished the house. Something in the room moved.

The closet door burst open and a werewolf shoved out, scrambling over the spellwork, his paws getting burned and his body taking the brunt of the next assault. I could see the metal tear through him, revealing a bloody ribcage. He yelped, but kept moving until he was right at Nick's shield.

Nick wavered. The wolf pawed at the shield and I put a hand on Nick's shoulder. Drawing on the air again, I shoved as hard as I could, creating a jet stream that forced the explosion away from us just long enough for Nick to open the shield and let the wolf past.

It collapsed on the other side and I looked down. Nick's teeth had bitten down hard on his lip, leaving a thin trail of blood down his chin. He couldn't hold out much longer.

The explosion blasted Nick's shield again, and I did the math. I couldn't carry both the wolf and Mallory. If Nick depleted his magic again, I'd have to save all three of them. No.

There had to be a way to disrupt the spell before it ate itself and left us buried in rubble. I reached out and listened. The circle was made out of pure iron.

It was thinner than I'd thought. He hadn't had to set it *under* the floor, just slightly hammered into it, an inlay of metal that had been hidden by all the books and papers and a now burned rug. I woke the iron with a hint of my magic, the infusion causing another explosion. Closing my eyes, I spoke to the iron.

I reminded it how tired it was, that it wasn't meant to deliver magic. Iron is dangerous to fae because of how much it drains magic, sucks it up like a sponge absorbing water. But then that magic just sits there until it's reabsorbed by the earth or fades from existence.

The iron remembered when it had been in the ground and exchanging magic with the world around it.

I held it and then gave it away. The metal sighed. *My purpose was to be a container.*

"You weren't meant for spellwork," I reassured it. Maybe that was part of why Woolworth had chosen iron. It contained vast amounts of its own magic, but couldn't move magic the way alchemy circles should.

No. The iron agreed.

"So, you could stop," I suggested. "Before you're fractured completely. Just let the magic go."

The iron considered it. Most of it was still in a circle, which meant that the magic it contained and the extra that Woolworth had added to activate the spell was sloshing around in it, a powder keg surrounded by matches.

What would take the magic? The iron asked.

It should go straight into the earth, where it would be reabsorbed, but I could tell the iron didn't want to poison the ground with whatever Mark had put into it. The well of my magic was empty, and I'd been trained first as a warlock. I knew how to take magic that wasn't mine and use it.

"Here," I said, reaching out. "I'll take it."

The iron reacted slowly, sending out a tendril of magic, and I remembered how Shannon had taught me to trade magic. At the time, I'd been giving her mine, since I had too much of it and not enough control. From the other end, accepting more magic than you knew what to do with was terrifying. All over again, I appreciated how she'd never once flinched away from me, even though I must have given her nightmares.

I pictured the magic coming towards me like a thread being spun onto a spindle. Small at first, but growing larger, I contained it in myself. My reserves filled, storm water reaching the floodgates. Still, I accepted more.

Mark's touch was a dark blot marring the pure white energy that the iron had contained before he welded it into his circle. I felt the iron wavering, the explosions faltering as it ran out of the fuel that was driving them. Finally, it was quiet.

Nick's shield was flickering, and I said, "It's okay."

With a gasp, a drowning man having finally found something to cling to, he dropped the shield, and his forehead bumped the floor. I felt overfull, like I was inflated with too much air. The magic had refilled me, but beyond what I thought I could hold.

How was Mark holding onto five people's magic at the same time? I searched for his poisonous darkness and wrapped my hand around it. I wanted to drain it into the earth, but that would do exactly what the iron hadn't wanted to.

Instead, I used it, pushing the magic to wake a tree I could see from the window. The tree blossomed, purple flowers bursting into bloom. It felt foreign, but I used the magic to grow the tree, adding nearly a full foot to its height. Using his magic felt like crying fire. It burned and dried me out. I felt filthy.

When I'd used all of his venomous power, I collapsed next to

Nick. I hoped that filtering the magic through the tree would be an antidote, and that I wouldn't be pouring the poison directly into the earth. Nick turned his head, eyes red.

"You should call the captain," I said. "This is a mess. Is this how all your dates go?"

He grunted a laugh.

"How about when this is all done, we go for dinner in L.A.?" he asked. "Somewhere no one's trying to kill us?"

"Yeah," I agreed. "Sounds good. You're buying, rich guy."

Below us, the door burst open, and I heard shouting. The cavalry had arrived, even without being called. Just to be safe, I laced my hands behind my head.

Forcing himself up, Nick answered the shouting voices. "Up here! Three civilians, all injured. We need paramedics."

"Hey," I said. "I'm fine."

"And I'll believe that when you've been checked out by a medical professional," Nick said. He greeted the cops as they came up the stairs with a warning. "Stay out of the room until it's been checked out by the alchemist on staff."

Black tactical gear and enough guns to take over a small government surrounded us. Nick's captain appeared, and I sat up, watching with interest as a thin woman approached from behind him.

"What's it look like?" she asked Nick. Her voice held the sort of respect that I'd expect from an alchemist addressing a King.

He started to push himself up against the wall, but clearly thought better of it and slid back down to the floor. "He had an unstable circle built into the floor. It reacted when we left the room and caused several explosions."

Then he looked at me. He clearly wasn't sure how to explain what I'd done. I rubbed a hand over my face and said, "I was trained as a witch, so I drained off most of the magic, and sent it back into the earth."

"You what?" Nick and the other alchemist gawked.

"That was the stupidest, most dangerous—" Nick said.

"How were you able to do that? That shouldn't be possible, a circle is self contained when it's set to run without an alchemist present—" the alchemist said.

"Zahide," Captain Tate said. "Go check and make sure the room is safe to enter."

As she walked past us, I could see she'd covered every inch of her clothes in circles. She activated five before approaching the doorway.

"You took the spell's magic?" Nick said. "That was so dangerous. You don't know what could have happened. You could have *blown yourself up.*"

"But I didn't," I said. "You alchemists always think that the worst is going to happen if you even touch someone else's magic. I'm fine."

Tightening his lips, Nick shook his head. Paramedics finally arrived and immediately began working on Mallory and the werewolf. Mallory was coming to, but the wolf was still unconscious.

"This is a mess," Nick muttered. "Who is this Woolworth guy, anyway?"

I pointed at a picture on the wall behind him. "That guy."

It was a picture of three people, Mark in a graduation robe framed on both sides by Adelaide and a very familiar alchemist. He was the one I'd seen at Acacia's hotel, the one in the Alchemist's Society. For a moment, Nick craned his neck, then pushed up and inspected the photo. He huffed out a breath.

"That's my Uncle Theo," he said. "I remember he had a kid, but I've never met him."

"Wait," I said, holding up a hand. "So, Mark Woolworth is a member of the King family?"

"I guess," Nick said, drawing out the word. "But I've never heard anyone mention him by name. And you said that we'd trained together? Or there was a photo of us together? I mean, I probably would have remembered meeting my *cousin.*"

I watched the paramedics calling for a shifter ambulance. The wolf moaned.

"Unless that was why Woolworth was pissed at his mom? He should have inherited all that legendary King power," I said. Nick threw me an annoyed look. "And instead he's left with dregs. Dad doesn't even recognize him to the rest of the family."

Slowly, Nick nodded. "That makes sense."

I squinted at the photo. "Uncle Theo isn't the one who's missing, is he?"

Nick's eyebrows shot up. "Yes. He is." Pulling out his phone, he tried a number, but it wasn't picked up. He frowned and scrolled to a new contact. "Sam. Did you find Theo? Okay, I need you to listen carefully. You need to call the police. Now. Tell them he's missing, and that I told you it's involved with a Paranormal Crimes case."

He hung up and began texting, his eyes on his phone.

"Who're you texting?" I asked.

"Everyone in Paranormal Crimes," he said. "One of them has to be free to track down Theo before—"

"Listen," I said. "I've been thinking about everything and I couldn't figure out what he was doing. So, he collects this power. Makes it his. Why? To what end?"

"Maybe he just wants to be the strongest," Nick said. "Be as strong as any of us Kings."

"Maybe. But how does he *prove* that?" I waited for the beat to sink in. "What if he calls up one of those demons from the demon realm? You said that would take a storehouse of power. No better way to prove himself as the most powerful guy in the room than to summon one without breaking a sweat."

Nick was frowning, his head tilted down. "You think that he's targeting the Alchemist's Society meeting tomorrow."

"Yeah, and maybe he wants to make sure your Uncle Theo has a good view of the son he abandoned ascending to the throne," I said.

As a paramedic taped down a bandage, the wolf yelped and transformed back into a naked man. A very familiar naked man.

"Are you kidding?" I muttered.

Dieter Rossi, the guy who wanted me dead more than anyone else in San Amaro, blinked his eyes open, staring at the ceiling in a daze.

"Dieter Rossi," I said. "Will you look at that?"

"You," he growled, but didn't move more than a twitch as the paramedic began his examination again now that he was fur-less. "Why can't you just die?"

"I'm that kind of guy," I reassured him. "Hard to kill. God-like, someone might call me."

"Cockroach," Dieter countered. Nick snorted, and I glared at him.

"Okay, Dieter," I said. "But you're about to discover exactly how mortal you are. So, good luck surviving when you have two packs coming after you."

"What?" Dieter asked.

"Well, I mean, you aren't even holding him for anything, are you?" I asked Nick.

Still examining the photo, Nick glanced down. "No. Right now, you're considered a victim."

"And you probably don't offer most victims protection in the hospital, do you?" I asked.

"It depends," Nick said. "We might."

"What does it depend on?" Dieter asked.

"Whether you're in danger," Nick said. He looked at me, and I could see his amusement at how easy Dieter was to play. "Are you in danger, Dieter?"

"Yeah, I'm in danger," Dieter said. "Almost got blown up!"

His wounds were healing, the skin closing up, and the two paramedics began talking over their next options.

"Really?" I said. "From who?"

"You just said it, from the SoPa and the Five Dragons." Dieter grinned. "I'll tell you all about them."

"That's nice, but that seems like a job for... oh, man, Detective King, what was the name of that team again? Criminal Gang and Pack Department?"

"Division," Nick corrected. "I could give you their number, but I think they're not too interested in little fish like you, Dieter. What do you even *know*?"

"I know all the drug routes," Dieter said.

"Because *you* were driving them," I said. "I don't think they're going to protect you so they can only arrest the guys who work under you."

Dieter's face was going pale, and I was pretty sure it wasn't from blood loss. "I'm a lieutenant with the SoPa, I'm valuable."

"Yeah," I said. "Keep telling yourself that."

"What do you want to know?" Dieter asked, wincing as the paramedics wiped off his wounds with antiseptic.

"It sure would be useful if you knew something about what happened here," I said. "I mean, if you confessed. Well, then he'd go into protective custody, wouldn't he?"

Nick cocked an eyebrow and pursed his lips. "Yes, if you confess and agree to testify against Mark Woolworth, then we can get you into protection."

"You might even get back into the SoPa's good graces if you help us find the guy who killed off their alpha," I said. "I'd start talking before one of the cops downstairs tips them off to what hospital you're headed to."

"Okay," Dieter said, glaring at us. He lifted a lip in a snarl. "Fine, I'll talk."

CHAPTER THIRTY-SIX

DIETER HAD BEEN MEETING MARK AT AN ABANDONED warehouse in an area of town surrounded by used car lots and small-scale manufacturing facilities. We figured that he wouldn't still be there, but if he'd had to abandon it quickly, then he might have left something behind.

This time, Nick insisted that we wear actual protective gear, so I was standing with my arms out scarecrow-style as Nick strapped a Kevlar vest on me.

"What I can't figure out is why we haven't found Acacia yet," I said, as he double-checked the straps and then smoothed a hand down my arm.

"The girl you were looking for?" Nick asked, distracted as he checked his sidearm. He re-holstered it and asked for the status of the support team on his radio.

They were still a few minutes out and so Nick leaned next to me against the car. He pulled out the snack pack that the department's alchemist, Zahide, had pressed on him. Apparently he hadn't quite gotten to magic depletion for the second time in as many days, but he was close enough that it had taken a lot of sweet-talking before Captain Tate let him lead the search.

"Yeah," I said. "I mean, we found the rest of his victims almost immediately once you knew to look for them. Why haven't we found Acacia's body yet?"

"Maybe he hid it because it might link him to the crime?" Nick suggested. "She *was* his student."

"Yeah, but he left Tim to be a booby-trap for us," I said. "I don't think he cares about subtle right now."

"I don't know," Nick said. "Is there a reason he'd keep her alive?"

I scratched at the back of my neck where the Kevlar vest rubbed. The sun was hot in the afternoon. Even with the ocean so close, summer in Southern California could be unpleasant.

"The summer solstice is tomorrow, isn't it?" I asked.

Nick glanced at me over the rim of his sunglasses. "Am I wearing a black pointy hat? Do I look like a witch who keeps track of that sort of thing?"

"Alchemists don't keep track of the solstices?" I asked, my nose scrunched.

"No," Nick said, shaking his head. "We don't need to. Phases of the moon a *little*, but my father always says that if you're relying on external factors like moon phases or seasons, then your magic isn't strong enough to stand on its own."

"Well, he sounds pleasant," I said. "I'm pretty sure that the solstice is tomorrow. Which means that the Summer Queen will be at the height of her powers tomorrow."

Nick finished off the snack pack and pulled out a second. He offered it over to me and I absently took a couple of pieces from it. They looked like dog kibble, and when I popped them into my mouth, they *tasted* like dog kibble, too.

Spitting them out, I said, "What in Hades' grey hell is that?"

"Regeneration bites," Nick said. He put another handful into his mouth, his teeth crunching down on them. The sound was like a handful of lug nuts in a garbage disposal.

"Let me guess, made by alchemists for alchemists, with everything you need to regenerate your magic and nothing that you don't need like *flavor* or *sugar*," I said.

"They're an acquired taste," Nick said. "My parents' chef makes special ones just for the family, but the mass produced ones will do in a pinch."

"I can't believe I kissed a mouth that put those in it," I said, wiping at my lips as though I could wipe away our kisses.

Nick laughed and then grew quiet. He frowned at a building a few yards away. We'd parked far enough from Mark's warehouse that he shouldn't have noticed us, but it was always possible he was running patrols.

"What is it?" I murmured.

"I think I saw a vampire," Nick said.

"This is the sort of place they like to hang out at," I said. Mostly empty, a few people coming in and out for work, lots of places to hide a body if you needed to.

If a rat could get up on two legs, dress itself like an eighties punk rocker, and talk like it had a mouth full of marbles, people would mistake it for a vampire. Sociopathic, disgusting, and willing to eat anything as long as it could bleed, vampires were my least favorite paranormal creatures.

That didn't mean that they weren't dangerous. One of them, you could fight off. Two and you're breaking a sweat. Once you get to three, you should run.

I watched as the vampire wove towards us. It moved with the slick grace of something not quite from this world. You could blink and it would be a few feet away, like a horror movie in real life.

Laurel had this knack for taking care of attacking vamps. I'd seen her take one down with twine and a pair of scissors. My magic was more defensive, although I'd been learning to use it offensively the past few days.

The SAPD policy was that officers could kill vampires if they were obviously feral and attacking. Most cops used that as an excuse to take potshots at vamps from the safety of their cars. Knowing Nick, he was going to wait until the thing was on top of us, teeth in our necks, before he took out his gun.

"Sir," Nick called out. "I'm going to need you to step back."

He held out his arm, his other hand hovering at his holster.

"Sir, do you understand me?" Nick asked. "Stay back."

The vampire cocked its head. It was wearing a torn black denim jacket and matching pants. The white shirt under its jacket was covered in brown stains I identified as blood. Its face contorted as it came towards us. Fangs snapped together, and it whined, neck curving up.

Slowly pulling out his gun, Nick aimed it at the vampire. "Do not come any closer. Please indicate if you understand."

"*Indicate?*" I said, reaching down to drag my fingers through the dust on the road, waking it up. "What are we, in debate class?"

"Some vampires are still mentally acute, but they've lost the ability to speak," Nick said. "Policy is to give them multiple ways to communicate and not limit it to a verbal acknowledgement."

"You're too nice," I said, pulling more dust towards me, until I held a mini sandstorm in my hand. "Most cops think that as soon as they see fangs, it's open season."

"That's against policy," Nick said, his eyes fixed on where the vamp had crouched down, fingers brushing the ground. The vamp glanced at us through a dark fringe of hair and hissed, teeth snapping.

I raised my eyebrow. "That's cute that you think everyone follows the same rules you do."

The thing was, some vamps could blend. It seemed to depend on how long they'd been alive, but I wasn't an expert. I'd met a couple of vampires who could talk, even hold a full conversation, but for every one who resembled their human selves, there were a few dozen reduced to walking predators. Creatures that moved with the sort of grace that made your brain think something was profoundly wrong.

The vampire scuttled backwards, eyes narrowed and hissing. Nick relaxed. I didn't. I could feel the dust nearby whispering about footsteps. A lot of them were coming this way, and I didn't think it was going to be good for us.

"Nick," I said. "Get ready."

Shoving off the SAPD windbreaker, Nick revealed arms covered in alchemist circles. He activated two, and a shield appeared around us, while the other sent up a bright light that had the vampire wincing back. They don't like bright lights any more than rats do.

The next two vampires came from behind us, but I turned and convinced the concrete to liquify just long enough to sink them ankle deep. Vampires are strong, but not werewolf strong. They'd need time to get themselves out of solid concrete.

Then there were four more that Nick took out with a sleeping spell. I watched him, sweat beading on his forehead. My stomach clenched. We should run, but there was no guarantee that they wouldn't track us or, worse, find some other victim.

"Call for help," I directed. "You're not in any shape to be fighting for too long."

"I'm fine," Nick snapped, but he pulled at the radio on his shoulder and requested backup. A body slammed against the shield and I heard a crack. I spun.

It was one of the vampires I'd sunk in concrete. That was impossible. It should have been stuck there for a while, if it could get out at all. Its bare feet were discolored from broken toes and bones where it had dragged its feet out of its shoes. How the vampire was even walking was a mystery.

"Nick," I said. I sent a jet of air to knock the vampire back. "Something's wrong."

Nick grunted and lifted his gun. He took a breath and spoke a word that lowered the shield around us. Then he was firing at the vampires, bullets flying as true as if they were spelled. Who knows, with Nick maybe they were.

I started whispering to the sand in my hand, reminding it of when it had been in a storm, when it had been drawn from the seaside and drifted over the air.

"If you did that again," I suggested, "you could rip their faces off."

The sand liked the idea of chaos, of bouncing against other grains until it had the momentum to do actual damage. With the wind pushing it, the sand whipped together, and the vampires coming close to me paused, trying to shield their faces.

The sandstorm was merciless, pulling more and more sand from the surrounding areas. Dirt and leaves got caught in the whirling, and two of the four vampires dropped to their knees, hands over their faces. The other two kept coming, even as they closed their eyes, blindly reaching for me, my scent impossible to catch with the wind.

Nick had downed four vamps on his side and was reloading. More were coming, slower now that they saw we weren't easy prey.

I searched underground and found a water pipe that was eager to flow. It burst upwards, sending two vamps flying. Nick picked off another one and listened to his radio.

"We are under attack," he yelled. "ETA?"

The garbled response made him bare his teeth and huff out a breath. "We need to survive until the SWAT team can get here."

A vamp reached me and I shoved a sharp gust his way, toppling him. He opened his eyes, cheeks scratched from the sandstorm. His eyes were dark and clear.

"Help me," he said. "Stop me."

"What?" I said. "What did you say?"

He clawed at his skin, as though trying to get under it. "He won't stop. He did something. I have to do this."

I could see his sharp nails scratching until his arms were

bleeding.

"Who did this?" I asked, anger brewing underneath my lungs. I wanted to scream the words, but that wouldn't help anything.

"Don't know. He gave us food, made us say thank you," the vamp said. He wasn't wearing the costume of a *Lost Boys* extra. Before this he'd been living his life, *blending*.

"Okay," I said. "Hold on."

My new powers still felt foreign, and I didn't know where they began or ended, just that they were more expansive than what I'd had before. The Windrose would have to be able to see obligations. Otherwise, how would he know if his judgements were fair?

I reached out and looked deeper. I could see all the things I usually could, the flow of water under my feet, the soft murmurs of trees and grass. But like the cord that connected the oak tree to the Windrose, I also saw threads leading away from the vamps. *Obligations.*

Nick's gun kept firing, and I saw more and more blink out, their obligations fulfilled by their deaths. Opening my eyes, the vampire in front of me had scratched almost all the way to the bone. He shrieked.

"I am *not* an animal." Which is not something that you hear a vampire say everyday. Sociopathic rats, all of them. Except for *this* one, apparently.

The magic in my blood *sang* and I felt the oak tree growing in my mind, its branches reaching out and behind me, Nick swore.

"Where did this *tree* come from, Parker?"

"I am the Windrose," I intoned. "I am the arbiter of justice and the sword of retribution. The one who tied this obligation around your neck has no rights to do so under fae law. His magic is stolen, his powers counterfeit. I determine you free."

The words took immediate effect and the vampires all sagged. The windstorm stalled with no power to feed it, and sand drifted to the ground. I wasn't sure where I'd found that language, because it sounded fae. *Old* fae.

Behind me, the oak faded as I released the Windrose powers. Nick retreated until he was at my shoulder, his gun still facing the vampires. "What was that?"

"I think it comes with the new job," I said, rubbing a hand over my face.

Most of the vampires were fleeing, their fluid movements looking a lot better when they were moving *away* from us.

"I'd ask where the tree came from, but then I'd have to ask about all the other trees," Nick said. "Is it like an arborist thing? Are we going to have a tree growing in the bedroom?"

Snorting, I said, "This one came from my mind. Or my powers? It has to do with being the Windrose, I think it's what ties the fae and the human realms together."

There was one vampire left, the one who'd fought the obligation with everything he had. His arms were shredded, and I knelt near him.

"You okay?" I asked.

"Thank you," he said, face turned towards the concrete. "Thank you. I couldn't stop myself. I had to kill you."

"Don't sweat it," I said. "I have some experience with the feeling. What's your name?"

"Luciano." He inhaled and then pushed himself up. "I should go. I can hear the police."

"Wait," I said. "Can you tell me where he is? The guy who pulled your puppet strings?"

"Warehouse over there," he pointed.

"Is he alone?" I asked, but Luciano took off, his movements jerky for a vampire. The obligation must have truly messed with him. It had turned him into the animal he clearly spent almost all of his time fighting.

Nick bent down, examining one of the vampires he'd shot. I walked over, unable to shake the sense of unease that was forming in my stomach.

CHAPTER THIRTY-SEVEN

THE SWAT VAN FINALLY CAME INTO VIEW, SURROUNDED BY A phalanx of cop cars. Mark clearly already knew we were here, but if he hadn't, the sirens would have given us away. Leftover sand from the storm I'd pulled together flew up as the vehicles stopped.

I raised my eyebrows when Zahide stepped out of the car, her coat long and stitched with circles. She had already activated a few, and looked around, like she was ready to do some damage.

"Vamps?" she called out.

"Gone," Nick said. He pointed at the corpses on the ground. "We'll need someone to come out for the bodies, though."

"I'll call it in," she said, ducking back into the car.

The SWAT team leader swung down from the van, and he and Nick had a rapid-fire conversation about the specifics of the raid. I squinted at the air, trying to feel anything over towards the building, but it all felt dampened. I couldn't feel anything, no water, no plants. It was creepy.

A cop sidled up to me, his dark blue uniform marking him as a beat cop rather than a member of the SWAT team or the Paranormal Crimes squad with their suits and Kevlar vests. I squinted at him and took a deep breath.

"Thistle," I muttered. "What're you doing here?"

"Lots of action, these police," he hissed. He looked as human as I'd ever seen, his beauty sanded down to near plainness. If I didn't recognize his eyes, he might have fooled me.

As though to show off, he blinked and even those were now plain brown. Zahide looked over at us and I moved so that my body blocked her view of him. Tucking my hand into my pocket, I said, "I'm looking for her daughter, so go back and tell your mistress I'll let her know as soon as I find her."

"That isn't my sole concern," Thistle said. "The Summer Queen grows weak."

"What?" I said. Shaking my head, I looked up towards where the sun was setting, orange painting the blue sky. "It's almost solstice. She should be at her most powerful."

"Should be, yes," Thistle said. "She's locked herself away, surrounded by only her most trusted guards. She is so weak that even a member of the crèche could kill her."

"What's causing it?" I asked. Looking at him, I wondered if Thistle had thought of murdering her, of using her weakness the same way she'd used her predecessor's.

"If it was known, don't you think that it would have been dealt with before this moment?" Thistle asked.

"So, why are you here if she didn't send you?" I asked.

"You are going to rescue Acacia, no? I am here to help." Thistle made a chittering sound and said, "I bring a lot of power, Windrose."

He was trying to *convince* me. This whole getup with the plain face and the forgettable eyes was all to tempt me into letting him help. Shrugging, I said, "Okay. Don't kill any humans, and if I hear that you put anyone under an obligation, I'll nullify it myself."

"That would be unjust," Thistle said, eyes narrowing. "The Windrose is just."

"Well, don't try me," I said. "My justice needs to be calibrated."

With a nod, he blended back into the crowd. Zahide was still watching him, but Nick and the SWAT leader called her attention, and when she looked back for Thistle, it was clear from her frown that she couldn't find him.

Nick came up beside me and I squinted at him. "You gave up on Spellwork and went for your gun pretty quickly."

"I'm fine," he said.

"You're exhausted," I said. With his back to the cops, I was pretty sure that no one could see me. I reached out and brushed a finger up his wrist.

Reflexively, he twitched a smile. "Yeah, but I can keep going. You should stay behind."

"After that display of fae magic? I don't think so," I said.

"They were all under obligation?" Nick said.

"The face-slap thing," I agreed.

"You aren't ever going to let me live that down," he muttered. "Are you?"

"Since I bet you can quote every regulation in the book, but fumbled on the word 'obligation'? Yeah," I said. "You're in for some ribbing."

"We're going to go in behind the SWAT team," Nick said. "Stay close to me and be ready. The only reason you're even here is because you're the fae expert and I convinced my captain that the spell was ancient fae."

"Close to true," I agreed. "I'll be good."

Nick narrowed his eyes, and I put up both hands, aiming for sweetness. Shaking his head, he gestured for me to get into the car. I slid into the passenger seat, picking up my satchel and putting it on my lap. If I was going to be getting into more fights, I'd need to restock my supplies.

Nick started the car, and we followed behind the SWAT van as it pulled out, driving right up to the building they'd identified as Mark's hideout. I'd packed lightly, thinking that we'd only be dealing with booby traps like the ones he'd set for us so far. After those vampires, though, I had a feeling that we were in for a much rougher ride.

The SWAT team flew out of their truck, a synchronized unit of black on black and gear designed for a battle field. As soon as they hit the sidewalk in front of the building, a blue light exploded, crackling. It was a barrier, similar to the one that Nick had used to protect us from the explosion at Woolworth's house.

Nick swore, as three of the ten men went flying. He jerked open his door and he and Zahide were both running for the barrier, calling off the SWAT team members with sharp commands.

Zahide yelled, "It's a Torino Barrier."

Shaking his head, Nick said, "No markers!"

As they discussed, I got out of the car. Whatever was causing the barrier to be so solid had muted all the spirits I could wake with my magic. They were on the other side, and whatever made up the barrier meant that I couldn't reach them.

Looking down, I wondered how far down the barrier went. It couldn't go all the way to the core of the earth. I felt down deep and winced when I heard a familiar voice wake.

Parker Ferro, you have survived.

Hi, yeah, good to hear from you. I'm actually looking for something—

Have you forgotten what you owe me?

No, no, of course not. But can you make your claim some other time?

Yes. I will. Your obligation to me must be fulfilled. For now, remember that the rules of human magic do not govern your kind.

The voice disappeared. It was an odd use of the word obligation. It didn't feel like a fae obligation, a compulsion, but rather an older, more formal way of saying debt.

Okay, great. So now I'd woken the thing that I owed, and it

didn't even help us. Then the ground trembled. I recognized it as similar to the earthquake that had helped me with Dieter.

The barrier flickered. The tremors disrupted whatever was keeping it intact, and Zahide's words came back to me. A circle was self-contained. It shouldn't lose magic or drain it off. But what if the circle was broken the way that it had been at Woolworth's house? I'd been able to take all the magic from that circle.

Approaching the barrier, I found a crack and shoved my hand into it. The magic screamed at me, a roar like a tornado. Reaching out for the first bit I could get my hands on, I pulled, spinning it on the mental spindle I'd created.

It wasn't the same as at the house, where the iron had helped feed me the magic. Instead of accepting, I was yanking, ripping apart a woven fabric and trying to wind the individual threads around my fingers. At first, the magic resisted, but then, like water finding an easier route, it trickled into me.

I was ready for it this time, and let it fill my reserves, then when it overflowed, sent it down into the greedy spirit beneath my feet. A ripple of satisfaction reached me as the voice drank and drank and drank. A hand clutched my shoulder, but I didn't want to look away in case I lost the slight edge of control I had. If that happened, I was as good as gone, ripped apart by the magic I was trying to sap.

The spell began to feel different, and I could sense more than see Nick's green alchemy spellcasting. He was trying to rip up the anchor points of the spell, but they were inside the boundary. A solid shake of the ground gave him a millimeter of access and his magic shot towards the nearest anchor point.

Unlike the spell at Woolworth's house, which had been designed to do damage as it collapsed, this one simply ceased to exist. With the anchor point gone, the magic just whispered out of existence. My ears were still ringing when Nick raced towards me, shaking my shoulders.

He was yelling, but it took a moment to make sense of the words.

"Are you okay?"

I nodded. "Yeah, fine. Filled up the tank, at least."

He shoved me back, and dragged his teeth over his bottom lip, before saying, "Don't do *anything* that stupid again. That could have killed you."

Still feeling the flow of magic coursing through me, like a leaf that had just barely survived river rapids, I followed him as he and Zahide trailed the remaining SWAT team members towards the building. Someone pushed through the door, and the SWAT team leader yelled for him to get on the ground, but the man kept coming, stumbling towards us, getting faster as he approached.

After another warning, the team opened fire, and I put hands to my ears, the echoing sound of rapid gunfire reverberating in my chest. The man kept advancing, and one of the SWAT team yelped, "Zombie!"

Zahide was already in motion, her hand slapping against a circle inscribed on her coat. It lit up deep red, and she motioned with the same hand. The spell sliced out, taking the zombie's head clean off. Her jacket was smoking, the spell burning itself out.

Then five more burst through the doors. They came rushing at us, and the SWAT team fired wildly as two members retreated back to the van for swords. I came up on Nick, fishing in my bag for something useful.

"I thought that no one taught alchemists how to raise zombies," I said. "Isn't it dark magic?"

"There's some necromancer cults still around," Nick said, pulling out his slender silver knife. He held it ready, but the SWAT team and Zahide seemed to have the zombies under control.

"Still, if Woolworth wanted to be the best alchemist in the world, where did he learn how to raise the dead? Or how to throw fae magic around?" I asked. My fingers wrapped around a rough piece of rope in my satchel, and I pulled it out. The fibers spoke to me, and I smiled. This was going to come in useful.

"Maybe he studied it for work?" Nick asked. "Necromancy is a field of magical studies because of its ties to old-world magic."

I hummed, and followed Nick and three SWAT team members as they continued forward, leaving behind the rest of the team and Zahide to deal with the zombies. When we entered the warehouse, Woolworth had shoved the remaining detritus from when it had been used to store construction supplies to the outer edges of the room, leaving a clean center for circles and other spellwork. He'd converted the whole space to his own personal alchemy studio.

Which was probably why Mark Woolworth felt confident standing in the center of the room, surrounded by circle upon circle, the magic so complicated that the spells were *rotating*. I'd never seen anything that complex outside of a movie theater. Beside me, Nick paled.

"This is only something a team of alchemists could do," he said. "We're going to need to call in every magic user we have."

He gestured and one of the SWAT team requested reinforcements on his radio while the other two circled Mark, checking for weak spots in his spell. I traced the massive outer circle with my eyes, unable to read the twisting words. My eyes caught on the two bodies at Mark's feet. One was struggling to sit up, and I saw it was Theo King, the man whose mess we were now cleaning up. I couldn't see the other one's face, but the hair looked familiar. *Acacia.*

Someone at my elbow made a hissing sound. I glanced over, unsurprised to see Thistle, blood on his mouth. Hopefully no one had seen him rip out the zombie's throat with his teeth. He pounded his fist against the outer circle, getting a burn for his trouble.

Then there was a low scraping sound. I looked up, and saw

something that nightmares were made of. It looked like the larger, angrier mother of the creature Nick and I had killed at Tim's apartment. Easily twice as long as Torres when she was in her dragon form, the demon was clinging to the ceiling with its claws, a reptilian tongue darting out from between its lips.

"Nick," I said. "He summoned another one."

The creature dropped down, burning itself on the outer circle, and it leapt onto the SWAT team. Nick tapped a hand to his arm and threw a spell that tripped the creature, allowing the cops to get a few shots off into its underbelly. That seemed to work; it was bleeding, but it spun, lashing out with sharp claws and a sweep of its bat-like wing.

"Can you do your circle again that burned the other one?" I asked.

Nick gave me an incredulous look. "Can you keep that one still long enough for me to do it?" he asked.

I shook my head no. The rope was still in my hand, and I let it unwind, the fibers each moving on their own across the floor. It took only a thought to reinforce them and then they were winding up every limb of the demon, wrapping tighter and tighter, a hair knotted around a finger. It wouldn't do much damage, but it would annoy the demon while we came up with a better idea.

I could see the demon whipping around in a circle, yowling like a cat as it tried to get the threads off of its body.

"What are we going to do?" I asked.

The question was impossible to hear over the noise of ripping metal, a screech of sound as the roof opened up like someone had taken a can opener to it. A very familiar dragon head poked through, her eyes locking on Woolworth.

CHAPTER THIRTY-EIGHT

TORRES LET OUT A ROAR THAT RATTLED THE ENTIRE BUILDING. I covered my ears and watched as the cops swung their weapons between the demon that was crawling towards them, bat wings dragging behind its lizard-like body, and the honest-to-Hades dragon above them. Torres's reptilian eyes narrowed, the slit of pupil blown wide as it adapted to the darkness of the warehouse.

Then she was grabbing at something near her claw. Hidden in the roof beam's shadows, there were dozens of demons. Each was the size of a large dog, and I imagined that if you got close, they could easily disembowel you. Nick's eyes darted around the ceiling, searching out all of the bat-winged creatures. Torres ripped off the head of the one she'd captured, tossed the corpse aside, and then glided down into the warehouse.

The space limited her, but she didn't need to fly far, aiming straight for Woolworth in the center of his glowing circles. With a scream, she glanced off a shining barrier. The circles created a dome above him, protecting him from anything dropping down. Smart if you'd released a nest of demons in your warehouse.

"Why are they moving?" I called to Nick.

"What?"

"The circles. Why are they moving?" I gestured to the spinning circles that surrounded Woolworth. With my other hand, I reached in my bag and pulled out leaves from some vines. It might save me from a couple of the demons, but after my experience at Tim's, it wouldn't last for long.

"It's a timing thing," Nick said. He pointed at the first two layers of circle. "He's got three spells running on his first circle. The only way that's possible is if they're moving. Otherwise you can only run one at a time."

"Wait," I said. "So, if the spells were frozen, we could get to him?"

"Yeah," Nick said. "But even if you iced the floor, the spells would still move."

"But if time stopped," I said. "Would they stop?"

Narrowing his eyes, Nick said, "Maybe? How is time going to stop, Parker?"

Before I could answer, fully shifted werewolves burst through the warehouse door, their muzzles wet with blood. I hoped it was from zombies, and not the SWAT team members we'd left outside. A familiar form bounded past me, snatching a demon out of the air as it dropped from the ceiling, its eyes on me and Nick.

Grunting, Nick raised his gun and fired at the demons, even as the wolves engaged them. I saw Thistle on the far side of the circle, his mouth moving as he darted around one of the demons. Its neck bent backwards and then he snapped a foot up, crushing its throat.

He was too far away. There was never enough time.

"Nick," I yelled.

Backing towards me, he glanced over, and whatever he saw on my face, his own expression darkened. "Parker—"

"Just, keep an eye out for me." I closed my eyes and reached past all the noise and spells and magic flying around. I reached past the wrongness of the demons in our realm and the call of the Far Realm that I sensed in the center of the circle.

In the background, there were the constants: the spinning of the earth, the movement of the heavens, the walls between realms, and *time*.

"Hey," I murmured. "Hello."

Nothing responded, but what interest did time have with me? I nudged it slightly. A gentle push of magic that got its attention. I felt the momentary focus, and I noticed a millisecond of silence, like the world had gone still. Then time moved on, continuing forward at the fixed pace of seconds, minutes, hours, days.

How did Thistle talk to something so much more massive than he was? How did he convince it to stop?

I shoved more magic at it. The too-full feeling I'd had since draining Woolworth's barrier magic faded. This time, the pause lasted for almost a full second.

"Hey," I said. "I'm going to need you to stop."

Curiosity brushed my mind, and a voice that was more of a deep rumble than anything auditory said, *It will cost you.*

Reaching into the wellspring of magic I had inside me, I pushed out, giving more magic than I'd ever used at once. Time froze.

I opened my eyes, continuing to feed my magic to time. Nick was looking at the frozen battle around him. He said, "Parker, what did you—"

"No time," I said. "Let's move."

Grabbing his hand, I yanked him with me, nearly tripping in my haste to get to the center of the circle. How did Thistle freeze time easily? Was time less greedy if you had more time to talk it into doing what you want?

Nick squeezed my hand and moved beside me, dancing us through the layers of circles, careful to avoid anchor points. He frowned down and looked back at the path we'd carved and then reached into his pocket and pulled out his silver knife.

With a quick slice, he severed one of the circles we were in, and then shoved me forward until we arrived at the inner circle where a frozen Woolworth was reaching down for Acacia at his feet.

Her nut brown skin had turned ashen, nearly blue, and I could see the warm yellow of her magic flowing out of her veins and into Woolworth's palm. *No*, I realized, seeing that the tendrils of magic were drawn from somewhere else *through* Acacia. The *Summer Queen's* magic flowed into his palm.

No wonder Woolworth had the power to do all this. If he was draining the Summer Queen at the height of her powers, he was tapping into an ocean of magic.

For a little boy, jealous of his powerful, acknowledged cousins, this must have been what he'd wanted his entire life. I pulled Acacia up. She was almost impossible to move, too heavy to even nudge.

She was stuck in time, her body couldn't move through it like Nick and I could. I was still a fountain of magic, feeding the voracious hunger of time.

"This one," I said to it. "I need this one, too."

It will cost you, Time repeated.

"I can pay," I said.

Instantly, the drain on my magic disappeared, and I could lift Acacia. I handed her to Nick. Around us, time flickered back into movement. A half-second here of shifting, another half-second a moment later.

"Go," I yelled. "If he finishes draining her, we'll have no hope."

Frowning, Nick took a stumbling step back, then sprinted for the outer circle. He got free just as I lost control of time and everything shuddered back into movement. Placing Acacia on the ground, Nick spun, reaching for the circles, but it was too late, the clockwork movement of Woolworth's circles was back in place.

I was facing Woolworth, and he growled in unhappiness as he saw that Acacia had disappeared. He turned to me, eyes narrowed. He didn't look like a junior professor anymore. Now he was a man with more power than anyone in the room and more anger than reason.

At his feet, his father moaned, a gag keeping him from speaking and rough rope binding his hands and feet. He'd struggled to a sitting position, but didn't seem like he was in good enough shape to manage more than that.

"You!" Woolworth yelled. "I should have killed you as soon as I saw you."

"Too late," I said. Behind me, I heard a crash like two galaxies colliding and I felt the circles freeze up.

Nick's little cut had just thrown a rock in the clockwork, and it looked like it was going to get messy. Woolworth heard it, too, and his eyes widened. I used his distraction to throw down the leaves I'd pulled out earlier. I'd crushed them nearly to dust by my poor handling, but I fed them enough magic that they sprouted and grew true.

Climbing up Woolworth's legs, they held him fast as he struggled to see what the damage to his spells was. He made a disgusted sound and waved his hand. It was like watching someone slice open reality.

I'd seen fae make doorways many times, but the way they did it was always clean. Theirs were neat arrangements with reality that pulled the Far Realm closer to Earth. This was brute force without any sort of technique.

Woolworth grabbed the Far Realm and yanked it closer. It was like driving a car through a wall and calling it a doorway. The two worlds screamed. My eyes widened as I heard the dissatisfaction of the Far Realm. Some of that was now my responsibility.

I was the Windrose. Justice and retribution were both in my purview.

"Stop," I commanded, finding that deep voice again. The tree was there before I even reached for it, a sapling growing fast around me.

Woolworth sneered. "You think you can stop me, *fae*? I killed that stupid old man who tried to take my power from me. I'll kill all of you. You're not even *human,* and yet *you* get magic in your bones."

"Oh, boo hoo," I said. "Tell it to your therapist. If you wanted power that much, why didn't you just join a coven?"

As he turned to me, I saw his control flicker, but only a moment. Reality was bending, like a plastic spoon held too close to a flame.

"And *dirty* myself? No. This is *mine.* I *own* this magic. And now I'll own every drop of magic that you're hiding in the Far Realm." He forced his hand through the doorway and I saw him draw the magic into himself. He wasn't doing it carefully, the thread on the spindle. Instead, he was pulling it out with greedy fingers, bloating with it.

The vines withered on his legs, turning to ash that he kicked aside with his feet. He snarled and tore open his shirt with his other hand, revealing a large circle on his chest. The pattern was familiar at this point.

"The Kings won't be able to deny me now. I'll be the most powerful alchemist in the world. My father can't reject me if I'm more powerful than even Robert King." He spit the words at me and I narrowed my eyes, watching for any weakness. I had to keep him from doing something dangerous before Nick's slice in the circles paid off.

"You know they won't," I said, inching close to him. His father's eyes widened. "You think witches are dirty? You're *filthy.* You only have other people's magic now. Even witches don't steal their magic."

"Shut up!" he yelled, pulling his hand out of the Far Realm to throw a blast of pure magic at me. Dodging it, I rolled and came up next to my oak tree.

There was something wrong with the tree. Normally it seeped with power, imbuing me with abilities and strength I hadn't had a few days ago. Now, though, it was like a washed-out projection of a tree, a ghost of itself.

I could see Nick out of the corner of my eye, trying to get into the circle, yelling something I couldn't hear over the noise of the battle. I glanced between Mark and the doorway he'd created. Whatever was wrong with the tree had to do with that.

There was too much power sloshing around in Mark right now. No matter how much he stretched, he couldn't take much more. It reminded me of the iron from his house. He'd stuffed himself with gunpowder. The right match might set him off.

While I was distracted by trying to figure out what to do with Mark, he'd pulled more magic and slapped a hand down on a circle I hadn't noticed. It powered up, Mark's magic a sickly red, and then I was dodging electricity.

A bright lightning bolt hit the tree, and it groaned, shaking the building. I let the tree go, and it faded, disappearing into a whisper of reflected light. The crackling of electricity reminded me of what Zahide and Nick had both said when I'd explained how I'd sapped the energy from the circle at Mark's house. Taking magic from a contained circle was dangerous.

Explosive, even.

I just had to get him to *touch* a circle. He was laughing as I dodged around the lightning, limited by the circles he'd drawn to keep everyone out.

"Awww," I said. "This is fun. I can't wait until you meet a real alchemist, though."

"What do you mean?" he said.

"You don't even recognize him?" I said, gesturing towards Nick. "He's your cousin, and this mess of circles doesn't even faze him. He's only waiting because we have a bet that I can take you out without getting a scratch."

Angrily, Mark slapped his hand down on the circle again, ready to push more power into it. I pulled tight on the obligation that sat between us.

It was weak. Barely more than a thread. It had nothing on the chains that had tied me to the Summer Queen.

Still, I had more power now than I'd ever had. I could make it work.

"*Drink*," I commanded.

The circle on his chest predisposed him to it, his other hand drifting close to the doorway to the Far Realm, but my command pushed him into touching the lightning circle. It was like nudging someone who was already bent over. They were going to fall, anyway.

The spell he'd drawn on his skin brightened at the command, and then Mark was drinking back the magic in the lightning circle. But the spell on his chest was greedy, and it pulled at the magic from the larger circles that Mark had drawn.

At the influx of magic, he screamed. The circle on his chest lit up white, and I saw it smoke, branding itself into his skin. As he drew magic from the larger circles, Nick's slice exploded, shattering the spell. Magic shot out, most of it disappearing into the ground, but some of it slamming back into Mark.

He made an inhuman sound and his whole body expanded outwards. For a moment, I was afraid that he would *actually* explode and leave everyone covered in blood and viscera.

Instead, the magic he contained detonated and released like an atomic bomb. It threw everyone back, even Torres and the demon. Everyone slammed against the walls of the warehouse, colliding with the shelving and pallets that Mark had pushed back. Theo King slid away as well, and Nick tried to catch him before he could get hurt, but missed him by a few feet.

I stayed in the inner circle by throwing myself down flat, avoiding the brunt of the explosion. After the wave had passed, I looked up.

Mark was on his back, chest smoking. His eyes were bleeding, and he blinked them rapidly, moaning. Not bleeding, I noted, *bloody*. The backfiring magic had burned out his eyes, and all it left was two holes in his face.

My eyes caught on a rainbow of light. Worse, the discharge of magic had left the doorway to the Far Realm open. In fact, as I looked, the opening grew and someone walked through.

CHAPTER THIRTY-NINE

THE WINTER KING CROSSED THE THRESHOLD FIRST, A COMPANY of soldiers dressed in silver armor following behind. His own armor was a pale silver so brilliant it looked almost white. Behind him, the Spring Queen entered with a few fae whose armor looked more decorative than useful, chain mail shaped like tree leaves, knives with hilts carved into the faces of animals.

Seeing the werewolves still fighting the demons, and Torres wounded, but still holding her own against the larger demon, the Winter King gestured and his men spread out, silver swords flashing as they began dispatching the demons.

I swore as the Autumn King followed behind, his own troop of soldiers wearing bronze armor and helmets that masked their faces. Behind him, the Summer Queen arrived. I could only tell it was her by the blue and yellow colors that she wore over her golden armor. The metal looked nearly paper thin, but I imagined it could stop a bullet. She had the most soldiers with her, their faces blank, and hands on the twin swords most common in the Summer Court.

Although both the Autumn King and Spring Queen followed the Winter King's lead and sent their soldiers to help the fatigued wolf pack, the Summer Queen kept hers close by, forming a protective circle around her.

"Windrose," the Winter King boomed, hand resting on his sword. "You have found our murderer."

Mark whimpered. I imagined what he must feel. The power of the fae in this room was tremendous, and with not a single drop of magic left in him, it must have been a reminder of what he'd felt his entire life.

"What justice will you mete out?" the Autumn King asked. His hand was wrapped around a spear, the blade at the end glinting in the light from the Far Realm.

"My daughter?" Her helmet muffled the Summer Queen's voice. She must have wanted to hide her weakness from her fellow monarchs.

"Safe," I said. I pointed to where Thistle had gathered Acacia into his lap, guarding her with a nest of thorny vines.

The Queen pointed, her jeweled fingers ungloved. "Fetch her."

Two soldiers jogged off, their armor like bells ringing as they moved. Thistle let the vines disintegrate as they approached, and he lifted Acacia closer to his chest. Cradling her, he followed one soldier back, as the other guarded their rear. The Queen nodded at his return.

"As expected of my most loyal servant," she said.

"My liege," he said, hands tightening on Acacia.

The fighting grew quiet as the fresh fae soldiers finished off the remaining demons. A mix of Winter and Spring soldiers dispatched the mother demon, the Winter soldiers attacking head on, while the Spring warriors darted in and out, making precise cuts that took out tendons and veins until the demon collapsed on its side and Torres ripped its head off with her teeth.

"Windrose, what judgment do you give this man?" the Autumn King asked again. He looked down. "I would have his head for what he has done to Timothy."

I wondered who Tim had been to him. A loyal servant? A

lover? Or did the Autumn King traffic like the Summer Queen and leave his child behind in the human realm to do his spy work?

Nick stood tense at the edge of the fae groups. The rest of the humans had moved aside, afraid of what the fae would do to them if they got noticed. If I did what I had to as Windrose—demand a life for a life—I wasn't sure that Nick would ever forgive me.

Mark had murdered so many, but Nick would want him tried in court, not by a horde of fae who would execute him here.

"I sentence him to a lifetime without magic," I said. Adelaide Woolworth had believed that the fae taught humans magic. So that circle that Mark loved so dearly had to have some ounce of fae still left in it.

I felt the oak grow behind me, and as the soldiers saw it, their eyes went wide. One dropped to her knees.

There was a pressure on my palm, and I was holding Malcolm's cane in my hand. The symbols for the four courts glowed on its head. Approaching Mark, I felt the magic of my position shift and tighten.

I touched the tip to his chest.

"You stole magic, Mark Woolworth," I said. "You won't ever draw a circle again."

He shrieked and the circle on his chest began smoking, the brand shifting to a new configuration. When it settled, I could read it. The symbols denied Mark any magic. I blinked, and the translation vanished, the tree behind me fading back into nothingness.

"And what will be done with his shell?" the Autumn King asked.

"Put him in prison for his lifetime," I said.

"No death," the Autumn King spat, as if goading me to change my mind.

I looked at Nick and hoped it would be enough. "A lifetime without magic is enough punishment for him."

The SWAT team leader had entered the warehouse, Nick's

captain behind him. Nick glanced over and then moved to stand next to his captain when Tate beckoned.

"Get him up," the Autumn King said, gesturing at Mark. "We will heal his injuries so that he might experience the fullness of his sentence."

"Great," I said. "Sounds like a plan."

Two soldiers held Mark between them, his arms thrown over their shoulders. His head lolled down, and he groaned.

"Windrose," the Autumn King said, nodding his head. He glanced to the Winter King. "Well, Balsam? Are you satisfied with the new fulcrum between our kingdoms?"

The Winter King stroked his beard, his other hand still resting on his sword. He looked me up and down, his eyes as cold as a glacier. Finally, he nodded.

"I am pleased with the outcome. It has been too long since my warriors fought against the beasts of the darkest realm." He waved his hand and his soldiers formed up again, then marched through the doorway. The Spring Queen followed, a smile on her face as she dipped her chin in goodbye to me.

The Autumn King led his soldiers back through the doorway, Mark's feet dragging on the ground as he was taken through the doorway he'd opened. Finally, the Summer Queen approached. She flicked up the visor of her helmet. Her cheeks were bone white. The only color on her face was her blue eyes, which caught mine.

"Congratulations, Parker Ferro," she said. "You have fulfilled the task I set for you."

"It's part of my job, now, isn't it?" I said, challenging. "The Summer Queen doesn't set tasks for the Windrose."

"Ah, yes," she said. "Windrose. Now you must be fair, just, and above all, *neutral*."

Her eyes flicked to where I clenched my hand on the cane.

"You cannot kill a monarch if you are being neutral."

"I bet I can find a way if you want to test me," I said.

She made a *tsking* sound and gestured for her soldiers to follow her back. Some color returned to her lips. Apparently, she was recovering quickly, with the solstice so close and Mark not stealing her magic anymore.

As the last of her soldiers disappeared, I expected the doorway to close, but it hung open, the torn edges glowing rainbow colors, like an aurora borealis up close. Frowning, I felt for the doorway and swore, "Hermes' winged sandals."

"What's wrong?" Nick asked, right at my elbow.

I jerked, startled, and he grabbed my arm to keep me from tripping. His captain joined us and looked at the doorway.

"That doesn't look good," he muttered, pulling a toothpick out of his pocket and setting it between his teeth.

"Whatever Mark did," I said. "It's actually moved the Far Realm closer to ours."

"Is it permanent?" Nick asked, eyes tracing the hole between our worlds. I could see him already planning how to contain it.

"I don't know," I said. "I can close the doorway itself, but I think it might mean that it will be easier for things to pass between the realms."

"On purpose?" Captain Tate asked.

The SWAT team leader joined us, his hands tight on his weapon.

I shrugged. "Or accidentally. Before we were on opposite sides of Death Valley. Someone could get across, but it was hard. Now, it's a crack in the sidewalk."

The SWAT team lead swore colorfully enough that Captain Tate sent him a frown. "You said you can close it?"

"I can try," I said.

I closed my eyes and felt for the tree that grew between realms. Its roots sat in two worlds, its trunk halved. It still felt ghostly, disliking the mix of worlds. Drawing on that feeling, I reached out and pulled at the edges of the hole.

It was like trying to put tissue paper back together. The thinness made everything delicate. I felt the first pieces catch, and then more, until it only left a pinprick of a gap. Opening my eyes, I bent down low and squinted at it. Maybe no one would notice, but I knew it was a bad idea to assume.

"It's as good as I can get it," I said.

One of the cops found the light switch and flooded the warehouse with dim fluorescent lighting, half the bulbs gone out and a few flickering. It illuminated a grotesque scene. The corpses of the demons littered the floor, their blood a strange purple color. A few medics had arrived, and crouched over injured cops, two paramedics undoing Theo King's restraints. I watched as they loaded him onto a stretcher and wheeled him out of the building.

Almost all the wolves had all slunk out the door, but Malik and Torres were waiting for us near the edge of the darkened circles.

At the door, I saw someone waving and recognized Chelsea, her face bright. A familiar woman had an arm slung over her shoulders, and it took a moment before I recognized her as Dieter's wolf on the side. It looked like the two had found out that they had something in common. I'd fear for Dieter's safety if he didn't deserve everything they had coming for him. Raising my hand, I waved at her and she and the other wolf walked out of the building.

I looked back to where Malik and Torres were speaking to each other, the alphas of two packs that rarely mixed with cops.

Nick saw them, too, and at my look, he excused us from Captain Tate and the SWAT team lead, now in the middle of a conversation about containment. They must have agreed with me that even a hole no bigger than a grain of sand was too much of a risk to leave unattended.

As we walked over to them, I wanted to ask Nick what he was thinking, but it seemed dangerous. What if he was pissed that I'd let Woolworth get away?

"That wasn't pack justice," Malik said.

"You can tell your pack that the fae took him. That's more than enough punishment," I said. "If you wanted to fight the fae monarchs for him, you should have said. I'd have sold tickets. Ten bucks to see the alphas of two packs get murdered."

Malik snorted, and I saw Torres' eyes narrow in amusement. "Ten bucks? I think you could do better."

"A hundred," I said. "He's punished. The fae will make sure of that."

"Windrose," Torres said. Her predatory eyes raked over me. "I think I like you a little more, now. If anyone's going to make his life hell, it'll be the fae."

I could feel Nick's disapproval, like a thundercloud booming in the distance.

"We good?" I asked Malik.

He offered his hand. I grasped his forearm, and he pulled me close, an arm around my back.

"Be careful," he murmured into my ear. "You always were a little too sneaky to make good pack, and you're going to need that, dancing with the fae."

He released me and took a couple of steps back, gesturing to two of his waiting pack members. Celia and Tara, I realized. I waved at them and Tara raised her hand in greeting while Celia shook her head. They followed Malik, a half-step behind him as he left. Torres and her guards were close behind, brushing past the SWAT team members entering the building.

"What's going to happen to him?" Nick asked.

I didn't pretend that I didn't know who he was talking about. "He's going to live the rest of his life without being able to wield magic. He won't get any magic back. That explosion looked like it messed something up in him."

"Is he going to be tortured?" Nick asked.

"No," I said. "Not physically. That isn't how the fae operate."

"Mentally?" he asked.

"What do you want me to say?" I said. "If I'd tried to get them to leave him here, they would have fought back. They don't listen to me yet, Nick. I could either let them kill him or let them take him."

"He should have faced justice here," Nick said, the edges of his lips pulled down.

"Yeah, well, should've is a world of regret." I shrugged. Digging deep, I found the honesty that had made me tell him about myself in the first place. "I don't want to lose you over this. I tried to make a decision that we could both live with."

Nick sighed, and I saw the frown on his face wasn't from anger, but worry. He lifted his hand and cupped my cheek, sliding down my neck to my shoulder. He tightened his hand once and then dropped it.

"This is going to be a mess of paperwork. You should get checked out by the medics. I don't know what you did, but it looked dangerous."

"It wasn't too bad," I lied. "Piece of cake."

"Sure," he said. "I'm sure if I told your sister about it, she'll order you enough food to feed an army."

"What, you're going to *tattle* to my sister?" I said.

"If you don't get yourself checked out?" he said, eyes narrowing. "Watch me."

I groaned and followed him out of the warehouse towards the ambulances on the street. "At least promise that we can go on a real date after this."

"Sure," Nick said. "Anywhere you want."

Grinning, I said, "I can think of a place real close. Does breakfast in bed, even."

"Does this place also have a pile of your laundry on the floor?" Nick asked.

"Not if you give me ten minutes," I said.

Nick leaned in and pressed a kiss to my lips. He tasted warm, like honey on a summer day. "Five. And I'll bring the breakfast."

CHAPTER FORTY

Of course Nick had to stay behind. I got cleared by the paramedics with strict instructions to rest and go to the hospital if I began feeling any effects of magic depletion. Zahide cleared me with a brief check before sending me home.

When he found out my plan was to call an Uber, Nick insisted on sending one of the uniformed cops working outside the building to take me home. It would have been cute if it wasn't a little overprotective. Still, given the way my finances were, I wasn't going to turn down a free ride.

By the time I got home, it was morning, the sun painting the sidewalk a warm yellow. I waved goodbye to the cop and then headed inside. Every part of me was ready to collapse into my bed, and when I got off the elevator, I winced.

Jeffrey Jenkins stood near my door. He had a large toolbox in one hand, and grinned when he saw me.

"Hello, Parker," he said. "So sorry to tell you, but your apartment has been having power issues! Probably won't get fixed until... oh, maybe next month?"

I clenched my teeth so tightly I could practically hear my fillings cracking. Behind Jeffrey, Shannon's head popped out of the door, her brown eyes going wide and then she was running towards me.

"I was so worried," she said. "I felt something going on, but I couldn't *get* to you."

"It's okay," I said. "I'm fine."

"Sure. I'm sure if anyone can survive in the dark it's you," Jeffrey said. "But just as a reminder, any open flames in apartments are forbidden."

I looked at Shannon and an idea formed. "Hades' breath, Jeffrey! Did you turn off the *power?*"

Pushing past him, I opened the door and revealed Shannon's bed inside. With the lights off, it looked eerie, her skin painted blue. She was breathing, but it was so shallow that I bet Jeffrey wouldn't even notice it.

"You killed Shannon!" I said, turning on Jeffrey. I ran to the body and lifted her arm, letting it fall with a solid thump back on the bed. "She was alive and you turned off her power!"

Jeffrey turned ashen, his mouth hanging open. "What— But— Who—"

"My mother!" I said. "She needed that power to live!"

"A little much?" Shannon asked, her hands on her hips. She raised an eyebrow and I shot her a narrow look. Cracking a smile, she squinted at Jeffrey.

He was looking around the room, panicked. "But, what? How—?"

"You'll have to tell people that someone died here," I said. "And I'll be telling the cops all about how I had power yesterday when I left, and *you* with the tools..."

"No," Jeffrey said, shaking his head. He backed away. "No. I didn't have anything to do with this."

One of my neighbors, one I didn't know by name so much as the fact that she always let her kids run in the halls, cracked open her door and peeked out. Her eyes widened when she saw my dark apartment, Jeffrey's tools, and what looked like a corpse. Hastily, she shut her door.

"I didn't kill *anybody*," he shouted.

Turning tail and running, he slammed open the door to the stairwell. Shannon's eyes narrowed. "I don't like the look of him. I think he'll be having *very* bad dreams tonight."

"*This* is why they kicked you out of your care facility," I said. Moving to the windows, I threw open the blinds and let in some bright morning light.

"Well," Shannon huffed. "What's the point of being a ghost if you can't haunt some people who deserve it?"

Shutting the door, I said, "Go ahead. If anyone deserves bad dreams it's that guy."

Giving me two thumbs up, Shannon walked through the door, hot on Jeffrey's heels. I glanced at her body, unsure if I should be creeped out by sharing the room with a shell. Making a face, I shrugged. I had bigger issues. My whole body felt sticky; a thin layer of grime had worked its way into every crevice.

Shower first then food, I decided. With the decision made, I headed for the bathroom, tossing all my clothes in a pile. The shower was glorious, even if I had to take it in the dark, feeling for the soap and washcloth by memory.

By the time I got out, morning light had bathed the bedroom a warm white and I picked out a pair of track pants and a t-shirt from a local band that Laurel used to like. I tripped over the pile of dirty laundry and groaned.

'Pile' was perhaps underselling its size. I'd put a load in the washer downstairs before making myself dinner. Breakfast. Dinfest?

Shoving everything in a laundry bag regardless of color, I hefted it and grabbed my keys before leaving my apartment. Halfway down the hall, a door creaked open. I turned, expecting it to be the neighbor that I'd scared with Shannon's 'corpse,' but it was Malcolm's door.

With a sigh, I shuffled towards the door, unsure what else the day could hand me. Stepping inside, I was back in the San Amaro hills, in whatever incredibly expensive house Malcolm had linked to the door in *Las Vistas*. I was pretty sure the actual house existed in the hills, but how did the doors work? And *why* did Malcolm need so many?

The house was still and I left my laundry near the door, blocking the door from shutting just in case the house got any funny ideas.

"Sorry I haven't been back. The past few days have been hard. But, I got the guy who killed Malcolm," I said. "So, if that's all this is, then you can... rest? You can go?"

There was a hissing sound and I followed it to the kitchen where the chef's stove had two pans on it; one held snapping bacon and the other was full of eggs. Both looked almost done and so I shut off the gas and grabbed a plate from the cabinet, serving myself a generous portion of each.

"This is for me, right?" I asked, bacon already halfway to my mouth.

A fork appeared on the counter and I took that as a yes. Pulling out one of the stools from the kitchen island, I sat down and began shoveling food into my mouth. I was so hungry that I barely tasted what I was eating. When my appetite slowed, I looked around.

There was less stuff than the last time I'd been in the house. In fact, other than the furniture, it looked like almost everything that was personal to Malcolm was gone.

"I think I'm getting a message here," I said. "You want me to move in?"

Tapping my fingers on the counter, I thought out loud. "This is the Windrose's house and I'm the Windrose now?"

Well, at least it had electricity, which was a step up from my current place. I stood, and started to give myself a tour when someone called my name from the entryway. Nick had one hand on the door, his other on his gun.

When he saw me, he sighed in relief.

"How'd you know where I was?" I asked.

He pointed at the laundry bag, which had my name written on it in large letters. I hadn't looked at it in so long that I'd forgotten. It was one of the bags from foster care. They'd use big bags like this because trash bags might tear, and they could fit all of our things in a bag like this. No folding necessary. Schoolbooks, clothes, toys, anything that we called ours would have to fit in the bag or get left behind.

I looked around the house, my eyes catching on the space for all my things. If I lived here, it would be *mine*, for as long as I was Windrose. No shoving everything in a bag necessary.

"What is this place?" Nick seemed hesitant to step inside, but I waved him in and shut the door behind us. When I looked, my laundry bag had vanished.

"You better be doing my laundry and not eating it," I muttered to the house.

"Parker?" Nick said, confused.

"I don't know, this house is sentient, maybe," I said. "This is where the old Windrose lived. I think I inherited it."

"This house is an apartment in your building?" Nick asked.

"That's just a portal or a shortcut or something," I said. "I'm pretty sure the house is in the hills. Don't ask me to explain, I don't know yet, either."

Nick looked around. "Well, it's certainly big."

"Yeah," I said. "I don't even have enough stuff to fill up this place."

"Really? I assume that you'll need one room just for your laundry," Nick teased.

"Okay, I was on my way to *do* my laundry when I got side tracked," I said. "How's your uncle doing?"

"He's still in and out of consciousness. I left Sam with him.

My dad is flying down tonight." He tightened his lips, like he wanted to say more, but kept silent.

"You should get some sleep," I said.

"So should you," he said.

He looked like he'd come directly from the scene; his skin had the same haze of dirt that mine had.

"Come on," I said. "There has to be a shower around here somewhere."

It turned out that there were several. We decided on the master bathroom, which had a pile of towels and scented soaps. While he showered, I went to make him food, deciding on a BLT to use the leftover bacon.

"Thanks," Nick said, taking the plate from me.

I pointed. "You're naked."

He had one of the thick towels around his waist and a few remaining droplets of water on his shoulders.

"My clothes were—" he made a face. "Can I borrow some from your place?"

"You *could*," I drew out the word. "Or we could enjoy what we have going here."

"And what is that?" he asked.

"Why don't you finish that and we can find out?"

Nick scarfed down the sandwich, whether out of hunger or desire, and followed me to the nearest bedroom. I pushed him back on the bed, and straddled his hips. His shoulders were broad under my hands, and black hair dusted his stomach, leading down to where he'd knotted the towel.

"Can I suck you?" I asked, the words awkward on my tongue. I wanted to just take him, but I remembered our first time, and waited.

"Yes," he said, leaning back.

Scooting down, I dipped my head and wrapped my mouth around him, enjoying the feel of his soft cock hardening between my lips. I increased the suction and moaned a little as he bucked his hips, a shudder of need. His fingers tightened on the sheets and I moved one of his hands to my hair.

He groaned, a desperate sound as he twisted my hair in his fingers. The sharp tug was perfect, grounding me and reminding me who I was with. He whispered my name, a mantra that sounded like he was casting me into being with magic.

When he came, it was hot and salty, and I swallowed it down, pulling off with a wet sound that made me grind my own dick into the covers. For a moment, I lay with my forehead on his stomach and felt his chest rise and fall, panting slowing after a bit.

"Come here," he coaxed, and he drew me up, until I was spread out on top of him. His fingers ran up and down my back, and the motion was so soothing, that I was sure I was going to fall asleep, hard-on or no.

After a bit, I felt his hand dip lower, teasing the waistband of my pants.

"Can I finger you?" he asked.

I was so relaxed that I was sure I was half dreaming. "Yes," I said to his chest.

He hummed, and I felt the vibration in my lips where they rested near his nipple. With a flip that was so fast I barely had time to blink, he'd turned us so he was on top, me still facedown under him. Shifting his weight back, he pulled my pants down just enough to show off my ass.

Slowly, he pressed a fingertip to my hole. It was dry, but I didn't protest. I trusted him.

When he pushed it inside, I gasped. It should have felt like a breach, but instead, it made me whimper. It wasn't enough. I shifted again, my dick leaking into my pants where I was trapped between the bed and Nick's weight.

"More," I said, the word pleading.

"Yeah, yeah," Nick agreed. He pushed in a second finger, still careful not to move them too much, and then curled them, hitting my prostate and rubbing small circles.

I cried out, pressing down into the bedding. His other hand worked its way around me and I felt his fingers tighten on my dick as his heavy weight held me down, his fingers still hitting me just right inside.

It was impossible not to come.

My vision whited out and when I came to, Nick was wiping me off with a wet cloth, his expression smug.

"Oh, please," I said. "I've had better."

"Oh, yeah?" he said.

"Yeah," I teased. "I'd give that a B plus. You're going to have to come back for some extra tutoring. It'll mean lots of practice."

"Maybe some more practice exams?" Nick said, sprawling next to me.

"Daily," I confirmed. I pressed a kiss to his lips and enjoyed his palm on my back where it had snuck under my shirt.

"I can do that," he said.

"Good," I said. "We'll start work after a nap."

EPILOGUE

"DIDN'T THIS PLACE MENTION SOLSTICE CELEBRATIONS?" I asked holding up the pamphlet featuring a nurse in scrubs helping a white, elderly woman walk down a hallway.

"Yeah," Laurel said. "Along with Christmas, Kwanzaa, and Chanukah."

"I mean, but still, that has to be like a... signal, right? That they're ok with witches?" I asked.

One of Laurel's eyebrows went up, and she opened her mouth before shaking her head. We were sitting in my living room, Silverwood cool and still around us.

"Our best bet is still Clearwater." She tapped on the brochure in the middle of the table.

Wincing, I picked it up, skimming the information again. "It's so *expensive*."

"I'm sorry," Laurel said. She pointed at me with narrowed eyes. "Are you suggesting we put a *price* on Shannon's safety?"

After I'd convinced Jeffrey Jenkins that he'd killed someone, the police and an ambulance had gotten involved. Shannon had been carted back to a hospital where a doctor had said, despite her adventure in my apartment, she was fine. Now, we had to find somewhere long-term for her, since her insurance wouldn't cover the hospital for much longer.

Clearwater was a local skilled nursing facility that catered to, per its literature, 'specialized clients.' Which, after a tour that showed off state-of-the-art werewolf-containment rooms for full moons, magical wards to keep out anyone intending residents harm, and specialized staff who were experts in everything from chimeras to age-related magic loss, was comprehensive.

"No," I admitted. "It's mostly all the paperwork. I mean, have you seen it? It's more paper than a grand-jury indictment."

Laurel shot me a narrow look. "Get over here and help me fill this out."

Someone knocked on the door and I held up my hands. "Oh, man, a guest! I'll be over here not dealing with *that*."

I gestured to the stack of paperwork and turned back to the door. Opening it, I found a suited Nick bearing a bottle of wine. With a grin, I leaned against the doorframe.

"Can I help you, officer?" I said. "Is my car parked illegally? Are you here to give me a *fine?*"

Rolling his eyes, Nick pointed to my car, parked in the circular driveway. The windshield was broken, side-view mirrors torn off, and it had a few werewolf-shaped dents in it. "That is a menace. It's not street-worthy and if I find out that you've been driving it before you fix it, then I'll make sure that you *do* get a ticket."

"It's on the to-do list," I promised. "If my rich boyfriend wants to make himself useful, he could buy me a new car."

With a put-upon sigh, he said, "Happy housewarming. I don't know why I bothered, but this is the nice stuff, so put it in a real wine glass. Not in a water glass."

"Come in," I invited. "You can help me find one."

The house was even larger than I'd first thought. When I'd gone back for my laundry, a few days after our showdown with Mark Woolworth, I'd found a new deed with my name on it.

Whether the house had made it or some fae that had been placed in San Amaro's city hall, I owned Silverwood.

After figuring that I might as well start making it my home, I even planted a couple of the seeds from the Old One tree in the expansive backyard. Nick had been concerned that I'd have talking trees that could see in my windows, but I assured him that trees didn't really care about what went on in my bedroom.

"How'd the facility tours go?" Nick asked, waving at Laurel in the living room. He followed me to the kitchen and I pulled down three wine glasses from one of the shelves and put them on the island that took up the center of the kitchen.

"Good," I said. "Most places don't want to advertise their stance on witches, but we can ask about hauntings. It's been... informative."

We were on our second day of tours and the haunting question had narrowed the number of candidates down to six from the ten facilities we'd visited. But of those six, Laurel was right that we only had one real choice. Nick nodded and searched for a wine opener, finding one in a drawer and peeling back the foil.

"I got some interesting news today," he said. "Derek McCallum's house is off the market."

"Someone bought it?" I said. "Good luck to them. We left behind some impressive bloodstains." Nick was quiet. I stared at him and said, "You think McCallum is back."

"Yeah," Nick said. "Or planning to come back."

The news made me huff a sigh. I knocked a fist against the marble counter and said, "Well. That's going to make things interesting."

"Yeah," Nick agreed. He reached out and put his hand on top of mine before turning back to the bottle of wine. "The department is forming a task force related to the Far Realm rift. Captain Tate nominated me to be the Paranormal Crimes representative on it."

"Really?" I said, watching him pour our glasses. I went to the refrigerator and pulled out a cheese tray that Laurel had brought over for lunch. Setting it on the counter between us, I took a slice of cheddar. "Congratulations. That sounds like a promotion?"

"It's... good. For my career," he said. "It means that I'll be noticed more."

"I don't notice you enough?" I said, leering at him.

He smiled into his glass and I picked up mine, offering him a toast. "Congratulations, Detective King. You're on your way to being Chief of Police King," I said.

He rang our glasses together and I leaned in to seal it with a kiss when we heard a voice.

"Windrose?"

I sighed. Nick had stiffened and his hand was hovering near his hip, even though I knew that he kept his firearm in a safe in his car when he wasn't on duty. Touching his arm, I set down my glass. "Take the wine into the living room. You can help Laurel fill out some paperwork. I'll deal with this."

"Parker," Nick said, eyes soft.

Leaning forward, I kissed him, his soft lips a promise of more fun after Laurel went home. "I've got this."

Unhappily, he picked up the wine glasses and headed for the living room. With a sigh, I headed in the opposite direction. Shannon was hovering near the room that led to the Far Realm, her brow furrowed. "She came through the Summer door."

"Thanks," I said.

Walking in, I noticed that my throne was already formed, the massive oak more solid than it had been the last time I'd pulled it into existence. My eyes widened when I saw who it was.

"Acacia," I said, taking a seat on the throne. The cane leaned against it and I picked it up. I still wasn't sure how everything worked, but I knew that either the tree or the cane gave me the gravitas and the language I needed when playing my new role.

"Windrose," she greeted, bowing her head.

"You can call me Parker," I said. "What can I do for you?"

She frowned, her hands clasped behind her back. She'd pulled her dreadlocks back into a ponytail and her skin had a golden hue that looked healthier than the last time I'd seen her. Her blue eyes were striking in her face, and it spoke to her parentage that I could feel the magic under her skin.

"I feel like I owe you a debt," she said. "For saving my life."

"No," I said immediately. "No obligation between us. I was just doing my job."

"I'd like to repay it," she said, ignoring me. "And make sure that you're... *informed* about some of the politics of your position."

"What politics?" I asked.

"You think you're a half-blood, like me," she said. "A changeling left behind by a careless fae. Of no court."

"No one's ever claimed me," I said, carefully. "Even when I went to the Summer Court."

Acacia spoke slowly, like she was choosing her words. "The old queen, Queen Aster, once had a child with her consort. Her *fae* consort. The child was stolen from her when it was an infant. She spent years searching for him. When she found you, she thought *you* might be that child."

"She never said anything," I said. "She would have told me."

My chest was tight, bands of pressure were crushing my ribs and my knuckles on the cane were white.

"Would she? If she wasn't sure who'd raised you and what your motives were?" Acacia asked. "I wanted you to know. The information makes us even."

"Am I Aster's son?" I said, the past taking on new meaning.

"I don't know," Acacia said. "But there was a reason that my mother freed you. And a reason her ploy worked."

She bowed and exited through the Summer door. I sat on my throne, hands tight on the cane. The tree around me shivered.

"Parker, you okay?" Nick asked. I looked around. The light was different. It was darker. Nick was crouched in front of me, his hands loose and expression concerned.

"Yeah," I said. I forced a smile and stood, the tree disappearing. I brought the cane with me and headed out of the room. "You guys make any headway?"

"Well, kind of," Nick said. He offered his hand and I took it. "Laurel seems to think that we should ask if the staff that will deal with Shannon are witches and I had to point out that's illegal and now I think she's mad at me."

I laughed. "You're such a rule-follower."

"Parker, it *is* illegal to discriminate based on religion." Nick was smiling though and I felt something in my chest relax. I would deal with Lilacina some other time. For now, I was going to enjoy the expensive wine my boyfriend had brought over and some cheap takeout.

Parker Ferro.

The voice rumbled in my bones.

I have come to demand my payment.

———

Book 2 of San Amaro Investigations coming Summer 2021.

To get a free 17k short story showing how Parker and Nick met, sign up for my newsletter here.

Join my Facebook group, The Kai Butler Brigade to hang out, chat, and catch snippets of what I'm writing.

Printed in Great Britain
by Amazon

56982513R00210